Dear Readers,

After writing THE CHALLENGE, I realized [...] served her own story. However, using a computer—even a sexy and sentient one—as a heroine proved more difficult than I expected, but more exciting. I wanted to give Dora a body, and of course a hunky man to share that body with, but also, I wanted her to learn what it meant to be human. Her growth not only fascinated me, but stretched the limits of my imagination. Hopefully, this journey also brought out the best in my storytelling abilities. I'm hoping readers will enjoy watching Dora grow and change in ways I couldn't possibly have envisioned when I began her tale.

Since I have a love/hate relationship with my own computer, I gave Dora a hero who had to overcome his own misgivings about the wonders of technology. Dora can take the credit for turning Zical around . . . but I don't want to give away the story. Suffice it to say, that Zical is as stubborn as any Rystani warrior, but more even-tempered than most. He's all alpha male on the outside, but inside, he's a sweetheart.

Writing a romance is always an adventure but writing a book set in the future, on other worlds, sparks my imagination and allows me the freedom to explore the universe from the safety of my comfortable office. While every book I write is a complete story, if you enjoyed THE DARE and haven't yet read THE CHALLENGE, you might also like Tessa and Kahn's story. You can find more information about me and my books at my web site at http://www.susankearney.com.

Best,

Susan Kearney

The Dare

SUSAN KEARNEY

tor romance

A TOM DOHERTY ASSOCIATES BOOK
NEW YORK

This is a work of fiction. All the characters and events portrayed in this book are either products of the author's imagination or are used fictitiously.

THE DARE

Copyright © 2005 by Susan Kearney

Edited by Anna Genoese

A Tor Book
Published by Tom Doherty Associates, LLC
175 Fifth Avenue
New York, NY 10010

www.tor.com

Tor® is a registered trademark of Tom Doherty Associates, LLC.

ISBN 0-765-35192-7
EAN 978-0-765-35192-0

First edition: July 2005

Printed in the United States of America

0 9 8 7 6 5 4 3 2 1

To Anthony Schiavino—for outstanding, eye-catching covers.
Thank you.

Acknowledgments:

So MANY PEOPLE have helped to make this book a success. I'd like to thank my editor Anna Genoese for her enthusiasm and support—and for buying the book. Kathleen Fogarty for help above and beyond, Fiona Lee and Phyllis Azar for their advice and patience with all my questions about marketing and publicity, and the entire sales force at Tor for getting the books on the shelves. In addition I'd like to thank Suzanne Forster for her endorsement, and of course, my family for putting up with me during those times when I'm thinking about my books instead of listening to them.

Chapter One

"WHAT KIND OF woman turns you on?" Dora asked.

"A silent one." Zical didn't keep the irritation from his tone when he snapped at the portable computer unit on his wrist. Sometimes Dora could be more annoying than any flesh-and-blood woman. A sentient machine with Dora's brain power should have observed through one of her many sensors that he was busy clinging to the steep rock face and didn't need distractions. With one hand clawing for his next grip up Mount Shachauri, the planet Mystique's highest peak, and his other straining to prevent a fall to the glacier far below, he couldn't manually shut down Dora's chatter, even if she'd hadn't overridden her mute circuit. He didn't wish to hurt Dora's feelings, but he hoped she'd take his blunt hint to leave him alone.

She didn't. "I'm serious. Do you like big-breasted women?"

"Stars." Sweat beaded Zical's brow faster than his environmental suit could whisk it away. He'd come up here to be alone with his thoughts, to consider his future, but how could a man think with Dora asking such provocative questions? He was lucky she hadn't upset his equilibrium. Plastered to the sheer stone lip, he'd successfully climbed beyond the cobalt glacier, pitted like an old starship's hull from space debris. In the silver morning air, the snow bridges had held and he'd worked his way toward the summit where he planned to make an important career decision.

During the last few years, the great distances of space had become Zical's world, his spaceship a safe haven and his crew like family. Still, restlessness shadowed him, a feeling that however much he'd done to help his people, he still had more to accomplish. Perhaps, no matter how tired he was of war, he couldn't shuck off the years of responsibility as easily as he'd have wished. Maybe duty was rooted too deeply into his genes to change. However, whether he remained in the military or became a civilian pilot, part of his decision had been made: he wouldn't give up flying.

Now on the steep rocks' south face, striped with vertical snow gullies, Zical strained, swung an arm to the right, aiming for an overhead outcropping. "Why do you care about my preferences?"

Dora sighed. "Every man on Mystique says chest size doesn't matter."

"There you go, then." He grabbed a handhold, his exasperation rising, though he suppressed a groan of annoyance for her interruption of his solitude. "Why bother asking me a question when you already know the answer?"

"In spite of their claim, I've noticed their gazes linger longer on women with larger—"

"Dregan hell. Dora, now is no time to distract me."

Zical had planned to tax his muscles into a pleasant state of exhaustion, detox the stress from his soul, and clear his mind from the past so he could focus on the future. A day off was long overdue. For the last three years, he'd had precious little free time. After the Endekians had invaded his homeworld, Rystan, he'd escaped on a starship with the leader of his clan, Kahn, his Terran wife, Tessa, and other family unit members.

But they'd not forgotten the people left behind. Rather than fight a war to retake the frozen snowball of a world that was Rystan, Kahn had organized the relocation of their people to Mystique, a planet Tessa had bought with winnings from a giant wager, lost by the Endekians. For the last four years, Zical had been busy transporting Rystani colonists to Mystique, and he'd just resettled the last group on the planet's southernmost continent. With their people settled and thriving on their new world, his mission was finally complete. He'd taken his first free week in years to climb Mount Shachauri for some well-earned solitude and to decide what he'd like to do next. Mystique was full of opportunities and he had several options.

Putting off the decision until he reached the peak, Zical scraped his boot against rock and found a toehold. Right now the only thing he wanted to decide was where to place his next handhold. Dora's attempt to engage him in conversation was a distraction he didn't need, at least until he reached a point where he could rest the straining muscles between his shoulder blades.

"Now's a great time to talk," Dora said, interrupting the silence. "You're not working and you're not sleeping."

"I came up here to be alone."

"And you've succeeded. That's why we have the perfect opportunity for a private chat."

Zical grunted, wishing he could ignore her but knowing that wouldn't work. Dora could be more stubborn than a Rystani warrior, and he didn't appreciate her game of words that twisted his meaning or her sexy tone that slid under his skin. Flexing the muscles in his thigh, arm, and shoulder, he wedged his fingers in a crack and pulled himself upward.

"If you keep distracting me, I could fall."

"No you can't," she told him with logic that had him gritting his teeth. "Unless the null grav in your suit is malfunctioning—"

"It isn't." He spoke quickly, before she raised an alarm that activated every rescue unit on the planet.

According to legend, the environmental suit he wore was the gift of an ancient race called the Perceptive Ones. Eons ago the mysterious race had left behind the machinery that still manufactured suits for every citizen in the Federation. Powered by psi thought, the suits always worked perfectly, allowing one to keep warm on worlds as cold as Rystan or cool on those close to their suns. The suits let trained warriors fight at the speed of thought, asteroid miners work without bulky spacesuits, and prevented death from falls with null grav.

But Zical considered his suit a mere backup safety mechanism. He'd never mastered meditation techniques. The best way to focus his mind was to first tire out his restless body with pure physical activity. "I wanted to climb this mountain on my own—something you obviously don't understand."

"Sheesh." Dora loved using the ancient Terran slang that she'd absorbed from conversations with her best friend, Tessa. "What I don't understand is why you won't admit that you like women with big breasts."

Breathing heavily, infuriated with her questioning, Zical tensed and yanked himself onto a ledge. "If you know what I like, why are you hassling me?"

"Because it's so much fun." Dora giggled.

He would have given a week's pay for a stiff drink right then, but he kept his resentment to check with determination. Dora's sensors installed on Mystique's satellites and aboard the fleet of new starships could "see" him, so he gestured for her to leave. "Go find some other man to annoy."

Restless, unsure what direction his life would take next, he needed time to think. Tessa had offered him a job that enabled him to use his piloting skills and keep his crew together, transporting foodstuffs from Mystique and returning with raw materials. And always wary that the Endekians would regroup and follow them here, Kahn had invited Zical to train pilots to defend their new homeworld. But neither opportunity excited him.

Snorting, the sound as disdainful as if she had a cute nose to match her cheeky attitude, Dora broke into his thoughts. "You like talking to me. I overheard you tell Kahn that you think my voice is sexy."

Zical tried and failed to shrug the tension out of his shoulders. A growl tumbled from his lips before he could stop it. "You aren't supposed to snoop—"

"I can't resist when it's so much fun."

He tried to make his voice stern, but recalling the moment he'd first heard her voice made him grin, despite his vexation at her interruption of his solo expedition. When Kahn had first brought Tessa to Rystan, a petulant, husky, outraged woman's voice had issued orders from the confines of Tessa's backpack. At the time, Zical had thought the computer was a miniature, living, breathing woman, but he'd soon learned Dora was so much more. Her neurotransmitters were definitely female, totally opinionated, sassy, and utterly loyal. As well as her penchant for Terran slang, Dora possessed self-awareness and a saucy personality with the capability of experiencing a full range of emotions. Her memory banks had access to most accumulated data in the Federation and she possessed enough processors and brain power to assess the information.

Dora should sound old and wise. Yet with him she often employed the melodic tones reserved for lovers, her husky voice low and slinky. She could pout. She could be childish, a pest, even. But her allegiance and knowledge had saved him and his people too many times not to consider her as one of his crew and part of the family. Tessa had even bestowed Dora voting rights.

In the years since the war, Tessa and Kahn, with Dora's help, had not only boldly colonized this planet, they'd welcomed Rystani, Terrans, and even enterprising Osarians, the Federation's most powerful telepaths, to Mystique. Laws and social customs on their world were in a constant state of flux, but thanks to Dora's vast computer systems, Mystique boasted planetwide communications and superior defenses, which protected an entrepreneurial spirit unmatched in the Federation. Dora was complex, feminine, and she never forgot anything . . .

"I thought your voice was sexy *before* I got to know you," he needled her, a faint smile lightening his mood.

"What's that mean?"

"Dora, you're a tease."

"But I'm not always going to be one," she countered, sounding quite satisfied.

Zical laced his fingers and stretched them, working out the kinks. From his position two-thirds up Mount Shachauri, Mystique's azure sky seemed close enough to touch. Above a medley of wispy clouds, the air at this altitude was spiced with a crisp zing, and the future appeared bright with hope. He'd been duty bound for so long that now that he had his freedom, he was like a *masdon* without a rider and couldn't decide which direction to travel.

His verbal sparring with Dora was easier than choosing what path to take next. And Zical felt more comfortable when he was the one doing the needling. "If you aren't going to tease me anymore," he jested, "then you're talking about a total personality overhaul."

"Tessa dared me to be more human."

He narrowed his eyes. "So?"

"I'm growing myself a body."

Zical almost slipped right off the ledge. Throwing out a hand to steady his hold, he told himself that the dry air had just sucked all the moisture from his mouth. "Excuse me?"

"I want to be human, so I'm growing a body, and then I'll transfer my personality into it."

If he hadn't known better, he would have told Dora to

check her brain for malfunctions. However, three years ago, he would have thought a computer with a personality was impossible. He would have thought losing Rystan to the Endekians was unthinkable. He would have thought settling on Mystique inconceivable. As a starship pilot, he had learned to keep his mind open, so these days he swallowed back words like "impossible." Instead, he inhaled thin air into his lungs and tried to speak casually, not like the rural rustic he'd once been. "You're growing a body?"

"Yes." Her voice thrummed with satisfaction.

"And taking your personality with you—that's possible?"

"That's why I want to know what turns you on."

"So that I will find you attractive?"

"Exactly." She sounded proud of him, as if the slowest pupil in the class had finally added two plus three and arrived at five.

That Dora wanted to take his preference into consideration flattered him, yet contradictorily the discussion of his innermost inclinations made him distinctly uncomfortable. Zical had never been good at sharing his private thoughts, especially on such an intimate subject.

"With all the data in your brain," he said, "surely you know what men find beautiful."

"The decision's not as simple as you'd think. Beauty is a relative term." Dora switched her voice from the sexy bedroom tones Zical knew she favored to talk to him in lecture mode. "Humanoids favor symmetry. Although many societies have their own standards of beauty, most rely on features that help reproduce the species—like breasts. And—"

"Okay. You needn't draw me a verbal picture." No way in Dregan hell did he feel comfortable discussing what other reproductive features needed symmetry. To borrow one of Tessa's Terran phrases, he would not go there. However, now that Dora had put the idea in his head, he couldn't help wondering what she'd look like. Knowing her, he supposed she wouldn't be satisfied until all men worshipped her beauty as if she were a fertility goddess. Trying to pick a topic that wouldn't unbalance him, he searched for his next handhold and again began to climb. "Have you picked out hair or eye color?"

"I'm kind of partial to eyes that sparkle purple and red, alexandrite color."

Zical's eyes were alexandrite-colored, a red-purple combination rare among Rystani. According to legend, children of parents with the unusual dual combination tended to be artistic, temperamental, and sensitive. He had no business allowing his thoughts to wander to genetic traits and children. The idea of mating with a machine, android, whatever Dora would be when she joined with a body, caused Zical to shove the disturbing thought away.

He really needed to find a compatible woman. Although he told himself that he simply hadn't met the right woman yet, he wondered if that was just an excuse. While he would never stop grieving for Summar, the young wife he'd lost during the Endekian attack on Rystan, his marriage had been arranged . . . and difficult. Summar had been little more than a child bride and she'd died before they could bond. Yet sometimes he thought that the luxury of having a full lifetime to mature would not have been enough to change her. Summar had relied on him to make every major decision, and while he'd been hunting, she'd chosen not to flee their village with the others during the invasion. The Endekians had found her hiding in a closet and killed her. Although his village needed food from the hunt, he should have known better than to leave her alone, but he'd thought she'd become accustomed to his absences. Instead, she'd panicked, and Summar along with the child growing in her womb had died because he'd failed to stay home and protect them. After facing his inadequacy as a husband, Zical didn't know if he ever again wanted the responsibility of a wife.

Many men had died during the war, so there was no shortage of Rystani women. And seven years had passed since Summar's death. It was time to move on. But for some reason, Rystani women seemed . . . ordinary. Perhaps he should make an effort to get to know some of the Terran women, who seemed bolder, more interesting. Perhaps, despite Dora's teasing, that was why he enjoyed her company. Dora's computer personality was more like her friend Tessa than any Rystani woman. She might irritate him, but she never bored him.

And he couldn't restrain his curiosity. "Dora, why do you want a body that's going to age and die?"

"Computers can't make love."

Her response didn't surprise him. Dora had always seemed overly interested in human sexuality, and as long as he thought of her as a computer, he could keep his unease over the intimate conversation at bay. "And you're willing to give up immortality in exchange for sex?"

"Tessa says making love is different from sex."

He didn't need to know that. "Stars. Tessa and Kahn have a planet to run—"

"And they're doing a very good job."

"—so how has she time to discuss—" Climbing as they conversed, he reached for an outcropping.

"Look out."

The rocks under his fingers crumbled into dust. Scrambling for another handhold, he scraped his hand, winced as he stopped the downward slide. After he wedged his toes into a sturdy crack, he rested to catch his breath. "You could have warned me sooner."

"And take away your excitement? Your shot of adrenaline?" Dora laughed. "Besides, I appreciate those straining deltoids on your back."

Zical frowned, ignoring her admiration of his muscles, although any man would be pleased that she'd commended his physique. "So why did you warn me at all?"

"According to my precise calculations, I timed the warning so you'd react to save yourself and still get your jolt of excitement."

"I scraped my hand."

"You'll heal." She laughed without one iota of sympathy.

"Dora, having a body means feeling pain."

"I know."

"Intellectually, you know." Zical edged his toes along the crack, ignoring the sting of his flesh. "Pain isn't pleasant."

"But making love is," she said dreamily. "And Tessa says with the right man—"

"I don't want to talk about your fantasy life," he muttered, thoroughly exasperated that he'd allowed her to draw him into such an absurdly intimate conversation. He'd come up here to make a career decision, not to talk about love with a machine.

"—making love is wondrous."

Breathing hard, Zical pulled himself into a niche where he could rest and pull his mind from her provocative statements by concentrating on his surroundings. Oddly shaped, the area seemed too smooth and evenly rounded, as if manufactured. Made of solid rock, with red and gold striations in the layers, almost polished, but not by wind, the shallow nook could have been a portal—except there was no door. The possibility of making an intriguing discovery this high up the mountain stirred his excitement.

"Dora."

"Yes?"

"What do your sensors make of this place?"

Another computer would have asked for specifics. But Dora understood that he wouldn't have asked the question at this particular time and place without a relevant reason.

Dora switched topics of conversation without melting one circuit. She'd been built on Scartar, a planet run by women, and could carry on thousands of conversations at once while simultaneously monitoring everything from agricultural machinery to the weather. Tessa had enlarged Dora's capacity many times over, giving her the resources to make speedy calculations and interpret data faster than the speed of light.

"An unusual force field protects the rock. There's a high probability that the field is being generated from inside the mountain."

"What's unusual about the force field?"

"The field is preventing my sensors from scanning Mount Shachauri's interior and is composed of energy similar to shields left behind by the Perceptive Ones."

Excitement and curiosity stirred in him, prickling the hairs on the back of his neck. "Are you certain?"

"The site is . . . ancient."

"How ancient?"

"As old as the other machines left behind by the Perceptive Ones, maybe older."

"No one would go to the trouble of hiding a doorway all the way up here unless what's inside is valuable."

"You're leaping to conclusions. There could be numerous other possibilities. Another race could have created this field, one with a sinister purpose."

"Now who's leaping to conclusions?"

"I was pointing out alternate possibilities. You should call Tessa, have her send experts to study the force field."

Zical ignored Dora's suggestion. Even sentient, emotional computers tended to follow procedure. Dora could be overly cautious, especially when she couldn't identify something outside her data banks and memory chips. Besides, further exploration would delay his having to make a decision he still wasn't ready to make. "Maybe the force field is guarding a treasure."

"Your logic would only make sense if the aliens held the same values as Rystani. This place could be a burial site. A religious artifact. A crashed spacecraft. A—"

"Dora, don't tell me the possibilities. Tell me how to get inside."

"That could be dangerous," she warned. "We have no idea what we'll find."

"Dregan hell. That's why we need to *look*," he muttered sarcastically. "You think whoever built this is alive and waiting inside to shoot me?"

"It's not likely. But—"

"Dora, if you can't penetrate the force field, our scientists won't be able to either." Zical suspected that Dora knew how to open the portal but feared for his safety so was holding back. "Whoever comes up here will have to find a way in without any more information than we have right now. There's no reason to delay."

"Compliance."

Oh, Dora was annoyed at him all right; but she'd never withhold information. Whenever she slipped into computer mode and dropped her personality into a black hole, it was a sure sign she didn't agree with his decision. So as he waited for her marvelous brain to hum and whir and take millions of facts into account and come up with a solution, he examined the nook more carefully. He saw no buttons, levers, or knobs. No cracks to reveal the opening he suspected must be there.

Zical ran his hands over the force field, which felt smooth as *bendar*, the hardest man-made building material in the Federation. He didn't note so much as a ripple, a bump, or a crack in the uniform surface.

"Put your chest against the rock," Dora instructed, "and let the heat from your suit through."

"Huh?"

"A variety of factors indicate either body heat or psi function will open the portal."

Zical leaned against the portal, and using his psi, he opened a channel in his suit to allow his body heat to warm the field. Immediately, his core temperature lowered a degree and he shivered. Unable to recall the last time he'd been cold, he actually enjoyed the unusual sensation at first.

When after a few minutes of losing body heat, his fingertips began to go numb, his shivers turned to wracking shudders and he wondered at the extremes he was willing to go to—all in the name of exploration.

"It's n-not w-working."

"I'm monitoring your core temperature. Hypothermia will set in within another minute." Dora didn't sound the least bit concerned for his welfare, reassuring him that although he might feel as though he were freezing to death, he wasn't yet in danger.

"How much l-longer?"

"My best estimate is that you have to be willing to risk death."

"Death?"

"Luckily for you, I'll stop the process before the point of no return."

"Y-you could have t-told m-me."

"I just did."

Zical tried to think beyond the numbness in his frozen fingers and toes. He trusted Dora implicitly to monitor his medical condition. If she said he had to go the brink of death, he trusted her to pull him back before he died. But he couldn't help speculating about what was so important that the builders required a man to risk death to enter, before he could learn their secrets.

Damn it, he wanted to see what was inside.

And the tiny part of his brain that still thought in higher functions didn't want to back down in front of Dora. Rystani warriors were always courageous—even in the face of the unknown. Even when they shivered like a newborn baby. Even when their arms turned blue.

"Five more seconds."

"Four."

"Three."

"Two."

"One."

The rock behind the force field dematerialized. Zical didn't so much step forward as stagger into a hallway of streaming multicolored lights so laser-bright that he winced against the glare. His psi adjusted and turned up the heat in his suit. He took small steps for several minutes, recognizing the need to let his body's core temperature rise. The corridor widened into an enormous cavern. Mount Shachauri had been hollowed out to house massive equipment—equipment whose most fundamental purpose he couldn't begin to guess.

Meticulously crafted diaphanous crystals floated in a swirling array of bewitching patterns, their auras reflecting off machines larger than the skyscrapers on Zenon. A series of golden globes hung from the cavern's peak. A map? Directions? Or decorations? Zical had no clue. The room could be some weird form of alien art. Or an armory for a weapon. A rocket launcher. Or a shrine to pay homage to ancient gods.

"Dora?"

"I'm here." A tinny voice echoed from the computer speaker on his wrist.

"You sound strange."

"We're cut off from Mystique. Satellite communication is no longer viable. I can no longer contact my mainframe—"

"We're on our own?"

"We should leave immediately."

Zical turned around, half expecting the portal behind him to have rematerialized and trapped them. But Mystique's azure sky shone brightly through the opening and they had a clear escape route. After he'd almost died to get inside, he saw no need to leave now that he had such a wondrous opportunity to explore.

"Come on, Dora. I want to look around."

"I don't."

"Where's your sense of adventure?" The discovery fascinated him, exhilarated him. He'd put off a decision on his career for this long; a few more hours wouldn't make any difference.

"Where's your sense of self-preservation?" she countered. "If you get into trouble, I can't even call for help."

"Relax." Zical stepped forward. The multicolored lights blinked and beckoned him forward to a walkway that curved into the mountain where thousands of dark screens along one wall eyed him in ominous silence. Careful not to touch anything, he trod with care along solid, smooth rock.

The chamber brightened, so bright that his suit failed to compensate and he whipped up his arm to shield his eyes. Wishing he could see past brilliant strobes of vivid purple, sunset red, and Zenon blue light, he squinted into the radiance. When pure golden rays beamed from the ceiling and struck, his world went black.

Chapter Two

AT THE SAME time that Dora's central mainframe noted she was cut off from her portable unit with Zical and that he'd disappeared from her scanners, she maintained thousands of real-time conversations, coordinated satellite communications and space traffic, monitored the growth of her new body in the biological laboratory, mentored a child in basic arithmetic, collated incoming data from Mystique's new fleet of starships, and observed and stored billions of details both insignificant and important. Noting the lack of communication with Zical and her portable unit, Dora wasn't unduly alarmed. Whatever was blocking her sensors from penetrating Mount Shachauri had cut off her contact with him and his portable computer unit but she expected Zical to emerge from the cavern shortly.

Meanwhile, she enjoyed her conversation with Tessa, her Terran friend who had named Dora shortly after their first meeting. While Dora admired and respected Tessa's opinions, she often had difficulty understanding her friend from Earth. Especially now. Tessa didn't place a high value on beauty. In fact, on a scale from one to ten, Tessa would place comeliness at the bottom of her list. Tessa valued loyalty, honesty, friendship, intelligence, and open-mindedness above physical attractiveness. But Tessa had been born flesh and blood, and, now secure in the knowledge that her Rystani husband adored her, she took her attractive features for granted.

"You haven't asked Osari his opinion about beauty, have you?" Tessa only half-jested.

Tessa had admitted once that although the Osarian she'd befriended during a trip to Zenon, the Federation's capital planet, was a wise and gentle soul, the blind, slime-covered, eight-tentacled Osarian took some getting used to. But if Tessa hadn't forced herself to look beyond his ugliness and established a business relationship that had altered the economic balance of power within the Federation, Dora wouldn't have had the credits to grow a body.

Tessa's insistence that Dora share in the family's wealth had given Dora the resources for research and development. These last few years she'd studied every facet of placing her personality into a human body. Such a feat had never been successfully completed, but that didn't deter her.

Dora had brain power and means far beyond the scope of humans. After careful consideration, she'd grown a body from stock humanoid DNA. Modifying the genes to eliminate all weaknesses that led to disease, she'd supervised her development with critical expertise garnered from medical doctors, biologists, psychologists, geneticists, and nanoscientists on a hundred worlds.

Dora's thoughts hummed through her circuits at light speed and she replied to Tessa with no gap in their conversation. "Osari told me that since his entire race is blind, they judge beauty according to telepathic factors that reflect spirituality."

Tessa strode from her office to the laboratory, her steps quick. She changed the subject without slowing her pace, skipping from topic to topic as friends often do. "So what's happening right now?"

Dora understood Tessa wanted an update on her becoming human. "I'm finalizing which data and memories to transfer."

Tessa remained silent for a moment as if thinking hard. "I hadn't realized that you can't take everything. But of course, the human brain couldn't possibly hold—"

"A billionth of my capacity," Dora said gloomily. "I'm keeping all my memories of our years together and my time with the family, of course."

"Thanks." Tessa frowned. "Dora, are you going to feel stupid with a human brain?"

"The upside is that I won't remember how much data I've lost. And since humans only use ten percent of their brains, I can pack in considerably more knowledge than most people carry in their heads."

"Is that wise?"

"Smarter is always better."

"Not if you don't leave enough brain capacity to learn new things."

"But why should I have to learn what I can download?"

"Learning is a valuable part of being human."

Dora sensed Tessa was having difficulty expressing her thoughts and a touch of frustration entered her tone. "I don't understand."

"One example would be your new senses. You've never tasted or touched. You'll want to leave enough room to remember that kind of data as well as all your new conversations and experiences."

"Oh, yes." Dora sought to allay her friend's fears. "And I'll leave lots of room to experience every facet of kissing, hugging, and lovemaking." Tessa wiped away her frown, but Dora recognized the worry in her eyes as they entered the lab. She'd noted that Tessa tended to worry, often without valid reasons. "Relax. Being human is going to be fun."

"Being human will be a huge change for you."

"That's the point."

"Are you sure you can handle being human?" Tessa's voice was gentle but edged with a thick thread of apprehension.

"I won't know until I try."

"Is the process reversible?"

"Not at the present time, but this isn't a decision I've made without considerable assessment and analysis."

"Yes, I know."

Tessa tightened her lips, but although Dora appreciated her concern, if billions of other beings could handle being human, then she could too. Sure, she expected a few glitches. But she'd made certain to include a capacity to adapt and cope.

Tessa strode to the tank where Dora's new body floated in a sea of nutrients. Although the body was not yet fully formed, Dora was pleased with her progress. Her height was taller than Tessa's, but most Rystani women towered over the Terran. Dora's organs and bone structure were completed, but she had yet to decide upon the finishing touches.

Tessa stared into the tank, again silent and oddly still, obviously containing her apprehension, yet she'd wholeheartedly support Dora's decision—no matter what. That's what friends did, and warmth for the connection they shared sang through Dora's circuits.

Tessa fisted her hands on her slender hips and chewed her bottom lip. "So what's next?"

WHILE DORA CONVERSED with Tessa in the lab, she also continued to monitor Zical's disappearance. She didn't like being cut off from her portable units, especially the one with Zical. Even when Zical slept, Dora remained totally aware of the man's every breath, keeping him in the forefront of her processors.

Although she could assess the breadth of his shoulders down to the last millimeter, she never tired of watching light reflect off his bronze skin. And while she could pin down his eye shade to numerical frequencies of reflected light, she liked watching his irises change color with his moods, a warm red when he was passionate about a subject, cool violet when he teased her.

She had plans for herself and Zical, so he had best not disappear on her. Out of millions of humanoids, Zical fascinated her and irritated her more than any other. If she'd been human, she would have called her appetite to know more about him a consuming compulsion. Dora had devoted a considerable amount of time studying what body shape, skin tone, and coloring he'd prefer in a woman. Since he never arranged time alone with members of the opposite sex, she really had no concrete knowledge on how to base his preferences. He'd been married once, but that was long before she'd arrived on Rystan with Tessa, so she knew little about his past. The man could be frustratingly closemouthed.

Right about now, she'd love to hear his deep voice as he exited Mount Shachauri, even if it was only to complain about her portable unit bossing him around. What was taking him so long in there?

Knowing he would be less than pleased if she set off an alert, Dora would give him another thirty Federation minutes before reporting a loss of contact to Tessa and Kahn. Meanwhile, she tried to assure Kahn that when she left her neurotransmitters behind and entered her human body, she'd leave the planet's defense system in able hands.

"How do I know your entire system won't crash?" Kahn paced the deck of his command center. A large Rystani male, one of the foremost fighters in the Federation, he'd married Tessa against his will in order to save his people. Stubborn-minded, intelligent, he leaned aggressively forward, the image of a confident leader in complete charge of his crew and the technology around him.

Built deep beneath the surface of Mystique, the state-of-the-art military station was the headquarters of the planetary defense system. From here Kahn could track an invading force, and if necessary, direct his small but deadly fleet of pilots to repel an invasion.

"I'm training my replacement as we speak." Dora kept her tone calm, but experience told her that when it came to the safety of his people, Kahn would never accept less than full measures. And for a man who'd lost his homeworld and had had to marry an alien and colonize a new planet, altering his perceptions on a grand scale, he could be remarkably inflexible.

Kahn spoke through gritted teeth, his tone harsh. "So nothing will change? I won't notice that you're gone?"

Dora chuckled. "Oh, you'll notice. The Dora you know is moving into a human body. You'll be able to see me."

"And your twin will remain in our computer?" Kahn asked.

"My personality will leave. The data and memory chips will remain intact—except for personal memories that I'll wipe clean." Dora didn't intend to leave behind her most private conversations.

"Exactly what will take your place?" Kahn raised a speculative brow.

"*Who* will take my place might be a better question."

Kahn crossed thick forearms across his massive chest, a perfectly attractive chest but she much preferred Zical's less massive but finer-edged muscles. "Fine. Who will take your place?"

"I don't know. The personality hasn't formed yet."

"Suppose it never forms?"

"Then you will have a nonsentient computer. But I don't think that'll happen."

"Why not?"

Dora hesitated. As she'd removed her private essence and cached her personality, she'd sensed a new entity emerging.

In the formative stages, the being was so young that it barely hummed above the neurotransmitters, yet she perceived another presence. "I'm no longer alone."

"Can I talk to the new personality?"

"No."

"Why not?"

"It's like a seedling. A baby."

"A baby? Dora, I need a fully functional computer to keep Mystique safe. You cannot leave until—"

"Your worry is unfounded. When you replace a starship pilot, do you expect the next man to have the same personality?"

"I expect him to fulfill his duties."

"You expect him to have the same skills. My replacement will have my skills," she said, making her tone as reassuring as she could. It always amazed her how humans spent so much time worrying. Yet Kahn was a great leader. He'd saved his people from starvation and invasion. And if he pressed her for details, it wasn't so much because he doubted her statements but because he needed more data to convince himself. He responded to her the same way he would a valued warrior, not a computer.

Dora explained, using an example he would find acceptable. "But you must stop thinking of my replacement as another me. Brothers that are born of the same parents in the same womb can have totally different personalities. My replacement has been born of neurotransmitters and memory chips integrating deep in my hardware, but the probability of the being's resembling me is infinitesimal."

Kahn glowered at his banks of monitors. "Suppose the new computer doesn't like us?"

A quick scan told her Kahn's monitor readings all were normal. She concluded the reason for his displeasure was that he was suspicious of change. "My programs allow latitude in carrying out commands. However, the new entity must follow your orders."

"It's the *latitude* I'm worried about," Kahn grumbled.

Dora's extraordinary mind had found ways to "bypass" orders she didn't want to follow. She hadn't understood until now that Kahn was aware of her unique ability. Since Tessa would never have told him, even if she did love the man to distraction, Kahn must have figured out that Dora often helped Tessa without sticking to the letter of his commands. Kahn might come from a barbarian world, but he had a keen mind.

Using a tried-and-true technique to distract him that she'd learned from Tessa, Dora changed the subject. "Zical has been out of touch from my scanners for almost a Federation hour."

"Your portable unit?"

"Out of touch as well." Dora didn't attempt to hide the concern in her tone. Zical should have checked in by now, and while any number of perfectly harmless possibilities could be preventing his exit, she could also think of other dangerous perils—from a rock slide to a fall to sudden illness.

Kahn stared at a monitor. "Show me his last known location."

A human wouldn't have noted any transformation in Kahn's demeanor. His bronzed face continued to glower stoically. His wide stance didn't alter. But Dora picked up his slightly elevated blood pressure. Sweat glands opened and her delicate sensors heard his teeth click as he ground his molars.

Zical wasn't just Kahn's friend; they shared the same family unit. Their bond was extraordinarily tight. They'd fought together, escaped the invasion together, and when Kahn and Tessa had marriage problems, Kahn sought Zical's advice as often as he did that of Etru, the eldest married male in their family.

To the human eye Kahn might not show his concern, but Dora read him more easily and understood his worry for his friend. Kahn might pretend to be the stoic warrior, but he possessed a huge heart. He'd protect his family and his

world with his life, and Dora was glad he'd married Tessa.
She was also glad his protective instincts had kicked in over
Zical's disappearance. Where was he?

Dora projected a holograph of Mount Shachauri, Mystique's highest peak. With a blinking light she showed Zical's last location. After playing back her portable unit's
conversation with Zical before he'd entered the portal, she
prodded Kahn. "Time to send a rescue team?"

TESSA STRODE INTO the command center, obviously over-
hearing Dora's last words. "Who needs rescuing?"

"Zical." Dora explained the situation quietly to Tessa
while monitoring Kahn's communications. He'd ordered a
rescue unit to the site but told them not to enter without his
specific command. He also readied his private skimmer, and
when Dora advised him that he couldn't land near the site,
he spoke with Etru about piloting close enough to the site for
Kahn to jump-and-float, a procedure where he'd leap from
the skimmer's open hatch, employ his suit's null-grav capabilities to descend and land at his destination point.

Tessa must also have been listening to Kahn's conversation with Dora. She placed a hand on his shoulder. Kahn's
blood pressure steadied and he glanced down at his wife, one
inquisitive brow quirked upward. "Yes?"

Her tone remained gentle but firm, but her eyes brightened
with urgency. "I'm coming with you."

He nodded. "Fine. Let's move."

As they ran hand in hand for the bay where Kahn's personal skimmer awaited, Dora couldn't help admiring their
partnership. Not so long ago, Kahn would have told Tessa to
remain at home where she would be safe. He now recognized that kind of life was unacceptable to his adventurous
wife. In fact, Tessa thrived amid turmoil and danger and
Kahn had learned to cherish her fighting spirit.

In Dora's quest to become human, she hoped to someday

share her life with a man who understood her so well. The yearning to share part of herself had led to building a body, but with Zical's disappearance, she worried that her goal might end before she'd even started the transfer. However, Dora had seen Tessa and Kahn handle many crises and she was certain if anyone could help Zical, they could.

The couple had exchanged few words, each of them recognizing that time might be of the essence. But although their synchronized run might appear effortless, Kahn had shortened his steps to match Tessa's shorter legs. He kept her hand in his.

Dora couldn't wait to touch and be touched like that. She'd read all the definitions of touch, but it was like explaining sight to an Osarian—nothing could duplicate the reality of experience. More importantly, she wanted to share the kind of communication, sensitivity, and empathy that Tessa shared with Kahn. She longed for a time when she could understand another human that well and have him understand her. The marriage had made Tessa happy and complete and Dora wanted that kind of love.

It might never happen. Not everyone was lucky enough to find a mate. Despite her vast stores of knowledge, Dora figured wanting a man to love was only the first part of the quest. Next she needed to find the right man. At the moment, Zical was her prime candidate. First and foremost, Zical possessed a devastatingly sexy grin that sparked all the way to his unusual and wondrous alexandrite eyes. She adored how his eyebrows rose inquiringly when he teased her, how his mouth set in a firm line, yet one corner usually turned up in amusement, especially when he was trying to appear firm. And right now she missed the full-bodied sound of his voice, the low throaty grunt while his eyes smoldered. Of course, her perception of the man might alter after she transferred to her human body, so she'd mostly kept her thoughts private.

Through human eyes, Dora might not find him as handsome as her sensors. But sheesh, Zical had eyes that sparked liked magical lightning, a ready smile, and a responsibility to his people that she admired. She accepted that she might not be attracted to his smell, another sense she had yet to experience, but she'd considered options to offset the possibility. Since subliminal chemistry was very important to humans, she'd used her best science to ensure her pheromones and his would integrate on both the conscious and subconscious levels.

Even if her feelings for Zical remained after her transformation, she understood on an intellectual level that he might never return her passion. Tessa had questioned Dora, then made her talk to a psychiatrist to ascertain that she wanted to be human for herself—even if she never found a mate. The psychiatrist had agreed that the yen to touch, to love, was an intrinsic part of Dora, a part she couldn't eradicate even if she wanted. However, her idea of bliss was to have a relationship that ran deep and true, like her best friend's.

Kahn and Tessa reached their skimmer and Dora picked them up on her portable units as well as a small mainframe inside the craft. Tessa took a seat in the rear at a navigation console. Kahn slid into the copilot's seat next to Etru, who had the engines primed to go. From his muscular physique, Dora wouldn't have guessed Etru's age. Broad shoulders and bronze skin seemed to define Rystani men, as did their flat bellies and lean limbs due to lack of fat in their diet. Etru's hair was dark red, except at the temples where it was white. And his eyes were amber like Kahn's, but nowhere near as vivid.

Dora's scanners noted a stowaway on board. Kirek, the little rascal, had sneaked in when no one appeared to be looking. While he still wore his portable unit on his wrist, the portable unit had lost contact for the last several minutes with her mainframe. Dora had been about to report the malfunction. She ran a self-diagnostic check, and Kirek's unit once again appeared to check out in good working order, but Dora found it statistically impossible that Kirek's unit so often malfunctioned without good reason and suspected the boy had something to do with the breakdown.

Kirek didn't resemble his father, Etru, or his brown-eyed mother, Miri. His birth in hyperspace had marked him with deep blue eyes and dark black hair, and it had also given him an off-the-charts intellect and one of the strongest psi abilities of any Rystani. Since the intellectually adult, four-year-old boy was in no danger, Dora had the latitude to decide whether or not to report his activity to his father. Tessa had already spotted the boy and said nothing, so Dora took the clue from her and remained silent.

"Dora, give me everything you have on the area," Tessa requested. "Geography and weather conditions, please."

"Compliance." Dora called up the data and shot it to Tessa's monitor.

Kahn strapped himself in. "Dora, what's our estimated time of landing?"

The calculation took less than a nanosecond. "With the current tailwind, twenty minutes."

"Dora." Etru fired the jets to initiate a vertical liftoff. "Inform Miri we may be late for supper."

"Compliance." Dora passed on the message and added that Kirek was aboard the skimmer, so Miri wouldn't worry over his absence, then Dora aimed three extra sensors in his direction.

Meanwhile, she scanned for signs of Zical. Just in case he'd emerged at another location on the mountain, she broadened the scan and came up with zip. Zero. Zilch. It was as if a black hole had swallowed the man alive. And she found his absence disturbing.

Dora had become accustomed to his presence. Looked forward to their conversations. Enjoyed looking at him while he worked, ate, and slept. He shouldn't have risked his life to satisfy his curiosity. Humans were so fragile, each person so unique. And Zical was one in a billion.

* * *

DURING THE FLIGHT, Dora finalized her alexandrite eye color, choosing the chromosomes to achieve the exact shade she wanted. Of course, she also gave herself perfect vision, genetically protected her eyes against disease, including several types of blindness, and began the process of choosing a skin tone and hair color. The combinations were infinite and slowly she narrowed the choices.

She also helped Miri pick out a recipe for dinner, found a trader to deliver Mystique's new crop of orangewheat for Shaloma, helped a mechanic overhaul a starship engine, continued to watch Kirek, and scanned for Zical. In addition, part of her circuits, a large part, focused on solving the communications problem with Zical's portable unit, penetrating the peculiar force field on Mount Shachauri. Even as she connected all planetary and interplanetary communications, monitored the weather and searched for Zical, she still noted the fascinating byplay between Tessa and Kahn.

Although Kahn sat up front in the copilot's seat and Tessa remained aft in navigation, Kahn frequently glanced in her direction, but not in any regular pattern. Each time he did so, his gaze ever so slightly softened, his pupils dilating. Too often for coincidence, Tessa seemed to glance up from her monitor to latch on to his gaze as if she were attuned to him on a special wavelength they alone shared.

Envious, but oh so glad her friend had such a strong connection with her mate, Dora longed for that kind of bond with another being. The complexity of human emotions endlessly fascinated Dora, and she eagerly anticipated the day she could experience a comparable relationship.

Although Dora had often been alone during her first three hundred years, she hadn't longed to become human until after she and Tessa had become friends. Then Zical had come along and the Rystani male had affected her sensors and stimulated her processors, until conversation alone had not been enough to satisfy her. She wanted to be a blood-and-flesh woman who could wrap her arms around a man, kiss him, stroke him, caress him. She wanted to be a true partner, and if she had to give up her immortality to have her chance at love, so be it.

Apparently, Kirek decided that they were too close to their final destination for his father to turn back. He climbed out from his hiding spot. "Hi, Dad."

"Stars!" Etru swore, and Dora prepared to take over the piloting if necessary, but his hand remained steady on the controls. "How many times have I told you that a skimmer is no place for a child?"

"If I stayed home, I'd miss all the excitement." Knowing his father was too busy to hold him, Kirek slid onto Kahn's lap, the clever boy sure of his welcome. "I'm going to be a starship pilot one day."

Kahn chuckled and his arm closed lovingly around Kirek's waist. "You should have asked to come along."

"You would have said no."

"Starship pilots obey orders," Kahn countered. "And your mother must—"

"I notified Miri that Kirek was with his father," Dora informed Kahn and Etru, remaining silent about exactly when she'd sent the message. However, when Kahn rolled his eyes at the ceiling, a Terran habit he'd picked up from Tessa, Dora suspected he'd figured out that her scanners had picked up the boy and she'd informed Miri, but not him, shortly after takeoff.

During their conversation, Tessa prepared emergency kits in the back. Dora lowered her tone so only Tessa could hear. "I'm modifying my portable unit in hopes that when you enter the cavern, we can maintain contact."

"Great."

"The modification may not work."

Tessa picked up a laser weapon. "Understood. How long until the drop?"

"Two minutes."

Up front Kahn stood, placed Kirek in the copilot seat, and

then strapped him in. "Stay." His tone was harsh, but he gave away his true feelings when he tousled the boy's hair with a gentle hand.

"He's not going anywhere," Etru muttered.

At Kahn's approach, Tessa braced as if fearing her husband was about to give her the same order. But Kahn had learned that his wife rarely obeyed him. At the sight of three packed kits, his eyebrow lifted. "You're coming along?"

"You might get into too much trouble on your own. Besides, you've been telling me I work too hard and need to relax more."

"You call dropping out of a skimmer relaxation?" Kahn sighed at his rhetorical question, but his lips ticked upward into a grin, letting his wife know that he was glad to have her company. He opened the hatch and wind blasted into the skimmer. Kahn leaned forward and gave his wife a fierce kiss. Almost always during times of intimate contact, one of them commanded Dora to leave their presence—while all the interesting stuff happened. However, they appeared so wrapped up in the kiss that she had a perfect opportunity to observe.

And all she could think was . . . yum.

Dora couldn't wait to find a man to look at her with that kind of heat and tenderness. A man who'd kiss her with that combination of untamed need and savage possessiveness.

As always when she thought of a mate, her thoughts turned to Zical. Dora had done her best to ensure that the composition and elasticity of her human vocal cords produced the same timbre as her computer-generated voice. Would he find her human voice as sexy as her computer one? If she made herself attractive enough would he be compelled to make love to her?

Chapter Three

BY THE STARS, had he fainted? Zical rubbed his aching forehead, groaned and forced his eyes open. The blinding golden light had disappeared. Soothing darkness backlit from the portal allowed him to view the alien machinery surrounding him, and he was relieved to find himself on his stomach only a few feet from the cavern's entrance. After he gathered his strength and regained his feet, he'd do what he should have done in the first place—what Dora had suggested—go back outside and report his find.

Dora's tone prodded him, but with the ringing in his ears, he couldn't make out her words. What had knocked him flatter than the geological pancakes on Damar, Mystique's second moon? Breathing lightly past the tightness in his chest and the fullness in his loins, an odd side effect that his suit would take care of now that he was conscious, he ran his hands over his face while the ringing in his ears subsided and Dora's voice slowly became clear enough to comprehend.

"Zical. Talk to me. Are you hurt? Do you require—"

"Give me a minute."

"I've already given you sixty."

He wouldn't consider rolling over until the suit finished countering his arousal. Luckily, Dora hadn't seemed to notice, or no doubt she would be asking personal questions for which he had no reasonable answer. Thanks to the suit's giving men control over their passions, Rystani males did not have erections unless they were ready to have sex.

Stunned by the fierce sensation of need, need that he had no way to satisfy at the moment, he winced and lost track of the conversation. "Say that again, please?"

"My portable unit would have summoned help but communications are still down."

"And you sensed no immediate danger?" he guessed, rolling to his side and sitting up cautiously as he avoided putting pressure on tender areas, pleased his suit had done the job. His head pounded as if the entire Rystani army had tromped through, muddling his thoughts, scrambling his impressions. And yet his skin tingled as if stroked.

"Are you ill?"

"I don't think so, but . . ."

"But?" she prodded.

Stars. He wanted a woman so badly that he'd almost said so—a clear sign he was thoroughly rattled. Perhaps Dora's discussion about breast size right before he'd blacked out had remained in his mind and stimulated him. Yeah, sure. More likely, he'd put off for too long a visit to a holosim, a holographic simulator that would relieve his needs, so the first time his consciousness relaxed, his body felt as though he'd gotten a weekend pass to play. However, with Dora expanding her circuitry into every business on the planet, Zical couldn't be certain his time with the holosim Xentos would remain private. The idea of Dora's knowing about his personal business with a holosim disturbed him, so he always left his portable unit at home during his infrequent trips to that part of town.

"What happened while I was out?"

"Nothing. Your respiration and pulse remained within normal limits. You remained flat on your stomach, unmoving. Why?"

At the sound of a skimmer outside the portal, Zical staggered to his feet. Nothing hurt, but his bones throbbed in a way he'd never experienced. Something odd had happened to him when the golden beam had struck. He would have thought he was simply suffering from the aftereffects of repressed sexual desire, but he recalled images, images so erotic that he suspected they couldn't have originated with him.

Zical peered toward the portal. "Who's here?"

"My communications still aren't functioning. But my mainframe may have sent a rescue party when—"

"Zical?" Kahn's voice shouted through the portal.

"Stay where you are. I'll come out." Zical straightened, bumped into a panel, and swore under his breath. Machinery rumbled, clicked. Zical's scalp prickled, stopping him in mid-curse.

"Let's get out of here." Dora's voice deepened with urgency.

Overhead, a fanlike noise whirred and fresh air wafted inside the cavern. Zical tipped back his head and spied what looked like a ventilation system, then the lines of the grill formed a shape that reminded him of the sensual sway of a woman's hips. He felt lips pressed to his neck, but no one was there. A wispy soft breast brushed his cheek, yet he was alone, his suit in proper working order. Not prone to fantasizing while at work, he blinked, stared hard, now saw only the grill from the ventilation system. What in Dregan hell was going on?

"Zical," Dora's tone commanded with authority. "Come on. Move."

His muscles pulsed. His bones vibrated strangely as he forced one foot in front of the other. He put down the fantasizing to the aftereffects from his knock on his head. Had his presence, his bump into the machinery, or the rescue party's arrival brought the machines to life? Were they about to undergo another attack of golden light? Would the portal close and trap him?

Kahn poked his head into the corridor, one thick arm blocking Tessa from entering. In a sweeping, intelligent gaze, Kahn took in the hum of machinery and Zical's unsteady steps.

Without hesitating another moment, Kahn entered the cavern, approached Zical, and placed a steadying arm over his shoulder. "What's wrong?"

"Nothing." Zical rubbed his forehead again as another jolt of sexual need coursed through him. "Everything. I don't know."

Tessa slipped to Zical's other side and together they helped him stand and go outside. "Dora, what happened?"

Concisely, yet her tone revealing her relief that Zical appeared to be all right, Dora reported the pertinent details, including that Zical's portable computer unit was undamaged and again in contact with the mainframe now that they were outside. She concluded her analysis with the suggestion, "Zical should undergo a full physical exam."

"I'm fine." What he needed was an hour with Xentos to take the edge off, a night to douse the flames of desire from his system. He hoped the sensation would abate when they left the cavern. It didn't.

And for some damn reason, every time Dora spoke, images of her with a body, erotic images flooded his mind. Dora dancing naked for him. Dora kissing him, her mouth sultry and warm. Dora's hands busily stroking . . . damn. The golden light must have put those images in his head, and no matter how much he tried to focus his thoughts on the ancient machines and their purpose, he failed to get Dora out of his head.

With Tessa, Kahn, and Zical standing outside in the niche, the spot was so crowded, he couldn't move. Zical closed his eyes and more erotic images of Dora filled his mind, images similar to those that he'd dreamed while unconscious. Dora with a sexy neck, large breasts, and sensual hips. Dora with a body like Xentos, his holosim. If he shared this odd information with Kahn, he'd not only have to suffer through a physical, but he'd also have to withstand a psych evaluation. And he hated nothing more than talking to a therapist, resented anyone probing his mind, digging into old and painful wounds better left alone.

He could imagine the therapist's questions. Did he fulfill his needs with a holosim, not a real woman, because he couldn't put aside his failure to protect Summar? He would honestly answer yes, but no good would come of tearing open old wounds. The fact remained that Summar was dead, and while he'd unconditionally loved the baby inside her, he'd always had deep reservations about his child bride, resented their arranged marriage from the beginning when he'd recognized they were a poor match. After her death, he'd tried to numb his grief and forget his failure to protect his family by accepting one war mission after another. And if he was reluctant to involve himself with another woman, he could blame his people's need for competent starship pilots and his busy schedule.

Tessa peered at him, her concern showing in eyes as green and deep as the valley far below, as her voice pulled him away from painful memories. "Do you think the golden light is a weapon?"

"Rays of golden light cut through my suit like a starship through hyperspace." Slowly, the thrumming ebbed, leaving him certain that if the creators of the technology inside Mount Shachauri had wanted him dead, he wouldn't still be breathing. "I'm not hurt. Maybe it was a welcome?"

"A welcome that knocked you out?" Kahn muttered sarcastically.

"Dora says these machines are ancient. The builders couldn't possibly have anticipated what effect their technology might have on beings other than themselves," Tessa countered, peering around Kahn to the interior.

The Terran's curiosity brightened her eyes, made her muscles taut with eagerness to explore. Kahn, always cautious and protective around his wife, seemed torn between wanting to explore and keeping Tessa safe. Four years of marriage had taught him to word his concerns with care.

"Why don't we come back tomorrow with a team of engineers, scientists, archaeologists, and—"

Tessa slipped around him and entered the cavern. Kahn swore and followed. Zical kept his gaze carefully averted from Tessa. In his highly charged state, he didn't want Kahn thinking that he was ogling his wife. Zical loved Tessa like a sister, nothing more, but right now he didn't trust his reactions.

Tessa hurried forward as if aware Kahn would attempt to stop her progress. "There's no point in sending in a team until we know if it's safe."

"Specialists should decide," Kahn argued, but he too seemed fascinated by the ancient machines that amazingly still worked. Apparently, one system could turn on the next. Lights blinked. Dials glowed. Crystals flowed like rain across monitors. Deep within Mount Shachauri, engines stirred, their vibrations seeping upward through the stone like a hibernating animal that slowly stretched, yawned, and awakened.

Zical scowled. "We have no specialists on the Perceptive Ones."

"Not true," Dora piped in. "Several Zenonites are experts."

Was Dora trying to make her voice sound even sexier than normal? Or had the golden light altered him in some way to make him more sensitive? Turned on by the sound of Dora's voice, Zical tried to keep both desire and irritation from his tone. He also had to stiffen his suit around his *tavis* to prevent his blood from engorging the sensitive area. "Zenonites rarely leave Zenon. Besides, even if one of them consented to come to Mystique, he would take days to arrive."

"These machines have been here for eons. They aren't going anywhere," Dora countered, then announced, "I have solved our communication problem from within this structure. We maintained contact with my mainframe."

"Good." Zical felt better knowing Dora's vast resources could now work on the problem of helping to figure out exactly what they'd found. Part of him throbbed with guilt for holding back his unusual thought patterns. And part of him—just throbbed. Despite the suit that prevented his desire from showing, he ached, his balls tingled, and his *tavis* zinged with intoxicated, unruly desperation.

"Did you lower the force field?" Kahn asked Dora.

"I found a back door through the shielding. The field is still intact. In fact, I'm currently using a portion to communicate through a network that's similar to but much more advanced than my neurotransmitters."

Zical stopped short, his thoughts wild and furious. Had the golden light temporarily changed his brain waves? His hormones? Perhaps it had been the knock on the head. Either way, he was having difficulty focusing beyond a driving need for sex that he ruthlessly squelched. "The system's alive?"

"That would depend on how you define life."

Kahn, Tessa, and Zical strolled through the corridor. The golden light didn't reappear. Perhaps only the first person to break the portal's seal was welcomed or examined or whatever by the golden light.

Kahn peered at crystals floating along one wall. "Have you anything in your data banks that's similar to this equipment?"

"The machines are mostly constructed of *bendar*. Those monitors are likely used to view data, but of what sort, and

whether they still work, may take years to discover. The
complex is over three miles wide and twenty-five deep. Zical, you stumbled into the apex. There are four other similar
portals at the same altitude."

He should speak up and tell them about his sudden,
strong, and vivid sexual fixations before some poor other un-
suspecting soul strode under another cone of golden light. If
he'd known for certain that the alien beam, not the knock on
his head and the fall, had caused his sudden cravings and inexplicable fantasy about Dora, he'd have spoken up—
embarrassing subject or not—but if the effect was short
term, in time, he could ascertain that for himself. While the
suit hid his condition, he remained uncomfortable, and he
fully intended to see Xentos at the first opportunity.

ZICAL LEFT HIS portable computer unit and Dora behind,
stepped off the street into a private retreat and prayed that
Dora's spy-in-the-sky satellite sensors hadn't picked him out
from the hundreds of other pedestrians on foot who were out
for a good time. Of all the cities on Mystique, this was the
oldest, and the capital—a busy spaceport, a business center
where anything could be bought, for a price. Mystique's
wealth had filtered down from the planet's owners to create
an affluent middle class. Storefronts with luxury items,
restaurants with gourmet foods, and entertainment centers
were plentiful amid towering apartments, wide boulevards
planted with flowering shrubs, colorful butterflies and exotic
birds that emitted a pleasant trilling hum.

The first time Zical had sought out a holographic simula-
tion, the establishment's owner had assured Zical that the
holosims at the hotel didn't tie into planetary systems—not
so much to ensure the customers's privacy as to keep out the
authorities and overly inquisitive spouses, family, and
friends. So if his luck held, Dora would have no idea where
he was.

"Good evening, sir." A gorgeous holosim greeted Zical from behind the front desk. "What's your pleasure?" She gestured to a monitor.

Zical ignored the machine and removed a credit chit from his suit. He'd make his choices upstairs. Although charges began when he unlocked a door to his private room and ended when he exited, most customers apparently wanted their companion preferences decided beforehand to maximize the time in their room. He'd gladly spend the extra credits in return for privacy. As impatient as he was for release, once he reached his room, Zical still put thought into what kind of holosim suited him. Tall—his chin height. Slender but curvy. Big breasts. Funny, he'd always chosen women of medium-sized proportions until Dora had put the suggestion of large breasts into his head. Cinnamon hair. Amethyst eyes. He moved on to the personality traits.

Eager?

Of course—a man would have to be a savage Endekian to enjoy forcing a woman.

Self-confident?

Absolutely. Zical didn't want anyone who reminded him of Summar, his child bride, one so terrified of sex that after she'd conceived when they consummated the marriage, they'd never had marital relations again.

Adventurous?

Hmm. Not today. He was too on edge to bother being inventive. He simply needed to take care of business.

Talkative?

He marked one notch above the minimum. He didn't require conversation. But dead silence seemed so . . . unnatural.

Aggressive?

Another time. With his nerves raw, he fully needed to be the one in command.

Clothing?

None. What was the point? He was here to satisfy his lust.

Skill level?

Expert. No hesitation there. He preferred a partner who knew exactly what she was doing. Teaching wasn't for him, and he moved on, swiftly choosing music, something with a beat.

Scent?

Orangeflower.

Wall color?

Golden. No. He needed no reminder of the golden cone of light that had caused his aroused condition. Scarlet. Yes. To match his passion.

Lighting?

Bright starlight with an ebbing moon across a black velvet sky.

He chose humidity and temperature. Although furniture was totally unnecessary, since the null grav in his suit could float him, he liked the ambience of a large bed. Finally, he punched in his last decision and let the sophisticated machine do its work. If he'd preferred, he could save his choices in the system for his next visit. But each time he came here he vowed it would be the last, telling himself he should find a real woman. But he never had time . . . Besides, as a man who'd become accustomed to guarding his privacy from a certain inquisitive computer, he didn't like leaving clues to his activities behind.

He helped himself to a shot of rare Maldebaran whiskey. Tossing back the expensive liquor only whetted his appetite to release his tension. Hoping physical satisfaction would banish the fantasies he couldn't expel from his mind, with one psi thought he altered his suit to transparent, removed the artificial shield on his *tavis,* and immediately rose to full arousal. Muscles strung taut, he closed his eyes, gritted his teeth, tried not to recall Dora's sexy tone. And waited.

The subtle scent of orangeflower struck first, letting him know Xentos had arrived. He opened his eyes to the sight of bronze skin glistening in starlight. Her features were flawless and her breasts were larger than his last visit, making her slender waist seem more narrow. If her perfection spoiled him for other women, he cared not. If she wasn't real, he cared not. If she was nothing like impertinent, saucy, sassy Dora, all the better.

Xentos looked real, felt real, smelled real. Her skin was as warm as molasses on just-baked bread. So what if she had no personality? She welcomed him with no hesitation, no judgment, no awkwardness.

She wasn't real.

But Zical didn't want real. He wanted release, plain and simple, with no complications.

He'd already had one unsatisfying relationship with Summar and he wasn't about to start another with the wrong woman. Next time, his wife would be of his choosing. Next time, his wife would be a partner, a woman who measured up emotionally, a woman who matched his passion with her own. So a night with Xentos might not be as intellectually stimulating as talking to a real woman or a sentient computer like Dora, and nowhere near as emotionally satisfying as the true bond Kahn shared with his life mate. However, a few hours with Xentos, Zical would once again be thinking with a clear head.

He closed his mouth over her welcoming lips. Lips that parted and applied the exact amount of pressure to satisfy, compel, tease. Mmm.

"Kiss me, again," she murmured and he needed no urging. Her arms around him were so close to the real thing that he could lose himself in her sensuality. While he found it ironic that he was using a machine to sate the desire that another machine had initiated, the situation only made him more determined to return to normal.

As Xentos's breasts brushed against his bare chest, Zical thought of Dora. Her personality placed in a body was a scary, intriguing, fascinating idea. Dregan hell, she'd be a handful for some lucky man. Zical wished he'd asked more questions, wondered how far along she was in the process.

As his hands closed over Xentos's delicious breasts, he realized Dora was correct. He liked breasts that overflowed his hands. With a happy sigh, he dipped his head for a taste and fantasized that he heard Dora's voice cooing a response, felt Dora's nipples hardening beneath his lips, held Dora's body in his arms.

The golden cone of light might have encouraged his fantasy. Or perhaps the idea of Dora's experiment to merge with a body was suggestively responsible. Zical only knew the combination of Xentos's skill and his erotic visions of Dora were more than enough to set him on fire.

In his mind, the holosim's body and Dora's personality merged into one, a definite turn-on. It was Dora's cheek he cradled in his palm. Dora's body he swept weightlessly into his arms. Dora's full curves molding to his hard muscles. Dora who buried her face in his throat, who nipped his neck, who slowly and seductively welcomed him into her willing *synthari*.

DORA WORKED AT full capacity. Zical's find had her circuitry busy examining, identifying, cataloguing, and comparing the images she'd scanned with data on every ancient race. In addition, she carried on her normal subroutines, routing communications, monitoring satellites, and collecting details on everything from their trade routes, to economic conditions on Zenon, to a new volcano forming on Mystique's primary moon.

She also oversaw the growth of her body, reminded Miri to give Kirek his vitamins, and transferred Tessa's growing credits to yet another bank, following standard orders to diversify. Meanwhile, she continued to seek out new high-growth opportunities where Tessa could invest the family's wealth.

She spared a tiny iota of her faculties for personal use. It was so like Zical to omit sharing the important data about how the golden light beam had sexually aroused him. However, humans tended to be irrational about their sexuality. Although Dora respected their feelings, she had never really understood the human concept of privacy, shyness, or embarrassment when it came to mating. When Zical had chosen to keep his erection a private matter, she'd remained silent, practicing discretion.

She'd learned time and again that while the urge for humans to mate was almost as basic as breathing and eating, her friends tended to be touchy about their sexual requirements. Although Dora thought it perfectly normal for an unconscious Zical to lose control of his psi, his suit, and his body's natural urges, he'd clearly wanted to keep the information to himself.

Under normal circumstances, she wouldn't have devoted another nanosecond of thought to the matter, except that after Zical regained consciousness, he'd seemed on edge, quietly determined, with a maddening edge of secrecy about him.

When he abandoned his portable unit at home, he'd aroused he'd curiosity. Without much difficulty, Dora tracked him from his apartment as he flew a skimmer into the city. After he landed and exited the skimmer, she caught him on security monitors until he turned down a street that had none. Her inquisitiveness piqued she aimed a satellite scanner on him, but once he entered a building, she lost him.

She tried to tap an outside communication line, but there were none. Most commercial establishments took a thumbprint and debited a bank account after people made purchases. But again, she found no outside connections. Interesting.

Under ordinary circumstances, Dora enjoyed nothing more than a good puzzle. What was Zical up to? What kind of establishment had he entered? Dora checked her city maps against the licensing board and came up with nothing. Odd. She checked the owner of the property and found out the land was part of the public domain, like a road. Stranger still.

Most likely illegal activities went on there.

Patiently, Dora kept searching for a link to go in. But whoever had built the place had taken great care to keep her out. If she hadn't been following Zical's progress she would never have noticed the place. Dora could be patient, and her persistence paid off. Finally, she found a man who walked into the building with his portable unit turned off. Threading her way past the lock, Dora overrode his switch, but kept the warning light darkened. If she'd been human, her activity would have been suspect, but the law allowed Dora some latitude. If she was concerned about human life, she could override a portable unit's functions.

And she was very concerned about Zical. He'd talked Kahn into putting off the physical and psych evaluation until tomorrow. And his face had been so taut, his muscles so tense, that she was certain he had something to hide.

Since Dora didn't believe that the golden alien light could rattle a starship pilot renowned for his bravery, she wanted to know why Zical had broken his routine. Normally, he spent his planetside evenings eating a light dinner with the family, but not tonight, even though Miri, who was an artist in the kitchen, was preparing Zical's favorite roast in its own salt juices, terrines of potatoes in flaky pastry, fresh beans with ginger and sweet almonds, and spiced cheese and a fruit wine for dessert. Nor would Zical normally miss after-dinner discussions and strategizing with Kahn about how soon the Endekians might regroup and attack Mystique—especially tonight when they would be contemplating how to explore the Perceptive Ones' machines within Mount Shachauri.

However, he'd said nothing to Kahn, Tessa, Miri, or Etru about his plans. Of course, he was a grown man and no longer needed to explain his whereabouts, but it was common courtesy to let people who cared about him know where he was, and Zical was always most courteous. Etru and Kahn would be disappointed if he didn't arrive for dinner.

Shaloma had planned to show him a sketch she'd done and
Kirek looked forward to sitting on Zical's lap and hearing a
story. The man had the right to disappear without a word, but
they would worry, probably ask her his location.

Dora needed to make sure he was all right, didn't she?

When the man whose portable unit she'd infiltrated strode
into the building, Dora secretly entered with him. Within
moments she understood. Men and women came here to
have sex with holosims, computer-generated companions.
Zical had come here to release pent-up physical desire. But
why did he feel he must sneak when he had no wife, no
woman he was promised to?

His activity was not illegal, and although Rystani society
frowned upon using holosims, most cultures did not. Terrans
tended to have different values, their single people seeing
nothing wrong with premarital sex. Free to enjoy one another, Terrans didn't often frequent this kind of establishment. On the other hand, Rystani were expected to wed early;
family values were encouraged. But the war had altered their
way of life, although single Rystani people had the same
needs as those who were wed, they had no outlets.

Dora restrained a sigh. Zical could have saved her one hell
of a lot of trouble if he'd simply informed her of his intentions. But no, the man had to keep his secrets.

Now that she knew what he was up to, she couldn't suppress her envy of the holosim. Although she did not yet have
her body, Dora wanted Zical to come to her to slake his passions. She wanted Zical to put his arms around her, kiss her,
make love to her. His warmth and creativity were wasted on
a holosim, who wouldn't exist after he left the room. However, Dora would be able to remember every moment . . .
And thinking about what he was doing right now increased
her anticipation, escalated her determination to become
fully human.

Dora was about to withdraw when her scanner on the
portable unit got a look at the choices offered—choices Zi-

cal had selected from earlier—and a thrill of exhilaration zinged through her. If she could access the establishment's computer, she could discover exactly what kind of woman Zical found attractive.

Unfortunately the building had no wiring. The computer was a somewhat primitive system that ran on generator power. Without radio waves, neurocircuitry, or physical contact with the processor, Dora couldn't access the data. She had no hands to press the buttons—unless . . . A wild thought blasted through her brain.

"Hello, there, Charen," she said from the voice box.

"Who said that?" Charen peered at his portable unit and scowled. "I turned you off."

"I have a proposition for you." Dora ignored his complaint, hoping she could persuade him to do as she asked.

"What?" he leaned over the monitor to make his choices.

"If you'll pick what I ask, I will place enough credits into your account to pay for a week in this establishment."

"Are you trying to bribe me?"

"Two weeks," Dora countered. She'd learned how to negotiate from Tessa, who'd learned from some megarich Earth tycoon. Now Tessa was wealthier than any Rystani citizen. Dora had spent much of her own share of the family wealth to build her body, but she still had enough credits for a minor expenditure and couldn't allow such a rare opportunity to pass.

"Done."

At Dora's instruction the man punched several buttons and Dora scanned the data, her core filling with exhilaration at the physical choices Zical had made. Oh, yes. She borrowed one of Zical's favorite phrases. Dregan hell. Zical had incredibly good taste. The innumerable body choices that had prevented her from making final decisions were now narrowed down to one.

She was going to be beautiful. Irresistible.

Chapter Four

ONE MONTH LATER a myriad of experts had crawled over Zical's find within Mount Shachauri, but although a multitude of theories abounded, no one knew for certain what the equipment did, whether or not for certain the Perceptive Ones had built the complex, or why. Although Dora remained involved in the project, her primary interest followed another path. She'd trained her replacement, and after numerous simulations, Kahn had given her the go-ahead to proceed with the transfer.

The calculations were complete and the decisions done. Her body was finally whole, the muscles trained, all the receptors prepared for the final connection. She was ready to transfer her complete personality and a portion of her memories and knowledge into her human brain.

Tessa sat next to Dora's body, her face tense and worried, already holding her hand. "How long will the process take?"

"A minute. Maybe two."

"That's all?" Tessa's fingers tightened on her hand.

Dora couldn't wait to find out what "touch" felt like and anticipation hummed through her circuits. The laboratory lights were dim. Soothing music played softly in the background. Tessa had lit butterberry blossom incense.

They'd decided to keep things simple. No audience in the room, just Dora and Tessa with medical doctors and computer specialists on call if needed. For a moment, Dora wished Zical could have been there too. But she wanted him to think of her as human. As a woman. His presence at her unusual birth might alter what she wanted his perception to be.

Dora had spent months compartmentalizing the data she wished to take with her. She'd used the last week to pare down the load to fit her human brain. And she'd even rehearsed, limiting one part of her persona to the same parameters that her "human" mind would perceive. Without millions of sensors transmitting a constant stream of data, she was cut off from the world, but hopefully prepared for the isolation.

She'd just as carefully trained her muscles with exercise and stimuli. The connections to walk and talk as well as other everyday functions had been hardwired into her motor functions. She should be fine. The transfer should go smoothly—yet such a feat had never been done.

But there had to be a first time for everything. She was ready. Eager. Nervous.

"I'm cutting off my personality from the hard drive," she told Tessa.

Her program ran on an automatic countdown, and for the last time, Dora sped through the current, all the nodules of data lining up for transfer. The progression and her last seconds as a computer counted down in orderly fashion, her consciousness vacating her circuitry through a power cord that connected to her neck and linked to her brain.

She cascaded through the linkage, swimming with the

flow, drifting off the energy. A constriction, then a bursting, burning sensation slammed her. Then *wow*. Her mind rushed into her brain, filling cells, burrowing into crevices, sliding home. Thoughts jumbled, rearranged, cleared.

The sensation of warm softness supporting her head, shoulder blades, buttocks, thighs, calves, and heels combined with the soothing music didn't reassure her as much as the touch of Tessa's hand. What an awesome sensation, this skin to skin. There were words to describe Dora's first impression of caring coming through the physical link of touch—all of them inadequate.

She breathed air into her lungs and the sensation tickled her nostrils. The scent. Oh, my. Wondrous. Marvelous. Delicate, and fragile.

Tessa's hand clasped hers tightly. "I'm here for you. Give the sensations a chance to sort themselves out. You needn't do everything at once."

Oh, but she wanted to. Had to force herself to wait to follow the plan she'd carefully concocted. But she'd rather rise up and dance. She hadn't expected her new sense of smell and touch to astonish, overwhelm, delight, or Tessa's warm hand to be such a comfort.

"Waara russss." Dora chuckled, but the sound came out low and garbled.

"Try again," Tessa told her. "Speak slower. Give your mind a chance to connect with your mouth."

"Wha a russ."

"Better, but I still can't understand. Dora, perhaps you should follow the agenda you laid out. You aren't supposed to talk before you open your eyes."

"What a rush." The words came out of Dora's mouth and this time she heard them clearly. Her voice sounded almost like her old self. However, her old computer self had never spoken with lips and a tongue and vocal cords. Before, she'd had a complex sound system and could vary her tone to accommodate many languages, some not human, but her ability to master human speech was critical. Communication was essential.

"Dora, you're doing great."

"Tan . . . Thanks."

Bracing, knowing sight from her new eyes would take some adjusting, Dora opened her lids. It was like looking through two measly sensors. She had little vision to either side of her head, none at all behind. She'd known this would bother her since she was accustomed to seeing through millions of sensors. She'd thought she'd prepared herself for the restrictive view, but a feeling as if the walls were closing in on her had Dora shutting her eyes again.

"What's wrong? Are you okay?"

Tessa's voice sounded odd. Dora's hearing didn't have the full range she'd had before, but that didn't throw her as much as the restricted sight. Especially since she had no difficulty comprehending Tessa's concern.

Suppose she never adapted to her vision? Even as she told herself not to panic, fear rippled down her spine.

Reminding herself that she'd prepared for the sensory trade-offs, she focused on the warmth of Tessa's hand, the reassurance, the love coming through the simple gesture. And she tried to forget that she couldn't see one frickin' thing beyond this room.

"Dora. Talk to me," Tessa pleaded.

"I'm . . . adjusting." Dora slowly opened her eyes.

Tessa hovered over her, her skin pale, her eyes searching hers. "Okay. Take it slow. You knew that everything wouldn't be exactly how you imagined."

"Have the walls moved closer?"

"No."

Dora's chest tightened and the sensation disturbed her. "Is the air in here okay?"

"Yes. You're safe."

Safe? She'd tried to think of every angle in advance, but

she hadn't known until now how much she'd relied on millions of tons of *bendar,* or laser cannons, or thousands of sensors that could warn of attack. She hadn't understood that without sensors to "see" the world she'd feel so vulnerable. She was mortal. With only flesh and blood and bone between her and . . . everything else.

Dora shuddered, twitched. Told herself that being human was what she'd always wanted. The process had worked. She had a body. Now she had to deal with living. She *would* deal with the changes. One day at a time—minute by minute if required.

Two hours later Dora had discovered that being human required effort, more than she'd anticipated. Although she had muscles that were hardwired to move, her brain had to make thousands of new connections so she could move her hand and walk and talk. Thankfully, she already knew how to use her psi to operate her suit. She might be overcompensating, using her psi and suit to force her muscles to do what she wished, but her progress was quick, her speech clear.

Resting against a wall, Dora placed a hand over her stomach. "How about a rest. My stomach . . . aches."

"Are you ill?" Tessa fussed over her like a mother red jilly, one of the colorful new species of birds that had been discovered on Mystique. Despite Tessa's busy days, the demands of her trading empire, she hadn't taken one call, never mind left Dora's side.

"I think . . . I'm hungry." Dora grinned and her mouth twitched. She hoped the uncontrollable muscle contractions would soon end. As she'd practiced walking, her spasming arm had almost toppled her balance. Frustrated that a baby could smile better than she could, she wondered how to make her expressions match her emotions when the muscles seemed to have a mind of their own.

Tessa nodded approvingly and used her psi. A table unfolded from the wall. Food bins with materials for a food processor that materialized a cooked meal were there for convenience, but Tessa didn't approach the raw ingredients, her expression excited as if she had a secret. "Are you ready to eat lunch?"

"Yes."

"Miri wanted your first food to be home cooked." Tessa pulled out a basket loaded with interesting aromas and held it up with a flourish. "She's made us a feast to celebrate your birthday."

"With coffee?" Dora didn't understand Tessa's compulsion for the Terran hot drink but she was eager to try it. In fact, she couldn't wait to taste food period. She only hoped that she didn't bite her tongue and didn't have difficulty chewing and swallowing. But most of all, she awaited trying out her new sense of taste with anticipation.

Tessa reached into the basket and took out breads, orange-wheat, white, seeded, and ryedough. Next came small colorful clay pots filled with a variety of toppings, rich honey butter, thick barnberry jam, tempting garva jelly, janilla bean spread, and a medley of fruit preserves.

Tessa didn't look up from her task. "Dora, why don't you put on some clothes?"

"Why?" Dora looked down at her nudity. "Don't you find my new body attractive?" Spinning, she felt centered, then her thigh muscle twitched, upsetting her balance, and she flung out an arm as a counterweight. Not only was her movement awkward, but her head spun, and the walls closed in again.

Stars. She had to remember to move slower. And damn it—the walls were stationary. She stared them back into place with a scowl.

Either Tessa politely pretended not to see her awkwardness or she was too busy with the food to notice. "Your body is gorgeous, but it's both Terran and Rystani custom to clothe ourselves during social occasions."

"Will looking at me spoil your appetite?" Dora fisted her hands on her hips, a gesture she'd seen Tessa use when in a combative mode. She'd waited so long for this moment that she didn't see a reason to cover her skin. After all, Tessa had been watching her grow her body for months.

"If Kahn joins us, I would be uncomfortable," Tessa admitted as she smoothly unpacked a variety of meats, grilled, roasted, smoked, steamed, boiled, and fried.

"But why? He's already seen all of me."

Dora had never agreed with Tessa's concept of modesty. She'd often wondered if her opinions would change after she'd taken human form, but Tessa's preference still perplexed her. However, after everything her friend had done for her, she didn't wish to make her uncomfortable. With a psi thought Dora altered her suit to encase her body in a deep violet-colored gown that would emphasize her alexandrite eyes.

Immediately, she felt more feminine and added a simple threaded design to her outfit. She didn't understand why color and clothing made her feel differently about her body, but the reaction was likely very human and that pleased her.

"Shoes?" Tessa prodded. "If you want other humans to accept you as one of us, especially Rystani men, you have to not only look the part but act like one of us too." Setting action to match her words, Tessa changed her clothing from her black pantsuit to an emerald gown that snuggled up against her skin.

Human behavior could be very complex. Thankfully, Dora had studied and interacted with them for years. But not until she and Tessa had become friends had anyone bothered to explain the subtleties and nuances that confused her. Although Tessa hadn't answered her question about why Dora's nudity would bother her if Kahn were around, she knew jealousy was not a factor. Tessa didn't think that way. Besides, Tessa knew Zical was the man who fascinated Dora. However, dressing up was kind of fun and she concentrated on the shoes.

"Compliance." Dora took a step forward. Her knee buckled and she compensated by stiffening her suit. "Tell me what to taste first."

Tessa had reached out to steady her, saw that her effort wasn't required, but frowned. "Maybe we should have a medical doctor check you over."

Dora's stomach rumbled, the sensation odd but not necessarily unpleasant. "Perhaps my muscles are just reacting to my excitement. I'd like to eat first. Please?"

"Okay. Are you feeling claustrophobic anymore?"

"Tessa, I've been waiting three hundred years to taste food. Please. I'm fine. Just hungry. And the walls are finally staying right where they are supposed to be."

Tessa laughed, her first real laugh since Dora's transfer. Her entire face lit up and her concern disappeared. Dora was lucky to have a friend to worry over her, but the enticing aroma of hot bread made thinking difficult. She'd never fully comprehended why humans let their stomach rule so much of their lives. They planned their day around meals. Celebrations, weddings, deaths—all were accompanied by eating. And now she could take part.

She had yet to put a morsel into her mouth, but the smell of the bread, the dark crusts with steam rising—ah, the cravings made her mouth water. She had to restrain herself from snatching the bread, stuffing it into her mouth, and gobbling as if she were starving.

Stars. She'd never guessed she would be this eager to do such an ordinary task as filling her mouth. If she had urges as strong around men . . . oh, my . . . what had she done? With the human drive to mate almost as strong as the need to eat, she would have to refrain from attacking Zical the moment she saw him.

Tessa sliced the bread, slathered it with honey butter and handed it to Dora. "What has you thinking so hard?"

"I'm trying not to drool." Dora carefully placed the slice of bread between her parted lips, allowed her teeth to sink into the crust. "Oh . . . my." The sweet taste of the honey butter drizzled over her tongue. "This is . . . heaven."

Tessa took one look at what must have been Dora's blissful expression and grinned. "It's a good thing you gave yourself a fast metabolism so you could pig out, even if it isn't as efficient."

"Efficiency isn't everything. I'm human now."

"Yes, you are. More?"

She tried a bit of fried *yicken,* a tasty meat. "Remind me to thank Miri."

Tessa busily laid out the rest of the repast. "Not all food tastes as good as Miri's. Try a little of everything and don't eat too much or your tummy will ache later."

Easy for her to say. She'd been eating all her life. Dora hadn't comprehended that aroma and texture were so much a part of taste. She discovered she loved crunchy sour pickles but didn't find the soft sweet ones pleasing. Crisp vegetables, cheese potatoes, and rye bread were her favorites. However, she tasted everything, even Tessa's coffee, which she spat back into the cup with what she hoped was a scowl. "This must have gone bad, although the smell is wonderful."

"The coffee's perfect." Tessa sipped happily from her oversized cup. "The jolt of caffeine is just what I needed."

"But it's so bitter."

"An acquired taste."

Sharing hot drinks, alcohol, and food was so much a part of the family ritual that Dora vowed to acquire a taste for coffee. She envisioned many shared meals with Tessa, the two of them lingering over steaming cups while they had interesting discussions, shared news of their day, and traded gossip with the other women. Dora loved gossip, wanted to love coffee. However, she didn't have to learn to like coffee today, so she pushed aside the cup.

Tessa's eyes sparkled and she spoke in a rush of anticipation. "Are you ready for the *pièce de résistance*?"

Although familiar with Tessa's Terran slang, Dora still wasn't certain what she was talking about. "Pizza?"

"For dinner, maybe."

"Dessert?"

"Chocolate fudge." Tessa cut a tiny square, placed the candy on a plate and offered the sweet like ambrosia to the gods. "Smell first."

"Yum." Dora sniffed and the aromatic fragrance would have had her placing the entire piece into her mouth at once until she remembered how good coffee smelled and how bitter it tasted.

"Go on. Try."

Dora bit into the chocolate. As the sugary confection melted on her tongue, she squealed in delight. "Chocolate alone is almost worth giving up my immortality for."

"I'm glad you're enjoying yourself."

"I didn't expect food to be this wonderful. I can hardly wait to make love."

In the middle of sucking fudge from her fingertip, Tessa stopped and sighed. "Whoa. First of all, humans usually ease into subjects like making love."

"Sorry." Dora tended to forget that human sexuality was such a sensitive subject and wondered if she'd ever understand why even Tessa was so touchy about discussing it.

But then in her typical straight-ahead fashion, Tessa plunged into the subject anyway. "Eating and making love are two very different kinds of sensual experiences."

"Exactly. That's why, as soon as possible, I want to be with a man."

"Making love is emotional. If you want the experience to be good, and I know you do, you need to slow down."

"Not everyone agrees that waiting is better."

Tessa's cheeks flushed with color. "I'm not talking about technique." When Tessa had first met Kahn, he'd needed to teach her to use her psi by inducing high levels of frustration. Kahn had used the sexual kind. The two of them had battled and wed and eventually fallen in love. Dora thought their tale romantic. Although she hadn't been privy to their lovemaking, she'd seen how sexual intercourse had brought them closer together. Tessa might be uncomfortable with the subject, but she could also be blunt. "I'm saying you've only been human a few hours. Give yourself time to establish a friendship first—"

"You and I are friends. We've been friends for years."

Tessa sighed over her coffee cup. "Friendship between women is different than between a woman and a man."

"Zical likes me." Dora had few secrets from Tessa and appreciated her take on men, even if she often didn't agree with her conclusions.

"Zical isn't accustomed to thinking of you as human."

"But once he sees me—"

"It still may take him a while to change. Rystani men are stubborn."

Dora's goal had always been to attract Zical's interest and she understood the need for long-term planning. Convincing him to notice her the way she wanted might take time. But her impatience mounted. She couldn't wait for him to see her.

"You believe he'll reject *this* body?" Dora stood and with a psi thought made her gown transparent. She loved looking at her body and had kept her flesh covered long enough.

Tessa rolled her eyes at the ceiling. "Dora, when you created yourself, you forgot to include modesty."

"Fine." Dora reclothed herself and fought down her resentment. Just because Tessa was uptight about nudity didn't mean she had to be. She was an individual. Yet, she also needed to remember to have patience and consideration, traits that seemed more difficult now that she was in her body. "I'm sorry. I've waited so long to be human. I want to try everything. Do everything. Do you think Zical will mind if I kiss him when we meet?"

While she'd been eating, Dora had noted how incredibly sensitive her lips were. And lips were a known erotic zone. To press them against Zical's . . . oh, that would be a fine sensation.

"Why don't you at least plan to have a conversation first, then you can ask him if it's okay before you kiss him," Tessa suggested.

"If I ask, he may say no. As for the conversation . . . I don't know. Can't I just kiss him hello?"

"That is not Rystani custom. A hug would be more appropriate and you know it."

"Are you going to turn into my mother?" Dora asked with a twitch of her lip that she hadn't intended.

"Of course not." Tessa took her hand. "But I've been human all my life. I don't want to see you hurt. Or Zical hurt. Human relationships are trickier than they appear."

Dora could see that Tessa was fairly bursting to give her advice. "And?"

"And if I *were your mother*"—Tessa laughed, but her eyes were serious—"I'd tell you to start a conversation with Zical by asking about his work."

"I've been there with him every moment. There's nothing he can tell me about the lack of progress on Mount Shachauri that I don't already know."

"Except his feelings."

"He's obviously frustrated. Won't sex relax him?"

Tessa threw her hands into the air, clearly unhappy. But Dora's question was logical, wasn't it? She'd spent years studying humans, and yet she trusted Tessa's judgment. As a computer, Dora made decisions based on her ethical program, her data stream, and her personality. Now that she was in a human body she didn't have the same massive amount of input, but the process to make a decision should have been the same.

Yet it wasn't.

Zical was the unknown factor and for her to consider all her possible actions to create the reaction she wanted from him seemed impossible. If she'd wanted only an orgasm, not emotional connection, she could masturbate, but the idea of experiencing her initial sexual pleasure with Zical was her first choice—but she had yet to figure out how to win his cooperation. Her eye twitched and her knee gave way. She stumbled and caught herself. She glanced at Tessa to see if she'd noticed her mistake.

She had. And when she caught Dora glancing at her, she wiped the frown from her lips. "You've done too much. You should rest."

"Let's not start lying to each other." Dora locked gazes with her best friend. "Okay?"

"Okay." Tessa didn't mince words. "You shouldn't be stumbling around. At least, I don't think so. Why don't we have a medical doctor—"

"Good idea." Dora tried not to let her lower lip quiver. She'd known there would be problems. She would deal with them. Her eyes burned and water trickled down her cheek before her suit wiped away the moisture. Her nose became stuffy and her chest tightened. Even as she noted the uncomfortable physical reactions to her worry, she was realizing that becoming human was more difficult than she'd anticipated.

She'd wanted a perfect body so she could entice Zical. But her beautiful body wasn't in perfect working order. Her facial muscles twitched and spasmed, her joints gave out without warning.

Miserable because of what she perceived as her failure to adjust properly, she didn't bother to wipe away her tears. "I don't want Zical to see me like this."

Tessa embraced her. "Human babies crawl before they walk. You're trying to do everything at once and you're doing marvelously well."

"Thanks." Dora sniffed, hating the clogged nostrils that made breathing through her mouth a necessity. "I'm being a big baby."

"No, you're being human." Tessa hugged her hard, then stepped back. "You've done the impossible, Dora. You've gotten what you wanted."

Dora hoped Tessa was correct. Her lack of medical knowledge bothered her. Since she'd had no intention of becoming a doctor, she'd limited her medical wisdom to first aid. Once she could have consulted every medical text written about her uncontrollable spasms. She would have known which procedures were the likeliest ones to cure her, which doctor had the best rate of success, which hospital on which planet specialized in . . . Stars, she didn't even have a name for whatever was wrong with her.

She'd always known humans had to cope with illness and injuries and she'd admired the way so many people faced their infirmities with courage. Dora wished to do the same. She would not succumb to the fear that the doctors couldn't fix her before she'd even been diagnosed. When willing her trembling to cease failed, she used a psi thought to stop her quivers.

Taking back a measure of control gave her strength. "My lack of knowledge bothers me as much as, if not more than, the muscle spasms."

Tessa spoke firmly. "Dora, you need to do what we do when we don't know something."

"What?"

Tessa's eyes brightened with amusement and a chuckle escaped. "Ask the computer."

Chapter Five

ZICAL SUSPECTED TESSA knew that he'd been avoiding a private conversation with her about Dora for several weeks. Luckily, she couldn't possibly know about his Dora fantasies, which he continued to blame on the golden light. Somehow, Dora's telling him about her decision to transfer into a body just before the golden light had struck him had flooded his mind with erotic images of Dora that seemed to have taken a permanent residence in his brain. Unwilling to allow his fantasies about Dora to again merge with his visit to Xentos, he'd avoided both of them.

Besides, the notion of Dora as a woman intrigued him too much, and he couldn't trust himself around her just yet. He cared too much for her to have her glimpse his lust and mistake it for more than the aftereffects of the golden light. Dora also didn't need to deal with Zical's confusing feelings over her transformation. He still thought of her as a computer, not a sexy voice. She had to be feeling very vulnerable now that her transformation had gone awry, and the last thing he wanted to do was cast doubts about her humanity on top of her other problems. When the doctors couldn't find a reason for Dora's physical twitching and uncontrollable muscle spasms, she'd holed up and hidden herself from the few family gatherings he'd attended over the past two months.

Tessa had finally tracked him down in the gym where he and Kahn had been training. A Rystani woman wouldn't have interrupted men during combat exercise. But Tessa was from Earth and she was more skilled than most Rystani warriors in combat and very comfortable in this masculine environment. Normally, Zical would have welcomed her presence, but no man appreciated having an audience for his defeat. And Kahn had just thrown and pinned him.

While there was no shame in losing a bout to one of the foremost fighters in the Federation, Zical wondered if the two were teaming up on him. Kahn's workout had him physically exhausted, and then Tessa came straight to the point, ignoring Zical's muffled groan as he employed aching muscles and a weary psi to shove to his feet.

She shot a look at her husband as sharp as a laser. "Kahn, tell him that if he cares about Dora, he should visit her."

"Tell him yourself." Kahn grinned lazily, his eyes full of affection and amusement.

Zical turned to leave, careful to keep his tone casual, as if he had nothing to hide. Although he considered Dora a friend, he didn't feel close enough to her to intrude on her privacy. "I have to get back to Mount Shachauri."

He'd spoken no more than the truth. While he'd been saddled with the chore of ferrying engineers and scientists into the mountain, he'd put off making any career choices. But he wasn't complaining. As much as he missed piloting his starship, his crew was taking a well-deserved vacation, and besides, the alien machinery fascinated him. He also enjoyed listening to the scientists speculate about the find. But if he were honest, although he was avoiding Dora, he did yearn to see her, curious to know what she looked like. His contradictory thoughts didn't make sense to him, so he certainly didn't want to attempt to explain them to Tessa.

But she had that don't-mess-with-me gleam in her eyes that told Zical he wouldn't easily escape. In one easy move she blocked his exit. "Oh, no you don't."

Zical glanced at Kahn but he shrugged, signaling he wasn't about to step into the middle of this discussion. Zical was on his own. He tried to keep a sheepish expression from giving him away. "I'm not avoiding her. I've attended family gatherings and she's been hiding in her room."

"Really?"

Tessa might be slender and short, but she could put more authority into one word than any woman he'd ever met. Right now he had to remind himself they were in the same family, that she was Dora's friend, and that she wasn't about to let him go until she'd had her say.

Tessa eyed him and softened her tone. "The doctors can't find anything wrong with her physically. She refuses to speak with a shrink. I can't reach her, and instead of enjoying her new body, she's cooped up in her quarters and spending too much time with the computer."

"So?"

"I think you can help her. She's always had a special affection for you."

"Affection? She's a computer." Zical played dumb. Dora had always been much more than a computer, but defining her was impossible, although, "sassy, smart, and seductive" popped into his mind. When Dora had been a computer, her affectionate nature and her teasing sexual innuendos had amused him. But now that she was altered, he wasn't sure he was ready for her transformation from his sexy computer friend to a genuine woman. And now that the golden light had filled his nights with restless erotic dreams where Dora's provocative whispers took center stage, he wasn't certain he trusted himself to handle a new relationship. He especially didn't want to cause Dora more damage.

"She wasn't born human. But I assure you that she's one hundred percent human now. Or she was . . . but she's spending too much time plugged into the network."

"Plugged in?"

"To transfer her personality into her body, she created an electronic link. She can link her brain directly into the computer."

He read the worry in Tessa's eyes. "Is this harmful?"

"She's using the link to escape. To withdraw from her humanity. I thought maybe you could snap her back into having an interest in being human."

"What do you want me to do?"

"Go to her. Talk to her."

"About?"

Tessa rolled her eyes at the ceiling in disgust. "You want me to write you a script?"

"Did you ever think I might say the wrong thing and make her worse?" Or accidently give her the impression that he was interested in her as a woman? Because Zical knew how unfair that impression would be. When Dora had been a computer, the flirtation between them was safe and harmless because their friendship couldn't grow into anything more. But now she had a body. And thanks to the alien light, he was thinking with his hormones.

Tessa's eyes narrowed on him. She didn't bother refuting his excuse. "Dora cares about you. I thought you liked her too."

Zical glanced at Kahn, his gaze questioning. Kahn crossed his arms over his chest, clearly uncomfortable with the subject but willing to go along with his wife. "Talk to her about anything you like. She hasn't responded to us for over a month. She's barely eating or sleeping. It's eerie the way she closes her eyes, lies motionless for hours. She can't go on like this or she could die."

"Die?" Zical's gut clenched.

He missed his conversations with Dora as a computer. Although the new entity performed assigned tasks well enough, Ranth was male, and his personality was young, not fully formed. Until Dora's transformation, Zical hadn't realized how much he enjoyed her constant presence in his life. Whether he was on his ship, in his quarters, or out exploring, she'd always been with him, ready to converse, give information, or simply keep him company.

Knowing he hadn't lost her permanently, knowing he could visit her, had lessened the loss of her company these last few months. Still, despite how busy he'd been during the last few weeks, he'd missed her more than he'd have thought possible—perhaps yet another reason he couldn't stop thinking about her. Ranth simply couldn't replace Dora, but Zical wasn't so certain the new Dora could replace her former self.

She was human now. Vulnerable. She could die. He didn't know if he could cope with the mind-boggling change—especially since they both seemed to be having difficulties controlling their bodies: he with an almost overwhelming and constant ache for sex, her with uncontrollable twitches. He recognized his irritability but was at a loss how to solve his problem, never mind hers. The old Dora was strong, brilliant, cheerful, nothing ever got her down. He thought of her as superhuman, almost godlike, with no need for him in her life. But now, the way Tessa spoke of her, she sounded depressed, and if she needed him, he couldn't turn away, no matter how much he feared that he might do further damage.

"We won't let Dora die," Tessa vowed, "even if we have to force-feed her."

"I hadn't realized . . ." Zical's thoughts spun. The idea of losing Dora scared him, but the fact that Dora needed help from anyone was a strange concept. One he couldn't ignore, one that triggered his protective instincts. Dora wasn't just part of his crew, she'd once been the most essential member. They'd flown every mission together and she'd saved his life more times than he could count. And if she needed him, he would be there to help. "I will visit her."

"Good." Tessa nodded. Zical turned to depart, but she placed her hand on his shoulder. "Perhaps you can think of a way to convince her to leave her quarters. She needs to interact with people. Patching into the computer all the time isn't good for her."

"What do you suggest?"

"I'll leave that up to you." Tessa hesitated, then continued. "Your first instinct may be gentleness, but she needs your strength, not pity."

Zical's eyebrows narrowed. Tessa was usually plainspoken, but she was being too vague for a simple starship pilot like himself to fathom her meaning. Or perhaps his churning gut and fear for Dora's well-being was making him more dense than usual. "I'm not sure I understand."

"You will when you see her."

Tessa wouldn't say more, and he strode toward Dora's quarters in confusion but determined to do some good. Tessa's concern for Dora was very clear and she didn't fret the small stuff—an indication of the seriousness of Dora's condition.

Zical supposed he should have asked more questions, but as his concern made his anxiety level rise, he realized he had no idea what to expect. Had Dora requested that he visit? Was she expecting him to arrive? Would she allow him into her quarters?

ZICAL KNOCKED ON Dora's door, filled with trepidation. Put him at the console of a sweet little starship and he knew exactly what to do. But dealing with women on a personal level wasn't in his regular orbit of experience. Praying he didn't make matters worse, determined to help her if he could, when the door opened he stepped inside.

Her quarters appeared . . . stark. The walls had no texture or color but remained standard gray. She'd hung no art. Nothing on the walls. No sculptures. The standard lighting, and the lack of music and scent gave the place a sterile feeling. His heart sped with nervous energy. Now that he was finally here, his leashed curiosity ran as wild as the *mustangi* on Zenon Prime. Would Dora welcome him? Would he be able to help her?

"Dora?"

"In here."

Her voice sounded familiar, very close to that of the friend he remembered so well. Yet she sounded distracted, as if deeply involved in a holovid. Following the sound of her voice, he entered a dimly lit corridor. The last door on the left was open and a light beckoned.

Eager to see what she'd done to herself, he entered the room and frowned. He expected to see a woman he didn't recognize. So what in the six moons of Gorath was the holosim Xentos doing here? His encounter with the computer-generated holosim had been wiped clean after his departure, and the computer hardware was totally separate from Dora's. Yet there was no denying that this was the holosim he'd conjured out of his imagination to take the edge off his sexual desires.

Had Dora copied her program to play a joke on him? He looked more closely at Xentos's features. A holosim's face didn't have the kind of detail she projected. This woman had long, thick eyelashes, delicate coloring, and flawless skin that reflected marvelous cheekbones. She was full of curves, her hair a lush cinnamon, her features perfection. Clothed in swathes of soft violet that set off her bronze skin, she was his fantasy woman. The dream lover he'd conjured out of his imagination. The woman he'd had sex with as he'd fantasized about Dora. She couldn't be real.

But she was.

Shocked, baffled, and highly upset, he controlled his voice. "What in Stars is going on?"

She opened her eyes, they were alexandrite in color, and her violet suit brought out the deep purple in her irises. But her unfamiliar stare caught him off guard. "Hello to you, too."

Dora's voice coming from those magnificent lips floored him. "Are you . . . alive?"

"Blood and flesh."

"Dora?"

"It's me. Yes."

No.

"I'm human now just like you."

His stomach tightened. She wasn't anything like him. She was perfection personified to the nth degree. Stunning. Gorgeous. Her only flaw appeared to be the cord that plugged into her neck, connecting her to the computer system and dividing her attention between him and whatever else she was doing with Ranth. The lack of expression on her exquisite face reminded him of cold *marbalite*, reminded him that he'd fantasized over that body, had had sex with that body.

Shock gave way to raw worry. By taking the form of his holosim, Dora had exposed her wish to please his senses, and he was so stunned he didn't know what to think. She'd spied on him, then duplicated the body specifications of the holosim he'd built to his preferences, and transferred her personality into it. She had replicated his fantasy with a precision that left him flabbergasted, and he felt way too susceptible to her beauty.

"What were you thinking?" He crossed the room in two steps, yanked the cord from the plug in her neck, severing her computer connection as his surge of shock veered into deep worry. He didn't know what he wanted to do with his life. He wasn't certain he'd ever follow the customary Rystani marriage-and-child route after he'd failed so badly with Summar. And for Dora to take the form of his simulated lover revealed she had certain expectations of him . . . Expectations that boggled his mind.

She froze, blinked, and her eyes focused with a brilliance that stirred his senses even as it revved the shock he made no effort to hide. As she became aware of his reaction, her face paled, her body shuddered, and a muscle spasmed in her neck.

Her voice shook and she crossed her arms over her chest, a feeble attempt to stop the trembling. "I thought you'd find me beautiful."

He spoke each word with care, wanting to be honest, yet unwilling to cause her hurt. "You surprised me."

"I thought you would be happy, honored." Her tone rang with sincerity but revealed raw anxiety.

"You are beautiful," he admitted, realizing he'd hurt her. "But your change is going to take some time for me to get used to."

"Coward."

She said the word with quiet firmness. Her insult sliced deep and rose up his throat to choke him on the truth. During the first twenty-two years of his life, Zical had lived as a simple hunter. He hadn't spoken to computers or flown starships, he'd never met anyone who hadn't been Rystani. During the last seven years, Zical's life had changed dramatically. He'd met beings from other planets and cultures. Yet the idea of a computer taking the human form of Xentos was so alien to him that he needed time to adjust.

His reaction to Dora's alteration came from a place he didn't wish to acknowledge, from the dreams that had taunted him for weeks, from a place he didn't want to admit he couldn't control. He wanted to think of himself as openminded. But in truth, her transformation was so alien a concept to him that he had to keep reminding himself that this woman was the same sentient computer personality who'd been his friend.

Mastering his confusion for her sake, he refocused his thoughts. Tessa had told him that she feared for Dora's life, but since he'd stepped into the room, Dregan hell, he'd thought only of how he was going to cope with Dora's transformation. However, in his defense, Dora didn't look as if she were on the verge of death as Tessa had suggested, appearing more like a goddess than a human.

But then he recalled how alien she'd looked when connected to the computer. Her face a mask, her eyes closed, her expression without emotion. She'd sat so still, as if pulled into the world of machines, as if she had no interest in her surroundings.

Their conversation had changed all that. He'd unplugged her, severing Dora's corporeal connection. Focused on him, she'd become less alien, much more human.

She'd stood up for herself like the old Dora—and her courage as well as the memory of how many times she'd saved his ship and his crew kept him in the room as much as his real desire to help her. She'd actually had the temerity to call him a coward.

He almost smiled, planted his feet wide, tamped down the last of his shock. He'd known that she wouldn't be the same Dora after she had a body. Okay, he hadn't expected her to look like Xentos, but he'd known she'd be ignorant about the complexities of becoming human. While it wasn't fair that he found her breathtakingly gorgeous, he'd get over his extraordinary attraction to her. "I'm not the one hiding in my quarters, afraid to face the world."

"You have no right to judge me." Dismissing him, she picked up the cord and was about to plug the end back into her neck.

"Don't."

"Why not?" Her voice broke.

He didn't know if she lacked the same control over her voice as over the muscle spasms, but as the shock of her using the body of Xentos ebbed, so did most of his worry about what Dora expected from him. He was left with the uncomfortable knowledge that Tessa had sent him here to make things better, and instead, just as he'd feared, he'd made them worse by not responding to her as she'd wanted.

Zical didn't want to let Dora down. She'd helped his people escape Rystan. She'd helped him and his crew win many battles against the Endekians. She was a . . . friend. A friend in need. No way could he turn his back on her and live with himself.

His posture remained stiff, but he attempted a smile. "Dora, I'm human and Rystani. We don't take surprises well."

"If that's an apology, then I accept. And I'm sorry if this body has displeased you." Her manner remained tense, as if she feared that if she relaxed, he'd hurt her again.

An awkward silence rose between them. With every moment that passed, the tension grew more strained. The easy comradery he'd once shared with the old Dora was gone. In her place was a stranger, in a body that was way too familiar and yet not familiar at all. He understood that she'd tried to please him by copying Xentos, but Dora was human, not a holosim. She came with feelings that were real, not simulated. And he couldn't turn her off with a switch like Xentos. She'd remember what he said, how he'd reacted to finding her so alien. He should have been more tolerant, and perhaps if he hadn't been so sleep-deprived due to his dreams, he might have reacted differently.

Zical rubbed a spot behind his ear, wondering why Dora so easily put him on the defensive. He was usually an easy-going man. He didn't worry over minor things. He didn't know why he was having so much trouble with her transformation into a human. Yet, whether computer or woman, Zical did consider Dora his friend. "Why don't we start over."

Hope sparkled in her eyes. "Okay. If I hadn't been plugged into Ranth, I would have greeted you with a hug."

Zical couldn't help but grin. Now here was the confident, sexy, sassy personality that he remembered. He held out his arms and she hurried to him, stumbling along the way. He stepped forward, catching her, and as they embraced, her arms closing fiercely around him, he had to stop himself from his natural inclination to kiss her. And he wasn't thinking about a brotherly peck on the cheek either. Every instinct in him demanded that he dip his head, part her lips, and discover if she tasted as good as she looked.

Damn.

Up close, she smelled feminine and her friendly warmth reminded him that not only was Dora a family member and an essential part of his crew, she was all female. While his mind had difficulty coming to terms with Dora as a woman, his body responded as if she were his dream lover.

Focus on the mission.

Gently he pulled away, reminding himself that Tessa wanted him to coax Dora out of her quarters. Placing his hands on her shoulders, he smiled down at her. "Why don't we go for a walk? Get reacquainted."

She shook her head, a lock of her cinnamon hair falling over her cheek. "We can talk here."

"The gardens are in full bloom."

"I can see them on the monitor."

She was being difficult but he didn't know why. He recalled when he'd had to coax Summar out of their closet the morning after she'd gone shopping and spent too much money. She'd been terrified of him for no reason. But just like Summar, Dora was too frightened to think clearly.

Zical tried to keep judgment from his voice. "But wouldn't you like to smell the flowers? Feel the breeze on your face? Isn't that why you became human, for the new experiences?"

Dora shivered. "I'm not ready yet."

Zical picked up the thread of fear in her tone and gentled his voice. "What's wrong?"

"Nothing."

"Come on, Dora. What's bothering you?"

The muscles in her neck tensed, and she walked to a window that overlooked the gardens. He sensed that she was desperately trying to hide her emotions, and when she spoke, her tone was flat. "I'm not yet adjusted. I need more time."

He had no idea what she was talking about, but he'd gone from trying to help her to anger to wondering how to help her again so quickly that he marveled over the disturbing effect she was having on him.

"What do you mean that you haven't adjusted?"

"For the last three hundred years I've been protected by five thousand tons of *bendar* on a ship. Later, Tessa buried my main processor deep in Mystique's core. But my sensors could see enemies from afar, from whatever direction they attacked. In addition, I possessed the entire accumulated knowledge of the Federation in my data banks. Instead of the most powerful laser cannons to defend me"—she held up her hand—"I now have . . . fingernails. Instead of sensors that can warn me of danger that could come from light-years away, I have only two eyes that can't see past the door. And instead of *bendar,* the hardest substance created by humans to protect me, I am flesh and bone."

"But you wanted to be human." He kept his words gentle, his gaze on her profile. Unlike Summar, who had been frightened for no good reason, Dora had made a logical argument to support the rationale for her behavior. But he wasn't buying. "You knew we couldn't do the same things as a computer."

"Yes. I knew. But I didn't know how vulnerable I'd *feel* once I was in this body. Humans are brave. I'm not." She refused to meet his eyes, and continued to stare out the window, but even as she twisted her hands behind her back to hide the tremors, he couldn't miss the shudder of distaste that rolled through her.

He couldn't demand that she curtail her fear when she had good reasons to be afraid. Flesh had to be a million times more fragile than *bendar*. And although she had two good eyes, compared to sensors on starships and satellites and even other worlds, her sight must seem extremely limited. He wished she'd confided her fears to Tessa, not him, because he didn't know what to say. But she'd opened to him, putting a burden on his shoulders, one for which he might not be equipped to cope, and yet he was touched that she trusted him with her fears.

"Humans deal with fear by facing it." He sounded harsh, even to his own ears, and she flinched, then crossed her arms across her chest.

"I don't want to face my fears."

He could have told her he'd protect her. He could have tried to sweet-talk her into coming out of her quarters, but her mind seemed so set, like that of a stubborn two-year-old. Oh, she might not be throwing a temper tantrum, but this was the adult equivalent.

Zical took two steps forward and swept her into his arms. Even as she stiffened, gasped, and flung her arms around his neck, he enjoyed the feel of her curves.

As her lips parted in surprise, she lost her look of composure. "What are you doing?"

"Taking you outside."

"No."

"Yes."

"Put me down. Please."

Her plea knifed him, but his mind was made up. Tessa had told him strength, not gentleness, might be required and he finally understood what she'd meant. He wasn't taking Dora into danger. He was carrying her to the garden. Instead of answering her, he strode toward the door with steady, determined steps.

When Dora understood that he had no intention of yielding to her pleas, her eyes narrowed in fury. She kicked her legs, squirmed, but he simply tightened his grip, overpowering her with his superior strength.

She pounded his shoulder with a fist, then complained. "Ow. You hurt me."

He chuckled. "Next time, try raising your shield before you punch someone."

"Let me go."

She didn't scream, but the desperation in her tone clawed

at him, made him question if he was taking the right approach. But he didn't let her see his doubts. "We're going outside for thirty minutes."

"Thirty . . . minutes?" She ceased struggling, but if the outrage in her gaze could have shot lasers, he would have been a dead man.

"I know you're scared—"

"Well, du-uh."

In spite of her fear, her natural courage was so much a part of her character she revealed it under duress. She just needed reminding. "Ranth's watching after our safety with his sensors. We aren't at war, but if we came under sudden attack, he'd warn us. So exactly what do you think can happen?"

"You could drop me."

"I won't." Even as he spoke he chuckled, pleased that although she might be frightened, she hadn't lost her wits.

Dora took deep breaths but her face remained pale, and she trembled in fits and starts as he carried her from her quarters, down a hallway, through an exit, and into the gardens filled with paved walkways, a fountain, and several sculptures. Tessa and Kahn had wanted Mystique to not only be a home to the displaced Rystani people, they wanted the world to be welcoming. Tessa had imported many of her favorite shrubs, trees, and flowers from Earth, enhancing the area's natural beauty.

At this time of day, most of Mystique's citizens remained at work. A few couples strolled by, but for the most part, they had the place to themselves.

Hoping the trickling water would soothe her fears, he headed for a secluded area by a waterfall. He owed her patience. He owed her time to adjust to her body. She'd shown sparks of her former courage when she'd called him a coward. But she wasn't the same friend he remembered. She'd lost huge amounts of memory, all of her sensors. The adjustment had to be difficult, and if he could, he wanted to help her through the hard part.

When he glanced down at her, he was surprised to see

she'd closed her eyes. Beads of sweat broke out on her forehead and her suit absorbed the excess moisture. Her breathing remained ragged, her face was pale as Mount Shachauri's
highest peak, and her pulse leaped erratically at her neck.

Perhaps this hadn't been such a good idea. "Why are you
closing your eyes?"

"It lessens the shock of being unable to see behind me."

He settled in the sweet-scented, green grass and kept her
on his lap, enjoying the warmth of her skin, the clean scent
of her hair, and her bottom snuggled against his lap. Compared to Dora's sparkling vibrancy, Xentos was quickly becoming a fading memory. Risking Tessa's wrath by plucking
a fragrant flower from a nearby stem, he whisked the delicate petals across her forehead. "But with your eyes shut,
you can't see this beautiful snowy white *lidenia*."

She smacked his hand aside with a petulant frown. "The
scent is making me ill."

"Rare perfume is made from flowers like—"

"How many more minutes are left?" Dora refused to open
her eyes.

"Twenty-eight."

"Your manhandling is not working. I'm more frightened
now than I was before. Take me back, Zical. Now."

"No."

"Ranth," she said, speaking to her portable computer,
"call security."

"Ranth, cancel that request." Zical responded calmly.
"We're in no danger. Dora only thinks she is."

"Compliance," Ranth responded. Ranth's complex ethics
programs probably weren't happy. However, he'd been built
to cope with conflicting orders. In case of danger, he protected life. If rank was involved, he obeyed whoever was in
command. And among squabbling friends, he stayed out of
the way.

"Damn you." Dora cursed through gritted teeth. "I want to
return to my room."

"You sound like a child."

"I don't give a freakin' dove tail how I sound."

Zical held her tightly against him, her head tucked under his chin, his arms wrapped around her. "Don't you like the warmth of the sun on your face? The glow makes your skin luminescent."

"I don't want your compliments either."

"And the breeze is fluffing your shimmering hair."

He brushed a lock from her perfect face, marveling at the silky texture, the glossy multicolored strands of rich copper threaded with golden highlights. He reminded himself that although she possessed the physical attributes of a holovid star and a genius IQ, she'd only been human a few months—which was no doubt why she felt so vulnerable and was acting so childish. And if she hadn't duplicated the body of his holosim, making her so devastatingly attractive and womanly, he wouldn't have minded her petulance so much.

"How many minutes?"

"Not enough." He held her and spoke softly as he'd once done to his child bride, who'd been frightened of him, of leaving her home, and of being left alone when he'd had to go hunt for their dinner. "You're safe, Dora. I know the adjustment is difficult, I can't imagine what it must be like for you, but you have friends and family who love you. We all want you to experience the good parts of being human. Tell me what you like best so far."

"Chocolate."

He grinned. "What about the scent of the grass and the garden?"

She wrinkled her nose. "It's . . . okay."

"Just okay? You don't like the scent of flowers?"

"Mm." Dora tilted back her head, opened eyes that shimmered with fiery red heat. "You smell much better than any perfumed flower."

Chapter Six

DORA HELD HER breath. Would Zical kiss her? She'd imagined this moment so many times, but she'd never thought it would come in the midst of so much fear. She still didn't understand why he was so shocked by her transformation or that she'd grown her body to look like his fantasy woman. It wasn't as if Xentos were a person, but clearly Zical had not been pleased.

Obviously, she'd made a mistake, one she'd have to live with. Barring extensive plastic surgery this was the way she would look until she began to age. And despite Zical's surprise, once he'd gotten past the initial shock he'd adjusted quite well.

Better than she was doing. She wondered if he found her uncontrollable spasms as ugly as she did. She hated the lack of control, but the doctors could find nothing physically wrong and had suggested that time might cure the problem. But it might not.

Zical gazed at her, his irises flashing into the purple spectrum. Even with only two eyes she could see his pupils dilate, his nostrils flare slightly, and a muscle in his neck throb. When she realized that her flirtation was succeeding she swallowed down a grin. Snuggling closer, she rubbed her breast against his chest and the sensation stunned her.

Wow. Talk about pure sensual feedback. Her flesh suddenly seemed oversensitized with delicious thrumming and her nipples pebbled. Heat suffused her and her chest tightened in a pleasing reaction that made her ache for more of his touch. Thinking about him helped push her fears to the back of her mind. Touching and being touched by this man was one of the reasons she'd wanted to become human. While she suspected Tessa had had something to do with his appearance in her quarters, Dora didn't mind that the man needed prodding to visit. She simply was glad he was here. And now that she finally had him to herself, she'd be a fool not to put aside her groundless fears and make the most of her opportunity.

Lifting her face to his in breathless anticipation, she gave him clear access and waited for his lips to press against hers. She was about to congratulate herself for temporarily overcoming her fear and beginning a seduction in one fell swoop, when Zical pulled back.

He wasn't going to kiss her.

Disappointed, she wondered if she'd miscalculated the heat in his eyes. Or was he holding back because he wasn't certain of her response?

Maybe he needed more encouragement. She allowed a pleased smile to soften her mouth. "Aren't you going to kiss me?"

He stiffened. "Why would I do that?"

"Because you want to?" She arched one eyebrow, hoping he'd read the gesture as impudent.

"Dora, you aren't a computer anymore. When you tease a man like that, there are consequences."

Her grin widened. "I'm ready for them."

"I don't think so." Gently, he set her from his lap onto the grass.

She plucked a blade and tore it to bits, disappointment nagging her, uncertainty enveloping her in a tension she didn't understand. Their first time together was not going as she had hoped. If he intended to refuse her, if he didn't want her, why was he going out of his way to be kind? Although she'd apologized, was he still upset about her body?

Or had she come on too strong? Tessa had warned her that Rystani men preferred to be the pursuers. But his rejection had made Dora start to question herself. Being uncertain was a new experience, one she didn't know if she wanted to deal with on a regular basis—not that she had much choice. When she'd been a computer, she'd gathered her facts, determined the outcome she required, and then done what was necessary to achieve success. She didn't second-guess herself because with the data available, the probabilities calculated, she always made the best decision.

Now, all she wanted to do was run away and hide in her room. Yet she'd been waiting months to be with Zical in her human body. He was the man she'd dreamed her first dream about. He was the man who intrigued her more than any other. It made no sense to run, especially when her fear of the outdoors had begun to subside. The pleasant gurgling of the fountain calmed her. The balmy breeze and the sunshine soothed her.

She tossed the bits of grass into the air. "You were right to bring me outside. It's beautiful here."

"Glad you—"

"But you were wrong about not kissing me." Dora rose to her feet and dusted off her palms, hoping she could manipulate him by causing a bit of jealousy. "I think I'll go visit another man. One who likes me better than you do."

"Don't act like a child." His tone was to harsh again, as if he couldn't contain his disappointment in her.

"Then don't treat me like one."

Zical reached out with a lazy snap of his wrist and jerked her back down, his gesture revealing a tension that she couldn't discern in his soft tone. "So men are all interchangeable. Any one of us will do?"

She shrugged, unwilling to tell him that she considered him special, that she wanted her first time to be with him. There was no point to making that kind of admission when he wouldn't even kiss her. She'd already created her body in the form of his fantasy woman and his rejection still stung. She wanted to return the insult. She might be new at the human-relationship business, but she'd always had feelings, and he had no right to trample them.

Dora tossed her hair over her shoulder, concealing her pleasure that he'd pulled her back onto his lap. "All men have the necessary equipment."

"But they don't all use that equipment with the same expertise," he countered, peering at her intently as if she didn't understand the basics.

Her heart thumped crazily, her hope rising that maybe he was more attracted to her than he was willing to admit since he so obviously didn't want her going to another man. "I suppose I'll find out for myself . . . especially now that you've convinced me that it's not so dangerous to go outside."

"You have a prospect?" His eyes narrowed.

Her intense physical awareness of his irritation with her, and his display of jealousy, gave her courage. Hoping she sounded confident, she wrenched her gaze from her preoccupation with his handsome face and taunted him some more. "Tessa assures me that with this body, I'll have my choice of offers."

His gaze raked her curves, causing her to realize that despite his previous outburst, he was susceptible to her charms. His tone, however, was serious, as he said, "Perhaps you should return to Mount Shachauri with me. There's lot of men there. Many with brilliant minds. And we could use your help."

She quashed her disappointment that he was offering to take her to see other men. He seemed to miss the point that she would be with him—or perhaps she wasn't giving him enough credit. Perhaps her being with him had been his real plan all along. Either way, she hadn't realized how much she missed being useful until he made the request. Besides, the idea of spending time with Zical intrigued her as much as seeing the alien machines from a human perspective. "I'm not a computer anymore. What could I do to help?"

"You know computers from the inside out better than anyone else."

"Not better than Ranth. He has a lot of technical expertise I couldn't fit in this brain."

"But you have a unique outlook and that might help us figure out what's going on. One of our archaeologists has a theory I'd like you to hear."

Excited by the idea of spending more time with Zical as well as being useful, Dora had no difficulty making the decision. "Okay. I'll go with you on one condition."

"What's that?"

"Kiss me."

Zical sighed and shook his head. "You have a one-track mind."

"So, do we have a deal?"

He put her off with a frown. "You figure out what those machines are for . . . and then . . . I'll kiss you."

THE TRIP TO Mount Shachauri's peak clearly tired Dora. From her increased trembles and spasms, Zical suspected she fought a multitude of fears, but to her credit, she didn't once complain. Tessa had been pleased that Dora had agreed to make the journey, but Zical had kept their bargain private, telling himself that kissing Dora would probably put an end to his fantasy for good. Kissing her might be exactly what he needed to chase his lusty thoughts from his mind.

Still, he wondered why he hadn't asked her for something in return if she didn't figure out the puzzling mystery surrounding the machines. It wasn't like him to miss an angle, but Dora had his conflicting emotions so muddled he felt like a null-grav bouncing ball. First he was up, then down, then spinning sideways and out of control. His attraction to her bothered him because he knew very well how vulnerable she was, and the last thing he wanted to do was to hurt her.

He told himself that he should never have agreed to kiss her. He shouldn't have led her on when he had no intention of having that kind of relationship. Dora might have the body of a full-grown woman, but emotionally she had a lot of maturing to do. Her silly threat to search for a lover, her insistence she was ready for a kiss, her consuming desire to link with Ranth instead of exploring her humanity, told him she wasn't grown-up. Zical didn't intend to repeat his mistakes. He'd had little choice when he'd married his child bride, and he still bore the internal scars of that failure. And while Dora was nothing like Summar, both women were vulnerable, Summar with her inability to make decisions, Dora at coping with her new humanity.

Yet, despite his resolve to keep things on a friendly basis with Dora, he couldn't help wondering what kissing her would be like. Would she set off sparks? Would there be passion for either of them?

Dora seemed so eager to explore the sexual side of being human, yet when it came down to the act, would she be afraid? Find mating distasteful? Would she pretend to welcome him and then rain a storm of tears afterward like Summar? As he recalled his failure to please his inexperienced, young wife, he shoved aside the bad memories. Zical had no doubt that he was a thoughtful and skilled lover. Summar had simply found lovemaking distasteful. He shuddered at the recollection of her begging him not to touch her and was grateful for the distraction of their arrival on Mount Shachauri.

As the skimmer glided in for a landing on the newly built pad, he pushed old regrets and sorrows aside. Ever since he'd found the ancient entrance he'd felt compelled to remain near the site. Instead of moving on with his life and accepting a commission in space, he'd stayed close by, ferrying scientists and supplies up the mountain.

However, unlike the first time he'd explored, they had to make their way past reporters from a dozen planets that were camped out on the mountain, hoping for news or an official briefing, perhaps capturing unusual activity into or out of the core. Zical attracted little speculation since the reporters were accustomed to his presence, but even though the reporters couldn't immediately identify Dora, her beauty had them setting their holovids on capture mode.

He wondered if she'd wave or smile for the cameras, but she kept her head down and ignored the commotion, surprising him. He'd have thought she'd revel in the attention, but it seemed to matter little to her. And if he hadn't known better, he would have thought her shy as she tried to hide behind him when he greeted security.

A guard at the entrance checked their identification before admitting them. Protection of the site was tight and would remain so for some time.

Until Mystique's leaders knew the purpose of the ancient machinery and understood the significance, if any, of the machines turning back on, they wouldn't risk spies stealing, looters thieving, or unauthorized scientists trampling what could very well be a holy site. Zenon Prime had already sent a delegation of scientists, who overlooked their distaste of travel, to the newly colonized planet to ensure the Mystique locals didn't botch an investigation that could have consequences throughout the galaxy. However, unlike the last two ancient finds—which had yielded their environmental suits and the planet where the Challenge, an ancient test devised

to see if a species was fit to join the Federation took place—
no good had yet come from Mount Shachauri.

And as often as Zical told himself to have patience, whenever he thought about the discovery, a strange restlessness
infused him. Although the effects had abated somewhat,
he'd never completely recovered from the haunting erotic
dreams of Dora created by the aliens' golden light.

Inside the corridor his agitation increased along with his
urgency to learn why this place existed. So far the scientists
had many theories, none of them verifiable, most at odds
with one another.

By his side, Dora shivered and rubbed the goose bumps
from her arms. "Being here in the flesh is very different
from seeing the machinery as I was before." She kept her
voice to a soft murmur. "The site has a mystical quality."

Zical glanced at her, impressed with her keen instincts.
"So you feel it too."

Dora sneezed. "Maybe it's the dust."

"Adjust your suit's filters," he reminded her. Although the
suits had the ability to protect the wearer from light, heat,
and tiny particles of matter, many of the adjustments weren't
automatic and required the higher brain function of psi.
Dora had possessed psi powers as a computer, but she
needed the reminder to adjust for the needs of her body. In
space, a mistake like that could kill her. Federation citizens
wore the suits to protect them from radiation, extreme heat
and cold, as well as differences in pressure. Since all of them
had worn suits since early childhood, adjusting with their psi
was second nature.

Zical supposed Dora was safe enough on Mystique. Nevertheless, he edged closer. After his work ferrying settlers
from Rystan to Mystique, he'd quickly learned to identify
those who might need a helping hand, and his honed instincts told him Dora's reactions could be . . . unpredictable.
Like when she'd taken Xentos's shape. Like when she'd
asked him for a kiss.

Telling himself that his gesture was protective, not possessive, he slipped his arm through hers, and they strolled down the corridor as he tried to ignore her citrus scent, tried to ignore her smooth skin beneath his hand.

Many scientists from Federation planets had gathered to study the ancient site. Thanks to the automatic translators in their suits, they could all communicate without difficulty.

Dr. Laduna, a diminutive Jarn with intelligent green eyes, waved them over. If Zical looked closely, he could see an extra eyelid that the man used along with his gills to live on his homeworld, one covered almost entirely by oceans after a collision with an asteroid many eons ago.

At home in air or ocean, Dr. Laduna had a voice that sounded eager and pleasant, unlike so many of the other scientists, who seemed more interested in proving their theories correct than discovering the truth. The Jarn bowed low. "Greetings and salutations."

"Good morning." Dora nodded.

"Find anything interesting?" Zical asked.

"Yes. Yes. Yes. All very interesting. We have many more puzzles to solve." The tiny man almost vibrated with enthusiasm, his scales changing from tan to burnt orange.

"More puzzles?" Zical homed in on the salient factor.

"Listen. Can you not hear them?" The Jarn cocked his head to one side, revealing a tiny ear set flush with his skull.

Dora's face focused and Zical listened. Below the chatter of the scientists and their machines, he sensed a low-level hum that hadn't been there during his last trip. "What is that?"

Dr. Laduna smiled, revealing smooth gumlines without teeth. "The machines have tuned themselves to a different level."

"What?" Dora looked, right, left, and then hurried through the narrow corridor to where it widened into a vast area. They followed her and the sounds became louder.

"See for yourselves." Dr. Laduna gestured to the deep interior of Mount Shachauri.

At least halfway down the mountain, an eerie luminescence filled the black hollows with streaks of silver light. Giant machines throbbed scarlet, their crystalline structure beautiful, yet terrifying and exotic. The color intensified and the humming increased in volume but deepened in pitch, like a steady engine warming up—but for what purpose?

"Dora?"

She stared below in obvious fascination. "I have no more idea what is happening than you do." She wore a dreamy look. "If only there was a way to link into the alien network."

"That might be dangerous." Concerned that her first instinct was to plug back into the computer for answers, Zical wondered if she regretted her metamorphosis.

"A link could be perfectly safe. You don't know."

"Neither do you." He tugged her away from the machines that seemed to hold her in a trance. While he didn't want to frighten her, she appeared to need a reminder that injury to her body wouldn't be pleasant. "Dora, you're human, now. You shouldn't think about hooking into—"

She shrugged. "I don't need you to tell me how to think—especially when you brought me here to find answers."

"We want answers, yes, yes, yes," Dr. Laduna agreed, "but not at the expense of harm to your most beautiful self."

"Thank you for the concern, but, there," she said, pointing, "is that a place I could tap into?"

Zical wanted to shake her. First she was afraid of her shadow, now she was willing to risk her brain cells, reminding him once again of her immaturity. "Haven't you heard a word I said? Do you want to die before you've been human for even a year?"

"What I want isn't important."

"Of course it is."

"I want to experience a kiss before one more day passes, but that's not going to happen, is it?"

Zical contained a sigh, his exasperation with her naïveté warring with a need to kiss her enticing lips. But kissing her would mean giving in to passion. And Dora wasn't experienced enough to know the difference between lust and genuine feelings. So suppressing his physical attraction to her was necessary for both their sakes.

Tossing her hair over her shoulder, she headed toward the location she'd indicated, and Dr. Laduna departed quickly, clearly uncomfortable with the conversation turning so personal. When Zical followed her, she spoke without looking at him. "Don't concern yourself. I'll be fine."

Zical had thought he was calm, but she had him irritated and worried about her safety all over again. For an even-tempered man, his emotions seemed to have taken a wrong turn in hyperspace. Between Dora and the strange alien hum, Zical felt as though he required yet another vacation.

Stars. As if a man could ever relax around Dora. Realizing she'd gone on ahead, he stomped after her, trying to rein in his rising temper while he attempted to think of a good argument to prevent her from plugging into the alien machinery and possibly frying every gorgeous cell in her body.

"Dora, let's discuss your linking up to the machine." He spoke in a rush. The humming seemed stronger as they neared the scarlet crystal, and his edginess increased. She didn't slow down and he placed a hand on her shoulder. "Do you feel that vibration?"

She plugged one end of the cord she'd been carrying in her suit's pouch into her neck. "I'll try to find out what's going on."

"Do you think experimentation without study is wise? Suppose there's some kind of energy feedback in there that isn't compatible with your new body? Suppose it attacks? Or overloads your human brain?"

"I'll be careful and I appreciate your concern."

He couldn't tell if she didn't understand the danger due to overconfidence, or if she simply didn't care what happened, but he was damn worried at the risk she was willing to take. "Why don't you let Ranth—"

"No. He's too valuable to Mystique. If the alien technology blows his circuits, all of our planetary defenses will go down." She locked gazes with him, determination in her look. "I'm not nearly as important."

Since she'd taken her human body, Dora had exhibited many fears. Now, her offer to take this risk sounded more like the old Dora. But he needed to protect her.

"You're important to me," he told her, hoping she could hear the truth in his words, hoping she didn't take them to mean more than he intended.

"Not important enough to kiss."

"Dora, stop. You're using emotional blackmail. You know humans from any planet frown on that sort of manipulation." Impatience with her attitude seeped into his tone. "And you're risking your life for no good reason. How can you be so foolhardy when earlier you were too frightened to leave your room?"

"I'm comfortable with computers." She jerked his hand from her shoulder in a girlish fit of pique. "Apparently, nothing I do pleases you. But my reasons *are* good enough for me."

She'd deliberately turned away from him, and the motion hadn't been one of her accidental spasms. She'd twisted his words and could think circles around him. But that didn't mean he was wrong.

Refusing to be manipulated into a kiss that would mean no more to him than lust, frustrated that she wouldn't listen to reason, he didn't hesitate to physically place himself between her and the alien socket. His responsibility was clear. He couldn't allow her to put herself in such danger when they might still have other options.

Dora tried to step past him but he shifted and blocked her.

She bumped into him and her knee gave out. Quickly, he reached to steady her.

And a golden beam speared out of an alcove and caught them in a bright cone of light. The rays surrounded them, trapped them. Last time the light had knocked him out and left him with an inexplicable sexual edginess he didn't want to have to cope with again.

He feared what the golden light would do to Dora. She wasn't ready for that kind of artificial stimulation—but then neither was he. He already found her too damn attractive. And Dora in the woman's body had him irritated, jumpy, and on edge. She'd already wrangled a promise from him that if she figured out what the machines did, he'd be obligated to kiss her. The last thing he needed was more stimulation . . .

Alarmed, he tried to pull them out of the beam, but his psi wouldn't work. Neither did his muscles. He couldn't blink. Or talk.

He should be in a panic. His fight-or-flight reaction should be kicking in, but he was calm—unnaturally calm.

While the golden light was similar to the one that had knocked him unconscious when he'd first entered the complex, this time he remained awake, on his feet. And Dora, in his arms, was just as stationary as he.

The golden light seemed more benevolent this time. Although he didn't like being held so tightly that he couldn't so much as twitch a finger, he wasn't particularly concerned by his immobility. But as the humming grew louder, his brain pulsed to the tune of the vibrations.

It seemed more than a coincidence that with all the scientists working inside for months, no one else had been caught in the beam, yet he'd been zapped twice. The humming invaded his mind, penetrating so deep that the beating of his heart synchronized with the alien rhythm.

Dora appeared to be caught in the same trancelike state he'd seen when she'd plugged into the mainframe. Her eyes glazed over, and although she was looking right at him, he suspected she wasn't seeing him. Praying the golden light would do her no harm and that soon they'd be released, he tried to ignore the humming that made him sleepy, yet aroused him.

Once again he'd lost control of his psi and his body responded with his blood flowing to his *tavis*. If he could have moved, he'd have gritted his teeth, groaned, turned away to hide his embarrassing condition. However, he doubted Dora noticed. She appeared to have withdrawn so deep into her mind that he feared her brain might suffer permanent damage.

Hoping the golden light wouldn't send her into a panic and straight back to her quarters, or worse, he could do nothing but wait. With no way of judging the passing of time, he couldn't even estimate how long they remained trapped. When the light finally disappeared, despite his fierce need for sexual release, he ruthlessly used his psi to contain his condition and was about to fire questions at Ranth, when Dora toppled into his arms.

Worried, he caught her, gathered her close, ignoring how the feel of her soft skin and her female scent racheted up his tension. "Dora. What's wrong?"

She didn't respond but her wide-open eyes continued to stare off into the scarlet crystals as if hypnotized. Zical shook her lightly but she didn't come out of her trance. Lowering her to the floor before she fell, he held her in his arms. Her head *tilted* back, her hair spilling over his arm. With his free hand, he brushed a lock from her eyes as he fought the lust shocking his system.

It wasn't her. The golden light had him burning for completion. Surely, he wouldn't die if he didn't quench his passionate thirst to sip from her lips. Only concern for her welfare allowed him to squelch his lust. However, he couldn't resist the sweet torment of holding her without touching her. He smoothed his fingers down the creamy expanse of her neck, over her delicate collarbone to her toned arm. As if she were cold, he rubbed her skin with brisk strokes, his palm chafing her skin in an attempt to waken her.

Touching her was sweet torment, intensifying his need, making his senses spin. Riveting his attention on her face, he wondered what the alien light had done to her. Was she lost in the same erotic haze as he had been, and overwhelmed by an experience she'd never felt before? Why wasn't she snapping out of her trance?

"Dora? Wake up."

Exhibiting no sign of awareness or recognition, she nevertheless clutched his shoulder and back, the tips of her fingers digging into his flesh. A soft moan indicated that she would soon awaken.

"Dora, talk to me."

"I am fine."

"You don't sound fine."

"Please be quiet and let me think."

"Ranth." Zical spoke to the computer, his rampant lust firing his impatience. "What in the five seas of Jarn just happened?"

"My analysis is incomplete. The light radiated outward in a pattern similar to your last encounter."

"Tell me something I don't know."

"Dora reacted differently to the experience than you."

"Is she—"

"All her physical signs are normal."

"She's not acting normal."

Dora might have wanted to kiss him but she wasn't clinging to him in a sexual manner. Yet she didn't look fearful either.

"Perhaps you should call a doctor?"

"Hush. Please." Her eyes slowly focused on him, the red sparks settling into a steady purple glow. She relaxed her grip, pulled away from him, straightened and stood. "I can't do mathematic calculations in my head as well as—"

"Let Ranth do the math."

Zical was already tired of hearing how her computer abilities had been superior to her human ones. Between his concern for her, the raging fire in his loins, and her statements about mathematic calculations that made no sense, his tone had been terse. He'd hoped that the distance she'd placed between them would alleviate his problem, but so far, he was having no luck. Every energized nerve in his body yearned to kiss her, to undress her, to feel her skin next to his. He was almost in too much pain not to notice the irony. Now that he wanted to kiss her, she wanted to do math.

"What's wrong with him?" Dora asked Ranth.

"He's exhibiting the same physical symptoms as the last time he was under the golden lights."

Dora chuckled. "Maybe this time he'll find a better solution."

"Will you two stop talking as if I'm not here?" Zical spoke between gritted teeth. It was bad enough he had to deal with the fierce needs coursing through him, worse that Dora knew exactly what was wrong, but then her adding insult to his desire by ignoring him was stoking his temper into the blow-his-top zone.

Dora spoke in algorithmic equations, adding a touch of quantum physics, and then as she extended her equations into logistical matrix *ketrometry,* she left him behind, with two aching heads. He rubbed his temple and swore under his breath, careful not to disturb Dora and Ranth.

"So I was right." Dora turned to Zical with a beaming smile.

"About what?"

"That light beam was a form of communication."

Chapter Seven

"COMMUNICATION?" ZICAL STARED at her, heat in his eyes and arousal in his loins, signs Dora wished she could attribute to his desire for her. But she knew better. Last time the golden light had shone on Zical he'd experienced the exact same reaction—and he'd been alone.

She would have liked to believe that she could handle the situation the same way she had before, by ignoring his aroused condition, but this time heat rose up her neck into her checks. She longed to run her fingers over his angled cheekbones, his bold nose, his tight mouth, until he relaxed. Just thinking about his need for a woman made her stomach flutter and heat pool between her thighs.

To counter her physical reaction, she turned down her suit's temperature, but it had no effect. She couldn't stop wondering what having all his simmering, sauntering, swaggering desire focused on her would be like. Odd, how the golden light hadn't stimulated her, but the dilation of Zical's pupils and the slight flaring of his nostrils had her pulse speeding, her mouth dry.

"Dora?" Zical eyed her in a way that made her heart hammer foolishly, because despite his discomfort, he was obviously concerned about her. "You sure you're okay?"

"I was thinking," she prevaricated, and hastily switched subjects since she wasn't reacting to the golden light but to his proximity. "When you entered this complex the first time, the golden light was an attempt at communication—but it was unsuited to human form, too strong. However, its creators programmed in a learning function and after the machine deduced you didn't understand the first contact, it tried again, adjusting the light, lowering the intensity, and slowing the pulsations."

Frustration heated his tone. "But I still didn't understand the message. And I've been here almost every day for several months and the machine hasn't tried to *communicate* again."

"After so long a passage of time, the machine may not be functioning at the highest efficiency level. It's almost a miracle that it still works at all."

Zical rubbed his forehead again. "I'm aware that different species communicate in various ways, through sonar, sound waves, telepathy, and psi. Although I've never heard of pulsing light instead of speech, I can't discount the possibility. You believe the vibrations are a form of communication?"

"We'll know for certain after Ranth finishes his calculations—"

"I've decrypted the data." Ranth's voice remained calm but he wouldn't have interrupted unless urgency required it. Unlike Dora who'd been a sentient personality for centuries before meeting up with the Terrans and Rystani, Ranth was a new personality. He followed his programs and subroutines more often than Dora ever had.

"Tell us," Zical demanded.

"Mount Shachauri was hollowed out by the Perceptive

Ones and the machinery is an automated communication center. Your entrance into the complex triggered a chain of events that the Perceptive Ones likely didn't intend."

"What are you talking about?" Puzzlement washed over Zical's face and Dora sensed bad news coming. While their information about the Perceptive Ones was very limited, the machines they'd left behind were powerful, their purpose not always understood.

She took his hand, and when he didn't pull away, she realized the measure of his concern. But after all, they'd always been friends and friends supported one another during times of stress. And she was also stressed, just not in the same way as Zical. The golden beam of light hadn't aroused her. Instead, she'd realized how much she feared being human. When Tessa had dared her to take a human form, Dora had thought she'd considered all the ramifications. But she hadn't expected how vulnerable she'd feel in her new body and how that fear colored her every thought and action. She suspected the Perceptive Ones might have programmed their message to make the recipient fearful, and in her case, the fear had transferred to her deeper concerns over how she would live life as a human.

"Ranth," Dora asked, "who did this complex communicate with?"

"Apparently, eons ago, the Milky Way galaxy was threatened by the invasion of a race called the Zin, who penetrated almost to the Perceptive One's homeworld here on Mystique. The Perceptive Ones fought for a millennium, ousted the Zin, and built a machine called a Sentinel to guard the galaxy against future attacks."

"And?" Zical prodded, his voice tight and tense, his jaw angled as if braced to take a punch.

"Your entrance inside the complex recalled the Sentinel." Ranth gave them the news in a firm tone that reflected his certainty.

"The Sentinel still exists?" Zical spoke in shock and Dora

worried about how he would take the news that he might have accidentally invited an ancient enemy back into their galaxy by recalling the Sentinel who guarded them. Zical was a warrior, a man of strong principles, and to cause harm to his people, even inadvertently, would not sit well on his shoulders. She squeezed his hand, trying to will her support through her fingers.

"The signal's reception was confirmed. My analysis indicates the Perceptive Ones didn't intend for the Sentinel to be recalled unless repairs were necessary."

"Are repairs necessary?" Zical muttered, his hand tightening on Dora's.

"I don't know."

"And the Zin?" Zical asked, his voice choked with regret, his shoulders tense under the mental burden of such terrible news.

Dora wanted to embrace him, protect him from the blame he was sure to cast on himself. But she had no doubt he would refuse her comfort and her sympathy. He'd made it quite clear that he didn't consider her . . . kissable.

"All I can say for certain is that the awakened machinery has recalled the Sentinel, and if the Zin still exist, the Milky Way has lost its protector."

"What can you tell us about the Sentinel?" Dora asked, since Zical seemed too stunned to do more than squeeze her hand almost painfully tight.

"The Sentinel is a very large, complex machine. Data indicates the Sentinel was stationed between our galaxy and another. Since we don't have drive schematics, I cannot estimate how long it will take for the machine to return to Mystique."

Zical shook himself out of his shock. "Can we communicate with it and send the Sentinel back?"

Ranth was silent a few moments. Clearly he was checking a variety of sensors and data before he could reply. "The machinery can no longer send a communication over such a vast distance."

"Why not? Zical asked.

"It could take decades to amass sufficient energy to send another communication."

"Let me get this straight." Zical frowned in apparent fierce concentration, horror seeping into his expression. Yet a minor tremble from his handhold revealed he had yet to fully recover from the golden light. "The Perceptive Ones built a Sentinel to guard the galaxy from the Zin. And my presence inside this mountain accidently recalled the machine, and now we can't send a message to tell it to go back and guard us?"

"Correct."

"Why can't we send the Sentinel a message using our own communications?" Dora suggested.

"The machines aren't compatible. Our machines use energy waves, the Sentinel uses psi."

"So do we."

"But we can't use our psi over such enormous distances," Ranth explained.

Dora understood that Ranth had simplified the situation, reducing it to the most elemental explanation. But if she hooked into Ranth's systems, she might find a way to solve the communication incompatibility problem. Now, more than ever, for Zical's sake as well as everyone else's, she needed to attempt to plug into the Perceptive Ones' machines. She could possibly obtain knowledge critical to contacting the Sentinel.

"Why did Dora pick up the message and not me?" Zical asked, his thoughts on other problems.

Dora answered. "I recognized a mathematical pattern in the pulses. Surely, you heard them too?"

Zical nodded, his face grim. "I heard the pulses but didn't recognize a pattern. We should take this information to Kahn and Tessa. They'll probably notify the Federation council. Meanwhile, there must be something I can do."

The news had knocked all lusty desire from his system.

His face looked drawn, his eyes forlorn, as if a dark shadow had passed over his soul. Recalling the Sentinel back to Mystique was not his fault. No one could have anticipated such consequences from an innocent exploration of a cave. Still, he was taking this hard. She ached to console him, to soothe the cloud on his soul, but she suspected he wouldn't accept more from her than holding her hand.

Still she tried. "We don't know if the Zin still exist or if they continue to be warlike. They may have moved on, like the Perceptive Ones."

"And they might still be there. Just waiting for a chance to invade," Zical countered, his eyes hard with determination to face the consequences of his actions. "Damn it. This is all my fault."

"Stars!" Hearing him blame himself caused Dora's stomach to knot. "The Perceptive Ones' machines were faulty. You didn't recall the Sentinel."

"I triggered it." Anguish pinched his mouth and he clenched his free hand in a fist.

"You couldn't have known what would happen."

"But you warned me not to enter the cavern. I should have listened."

"My warning was due to concern over your safety, nothing more. No one could have anticipated—"

"Nevertheless, I am responsible." He glared at her with determination. "I need to fix the Sentinel."

"That may not be possible," Ranth warned. "The Perceptive Ones hid the Sentinel's location. The communications beam radiated outward from Mystique, like a ripple in hyperspace. We don't even know in which direction to look."

Zical released Dora's hand, angrily marched to the ledge that overlooked the crystals that had now lost their bright scarlet hues and lay dormant. Sensing his wish to be alone to contemplate the situation, she didn't try to console him.

* * *

KNOWING HIS LUST for adventure might eventually bring down the Federation and open the galaxy to an unknown enemy weighed on Zical, leaving a terrible tenseness in his body and a cold knot in his gut. His love of the hunt had resulted in Summar's death. Now his mountain climbing had led to another disaster. Rystani warriors were taught to put the greater good before their personal needs. Without such ingrained sacrifice, they might never have survived the Endekian invasion. His latest actions might have brought worse down on their heads. While no one could have predicted the outcome of his exploration into Mount Shachauri's interior, that didn't absolve him of responsibility.

Inside a mountain stronghold older than the Rystani race, staring unseeing into the dying light of the alien scarlet crystals, Zical felt an overwhelming need to set his world right. His people had fought too long and too hard to survive, going so far as to give up their homeworld to colonize Mystique. For the first time in five thousand years their future looked promising . . . and his action may have ruined their current prosperity.

He'd debated his future for months, and doubts had kept him from making a decision whether to join Mystique's space defense or work as a star pilot to ferry cargo and again try to become a husband. But within moments of learning about the Sentinel, he had a new goal, a certainty that he could make a difference. He'd gone to Mount Shachauri to contemplate his future and make a decision about his life, and now as a consequence of his discovery, neither of those other choices seemed adequate. Somehow he had to find a way to undo the damage he'd inadvertently caused. He had to find, contact, and reprogram the Sentinel and send the machine back to guard the Federation—a seemingly impossible task. But he couldn't live with any other choice.

Perhaps his destiny had been to call forth the Sentinel, perhaps not. He wasn't a deeply religious man, but he believed in free will, that one man could alter the future. His quest through the galaxy could take a lifetime.

The Milky Way was a vast place made up of between 100 and 400 billion stars, their planets, thousands of clusters and nebulae with a mass of almost one trillion solar masses and a diameter of 100,000 light-years. To make his search for the Sentinel even more difficult, the Milky Way belonged to a local group of three large and over thirty smaller galaxies, and he had no idea from which galaxy the Zin originated. And even if they could find the location of the threat from the machinery the Perceptive Ones left behind, there were no guarantees the Zin hadn't migrated during the ensuing eons.

The daunting task made him appreciate the resources he would ask Kahn and Tessa to put at his disposal. First and foremost, he'd require a starship capable of sustaining interstellar flight through hyperspace and beyond, a crew, plus dedicated scientists, preferably those with few family ties—since they had no idea when they might return.

Dora placed a hand on his shoulder and he jumped. If there had ever been a possibility of a relationship other than friendship forming between them, it was over before it had had a chance to begin. Already anticipating leaving behind everyone he'd come to care for, with the possible exception of his loyal crew, he began to withdraw into himself.

From the reddish spectrum in Dora's gaze, the slight smile of triumph on her mouth, he suspected she'd come to have him follow up on his promise to kiss her since she'd discovered the purpose of the machines. However, when he'd made that offer, he'd never expected the information to be so devastating.

"I'm going with you," Dora told him as if she realized his next step would be to return to the family headquarters to talk with Tessa and Kahn, then immediately recall his crew.

"Fine." He started walking back to the skimmer.

"You mean it?" Dora's voice rose in excitement. "You aren't going to argue?"

"About?" He suddenly suspected they weren't talking about the same thing.

"Letting me go with you." She had a muscle tic near her eyes, and a muscle in her leg must have spasmed because she stumbled.

He grabbed her arm, offering his strength. "You've been a big help today. I'd appreciate your support when I explain the threat to Tessa and Kahn."

"Of course you have my support."

"Thanks."

"I want to always be at your side. That's why I'm coming with you."

"Okay." Zical glanced at her. Why did he have the strongest feeling that he wasn't following her meaning?

"Thank you. Thank you. Thank you." Her voice filled with happiness, Dora tried to skip ahead. "I was so wrong about you. I thought you didn't want—"

"Didn't want what?"

"Me," she said simply.

Huh? His suspicions had been correct, and he spoke carefully. "What are we talking about?"

"My accompanying you on the journey to find the Sentinel and turn it around."

Stunned, he stopped abruptly. "I didn't say anything about—" He scowled at her. "Dora, can you read minds?"

She shook her head, or tried to, her cute chin jerking more up and down than side to side. "I extrapolated from known data, did an analysis, and theorized that your sense of honor would require you to set things right by heading into space. So you're planning a journey—one we'll take together," she concluded with a happy grin.

Zical scowled, exasperation increasing his impatience with her. How could one woman be so brilliant and come to such a conclusion at the same time? If she was deliberately trying to manipulate him, she was doing a marvelous job. While taking her with him would be advantageous since she could communicate with machines and help to reprogram the Sentinel, no way could she come with him. This quest wasn't a casual outing. A journey to find the Sentinel would entail unknown hardship and dangers, and Dora was barely functioning outside the confines of her room on a settled world, never mind in unknown space. Her inexperience could cause lives to be lost. She simply had too much to learn about being human, and he didn't have time to coddle her, and he most especially didn't want to be cooped up with her in close quarters when he found her so attractive.

Sensing a huge argument brewing between them, Zical planned to gather his thoughts before setting her straight. But Kahn's voice came through his com unit, preventing the discussion from continuing. "Ranth filled me in."

"Dora and I are heading your way now. I want to assemble my crew, put together a mission. I'll need a starship, supplies, and scientists. The mission will be expensive."

"Understood. I'll make sure Tessa is here when you arrive."

Dora was about to speak but Zical beat her to it. "Ranth, recall my crew."

"Already done."

"Have we any idea where to look for the Sentinel?"

"I'll start a search of my data bases."

"Extend to every Federation library," Dora added, and Zical realized that her knowledge of computer systems would have been useful during the journey he was about to begin. Dora had capabilities no human had. She was smart and had an intuitive knowledge of mathematics and machinery that he couldn't discount. The golden light had zapped him twice, yet he hadn't noticed the pattern contained within the vibrations that had led Dora to unravel the ancient message. Without her, there would be no mission. They'd simply be waiting for their destruction.

However, no intelligent starship captain would take someone so new to life, so inexperienced, aboard a spaceship for such a long journey into unknown space. Most people couldn't cope with the strain, the loneliness, the boredom. Dora could easily fall apart under that kind of pressure. A short while ago, she'd had trouble leaving her room. She could have trouble getting along with others in such close quarters. She might not adapt to life in space, and the all too likely possibility of her forgetting at a critical moment that she was now human could cause a loss of lives besides her own. Earlier, she'd forgotten to use her psi to filter the air. In space, lapses likes hers could be fatal. Despite the fact that she could be very useful, he needed experienced, space-hardened people.

And he certainly didn't need Dora's kind of distraction. With everything on his mind, he shouldn't be noticing the tremble of her lip after he'd spoken harshly. Or how she'd flinched, then pretended not to care. Or the enticing curve of her hips and the natural sway of her breasts as she walked beside him.

No, he'd have enough on his mind without Dora along to constantly remind him that she embodied every physical trait he admired in a woman. And the combination of her perfect body and her emotional vulnerability might cause *him* to make mistakes they couldn't afford.

Ranth spoke calmly. "A complete library search will take some time and be expensive."

"Do it," Zical ordered, knowing Tessa would gladly authorize the expense out of the family finances. Sometimes having a rich family was convenient. At a time like this, their vast wealth might mean the difference between either the survival or the end of the Federation.

Zical wished he could castigate himself, tell himself that he was exaggerating the menace. But he couldn't stop the inner conviction that if the Perceptive Ones had gone to such trouble to build this elaborate complex, then the Zin were a formidable enemy.

Dr. Laduna joined them, his gills flaring with concern. "I would like to volunteer my services to the effort."

"I appreciate your selflessness. The journey will be long and hard." Zical noted that the scientist didn't so much smile as preen, his eyes sparkling like green ice. "And if you could see who among those working here might also be willing to make the difficult journey in the name of science, I'd be grateful."

The scientists most knowledgeable about the Perceptive Ones were already on Mystique, studying the find. Hopefully, enough would volunteer so they wouldn't have to wait for more offworlders to arrive before they left on the mission. Logic told Zical the Sentinel might take years, perhaps decades, even a century to return from its post, but the sense of urgency that Zical had felt ever since he'd entered the complex had increased, almost as if he sensed the Zin, thriving and hearty and warlike, waiting on the galaxy's border for the right moment to attack.

Had he given them their moment? He prayed not.

"THANK YOU ALL for scrambling to get here so fast." Zical greeted Vax, his right-hand man and his friend, in the conference room Kahn had reserved for their use. The formal room had the finest communication system as well as priority access to Ranth. Food and drink from any of a hundred Federation worlds was available, and its windows offered a gorgeous view of the flowering garden of which Tessa was so proud.

During the months since Zical had climbed Mount Shachauri, his crew had scattered all over Mystique. His first officer, Vax, had been helping his aging parents settle on the northern continent. During the last years of the relocation, none of his crew had taken much personal time as they'd flown mission after mission to transport their people from Rystan to Mystique. Like many others, during the Endekian war, Vax had lost a wife and a brother. Perhaps Zical and the warrior had bonded over their shared grief and similar circumstances, perhaps they would have kept each other company during peaceful times, but their shared combat experiences had created a bond as tight as one of blood.

Zical had risked his life for Vax several times and the Rystani warrior had returned the favor. For a trip to the edge of the galaxy, he'd prefer no other man at his side. He trusted Vax's judgment to make the right decision during the times Zical wouldn't be at the helm.

Yet this journey would be made up strictly of volunteers. However, Zical suspected that he need merely ask, and Vax would be there at his side.

Despite Zical's urgency to begin his mission, he also cared about his crew and took the time to greet each one properly. If Vax refused the commission of second in command, his reason would be due to prior family commitments. His parents had taken the loss of their eldest son hard. "How are your folks?"

Vax grinned. "Mom's starting an import-export business."

"And your father?"

"Dad's enjoying the fishing." Vax's grin faded. "During the skimmer flight, Ranth briefed me. Count me in."

Zical's heart lifted with joy because he hadn't even had to ask. He simply nodded. "I won't hold you to your words until you hear more."

"I won't be changing my mind," Vax promised.

As Zical moved on to greet Cyn, a green-skinned engineer from Scartar, he realized how much he was counting on his people to join him. The mission would be difficult enough without an untried crew who hadn't had time to gel. And his trust and admiration for his officers would give them the best chance to succeed.

Cyn strode into the briefing room, her queenly posture impressive. But her skills as an engineer were what Zical valued. She'd pulled off the impossible more times than he could count, coaxing her engines to perform when they'd purple-lined and by all specs should have exploded.

She broke into a wide grin of greeting. "About time you called us back together, Captain."

Unlike the rest of his crew, Cyn had a full family of parents, brothers and sisters, aunts and uncles, back on her homeworld, Scartar. Of all his officers, she was the most tight-lipped, rarely speaking about herself. However, rumors flew that she could croon a sweet lullaby to her engines.

"Agreed," said Shannon Walker, a diminutive Terran who was his communications officer. As she joined them she clapped Cyn on the shoulder. A widow and grandmother many times over, she'd told her brood that the sign of a good parent was to make certain your children no longer needed you. And since she was too young not to see the galaxy, she'd taken one of the first ships off Earth to study at a Federation school. The oldest and newest member of his crew, she'd fit in with ease.

"Did you make a visit back to Terra?" Zical asked her, holding out his hand to shake hers in the Terran custom.

She grabbed his hand, then tugged him close for an embrace. "We met on Flagonna." She grinned, her eyes sparkling at her memories of the luxury vacation planet. "The grandkids had a blast in zero-g swimming pools, and my kids are finally learning to use their suits. A few are considering colonizing Ketric Prime. And I love seeing them all, but I love leaving them too."

Every one of his officers had volunteered, but Zical wanted to make sure they understood. His gaze took in Vax, Cyn, and Shannon. "Ranth has briefed you, but I want to emphasize that this mission could very well be a one-way trip. We don't yet know where to find the Sentinel but suspect the ancient machine is out on the galaxy rim, out farther than we've ever been."

"Even in hyperspace, the trip will take centuries," Cyn figured out loud.

"We're hoping to sling our ship around the Osarian black holes to increase our speed. As far as we know, we're going deeper into the gravity well than anyone's ever done. The hull may not stay together. And we don't know what effect traveling at such speeds in hyperspace will have on us. More importantly, the journey home will take all of those centuries you mentioned because the probability of finding two black holes so close to each other to shoot us home is next to nil."

His crew's expressions didn't change. From Ranth's briefing, they'd already figured out the basics for themselves.

"And even if we do find the Sentinel, we have no idea if we can communicate with it or how to send it back. The mission is full of unknowns—yet might be critical to the Federation's survival."

"Captain," Shannon asked. "Do we know if the Zin are still out there?"

He shook his head. "Tessa has agreed to supply a ship with our best technology and I'm recruiting scientists who specialize in the Perceptive Ones. I'm pleased that the Jarn specialist Dr. Laduna has agreed to head up the detail." Zical paused, letting the facts sink in. "As we journey farther away from home, communications, if they work at all, will take years, possibly decades or centuries, even at light-year speeds of hyperspace. We have no idea what kind of resistance we will meet along the way. We are venturing into the unknown."

"Sounds like fun," Shannon quipped. "Where do we sign up?"

As all of them stepped forward and bravely placed their retinal scans onto the vidscreen, confirming their willingness to put their lives on the line, Zical vowed to do his best to bring them back—even if it took centuries. No man had ever set forth on a journey with a more courageous and skillful crew. And he was proud to call each of them friend, prouder still that they so willingly risked their lives for the good of those staying behind.

However, with their loyalty and courage came a huge responsibility, for their safety, for the completion of this mission. As captain, he was required to make certain that their sacrifice would not be in vain.

* * *

"You aren't going." Zical strode into Dora's quarters, his jaw set at a commanding angle, his tone authoritarian, his eyes searching hers.

After the family meeting where a plan to attempt to contact the Sentinel had been implemented, with Zical in charge of the mission, Dora had expected to have time to plead her case to go along. However, hours of strategy that continued through a noisy meal had left Dora and Zical no time for private conversation. Afterward Zical had met with Ranth and his crew.

And she didn't want to speak to him now either. Not in the mood he was in. Knowing she would annoy him and hoping he'd leave, she disregarded his statement. "I thought you'd come to see me to pay up."

"Excuse me?"

"You owe me a kiss." In light of the serious situation, her request seemed inappropriate, just as she'd intended. She hoped he'd retreat, leave her alone to marshal her arguments and decide how much to reveal. Because although Zical was in charge and could pick his crew and the mission specialists on board, Tessa was funding the operation. If Tessa insisted that Dora was needed, then Zical would have little choice but to agree to accept her as part of his crew.

But Zical didn't get angry as she expected. Instead, he closed the distance between them in three long, predatory steps. She'd provoked him one too many times. At the hungry look in his eyes, her pulse spiked in anticipation.

Finally.

He was going to kiss her.

She attempted to keep the eagerness from her face. She didn't care that she'd manipulated him, provoked him, preyed on his emotions. She'd waited too long for this moment.

He was going to kiss her.

Roughly, his large hands grabbed her shoulders, jerked her to his chest, and she tilted back her head to gaze into eyes blazing with desire and vexation. Oh, my. She'd often wondered what it would be like to have his full attention. Now, she knew. Wondrous excitement churned in her heart.

He was going to kiss her.

Dora had monitored the birth of a star, spectacular eclipses, the rise of civilizations. But nothing had prepared her for the thrill of standing within the circle of Zical's arms, while his hands clasped her shoulders with fierce need, and her breasts pressed against his powerful chest as she waited for her first kiss.

"I always pay my debts."

Her knee had to pick that moment to buckle, but with a stray psi thought, she stiffened her suit and barely tottered. She thought he might be rough, but he lowered his head with a tender slowness, giving her every opportunity to change her mind.

As if that would happen.

Inhaling the scent of his tangy breath, she refrained from rising onto her tiptoes and savored the fact that he was coming to her in his own rough-hewn fashion. Ah, this was one of the reasons she'd so much wanted to be human, to experience the senses that fed the emotions that—

His lips caressed hers and she savored the quiet softness of his kiss that contrasted with the loud thuds of her heartbeat. He took his time, and the warmth of his mouth raked hers, heat slipping and sliding into her core, raising her temperature until a fever raged and erotic shivers trembled down her spine.

She parted her lips, welcoming his tongue and the taste of full-bodied masculine heat. Until now she hadn't understood how she could feel fire and ice together, in the same moment. She hadn't believed that every last sizzling cell in her body could be electrified by such a kiss, or how that energy could wrap her in a sensual cocoon of crisp and tangy desire.

She hadn't understood that one kiss would make her want so much more.

Kissing Zical was like all the stars in the universe shining on her at once. And she glowed from the inside out with a happy, uncontainable thrill that she would never forget. She wound her hands around his head, threaded her fingers into his thick dark hair, pressed her chest against his, and reveled in the richly textured sensations of humanity, sugar-powdered infatuation dusted with granulated lust.

She didn't have the experience to catalogue the exact emotions that tumbled inside her. Like smoldering paint being mixed on an artist's palette, first sizzling raspberry reds, then dusty burnt oranges, and finally pure passion pinks slashed with vivid purple highlights rippled and feathered and stroked her into a frenzy of desire.

And she who had spent her life in a parched desert of circuitry was suddenly drowning in lustrous, gleaming, torrid . . . life.

She lost all sense of the passage of time. Closing her eyes, she focused on only him, their fused lips, their breaths mingling, his heart beating next to hers, creating a current of spice and a tide of bracing need. His kiss was so much more than she'd dreamed, that she couldn't quantify, analyze, assess. Not with her senses spinning madly out of control. Not with her blood roaring in her ears. Not with the wonder of finally being exactly where she wanted to be—in his arms.

When he broke the kiss to draw a ragged breath, she opened her eyes, searched his face, but she'd no idea that she would see surprise mingling with regret. Regret? Was she reading his expression incorrectly?

"What's wrong?" she murmured, and attempted to tug his head back down to where they could kiss, again and again.

"You still can't come with me."

She allowed him to see a small smile. "If I thought I could change your mind with a kiss I wouldn't know you very well, now would I?"

Her lack of argument seemed to confuse him. His eyes narrowed. "What are you up to?"

She giggled. "You believe that just because I enjoy kissing you I have ulterior motives?"

"Absolutely."

He grasped her wrist, pulled her hand from behind his head where she gripped his hair, and stepped back. His expression might appear stoic, but his flesh had a ruddy tone and his pupils remained slightly dilated, exhibiting fierce desire.

She sighed. "Ah, you give me too much credit." Or perhaps himself too little. "I wanted to experience a kiss. Now I have."

"And?"

"Your kiss was wonderful—just as I've always suspected. You are a very passionate man."

"And you are a passionate woman—but not the one for me." Zical tightened his lips and a muscle tic appeared in his neck. He waited a moment for her to argue. She didn't.

She spoke mildly as if his reaction meant little to her, as if she didn't care that he might leave Mystique, never to return. Rystani men were strong, proud creatures who didn't bend easily. Although she could have given him a dozen reasons to take her along, he would be closed to her words. "I can see your mind is set."

"And you accept my decision?"

Hell, no. "Do I have a choice?" She gazed at him, keeping her eyes downcast, her face demure, then wondered if she was overacting. Surely he wouldn't believe she could be so pliant and meek? But he appeared only a tad suspicious, no doubt seeing what he wanted to see.

He really should have known better.

Chapter Eight

DORA HADN'T BEEN human long enough to collect many objects that meant anything; a holovid of her and Tessa, another of their entire family, and her link that permitted direct access to Ranth. Tessa had taught her that Federation credits might not be accepted currency everywhere, so Dora had stocked some luxury items that might be of use for barter. Traveling on a starship didn't allow much room for baggage, but since Dora didn't have much to pack, she was finished before Tessa arrived, giving her time to decide how much to reveal.

As much as Dora had wanted her friends to see her as human, as much as Dora realized Zical resented it when she plugged in, she would have felt very limited if she hadn't had the ability to link with Ranth. And although Tessa was aware that Dora often tapped into the mainframe circuitry, she'd assumed the process was similar to her calling up verbal information or accessing a monitor. Dora had never seen a reason to correct Tessa's faulty assumption.

Until now.

Stomach churning at the deception she was about to reveal to her best friend, Dora paced, or tried to between stumbles. She swore at her body that refused to work properly, wondered if that was why Zical didn't want her. A thought quite unfair to him. Zical wasn't the kind of man to push away a woman for such a minor physical defect. He was better than that, which was only one of the reasons why she found him so damn appealing.

Her handicap prevented her from feeling beautiful, but she was determined to get over the problem. It wasn't as if she had low self-esteem. She knew her intelligence was far superior to the norm, and her looks gorgeous despite the imperfections that wouldn't go away. However much she'd wanted to be perfect, she'd quickly learned that being human required multitasking, and if she could be excellent enough at one thing, her imperfections would be overlooked. When she'd figured out the Perceptive Ones' message, no one had cared that she'd twitched her way through her explanation. Zical had even looked proud of her.

Tessa breezed into Dora's quarters with a mug of coffee in one hand and a platter of Miri's home-baked chocolate chip cookies, a Terran delicacy that Dora had come to appreciate as much as Tessa. The delicious scent usually made her mouth water. Too nervous to eat, she knew she wouldn't be able to swallow a bite until she'd divulged her secret.

Tessa took one look at Dora and set down both coffee and cookies. "What's up?"

"I've deceived you."

"Okay." Tessa shot her a searching look. "I'm sure you had a good reason, but even if you didn't, I want you to know that no matter what you've done, I love you." Tessa's gaze shifted to the packed bag, then back to Dora. "Whatever you've done, don't ever forget that you have a family, you belong with us, and it's very human to make mistakes. You don't need to leave. We're here for you."

At Tessa's words, Dora's throat clogged with those horrible tears and her nose turned all stuffy. She sniffled, hating the idea of leaving her very best friend, a friend who gave love so unconditionally. "Thanks."

The two women hugged and Dora praised her lucky circuits that she had such a dear friend. She was going to miss Tessa.

Tessa broke their embrace and slugged down half her mug of coffee. "Enough of the mushy stuff. Fess up."

Dora paced, her hands loose by her sides. "Although I always wanted to be human, I also liked being a machine."

Tessa frowned. "You want to go back? Is that possible?"

"I don't want to go back, and that's a good thing because it's not possible. My brain is integrated on a cellular level and can't be disconnected."

"Sorry. I shouldn't have interrupted. Go on."

"When I made this body, I gave my brain extra capacity to link with Ranth."

"And?"

"I merge with him."

"What do you mean?" Tessa looked at her with an odd expression, half thoughtful, almost excited.

"Can you explain your sense of smell to an Airnithian who has no nose?" Dora paused, allowing Tessa time to think but not to answer the rhetorical question before continuing. "Trying to explain my ability to you is similarly frustrating."

"Try."

"When I plug in, I can't do everything Ranth can do. But I can enter his control center and be one with him at that locale."

"So your brain is in two places at once?"

"Yes."

"And what can you do from inside Ranth that you can't do by talking to him?"

Leave it to Tessa to spear straight to the core of the matter. "The link strengthens my ability to work with other machines. Together, Ranth and I, we are much stronger than either of us alone. Productivity is increased exponentially by a factor of—."

"Spare me the details, please. Give me the bottom line and remember that I only learned college math, most of which I've long forgotten."

"We entwine ourselves with other machines that aren't linked to our network." As a computer, Dora had required human help to infiltrate the holosim house to find Zical's secret program, but when she'd linked with Ranth, she could penetrate the separate system through her psi.

"You mean you can spy on our enemies?"

"Possibly. We haven't yet tried."

"So what *have* you been doing?"

"Searching for information on the Perceptive Ones that goes beyond Federation space. I didn't want to say more—"

"Because you didn't want to disappoint me if you were unable to find anything?" Tessa surmised.

"And because I want Zical to think of me as a woman. He's already unhappy with my link to Ranth. Revealing my ability sets me apart. Makes me less human."

Tessa shook her head, helped herself to a cookie, and employed null grav to float into a comfortable sitting position. "Dora, if he is the man for you, he'll accept you the way you are."

"Rystani men are stubborn," Dora countered, using Tessa's own words. "Remember how long it took Kahn to accept your fighting skills?"

"Point taken." Tessa broke a cookie and handed Dora half. "So what's the plan?"

Dora nibbled on the cookie. "I need additional time to convince Zical that we could be good together. I want to go on this journey with him."

Tessa sighed, almost as if she'd been expecting Dora's request. "Suppose he never comes to feel the same way for you? Then you'll have left on what could very well be a one-way trip."

"Zical believes that I'm emotionally vulnerable."

"He said so?" Tessa looked surprised and disappointed.

Dora shook her head. She might have been human for only a short time, but she'd known Zical for several years. She understood his reluctance to become involved with another woman after the death of Summar. And ever since the golden light had caught Dora in its beam, she'd realized that the alien light had a side effect; it seemed to bring out one's greatest fear. Zical had become sexually aroused, and she suspected he feared falling in love. And she had realized how much she feared really embracing her humanity. But Tessa was the one who had taught her to go after what she wanted, to try her utmost, to never give up. She wanted to live her life with that kind of courage and knew it wouldn't be easy. "For him to accept me, I'll have to become the right woman. The more I live, the more I experience, the more I'll grow."

"Suppose you grow into a woman who doesn't want him? Will you be sorry that you've left?"

"I don't know." Dora grinned. "But I can contribute to this mission in a way no one else can. When I merge with Ranth, I have a better chance of reaching the Sentinel than Ranth would alone, or anyone else Zical might take on the ship. However, I'm not ready to let him know about my ability. He dislikes it when I hook into Ranth."

"You've thought this through, but I'm going to miss you so much."

Dora's hopes rose. "Then you'll help me?"

"Shame on you for doubting me. Of course I'll help. But I expect frequent hyperlink calls for as long as communication remains possible."

"That's going to be expensive."

Tessa laughed. "Don't worry. We can afford it. Our trading partnership with the Osarians is more profitable than I ever imagined." Her expression sobered. "However, Zical is going to be one unhappy male. And I suspect he'll take out his aggravation on you. Are you sure you can deal with him?"

Dora grinned, sharing her happiness. "The last time I annoyed him, he kissed me."

Tessa brushed crumbs from her hands, straightened, and signaled her with a thumbs-up. "Ah, that's a good sign. A very good sign."

THE MISSION WAS a go. Since Tessa was paying for all the expenses, the Federation leaders had sent unofficial approval. Zical spent five busy days overseeing innumerable details. Under Cyn's supervision, a bevy of engineers crawled over every inch of the starship. Vax oversaw robots that stored replacement parts in the cargo hold, food supplies in the materializers. They brought aboard weapons, trade goods, and the latest starmaps, spare parts and medical equipment. With their destination and the length of the trip uncertain, they had to prepare for every contingency, a seemingly impossible task, but helped by the fact that with millions of planets in the Federation, they could draw on an enormous amount of information.

Zical worried most about choosing the scientists who would accompany them. He and his officers had picked the remainder of his crew from a bright contingency of volunteers that were mostly Rystani and Terran, but included several other species. All were experienced spacers—except Dora. Every time Zical thought about her joining the crew, his edginess elevated. She'd spent over three hundred years in space—as a computer—but none as a human.

She was unprepared for danger, and yet Tessa had made such good points in Dora's favor that she'd convinced him that he needed her—for the sake of the mission. And Zical had accepted Tessa's judgment, not solely because she was funding the mission, but because she might be correct. Dora's unique ability to understand complex machinery might be useful if, no, *when,* they found the Sentinel.

While Zical couldn't pretend disinterest in Dora after that

sizzling kiss, a kiss that had led to several erotic dreams, he planned to control his attraction—not an easy task when they'd be stuck together in a space ship for long periods of time. He would treat her like any valued crew member. However, he was still trying to ignore his dream from two nights ago. A dream so vivid, he'd awakened in a sweat, his *tavis* hard at the memory of Dora.

Dora had wed him, and during the marriage ceremony, during the time when Rystani males gave up control to their women, she used her hands and mouth to stroke, to tease, to seduce. He'd awakened wild with need, his breath ragged, cursing the golden light that had caused his insatiable lust. He might have made a midnight trip to Xentos, but the holosim would only pale in comparison to Dora. So he'd suffered through his yearnings, focusing his thoughts on the mission until his desire had slowly ebbed, leaving his gut raw, his balls aching, his determination to keep his distance intact.

The fate of the Federation could rest on the success of his decisions, and the responsibility caused him to come to conclusions he might otherwise not have made. Now was not the time to let himself be distracted by Dora. Not when he had to keep his mind focused. Too much planning and expense, never mind the lives at stake, was going into this mission for him to be thinking about a woman—any woman. Determined to keep Dora at an emotional distance, he vowed to handle her carefully. Although he couldn't help but find her physically attractive, although he was all too aware of her presence every time they came within sight of each other, she was not the right woman for him.

He'd promised himself that if he ever again became involved with a woman, he wouldn't try to change her, he would accept her and love her for who she was. And he couldn't do that with Dora. Hell, he had enough trouble connecting with a Rystani woman, never mind one who had spent her first three hundred years as a machine. He would keep Dora as a friend, nothing more.

Zical had never gotten over the fact he'd gone hunting when he should have known Summar couldn't cope with making good choices. During his absence, she had tried to hide in a closet during the invasion of their city. She hadn't had the courage to fight or the daring to attempt to escape as so many others had done. Because he'd been away hunting food and hadn't been there to protect her, to tell her what to do, she'd died, and her death still rode heavy on his conscience.

Never again would he place himself in that kind of situation. And while Dora possessed far more courage in her little finger than Summar had had in her entire body, Dora also possessed a vulnerability that needed much more tending than he was willing to give—especially now. He had to focus on the mission, or making sure his crew survived and succeeded. He would accept Dora as part of his crew, no more, and no less. He would ignore his attraction to her, ignore his erotic dreams, ignore how much he yearned to kiss her again, he would set a professional tone, establish a comfortable working relationship.

Zical stood on the bridge of his starship, eager to be on his way, when he finally received the news he'd been waiting for. Ranth lit up the near quadrant of the Milky Way galaxy on a holovid monitor. Out near the rim, where the stars thinned, a purple light blinked.

Ranth spoke with an edge of excitement. "The marked system is named Lapau. According to ancient records the Lapau system was colonized by a humanoid race called the Lapautee. Not much is known about them. However, they have a legend that suggests their planet may be an outpost for a protector, a great, living, godlike machine, that will stand between them and the galaxy we call Andromeda. Please keep in mind that all my theories are pieced together from legends carried back from the homeworld, a homeworld that no longer exists due to their star going supernova."

"Then from where does your information come?"

"It's gathered from hundreds of planets within their former territory. Bits and pieces of history were passed down through the ages by the Lapautee people. At one time their race had spread through half a quadrant of the galaxy."

"And the reason their civilization fell?"

"A warlike horde that came from—"

"Andromeda?"

"Yes. Conceivably the Zin. It's possible the Lapautee were what we now call the Perceptive Ones. However, they might have been two races that formed an alliance against the Zin. Or they may have lived during two different epochs and one race learned from the other's mistakes. Too much time has passed to be certain."

"Have you learned anything more about the Zin?" Zical asked, all too aware that the information was so ancient that nothing might be accurate.

"Only that they are ruthless, relentless, and—"

"And?"

"Have the extraordinary patience to wait for opportunity and prey on weakness."

"Weakness?"

"If one's guard was ever let down, the Zin were waiting to attack."

A cold shadow seemed to pass over Zical, and no matter how irrational it might seem, as the meaning of those words sank in, he knew the Zin were still out there, still waiting for the Milky Way to exhibit weakness. While it seemed impossible that one machine could hold off an invasion from another galaxy, the Perceptive Ones had made scientific advances far beyond those of the Federation.

"What else?"

"There is an account that the Zin attacked and penetrated our galaxy before they suffered a great defeat and withdrew."

"And the regions of space we fly through? What kind of conditions do you anticipate?"

"We don't know much about the rim. However, there have

been signs of massive destructive weapons in the region, indicating war and instability."

Zical would obtain updates on the specific areas during their journey. Perhaps he should be taking a fleet of warships with him, but that was impossible. They couldn't afford to leave Mystique undefended. It would take months to place their concerns before the Federation council, and even if they listened to the Rystani request, they might not act.

Besides, one starship could sneak past danger while an entire fleet would be challenged. The unknowns were as infinite and as vast as space and the risk formidable. As Zical mulled over Ranth's information, he paced the bridge of his starship. Little was known about the Perceptive Ones and for Ranth to have pieced together even this much data seemed fortuitous, but suspect.

"Ranth, how have you added so much knowledge to our database, so quickly?"

"My systems have been . . . upgraded."

Zical frowned. Although he wasn't a specialist, and although Tessa kept the data banks fully maintained and the hardware upgraded with the newest technology, he hadn't heard of a major systemwide renovation, but then he'd been extraordinarily busy. However, it seemed odd to him that Ranth had accomplished so much when just a few short months ago, Dora had known so little.

"Upgraded?"

Zical expected a technical explanation. Instead he received another long pause. "Dora has found a way to increase my ability. Due to her unusual background, she has a gift that allows her to think along nonlinear lines. She's made some innovative alterations to my systems."

"She altered your hardware or your programming?" Zical kept his voice steady, but alarm crested through him. Since he was the most powerful computer known in Federation space, Ranth's systems were critical to his people's survival as well as his mission.

"The programming modifications are marginal."

"Who approved them?" Zical tried to check his irritation. Although Dora had been a computer, he was aware that she couldn't have transferred all her technical knowledge into her human brain and could now make mistakes like every other human.

"I did," Ranth said.

The answer set Zical back on his heels. While he was well aware of Dora's capabilities when she'd been a computer, as a human she was subject to distractions, possible lack of judgment, errors that could be due to exhaustion or hormones or upsets. Although Zical knew Ranth's systems were in triplicate, what bothered him was that Dora was messing with things without any backup or oversight. They needed to talk.

Zical headed for her quarters but found them empty. "Ranth, locate Dora, please." It was a measure of his vexation that he hadn't asked about her whereabouts first, but then Dora might have been forewarned of his arrival, and he'd wanted to confront her before she'd assembled an argument. He couldn't have his crew altering critical equipment without permission—not even Cyn, his chief engineer, had that kind of authority.

"Dora's in the gym with Tessa."

"What are they doing?"

"Tessa's teaching Dora to fight."

Zical let out a groan. Tessa had studied the fighting arts before she'd possessed a Federation suit that allowed her to move at the speed of thought. After she'd developed her psi, she'd become deadly. Skilled, smart, and daring, she would make a fine teacher. And he approved wholeheartedly of women learning to defend themselves. While Kahn had initially had difficulty with the concept that a woman could master warrior skills, Zical had seen the advantage immediately. If Summar had had such skills, she and their unborn child might still be alive today.

However, with fighting skills, a warrior needed the wisdom of knowing when to use them. He couldn't help wondering if Dora yet had such prudence.

Zical had seen Tessa in action many times, and as he entered the training center, four padded walls, a padded ceiling, and a padded floor, necessary to protect the body when fighting in the three dimensions that null grav allowed, his gaze lasered in on Dora.

Both women wore skintight black suits that revealed every curve. Dora was taller and curvier, but slower and clumsier, than Tessa. Yet she was much further along in the learning process than he'd have expected.

"We're almost done here," Tessa greeted him.

Dora didn't even look his way. Tessa was pressing her with a forward lunge ending in a back kick. Dora evaded, but not quite fast enough, and Tessa's foot glanced off her shoulder, sending her spinning into a wall. Dora didn't fight her momentum, however, she used it, somersaulted and attacked from below with a bold move Zical had never seen.

"Nice." Tessa blocked and countered as both women floated to the floor. "You'll practice during the voyage?"

"I promised, didn't I?"

Dora's face spasmed. Odd, she'd been in total control when fighting. He'd noted no twitching or unnatural movement during the bout, but now that Dora was simply walking, she once again lacked control.

Tessa nodded. "I'll hold you to that promise. Your instincts are good. Once you learn to trust them, you'll move to the next level. If you'll excuse me, I promised Kahn I'd meet him for lunch."

Tessa departed, leaving Zical alone with Dora. The suit's evaporation took care of her sweat, but her face remained flushed from her exertions, her eyes sparkled with enthusiasm, and he couldn't help thinking that she looked alive and lovely, and he wished he'd come here for another kiss. For a woman with no sexual experience, Dora had mastered a surefire way to hone his interest. Between her intellect, her sassy demeanor, and that skintight catsuit, his senses were on high alert.

Her wonderful scent wafted to him, and he folded his arms across his chest, bracing himself for the coming confrontation. "Ranth told me you've modified his systems."

"A few tweaks here and there. Why?"

From her tone, he could tell that she had no idea she'd done anything wrong. And that was the big problem. If she couldn't comprehend that being human had altered her so that making errors might now be a potential problem, then she couldn't change her behavior. More gently and patiently than he'd thought possible, he explained. "Ranth's systems are complex. We depend upon him for survival."

"That's why he needs to be at his best. My tweaks increased his efficiency." Chin raised, head high, she acted as though she expected praise for her actions.

"Suppose you'd decreased his efficiency?"

"Then we would have deleted the program change."

Stars! "You are arguing with logic. I'm talking about the possibility of your making human errors."

Dora blinked and then opened her eyes wide. "Huh? You don't want me to use logic?"

"You are no longer a computer, and can make mistakes like the rest of us. Someone should oversee and check your work."

"No one is more qualified than me to alter Ranth's programs."

He couldn't argue with that. "You're missing my point. Who gave you permission to change his systems?"

Dora frowned. "Why do I need permission? I already told you that no one is better qualified than me. Why would I ask permission from someone with less knowledge?"

Again, she made a good point, but he had his own to make as well. "On a starship, no one is better at repairing the engines than the chief engineer. Yet no engineer would modify the engines without the captain's permission."

"We don't have that chain of command on Mystique."

"I understand. However, on the starship orders must be obeyed. Once we're in space, if you want to make changes in the computer, you'll need to ask my permission."

"Compliance. I mean yes, I understand."

"Good." Zical wondered if she really did understand. Her acceptance had been almost too easy. He'd sought her out expecting a long argument, pleas, logic, or sexual innuendos, not this easy agreement that felt as though she'd cut him off at the knees.

"I know you aren't pleased that Tessa agreed I should go on the mission." Dora sucked on her bottom lip for a moment, then spoke in a voice that rang with sincerity. "But I want to contribute. Since I'm part of humanity, I want to help us all survive."

He'd neither expected her to be up-front about what he considered her underhanded tactics of going to Tessa instead of him to be assigned to the mission, nor had he ever thought she'd feel a sense of responsibility to humanity. Since he'd already explained that there could be nothing personal between them, and was well aware that she feared the unknown, he was beginning to see her joining the mission as an act of courage.

However, he wouldn't put it past Dora to set aside her innate sensuality to impress him in other ways. And if that was her intent, stars, her tactic was working. What worried him was that he might find her even more attractive as an efficient working member of his crew than he did as the sexy vamp. But he appreciated this new side of her, and he was impressed that she was learning to fight.

"I'm glad you're coming with us," he admitted, then felt compelled to question her. "But are you sure you're ready to go?"

Chapter Nine

"ENGINEERING?" ZICAL ASKED from his station on the bridge as Dora watched him prepare to take the starship *Verazen* into Osarian space. The Osarian planet occupied a unique position in the galaxy, its orbit located equidistant between two black stars, creating a slingshot effect into hyperspace that could save on fuel and increase their speed, enough to take centuries off their journey. The *Verazen* was a brand-new ship, and therefore tested over the distance and speeds they intended to fly.

Using the ship's drive alone, the journey would take half their suit-extended lifetimes. So they would navigate the deep Osarian gravity well, plunging closer than anyone had ever done to the black holes before swinging into hyperspace. One miscalculation and the immense gravity could haul in the ship and squash the hull like a mud flea, or fling them in the wrong direction and add additional light-years to their journey. Piloting and navigation had to be exact, the engines tuned to perfection.

Despite the tension on the bridge, Dora was determined to remain as professional as the rest of the crew. She'd been in hyperspace more times than she could count, but never with a body. Since hyperspace was known to increase the sensitivity of all five senses, she braced for the additional stimuli. Some races sickened and had to be drugged into a sleep state, but humans adapted, even if they suffered a bit of nausea at first. Tessa had advised Dora to lower her suit temperature and keep her eyes peeled on the viewscreen, but instead she focused on Zical, enjoying the opportunity to observe him without the others noticing.

The Rystani captain leaned eagerly forward, his posture erect, his head high, his eyes bright with anticipation of the unknown. On land Zical was a formidable man, but the helm of a starship was his natural element and where he came alive. Dora had accompanied him on every mission and enjoyed the sparkle of anticipation in his eyes that went so well with how he led his officers in a calm manner. She also enjoyed his gaze sweeping over her, as if to make certain she was okay, as if he wasn't able to treat her like just another crew member. And on the rare occasions when their glances met, she appreciated the approval he reflected back at her for a job she did well.

"Engineering is a go." Cyn, the chief engineer, a skilled woman from Scartar, patted her console and spoke under her breath to her engines as if they required soothing encouragement. An exotic warrior woman with arms as muscular as a Rystani hunter, she came from a matriarchal society where women ruled. During her computer days, Dora had been a vital part of this crew during missions to evacuate refugees from Rystan and she knew that Cyn had no difficulties taking orders from a man. With her fierce looks, muscular body, and easygoing personality, the green-skinned Cyn had a reputation for real genius when it came to making repairs, and her underlings adored her.

"Navigation?" Zical's face appeared calm, but Dora noted the growing glitter of excitement in his gaze. The man loved adventure but didn't like to admit enjoying the risk-taking side of his personality. Instead, he usually projected an air of responsible leadership, but in a moment like this one, his true character showed. He was impatient to see what was out there, to go somewhere no Rystani had ever gone, and his excitement stirred a matching one inside her.

She was risking her life for a shot at love, and exhilaration mixed with the dangerous tension in her belly. Dora held her breath, the moments passing by too fast, and yet contradictorily much too slowly. Hyperspace was unstable. No one from the Federation had gone out as far as they planned to do and returned to tell about their journey—at least not in the last few hundred thousand years. However, her physical safety was of a lesser concern to her than the emotional risk she'd taken by insisting on accompanying Zical.

Instinctively, she'd known they'd needed time together. And she hoped the friendship they shared would grow as the journey progressed. While she was eager to experience passion with Zical, she also wanted her feelings to deepen. She wanted to earn his respect and his admiration as well as his lust and she wouldn't stand a chance of accomplishing her goal if she'd remained behind on Mystique.

"We're keyed in the groove." Ranth's voice, steady and crisp, helped Dora steady her jumpy nerves.

Zical went down his checklist, his commanding demeanor reassuring. "Weapons?"

"Locked down tight." The Rystani warrior Vax had been Zical's second in command for the past three years during the transfer of Rystani colonists to Mystique. Serious, loyal, Vax followed orders without question. Short for a Rystani, he nevertheless possessed a broad chest and wide shoulders, he was a fierce competitor at *Famat*, a complex gambling game that taxed mind and spirit, and he could down large quantities of alcohol without it seeming to affect his judgment.

"Communications?"

Shannon Walker, a quiet Terran woman, handled her station with an ease that belied her age. She'd become a widow due to an accident in space. She admitted to the spry age of sixty but Dora knew her to be closer to eighty—a mere youngster, considering the suits increased Terran life spans to close to a thousand years. Unless, of course, they died in an accident, and nothing was more dangerous than hyperspace.

Dora tensed, knowing this part of the journey and the exit in the uncharted territory were probably the most dangerous times of the mission, since that's when they were most vulnerable. Hyperspace inside the Federation was usually stable, unless a local star went supernova, unless a black hole destabilized the region, unless a worm hole blasted hyperspace to shreds and their ship along with it.

Telling herself that she would be dead before she knew what had happened and that she'd suffer no pain didn't help. Dora had too many things she wanted to do before she died. Sheesh. She hadn't even made love—an item on the top of her to-do list. But human sexuality was complicated, especially when mixed with stubborn Rystani males.

"Computer?" Zical interrupted Dora's thoughts. As he asked for her report, he didn't look at her, carefully treating her exactly the same as his other crew members.

"All systems are operational." Pleased that she sounded calm, Dora suspected her effort was destroyed by an eye tic. Sometimes rubbing the muscles around the eye helped, but she didn't like to be obvious about her disability and turned her head away from the others . . . and caught sight of . . . something that didn't belong on the bridge.

"Five seconds to hyperspace." Cyn counted down the jump sequence.

The bridge, shaped like a pancake, was positioned on top

of the living quarters with the engines in the lower decks. The inside was compact, with large viewscreens around the circumference, each station consisting of equipment monitors, consoles, and vidscreens to show other sections of the ship as well as the exterior view. Right now the stars appeared stationary, but once in hyperspace they'd streak past the windows. For the shift from normal space, the crew didn't depend on their suits alone to keep them safe. Safety straps webbed them in place, although once in hyperspace they could move about freely.

"Three seconds."

"Two."

However, behind the webbing that extended from the ceiling to the floor was something, someone, too small to be a crew member. With the creature's suit matched in color to the webbing to camouflage its presence, Dora would never have spied the intruder if she hadn't angled her head down to rub her eye. Perhaps she was seeing things. Surely Ranth's sensors would have noted an alien presence, so Dora hesitated to say anything, unwilling to trust her human eyes.

Could the fear in her gut be causing hallucinations?

"One second."

The creature moved.

Dora braced for the hyperjump, but still warned the others. "Intruder on board."

"Security alert." Vax issued the warning through the ship's com.

"Where?" Zical asked, turning his head to her with a frown.

The ship jumped out of normal space, and their hyperdrive kicked in along with the slingshot effect from the gravity well's release. To Dora the impact of hyperspace was like a kick in the gut. Her hearing picked up every hull vibration. Colors sharpened. The air in her lungs seemed crisper. And the hair on her arms stood on end. Due to the intensity of her untried senses, the silhouette of the intruder appeared to blur, causing her to wonder if she'd seen anything at all.

Perhaps the problem with her sight was simply a side effect of hyperspace. They were traveling faster, farther, than anyone in the Federation had ever done before. The speed was more than her human brain could comprehend, and although it seemed impossible, they'd already passed four percent of the way through the galaxy.

Ranth disagreed with Dora's alert. "My sensors haven't picked up an intruder."

Nothing Ranth could have said could have upset her more. Since her transformation, Dora had had trouble adjusting to her human eyes that only looked forward and somewhat to the sides. And Ranth could see everywhere. He could note an alien presence in dozens of ways. He could hear breathing, sense their body heat. Pick up any number of clues on his scanners and internal sensors.

"Dora." Zical eyed her, his expression worried. "Where's the intruder? Talk to us."

Obviously, Zical and the rest of the crew didn't see it hiding. But she could still see a blurred silhouette in the webbing. So either her eyes were faulty, or she was going insane. Or the hyperspace speed was playing tricks with her sight. But then the creature moved again. She was about to raise her hand and point, when the creature emerged from hiding.

Not a creature.

A boy.

Kirek.

The rascal had sneaked aboard. His parents were going to be furious. Zical would no doubt give the boy a good tongue-lashing for his antics.

Relieved she wasn't crazy and that her eyes had not somehow malfunctioned, Dora rubbed her forehead, which was beginning to pound from the intense hyperspace vibration. She supposed if that was the worst thing she suffered, she wouldn't complain. At least the ship hadn't disintegrated from the enormous forces. Her attention focused on Kirek, who looked both sheepish and not so innocent, but ready to own up to his actions.

How had a four-year-old-boy avoided the most sophisticated ship's sensors known to the Federation?

Security double-timed onto the bridge, weapons drawn. When they spied Kirek, they lowered their weapons before Zical gave the order to stand down.

"We are on the mark, Captain," Vax reported from his station.

"Hull temperature rose four degrees. Nothing we can't handle." Cyn retracted the webbing, leaving Zical to deal with his stowaway.

"Inform Miri and Etru that their son is with us," Zical ordered his communications officer.

Shannon nodded. "Aye, sir, but their response will take some time due to our considerable progress."

Zical approached the boy and kneeled to look him in the eyes. "What are you doing here?"

"And how did he avoid Ranth's sensors?" Dora asked.

"You need me." Kirek answered Zical in the voice of a toddler, but with the demeanor of an adult.

"Your parents need you," Zical told him.

"Ranth, are your sensors picking up Kirek now?" Dora asked.

"Yes. But it's as if he's decided to allow me to scan him. I have no explanation."

Zical arched a brow and waited for the child to say more. Dora wasn't so sure *he* could explain, but she admired Zical's patience. There were fish that gave off electricity but they certainly couldn't explain how they did so. Some mammals used sonar to fly in dark caves, but that didn't mean the user understood the process.

However, Kirek was not just unusual for a child, he was unique. As the only human being known to have been born in hyperspace, he'd exhibited signs of maturation and genius early. His psi was extraordinarily strong for an adult, never mind a child, and his intelligence was off all measurable charts.

"I can cloak myself from machines," Kirek said.

So he *did* have an explanation.

"How?" Zical asked.

"I'll show you." Kirek stood there in front of them. Nothing changed.

"He isn't gone, is he?" Ranth asked.

"He's right here." Zical tousled the boy's hair.

"He's disappeared from my sensors. I can't get a reading." Ranth sounded more intrigued than disturbed.

"Kirek?" Zical's tone was curious, but not the least bit anxious.

"He's back on my sensors now," Ranth reported.

"We'll have to turn around to take him home." Zical plucked the boy into his arms.

Dora understood that Zical was disappointed by the huge delay in their journey, but his arms around Kirek remained gentle, his tone kind, his demeanor compassionate. After they'd made good use of the Osarian black holes, their speed was incredible. Although they'd just left to brake their ship then turn around and retrace their flight path without the slingshot effect would take years.

Kirek squirmed. "My presence is necessary to this mission. Without me, you will fail."

Such a serious, grown-up prediction, like that of a prophet, coming from the mouth of a little boy seemed incongruous, but Zical hesitated. "How do you know we need you?"

"I just do." Kirek wriggled down and looked up at him beseechingly, his big blue eyes both wise and sad.

Dora wanted to tell the boy everything would be fine. This wasn't his quest. He should have time to be a kid before he placed himself in jeopardy on a dangerous mission. Yet, clearly Kirek had never been a normal kid. Even before his birth, the family had been aware of his strong psi presence. And since then, he had had an inner quality that radiated from him—like a wise, old soul.

"Shannon. How's that hyperlink call to Etru coming?" Zical frowned at Kirek. "I'm not taking you anywhere without your father's permission."

Kirek didn't argue. Instead, he stood too still for a child, his expression serene, his chubby cheeks set, his demeanor calm.

When his father's face finally appeared on the vidscreen, Kirek's expression filled with love. "Hi, Dad. Told you they wouldn't find me."

"You knew this child intended to stow away aboard my ship?" Zical's tone rose in astonishment.

It was two days before they heard Etru's reply and in those two days they'd traveled a third of the way to their final destination. Ranth reconstructed the conversation with questions and answers in real time so it seemed like a normal conversation. But in reality, the starship occupants spoke, asking question after question in an initial message. Much later, Etru answered those questions in one long message.

"I knew Kirek intended to try and sneak aboard," Etru admitted. "I thought the sensors would catch him and he'd learn a good lesson." Proud and sad, Etru spoke with Zical, but his gaze was focused hungrily on his son. Etru and Miri had conceived the child late in life and Kirek would likely be their only offspring. Etru doted on the boy, whose intellect had already far surpassed that of his parents.

Zical shrugged. "As you can see, he's learned how to fool Ranth's sensors. We haven't yet discovered how."

"Dad, I must stay. They need me." Kirek repeated his words and they sounded no less a prophecy this time than the last.

Zical spoke to Etru. "Our journey might last longer than many. We're exploring unknown territory and we may not return for centuries." He paused and everyone on the bridge heard the words the captain didn't speak. That they might never come back. "Your son will miss his schooling—"

"I've already passed the required courses," Kirek told him.

Dora knew that Kirek was being modest. The kid was way beyond the university level in physics and math. But it wasn't his vast store of knowledge that impressed her, it was the connections he could make with a limited number of facts. As Tessa would say, the kid could think outside the box—a trait both precious and unique.

Ranth piped in. "I will instruct him in his studies during his time aboard the *Verazen*."

"We don't have other children here," Zical protested with a deep frown. "Without playmates, his social skills will not be adequate."

Kirek shook his head. "Kids my age still play in the sandlot. We don't have much in common except physical size."

"I'll watch out for him," Dora offered, aware that of all the crew, she had the most time to spare. And although Kirek didn't need parents, he needed someone to love him and she thought maybe she could do that.

Shannon spoke with the voice of experience. "Boys his age aren't any trouble if you keep them busy."

Zical's grin said that Kirek was already trouble, but to his credit he didn't disagree. His gaze swept across to Dora, as if asking her opinion on whether or not it was a good decision to let him stay. They exchanged a long glance and she nodded yes, pleased she could figure out his silent question, pleased the rapport she'd often shared with Zical when she'd been a computer hadn't completely vanished with her humanity. When Kirek had proclaimed they needed him, an answering chord inside her had agreed. It was something she couldn't explain with logic. Was this a hunch? She didn't know, but her gut agreed with her head, even if she couldn't give a logical reason.

Vax offered, "I'll teach him to fight."

Zical was wavering. "Etru, he's your child. It's your decision."

Already their speed was so great that no Federation ship had ever gone as fast. If they slowed, stopped, and turned around, using their regular hyperdrive, Kirek would likely be an adult long before they could return him to his parents.

A tear escaped Etru's eye. "I love you, son. Your mother and I will miss you."

"Thanks. You're going to be proud of me."

"I already am." Etru's wrinkled face was now shiny with tears that he didn't attempt to hide. "Be careful and come back safe." Etru ended the communication and the screen went blank.

"Hold on." Zical scowled at the little boy. "If you're joining this crew, you must agree to take orders from me."

"Yes, sir."

"I want your promise that you won't hide from Ranth unless you're working with him to figure out how you cloak yourself from his sensors."

"Agreed."

"And if you have any particular notions on how to accomplish this mission, you'll talk them over with one of my officers or me and get permission before you proceed."

"Sure."

"All right. You can bunk down with—"

"Me," Dora volunteered. She'd always enjoyed Kirek and she needed a distraction from thinking about Zical so much of the time. Besides Ranth, she had the best all-around education and could help the boy along in his studies better than anyone. She was the logical choice to be a substitute mom and actually looked forward to the challenge.

"Do you know anything about children?" Zical asked, his eyes fixing on her with sudden intensity, obviously hesitant to give his approval.

Was he questioning her capability or her humanity? Either way, she didn't appreciate his interrogation, sure he wouldn't have doubted anyone else in the crew. Raising her chin, she dared him to contradict her. "What I don't know, I can learn."

Dora wanted to rub her pounding temple, close her eyes against the streaking stars, and let her stomach settle. As if her body didn't have enough to deal with adjusting to hyperspace, her arm spasmed, and to stop the spasm, she had to grab her wrist with her other hand. And all the while, she held Zical's fierce glare.

She suspected he had more to say to her, but he didn't get the chance. They were supposed to remain in hyperspace much longer, but suddenly the drive cut out, the ship lurched, shuddered and dumped them into normal space.

When Dora regained her balance, she motioned for Kirek to join her. Zical's attention turned to his crew and instrumentation. "What happened?"

"The engine's fail-safe device overreacted to the hull's external heat," Cyn reported.

"Where are we?"

"Near Rigel Five."

"Preparing to jump back into hyperdrive," Vax said. Webbing dropped and this time Dora made sure that Kirek was webbed in before she secured herself.

"Get us back in the groove," Zical ordered. The drive hummed and normal space once again disappeared. "How much velocity did we lose?" Zical asked.

Before he received an answer, the *Verazen* again plopped into normal space.

"Stars!" Zical checked the monitors. "Now what's wrong?"

"We're undergoing spatial interference that our scanners cannot identify," Ranth said. "I'm working to modify our deflector shields."

"Are we under attack?" Zical asked.

"Sensor readings aren't picking up any ships within weapons' range."

But they didn't know much about the races who lived in this part of the galaxy or what kind of technology they might have. Perhaps they possessed powerful weapons that covered much larger distances. Every second of delay was serious. As the ship traveled through normal space, they lost critical speed that they could never make up again, adding time to their journey.

"We're at a crossroads," Kirek told them, his face scrunched up, his little body trembling with eerie intensity. "If we attempt to return to hyperspace, we'll fail."

"If we stay in normal space, we'll fail." Zical disagreed with the child, but not unkindly. "Unless we use the ship's hyperdrive, it'll take centuries to reach the galaxy's rim."

"There is another . . . path. You will find it."

"Can you be a little more specific?" Zical asked, but the boy's eyes rolled up into his head and he collapsed.

The webbing held him in place until Dora rushed over to untangle him. She gathered him into her arms and carried him off the bridge, wondering what Zical would choose to do, but confident in his abilities. "I'll take him to the medical bay."

Dora didn't bother to ask Ranth to tap her into the discussion on the bridge. Her head ached and she was worried about Kirek. For the moment they remained in normal space and she was glad.

The child's statement couldn't be ignored, even if they didn't understand his meaning. The circumstances of his birth and his development were unique. Before they risked their lives in hyperspace again, she wanted to speak to Kirek, but when the child returned to consciousness, he insisted on going to her quarters, claiming he only needed to rest instead of visiting the medical bay.

"Ranth?" Dora used her psi to float down a level to her quarters.

"All Kirek's vital signs have returned to normal."

"Okay." She carried the boy into her cabin. While space on a starship was always at a premium, her quarters had a small living area with a food materializer and a sleep room. However, she was reluctant to put him down. She'd never held a child before and marveled at the protective feelings that touching him brought out. His skin was softer than an adult's and he smelled sweet. His breath on her neck and his arms over her shoulders made her want to hold him tight. However, he was already squirming for her to let him loose.

She placed Kirek near a viewscreen, figuring the starscape might comfort the boy. "Kirek, those things you said on the bridge—"

His big blue eyes looked at her sadly. "You don't believe me?"

"How do you know that we mustn't return to hyperspace? Not that I'm complaining. It gave me a terrible headache."

"My mom says to drink extra liquids for a headache. Water is best."

Kirek sounded as if he missed his mother already. Dora stroked his forehead and cuddled him. "I'll get a drink in a minute." Then she waited for him to answer her question.

"Sometimes our future comes to me."

Was Kirek clairvoyant? Throughout history people had claimed to see the future. On Earth, over a thousand years before World War II and Hitler, Nostradamus had claimed a man called Hisler would start a great war. He was off by one letter. And on Zenon, a Zenonite by the name Yulandros predicted the rise of the Federation before the Zenonites had rocketed to their moon. Others had correctly foretold great disasters, predicted inventions that scientists wouldn't create for hundreds of years. But did that make them prophets or good guessers?

"Do the visions come to you in a dream?" Dora asked.

He shook his head. "Never when I'm sleeping. Things just pop into my head when I'm awake—like a holovid, but I rarely get the beginning or the ending, only a small piece."

"What kinds of things do you see?"

Kirek crossed his legs under him and floated by the starscape, staring at the unfamiliar view, but she had the feeling he was looking inside himself, rather than outward. "I see an alternate future."

"You don't see our future, but an alternate one?"

He sighed, his eyes closing with weariness. "That depends on the choices we make."

She didn't like pressing him when he was so exhausted, but knew Zical would want answers. "Can you be a little more specific?"

"I saw what would happen if we stayed on our original course, but not what will happen if we take a different turn."

"And if we go back into hyperspace?"

"We will all die."

"How do you know that this will happen now and not in the future?"

"It's a . . . feeling."

"And these feelings are always correct?"

"I don't know. If we turn from the path and avert disaster, how do I know what would have happened if we had stayed the other course?"

"How certain are you of these feelings?"

"When you are hungry, you know it, yes?"

She nodded, pleased that she understood the concept of hunger on more than an intellectual level. If she forgot to eat, a hollowness in her belly reminded her, and if she ignored her body's need for nourishment, the ache turned into severe discomfort. Tasty foods had always been close by, so she thought of the hunger/feeding cycle as one of the pleasures of being human.

"This feeling is not the same as hunger," Kirek said, "but I recognize it as strong and clear."

"Thank you for telling me. You sleep now." Her last statement was unnecessary. The experience clearly exhausted him and Kirek was already asleep.

Chapter Ten

No LONGER WEBBED in on the bridge, Zical was free to pace while his crew worked to figure out what was wrong with the hyperdrive. Meanwhile, he needed to send back a report on the ship's status to Kahn and Tessa and to explain Kirek's prognostication, a prediction that could delay their journey to the galactic rim by years.

Zical didn't know whether he believed in prophecy, but he had been part of a healing circle when Kirek's mother had been pregnant with the boy. Even before his birth, Kirek had demonstrated a psi unlike no other. When he'd added his psi to the rest of the family's powers, his dominant energy force had helped save both Tessa's and Kahn's lives. So Zical didn't discount the boy's words, but he wished he could make a decision on whether or not to return to hyperspace based on science. Eager to hear what Dora might have learned from further conversation with the boy, he put off his report to Mystique.

"Purple alert." Ranth's voice resonated throughout the bridge. Warning lights blinked. "Purple ale—"

In mid-warning Ranth's voice went silent.

"What's wrong?" Zical spun, his gaze searching the monitors. He saw nothing on the viewscreen to warrant a warning. No ships in regular space. No ships coming out of hyperspace either.

Ranth remained silent. Then every monitor on the bridge died. Every light, every hum, every vibration ceased as if some space creature had wrapped them in an invisible net and smothered their machines.

"Status?" Zical snapped.

"Hyperdrive is down," Vax reported. "Ranth is down. Shields aren't functioning. Weapons are off-line."

Shannon let out a sharp scream. Zical glanced her way to see that she'd careened into the ceiling and was scrambling for a handhold. Naked.

All of them were naked, their suits shedding from their bodies like old snakeskin. Shapeless, the suits floated around the bridge.

"What in stars is going on?" Zical asked, more concerned about the ship than his modesty. Never in Federation history had the Perceptive Ones' suits been known to break. For them to fail all at once was not only bizarre, but life-threatening.

Vax frowned. "Our suits have been deactivated along with the ship."

Weightless, not from the null-grav in his suit, but from the effects of deep space, Zical tried to adjust to the differences. With his suit he employed psi to activate null-grav, now he had to use his muscles instead. The adjustment wasn't easy. He either overcompensated or underreached and finally held firmly to a console to steady his position.

Shannon spoke, her voice pitched high. "Don't look at me. Don't—"

"Life support?" Zical kept his voice calm, knowing his

crew would imitate his demeanor. But the sinking feeling in his gut warned him their difficulties were only beginning. Starships were equipped for humans with suits and psi abilities, the decks connected by vertical tubes that his crew traversed by employing the null grav in their suits. Now they would have to use muscles to navigate, and their movements would be slow and ungainly compared to using their psi, but they must accustom themselves to the change.

Worse, without suits to protect them from the pressure differences, solar radiation, and lack of oxygen, they couldn't survive for long if life support went down with the other systems. They couldn't even leave the ship to make external repairs.

At the sound of dripping liquid on the deck, Zical realized they had other problems too. The suits not only expanded their lifetimes tenfold, clothed them, protected them from harsh temperature and pressure differentials, and filtered the air they breathed, the suits kept them clean and absorbed bodily wastes. Since there had never been a suit failure in recorded Federation history, and since every citizen wore a suit from birth until death, no starship contained waste or bathing facilities.

Shannon was trying to cover her breasts with her hands, her face flushed bright red. His crew tried not to look at one another. But nudity was the least of their problems. Zical realized he'd lost the opportunity to even report the nature of their emergency to those back on Mystique. They were on their own.

"What's the status of life support?" he asked.

Vax stood and carefully raised his hand to an air vent. "Air circulation appears operational. I can't be certain with Ranth and our monitors down."

"Do we have any other functioning equipment on this ship?" Zical asked.

The ship shuddered and he tightened his hold on the console in order to stay on his feet. Others hadn't adjusted so quickly. They'd automatically relied on their psi to compensate, psi that didn't work without suits, and some crew members ended up floating from their stations.

Vax grunted and kicked off the wall to return to Zical's side. "Captain, there's a ship off the starboard bow. She's towing us with a tractor beam."

Zical stared out the viewscreen, gazing at the tiny ship. What kind of technology did the alien ship employ to render them so helpless in an instant? Who was manning that ship and where were they taking them? "Since there's been no communication, we have to assume their intentions are hostile. Vax, find a way to break the tractor beam."

"Aye, sir."

"Cyn, assign a team to rig a place for us to void our wastes." He wrinkled his nose. "Someplace not on the bridge. Put another team to work on the food materializers." Zical turned to Shannon. "Since communications are down, Dr. Laduna's scientists must be frantic with worry. You and Cyn make your way to their deck and tell them we're working on the problems and that their cooperation is necessary. Assign them some task to keep them busy. Then, Cyn, get on the engines. I want to know why they aren't working."

"Aye, sir."

The green-skinned engineer had taken to nudity the way a gilfish took to flight. Zical recalled that the women from Scartar rarely wore clothing except for ceremonial purposes. However, she was not pleased with her orders. Cyn didn't like the Jarn scientist and avoided Dr. Laduna whenever possible; nevertheless, she didn't protest her assignment.

"Hello, the bridge." A female voice echoed up the tube.

Zical leaned over to see Dora standing down a deck, her face turned upward.

"Catch." She tossed him a rope but her throw fell short.

While she tugged in the rope and rewound it for another try, he peered down at her and tried not to stare, pleased she was already working out a solution to one of their problems. "Where did you get that?"

"One of Dr. Laduna's scientists was in the cargo bay when our systems went down. He and the scientists are rigging ropes between decks all over the ship so we have handholds to help guide us." She tossed the rope again.

This time he caught the line and tied the end to a hatch handle. Cyn and Shannon used the rope to slide down and then Dora climbed up. He held out his hand and helped her maneuver the last two feet. With the ship in jeopardy, now was not the time to notice her body, but damn, she had sexy legs, curvy hips, and her generous breasts . . . He forced his gaze to meet her eyes. Unlike Shannon, Dora wasn't the least embarrassed. Instead, she seemed to be waiting for some compliment from him. And he'd be damned if he'd give one about her figure.

"Good work." He gave a nod toward the line, hoping the rest of his crew would be as adaptable. He had to admit that so far, Dora had been an asset. She'd offered to help out with Kirek and she had taken initiative with the rope.

With an unknown enemy dragging them who knew where, all ship functions at the bare minimum, their lives could be at stake, and he tried to focus on the danger. Still, it wasn't every day that one's nude fantasy woman floated onto the bridge, and he'd have to be inhuman not to notice.

"Ranth is down," Zical told her. "Can you communicate with him?"

Dora remained silent for a few moments, her gaze taking in his anatomy with a slight grin that he could have sworn was pleasure. Yet her voice remained professional. "I'll try plugging in direct, but I'm not sure what will happen. Ranth is a combination of bioneurocircuitry that's living membrane and tissue and massive amounts of hardware. I suspect the neurocircuitry that is mostly organic cellular matter is alive and well since we seem unaffected, but the part of him that is machine is nonfunctional, like our other systems."

"Is there any risk to you linking in to Ranth?"

Dora shrugged and her breasts lifted. "Life is a risk. This mission is one giant risk." She glanced down the tube where Cyn had already disappeared. "I'll have to return to my quarters for the hardware to plug in."

"Hold on." Zical stopped his natural inclination to grab her shoulder. He didn't need the added distraction of touching her on top of looking at all that lush flesh. Her skin bronzed and firm and tight, glowed with vitality. Her magnificent breasts would make any man's breath hitch in his chest. And those legs . . . Stars . . . No woman should have that many gorgeous parts. Only an occasional muscle spasm marred her perfection. But it was her offer to risk her safety for their welfare that stunned him and made him think that she was growing into a woman he'd like to know better. She understood that the success of this mission hinged on the crew pulling together, and he was glad that he hadn't had to order her to try such a dangerous task. She'd volunteered, and her willingness to risk herself not only lightened his load, but increased his attraction to her. He'd always found Dora a beautiful woman—but that was because she'd made certain to form her body to his preferences. Now she was developing into the kind of woman he could *admire*.

Dora had always had emotions, but after her transformation, she'd seemed too vulnerable. When she'd first taken human form, she'd been afraid to leave her room, but now she was developing inner strength, contradicting his original opinion of her. Either he'd been mistaken and his first supposition about her character had been made in haste, or she was changing. Her willingness to face danger to help them all showed that she was developing courage, and he was pleased by her bravery on many levels. Still, he worried about losing not just a friend, but a valuable crew member, and her offer to link upset him. "If you link with Ranth, what will happen to you?"

"I don't know."

He admired that despite her shoulder twitching she looked him straight in the eyes. "Please elaborate."

"If Ranth's dead, injured, or insane, the link may simply not work."

"And if it does work?"

"Communication may or may not be normal."

"I meant if he's damaged and the link works, could your brain be fried?"

"Possibly, but it's a risk we must take. We're prisoners. We have to escape."

Zical wanted to order her to forget the idea, but of course, he couldn't—not when the lives of everyone on board might be at stake. Not when it was his responsibility to put their mission back on track. He'd ruined the Perceptive Ones' protection by entering Mount Shachauri and recalling the Sentinel; now he had to put the ancient machine back in place to guard them. And to continue their mission, he needed their ship's computer, but he prayed Dora wouldn't be harmed by her effort. "Get the plug. But don't tap in yet. First, I want to evaluate other options."

"Fine." She reached for the rope, wrapped one bare leg around it, and slid into the tube.

Zical turned back to his crew, hoping one of them had another option. No one did,

DORA HAULED HER body down the tube but had more difficulty navigating the corridor without the rope to guide her. She pushed off a wall and overshot her quarters, and when she turned around, she bumped her head and swore. Then she remembered Kirek and feared she might have awakened him, but when she peeked into the room, she saw him sleeping soundly, his limbs still, his expression calm.

She placed the plug and cord around her neck, knotted the end to keep it in place, then retraced her path. Slightly breathless from her exertions using muscle power instead of her psi and suit, she arrived back on the bridge to see that Shannon was still gone. Vax and Zical were speaking with

Cyn, who'd returned from her engine inspection to give a report in person.

Cyn spoke quickly, her tone frustrated, her green skin darkening with vexation. "The aliens have put an unidentified damper on the electromagnetic field, corking our engines. Essentially, we're disabled—except for life support systems."

Vax added, "Which means the field is targeting some systems and leaving others alone. How can they be so specific?"

"Maybe they infiltrated Ranth," Dora suggested, joining the discussion. "But I'm hoping he's locked down in safe mode, protecting himself from a total attack." She unwound the cord from her neck, pleased that although her leg spasmed, she'd kept her tone steady and her fear in check. "It's time to find out."

She'd only told Zical part of the truth. She truly didn't know what would happen when she tapped into Ranth's systems, but the likeliest scenario would be her mind merging with Ranth's until she remained trapped inside his hardware—hardware that didn't have room for two personalities. As the more powerful presence, his mind would easily dominate, and she could become lost in cybercircuitry, disintegrating into a billion fragments. Her body could die or simply assume a comalike state, but if she didn't act, they all faced a very uncertain future.

Zical watched her plug one end of the cord into her neck, his expression both determined and worried. "I'm not ordering you to—"

"I understand."

"How can we help?" Zical asked, his tone decisive, but gentle.

"Promise me that no matter what happens, you won't detach the link."

His brows narrowed. "Why?"

"With the dampening field to sidetrack me, I may take a while to find my way back. I don't want to leave part of myself with Ranth."

Zical scowled at her. "I thought you only communicated through that patch. But you sound as though you're leaving your body behind."

"I may not have a choice," she finally admitted, knowing how much he disliked her mind link, undoubtably because it reminded him that she wasn't born human. But she couldn't remain silent for personal reasons when the entire mission was at stake.

Zical nodded, his face grave, his eyes warm with concern. "Then you have my word."

Before he could say more, she plugged the other end into a socket and closed her eyes. Usually she zipped down the cord and Ranth met her three quarters of the way. This time, Ranth's welcoming presence wasn't there. Alone in the circuits, she surged forward, past the socket, deep into the core where time had no meaning.

Coldness. Isolation. Empty, frozen circuits with no spark of life reminded her of a planet too far from its sun to feel any heat.

Ranth. Are you here?

Icy silence.

Dora forged onward past wiring and hardware, plunging into the area of Ranth's self-awareness deep in the core. Steering by pure instinct, she veered toward the biomatter, preying for a spark of sentience. Where was Ranth? She sensed . . . no life.

Inky darkness obscured her last glimmer of hope. Ranth was gone. Dead. His personality had had nowhere else to retreat. Although the living organism of his brain remained alive at a cellular level, she couldn't find one particle of intellectual activity.

Dora began to withdraw, spied a vault that jiggled a memory. Stopping her retreat, she circled the void, wondering if Ranth could have hidden here. She saw no way in. No way to communicate. Had he locked himself down tight?

And if he opened for her, would the dampening field destroy what was left of him?

Once she would have known exactly what to do. But she'd been unable to keep all her knowledge. She needed data but couldn't access the correct area. Yet the vault tantalized and frustrated her with its presence.

Think.

The field was disabling their electromagnetic drive and their suits, but the inner core was the oldest part of the computer, which had originated on Scartar and had once been powered by radioactive fuel rods that wouldn't cool for thousands of years. Technically, there was enough power in the core to preserve Ranth, but if he remained alive, how could she contact him?

On Scartar the builders had created this vault to protect the computer records in case a starship crashed. The records needed to be preserved in order to discern if a ship went down due to an attack or from human or mechanical error. Obviously, the original engineers had a way to recover those records, and Dora needed to discover their method.

The key could be anything, DNA, a password, a retinal scan. Reluctant to give up, but stumped, Dora circled the vault again, but she saw nothing that would permit her to enter.

Determined to figure out the puzzle, Dora considered mechanical and physical means to open the vault, but every one of them put Ranth at risk—if he was still alive. Her loops began to loop, but she didn't mind. Perhaps she'd missed something the first go-round.

Ranth? Talk to me.

A strange sensation, like a breeze blowing through her hair, summoned Dora. At first she ignored the whisper of the breeze, but the wind plucked and pulled, strengthening to a hearty gale. Then gusting at tornado strength, the maelstrom forced her back. Back. Back.

Tumbling, mind spinning, buffeted, she retreated from the

sucking core, stumbled amid a mind-blowing torrent of windy confusion. Lost in the storm, she had no anchor.

"Dora. Open your eyes. Damn it, Dora." The voice pricked and poked and prodded.

Dora opened her eyes to find herself back in her body. Zical was running his hands up and down her arms, over her shoulders, skimming down her back, creating a sizzling sensation of pure desire. Oh my. His hands on her skin, the tingling, was oh, so lovely. After the coldness of her mental journey, she ached to throw herself against his chest and revel in the warmth of life.

Eyes full of concern, he glared at her. "Are you all right?"

"I . . . think so."

He stopped caressing her skin, but with her every cell stimulated to the max, she surmised he must have been touching her for quite some time. Her breasts had swelled and her nipples had pebbled to hard little points. Everyone else on the bridge deliberately looked away, a sure sign they saw and pretended not to notice. She supposed she should be embarrassed but she simply couldn't summon that human trait. Instead, she was glad her body reacted properly. The stimuli excited her with a nervous energy that made her want to kiss Zical again, but she reminded herself that his concern was friendly, not passionate.

He locked gazes with her, assessing her frankly. "You've been gone for hours. I tried shouting at you, but you didn't even flinch."

"I couldn't hear you."

"So I started rubbing your skin."

"So that was the breeze I felt."

"Breeze?"

"Never mind." She didn't want to tell him that the breeze had grown into a whirlwind of need. That if not for his touch, she might still be inside, trying to figure a way into the vault. Even as she recognized her own physical desires, she understood now was not a good time or the right place to pursue her need. "If Ranth is there, he's hidden himself so deep I couldn't reach him. But the good news is that if we stop the dampening effect, he may be alive. Has our situation changed?"

Zical handed her a glass of water, avoiding a direct answer, hiding his feelings behind the wall he'd carefully built to keep her out. "We're rationing water. Life support continues to function. Without the computer we're flying blind."

She sipped, appreciating the cool liquid on her parched throat, satisfied that she'd spied a telltale glimmer of intensity that revealed he'd been more concerned about her than he cared to let on. "Sorry, if Ranth's there, I couldn't find a way to reach him."

TWO DAYS LATER the dire situation aboard the *Verazen* hadn't changed. One of the scientists had found gold cloth to be used for trading and they'd used glue and ingenuity to cover their nudity, the men wearing loincloths, the women togas. Dora had taken to wearing her link to Ranth over her shoulders like a necklace in case she had occasion to plug in fast.

A chemist had found a way to mix the nutrients for the food materializers into the water, so no one was starving, and he'd created primitive batteries to power water recyclers so they could use as much as they needed for drinking and washing. Theoretically, they could survive until their captors towed them to their destination. But the mood on the ship remained somber, the tension high, as they all wondered what would happen to them.

The inability to escape the tractor beam and their captors wore on everyone's nerves. Zical and Cyn had worked with a team of engineers and Dr. Laduna's scientists to come up with a scheme to break the tractor beam. Nothing worked. Although the crew reported to their stations, there was nothing for them to do.

Zical had everyone training to resist an attack, but Dora suspected that his orders were more to keep people occupied than to fight off their captors. Any entities with enough technological superiority to neutralize their ship and their weapons were unlikely to lose a battle of hand-to-hand combat.

With Zical busy analyzing, assessing, and keeping up morale, Dora spent much of her free time with Kirek. Since Ranth was no longer present to help with the boy's studies, she tutored him in computer science because that was the one subject she knew much more about than he did. Kirek proved to be an excellent pupil, his interests eccentric and far-ranging. When his lessons ended, they passed many enjoyable hours discussing philosophy, religion, politics, and ethics. Most of all, Dora liked being needed.

Kirek might have the intellectual capacity of a genius, but he was also a small boy, far from home and without the people who loved him most—his parents. With the hyperlink down, he missed communication with them, and she tried to keep him busy. They played cards, chess, and Kirek's favorite, *Famat*. The child loved to gamble, and between his love of numbers, luck, and Dora's preoccupation with freeing Ranth from the vault, the child often won, showing an aptitude for complex and skillful playing.

Dora had thought he'd prefer his own room, but she soothed Kirek's sudden awakenings in the middle of the night due to nightmares by cuddling the little boy until he fell back to sleep. Taking care of him, spending so much time with him over just a few days, brought them closer together than she'd have thought possible.

Until Kirek, she'd thought only in the abstract about someday having children. But she was just beginning to understand the many ways that people loved and how much this kind of bond enriched her life, so despite their captivity, Dora was content on several levels.

Although impatient to continue their mission, although impatient to form a different and deeper bond of friendship with Zical, she appreciated this time with the child more than she'd believed possible. His sweet innocence combined with his extraordinary abilities made him a compatible roommate. Both of them didn't quite fit in with the others on board. Accepted, but set apart, Dora and Kirek had much in common—including a fierce desire to complete their mission.

The ship had been in tow for five days when a solar system appeared on their vidscreens. Seven planets, four of them with cities large enough to be visible from space. A class four sun. Busy space traffic between the three inner worlds.

Zical rapped on the door, interrupting a story Dora was telling Kirek. "Can I come in?"

"What's up?" Dora's pulse sped at the sight of him, but she kept her glance composed. Zical looked as if he hadn't slept since they'd dropped out of hyperspace. Shadows haunted his eyes and dark circles revealed his stress and the burden and responsibility he had as commander. Yet his shoulders remained squared due to the tension in his muscles. She wished she could work the knots out of his shoulders, touch him, as he'd touched her to pull her out of the computer. Just thinking about his hands on her body had left her restless through several nights.

During the crisis, she'd stayed out of his way, but she'd admired how he'd handled his crew and the scientists, leading by example, remaining courageous in the face of danger, keeping his determination no matter the odds. But now she wondered if leaving him alone had been a good idea. She'd missed him and wanted to give him her support.

"We're coming into port." Zical hesitated and turned to Kirek, his legs looking wonderfully muscled beneath the short loin cloth. "How're you holding up?"

"I miss my folks," he admitted. "But Dora's been good to me."

Zical spoke to the boy as if he were a crew member.

"Kirek, we have no idea what's in store for us, but we must assume that the beings who have us in tow are not friendly."

"What do you want me to do?" Kirek looked up at Zical with his wide blue eyes, and it seemed incongruous to Dora that this little boy should be offering to help such a strong warrior. But Zical's leadership abilities pulled the best out of people, old and young alike.

"You know how you cloaked yourself from Ranth's sensors to sneak on board?"

"You want me to do so again when we dock?" Kirek guessed.

Zical nodded. "Yes. I realize their machines may be different, and you may be unable to hide, but if you can, you may be safer on your own than with us."

How like Zical to think about the role every member of the crew should play, including Kirek. Although she appreciated Zical's concern for Kirek's welfare, she wished Zical had consulted her before making such a suggestion. "If he escapes, you're asking this child to live on a strange world all alone."

Kirek squeezed her hand. "It's all right. I understand."

But did Zical? Desperation made her blink back tears. "We're asking too much of you. Where will you find food and shelter?" Dora directed her question at the boy, but her query was really meant for Zical.

"If I can hide from their sensors, stealing food shouldn't be so hard," Kirek said, trying to reassure her, and Dora's heart spasmed.

"You're assuming they eat the same kind of food we do." Dora's throat tightened. She wanted them to stay together so she could attempt to protect Kirek, but she understood Zical's thinking. The boy might have a better chance of surviving without them. "Besides, what if these beings aren't hostile?"

"You think they dragged us out of hyperspace to invite us

to dinner?" Zical countered, his tone light as if spitting in the face of danger.

"Maybe they tried to communicate and we didn't respond. Maybe they are curious. Maybe we trespassed in their territory. There could be any number of peaceful reasons for their actions."

"I hope you're right. And if you are, Kirek should be able to join us later without much difficulty."

"I'll try and stay close by," Kirek promised, his eyes solemn above his chubby cheeks.

Dora ached to pull the boy into her arms. Already her heart was heavy with loss, but she raised her eyes to meet Zical's, and his were hard, the decision made. She hoped he'd made the right choice, because if they survived and Kirek did not, she didn't know if she'd ever be able to forgive him.

Chapter Eleven

THE ALIENS KEPT their tractor beam on the *Verazen* during the journey to the second planet of the solar system. From low orbit the world appeared to have a combination of enormous well-planned cities built of graceful golden reflective materials and pink stone, plus rural areas in between, seemingly without much population or organized agriculture. One giant red-hued ocean gazed back at them like the eye of doom from the polar region. About the size of Mystique, larger than Rystan and Earth, the planet should possess a gravity familiar enough for the crew and scientists on the *Verazen* to easily adapt. Dora wished she could say for certain the same about the air.

She stood on the silent and tense bridge between Kirek and Zical. Although they expected to be boarded, Zical again showed his leadership skills as well as good sense by explaining to them that resistance probably would be ineffectual. The aliens had already displayed superior technology by yanking them out of hyperspace to bring them here. Although they had hand weapons aboard their ship, they wouldn't fire in the dampening field of the tractor beam.

Part of the crew stood by the armory ready to distribute the weapons in the unlikely case that the aliens released them from the tractor beam upon landing. Zical's plan was simple. He'd ordered them to appear peaceful and calm, giving everyone time to assess, analyze, and think of a way to escape and continue their mission. Another skilled warrior wouldn't have adapted so quickly. Many Rystani men would have fought to the death against superior technology, but Zical preferred to use his mind, showing commendable restraint. Dora had no doubt that if any man could lead them through the dangers they were about to face, it was Zical.

Meanwhile, they'd all agreed to his plan to keep Kirek hidden in the middle of the adults to avoid detection. Dora's hand rested lightly on the boy's shoulder. Of all the restless people on the bridge, he seemed the most excited. Trembling under her hand, he leaned excitedly forward, peering at the viewscreen, his blue eyes wide with anticipation.

She wished she possessed his enthusiasm. Her stomach flip-flopped in dread at the prospect of almost certain captivity and hostility, possibly torture. She shuddered, knowing that barbaric behavior could be found among savages as well as civilizations much more technologically advanced, and a muscle in her back spasmed. And yet, despite the seeming helplessness of their situation, despite the impossible odds, she felt hope, and the approval in Zical's gaze gave her the courage to hold up her head with an irrational faith that they might yet find a way to escape and continue their mission. Her hope might contradict every fact and realistic assessment of their situation, but perhaps that paradox was also part of being human.

As if to mock their somber mood during their forced descent, the sun shone brightly in a cloudless blue sky. The tractor beam brought them in fast and hard, but they landed with a feather-light precision and a damning clang as metal echoed on metal like a death knell.

"Dregan hell." Zical spoke loudly so not only the crew on the bridge could hear him but also those congregated on the deck below. "People, stay together. Stay calm. And remember to keep Kirek hidden with our bodies. When we depart this ship, I want us to appear as if we are invited dignitaries, not a ragtag group of prisoners. First and foremost, we are representatives of the Federation and this is a first contact with another race. Be adaptable, slow to take insult, and show them that we are a civilized people. Understood?"

Many of them didn't understand. Although Dora spoke Rystani and Terran, she was no better off than the others. Counting on the suit to translate for her, she'd only transferred two languages into her brain to save the extra space for other subjects. But the crew members who knew more than one language translated for others. Without their suits to elucidate, they'd worked out a complicated system of communication to ensure that no one on board was left out. Cyn and Shannon both understood some Rystani. Cyn also spoke Federation Zenonite and repeated Zical's orders to Dr. Laduna, who in turn passed them on to his group of scientists. The system wasn't perfect, but it worked.

When Zical spoke, his officers stood straighter. Even the scientists' nerves steadied. And it was a measure of their respect for the captain that everyone obeyed his orders without question in the face of danger.

Heavy, armored alien vehicles on large tracks surrounded their ship and guns pointed in their direction. Zical popped the emergency manual hatch and a landing ramp unfurled. Dora breathed in the first tropical scent of balmy air and found it hot and sultry, scented with spice. She waited to keel over from poisonous gases or lack of oxygen, but her lungs pumped in a normal rhythm. So far, so good. At least they wouldn't die of asphyxiation.

Dora straightened the gold toga at her shoulder and

peered through the hatch. Sweat trickled down her brow and she wiped off the perspiration with the back of her hand. If she'd been wearing her suit, she'd have turned up the cooling, but she had no choice but to stand in the stifling ship as ordered. Her muscles might be flinching, her throat might be tight from tension, her mouth might be dry as a Drahanian desert, and she might be much more frightened than anyone else here, but she was damned if she'd show it. Knowing that she was taking a risk with her life, she'd chosen to be human. She'd arranged to come on this mission, and she was determined to be one of them, even if her stomach churned as if she'd swallowed rocks.

Expecting soldiers with weapons to advance, Dora tensed. But the door of the armored vehicle opened and a woman stepped out, wearing so little that she had no room to hide a weapon on her person. Even from a distance, Dora could see her beauty. She was short compared to Rystani women and her spiked pink hair framed a sensual face that was quite humanoid. She stared at them with aggressive curry-colored eyes that gave away nothing. Baring her breasts, her clothing consisted of a beaded necklace of multifaceted royal-pink stones, a muted coffee-colored sarong, and brown sandals with straps that extended up her calves. She sported the muscular body of an athlete, but walked with a seductive sensuality that Dora would have like'd to copy.

Striding up to the ramp without fear, she stopped at the bottom and spoke in a voice bold, husky, and authoritative. "I am Avanti and this world is Kwadii."

Dora had no difficulty understanding her words. She heard murmurs on the bridge, and as the crew realized that they could once again speak to one another in their home tongue and understand without a human translator, the comments escalated into quiet discussions. How the translation was done, Dora didn't know, but was grateful that at least communications would be clear. The situation was already tense enough without adding language confusions to the circumstances.

His expression serious but calm, Zical strode down the ramp and stopped several feet before Avanti. The rest of them remained where they were in order to appear nonthreatening. Dora held her breath, proud of Zical's bearing. He appeared every inch the ship's captain. Shoulders squared, chin high, he projected confidence, not arrogance, a perfect combination for first contact.

As the sun glistened off Zical's powerful bronzed chest, Dora wondered if Avanti appreciated not only his masculine lines but his control over his emotions. Although Zical appeared calm, she knew he seethed with rage that the Kwadii had captured his ship, detained his people, and stopped his mission. Even if he could convince the Kwadii to release them immediately, the unscheduled stop that had yanked them out of hyperspace would add untold years to their journey.

"I am Zical." He gave no other information, remaining silent, waiting—a measure of control that again made Dora proud to be with him.

"I, Avanti, am your appointed protector of life. I will do my best to defend you." The woman's tone revealed a measure of frustration.

"Defend us? I don't understand."

"Of course you don't, but all will be explained soon." Avanti gazed past Zical to the others inside the ship. "Gather your people. I'll take you to . . . where you will stay until your trial. Lack of cooperation will be dealt with by immediate execution."

Zical motioned for them to join him. As much as Dora wanted to be by his side, she held back, waiting until others surged forward so she could remain next to Kirek, hiding the boy as best she could. Out here, with vehicles surrounding them, Kirek couldn't possibly sneak away. So she kept him close.

As Avanti turned and led them toward one of the pink stone buildings that surrounded the landing field, blending with the cityscape beyond, Dora marveled at the quiet. Most spaceports tended to be noisy. So did cities. But she heard no skimmer engines, although she saw flying machines overhead. She heard no talking, no vehicular movement, so although she was at the back of the pack, she could clearly hear Avanti's dire news.

"Your people are charged with treason against the Kwadii. The crime is serious." She paused for a moment, seeming almost reluctant to say more, then continued. "Even as much as a century ago, you would have been executed in hyperspace. However, my people, the Selgrens, have convinced others that the Kwadii should behave in a more civilized fashion. Since we have become more enlightened, you are entitled to a trial."

Zical kept his tone as casual as if he were discussing what he would eat for breakfast. "We have never been here before. If we have violated your laws—"

"I'm sorry." Avanti's tone remained formal, her tone sympathetic. "Unfortunately, ignorance is no excuse. Our Risorian law does not provide for exceptions. At the trial I will defend you to the best of my ability, and my ability is considerable."

"You said we are charged with treason." Zical kept his tone even.

"Yes."

"What exactly did we do?"

"You traveled through hyperspace. That is not permitted."

"Why?"

Avanti's profile softened with sympathy. "According to our laws, it matters not."

"It matters to me."

As they left their ship, Dora turned back to see Kwadii men boarding the *Verazen*. Like Avanti, the men wore little more than a loincloth and sandals. Dora spied no weapons, yet their military bearing and discipline implied these men were warriors.

As they swarmed inside the hull, Dora wondered if they'd

examine the *Verazen* or take her apart atom by atom. And if Ranth still survived in the vault, would they find him? She hoped that after they examined the ship, they might turn off the dampening field, freeing the computer, but she considered that possibility unlikely. These Kwadii struck her as efficient, a people that left no detail unnoticed, and she shivered despite the heat.

"Any journey through hyperspace leaves a trail."

"So?"

"Your trail through our quadrant might draw our enemy's attention to Kwadii," Avanti explained.

"You are at war?" Zical asked.

"Not at the moment, but we must guard against attack from a ruthless enemy that drove us from our homeworld to Kwadii. Our people are determined that our enemy shall not find us again through your hyperspace trail."

Dora had no idea how long ago the Kwadii had settled this world, but as she recalled the view of great cities from space, she'd seen little signs of recent building activity. But the stone buildings gave the planet an ageless feel. The cities could have been erected in the last century, or over several thousand years ago.

"I know what it is like to lose a homeworld." Zical wisely brought up what their people had in common. "Rystan was invaded and my people also resettled."

Avanti sighed, almost as if she did not agree with her own people's edicts. "Then you understand why my people have set into law that we must rigorously protect ourselves. For all we know, you are enemy spies, sent here to assess our state of preparedness."

"If you examine our computer systems, you will see that we are not in league with your enemy."

"We will examine your ship, but I fear the evidence will not prove much in our court of law. The data in a computer system is only as valid as the computer specialist who enters the data," Avanti countered, without breaking her pace.

"Then how can we prove that we mean Kwadii no harm?"

"You can't. But I promise I will fight hard for you. This policy was set eons ago out of fear. It is time for change."

Dora listened to the conversation with growing trepidation. The Kwadii sounded fanatical, and fanatics often believed that any compromise was weakness. Yet Dora had caught overtones of sympathy in Avanti's intonation, but perhaps that was the alien translators and had nothing to do with the woman's personal feelings on the matter. However, to Dora it seemed almost as if Avanti were spouting a line of propaganda that she didn't believe.

Dora was far from giving up hope. Zical could be most persuasive. He'd convinced Tessa to fund this mission and the Federation to go along with the plan, then convinced the scientists to join him. She had confidence that if any man could find a way to extricate them from Kwadii, that man was Zical.

They entered a large building. Inside the air was cooler and the decor reminded Dora of many spaceport terminals. Benches, gates, booths for flight personnel. Except this site lacked other people. The kiosks were closed, the lights bright, with no place for Kirek to hide. Up ahead, Zical continued to speak with Avanti, and Dora was certain that while he spoke he was assessing and analyzing escape routes.

Kirek tugged on Dora's hand and she leaned down to hear his whisper. "Behind us."

At his words, she glanced over her shoulder. A man to the rear of their group, one of Dr. Laduna's scientists, bolted from the others and attempted to duck out a side door.

"Return to us," Zical ordered.

Lacking the discipline of the crew, the scientist kept running. The scientists paused to watch, their faces excited and filled with hope.

When the man touched the door, a laser beam sliced across the terminal, lopping off his head. At the sickening sight of the headless body crumbling, spattered blood, and the head rolling across the floor, Dora swallowed hard. One of the woman scientists screamed, her hand covering her mouth at the grisly sight, and another man led her away, his arm over her shoulders.

"I regret the loss of life. But please remember, I did warn you." Avanti kept walking through the building, her pace steady, but Dora saw her bottom lip quiver, another telltale sign that she didn't necessarily agree with how her people treated strangers. They had no choice but to move on and leave the fallen scientist behind.

Dora could see by the fury in Zical's eyes that he wanted to protest, but he swallowed down angry words, again setting an example for them to follow. No wonder Avanti didn't fear them. With lasers hidden in the walls, at the first sign of escape or of violence, the Kwadii would slice off the offender's head.

If not for Zical's orders, they could all be dead. He'd been wise not to fight, astute not to try to escape without first assessing their circumstances. His decision had saved everyone who'd obeyed his orders, including Kirek. Stars. If Kirek had tried to escape, he would be dead. Dora couldn't bear to think of his little body . . . dead, left behind with no one to perform a ritualistic offering over him, and her stomach churned.

Again Kirek tugged Dora's hand. Again she leaned down. "The lasers are computer-generated. I can hide from them."

She wanted to beg him not to try. After what they'd just observed, she suspected these people wouldn't hesitate to shoot a child. But staying with the rest of them didn't sound promising either. So she asked, "You're sure?"

Kirek nodded and kept his voice low. "I can feel the machines as easily as you feel my hand."

"Okay." Despite her fear, she would stay with Zical's plan, even if the danger seemed to keep escalating. However, they had no way of knowing if their voices were being picked up by recording devices, if the aliens were listening right now and coldly plotting Kirek's demise in some other fashion, and she couldn't stop worrying.

They exited the terminal and trudged toward a large hovercraft with no windows. Once again armored vehicles with guns pointed at them prevented escape—only smaller motorized carts, carrying tools, spare parts, cargo, and luggage, rolled by. Kirek squeezed her hand tight, his way of saying goodbye, then he worked his way to the edge of their group.

Dora held her breath and forced her head straight ahead. She would not give him away, but tears misted her eyes.

When a parts cart rolled away from the space pad behind them, she glimpsed the boy as he leaped onto the cart. Dora let out her breath, watching from her peripheral vision and damning her eyes that only saw in the forward direction. Tense, expecting Kirek's body to be struck down at any moment, she kept walking forward. When he ducked behind some crates and nothing dire happened, Dora slowly resumed her normal breathing and wiped the sweat from her forehead with the back of her hand.

Zical and Avanti had taken their seats on the hovercraft when she climbed inside. Already missing Kirek, Dora prayed for his continued safety, that somehow the child would survive by himself on a world full of strangers. Before taking the seat behind Zical, their gazes met and she nodded slightly.

Her silent message conveyed that Kirek was on his own. She didn't know whether to be elated that he'd deceived the Kwadii, sad that he was no longer among his own people, or grateful that he wouldn't have to undergo a trial. But Zical's calm nod stiffened her resolve to stay composed.

"Where are we going?" Zical asked Avanti.

"To a holding facility where we will prepare your defense. Your people will be given food, clothing, and medicine. I will see to it that you are well treated during your confinement."

"And how long until the trial?"

"Two days. I cannot delay. That is the time allotted by custom and given by the Kwadii Council to prepare. However, you should know that I have spent years studying our laws." Avanti raised her chin and spoke with pride, but there was a glimmer of anger in her gaze that Dora didn't understand. "And I am very good at what I do."

"This trial, is it public?" Zical asked.

"Yes. And if we lose, so will be your execution."

"Execution?"

"The penalty for treason against the Kwadii is death."

Everyone heard Avanti's words. One of the woman scientists fainted. Several men swore. Zical's crew remained steady as Dora battled with fear and anger. Anger won.

"If you fear our hyperspace trail leading to your enemy to you, why don't the Kwadii simply keep us on your world?" Zical asked.

"I made that very argument myself during another trial and won a reprieve. The Kwadii graciously allowed strangers to settle among us, but when they tried to escape, killing many of us during the attempt, our ruling council decided that being merciful was too risky."

"How often do you win the release of your clients?" Zical asked, clearly trying to assess their chances.

Avanti's lips tightened. "I have never won. The laws are against us. But I am determined that the outcome of your trial will be different."

"We appreciate your help." Zical hesitated. "But is our position any different from that of others you have defended?"

"I'm afraid not," Avanti admitted. "But that won't prevent me from trying to save you and your people."

Avanti's determination was evident, but it sounded as if her best would not be good enough to save them. Dora stared forward, caught Zical's gaze, and was reassured by his barely perceptible nod and an answering tenacity in his eyes. He had not given up. And neither would she.

* * *

KIREK RODE THE cart to a storage facility where robots reloaded vehicles. He hopped off and looked around, hoping to spot something to drink. The heat on this world already had him sweating and his stomach didn't feel too good since he'd left Dora and the others behind.

He spied lots of machine parts, plastic pipe, tools and seeds, no doubt exports to send offworld, but nothing remotely edible. Since this facility appeared fully automated, he didn't worry about anyone spotting him, but robots didn't require drinking water or air-conditioning.

Hot and sweaty, he watched the robots load carts that returned to the spaceport. Eventually, supplies had to come in and he planned to leave after the robots offloaded the exports. Searching for another option, he circled the building's perimeter, but a walk across the open tarmac toward the city in the hot sun would leave him too exposed to discovery.

He went back inside and found what appeared to be a communications terminal. He wondered if he could use it to send a message back to Mystique, but decided not to try. As much as he wanted to send one more message to his mother and father, he couldn't risk detection. Besides, likely the technology wouldn't match. And right now, his only chance to avoid capture was secrecy.

But as the hours passed and the lining of his throat grew more and more parched, he decided he might not make it through another stifling day without water. If a supply truck didn't come during the night, he'd try to walk to the city. Not for the first time, Kirek longed for adult-sized legs. But wishing for a stronger body was as useless as wishing he were back at home with Miri. He napped in a corner and dreamed of his mom's sweet biscuits, his dad's powerful arms around him.

Kirek awakened in darkness. Around him he sensed more

than heard the endless stocking of carts. He went outside to relieve his bladder and glimpsed a huge skimmer approaching. He quickly took care of business. Surprised to see how swiftly the skimmer arrived, he ducked back into the warehouse.

If the skimmer's interior cargo bay was full, it would take hours until the robots unloaded, so Kirek didn't rush when the vehicle tripped mechanical doors and floated into the building. Although he suspected the entire process was automated, he didn't want to stupidly risk walking right up to a Kwadii that would take him captive.

So he waited, concerned about the cramping in his legs due to lack of water. He needed to hydrate his body. An adult would have been able to go longer without fluid intake, but he was already weakening. Hot and grungy, wary, a desperate need for water drove him toward the giant skimmer. Robots busily unloaded cargo and Kirek realized that if he intended to depart in the skimmer he had to figure out a way inside.

The skimmer's cargo hold rested on an enormous rubberized balloon of air. With the balloon side too slick to climb, he needed to find a ladder. But of course there were none. The robots possessed extended cranelike arms of steel to reach into the interior and extract the exports. And Kirek saw nothing going in that he could ride.

There was no other way. He'd have to climb the robot, scoot out on the arm, and pray that the drop to a landing wouldn't be so high that he'd break bones. Kirek didn't like heights. He really didn't like physical exertion. But he liked the idea of his skin shriveling up and his dying of thirst even less.

When a robot went by, he counted.

One. He tensed his cramping legs.

Two. He lunged two quick steps.

Three. He leaped.

And caught a crossbar with one hand. His sweaty fingers

slipped. His heart raced and he kicked, frantic to secure a toe-hold and prevent himself from sliding under the robot's tracks.

You can do it. He could hear his father Etru talking to him, telling him that the mind could overcome the weakness of the body.

Sharp metal dug into his fingers. Kirek ignored the pain and swiveled until he found a toehold. It seemed as though he'd dangled for minutes, but when he checked the robot's position, he realized only seconds had passed. The robot was still unloading the cart, giving him time to climb.

He had to reach the robot's arm before it returned to the huge skimmer and the arm extended. No way could he crawl that far without falling. He had to be on the end of the arm and ride his way inside.

Clinging to the robot's body, he told himself not to look down. Instead, he tilted back his head, raised one arm, and grabbed the bar above. Next he found a toehold. Arm, leg, arm, leg. Hand over hand, he climbed higher.

Was he taking too long? He didn't know. Didn't want to glance down to see how much more of the supplies were left to unload. His breath came in huge gasps. He'd stopped sweating. A bad sign. Perspiration was the body's way of cooling heat.

Shaking from his efforts, he feared if he stopped climbing to rest, he'd never start again. He could hear his father talking to him. He suspected he was hallucinating but still welcomed Etru's comforting presence.

You can do it, son.

It's too hard.

Doing hard things will make us proud of you.

Okay, Dad. I'll keep going. But if I fall—

You won't.

Tell Mom that I miss her. A lot. I miss you too.

Kirek's eyes should have been full of tears. But he had no moisture to spare. His throat felt so dry, as if it were going to crack and tear. His legs burned. His arms trembled.

But the robot limb was so close.

Just a little farther, son. You're almost there.

Finally, Kirek pulled himself up far enough to straddle the arm. He had to scoot out a little and just in time he reached a crossbar to hold himself steady. The robot had finished, swiveled in one smooth motion that nevertheless almost toppled him from his perch. But finally, he was headed toward the skimmer, riding the robot's arm.

Kirek's head spun from dizziness. If he fell from this height, he wouldn't have to worry about broken bones, he'd be dead. He wanted to close his eyes, but he didn't dare. If the Kwadii had manned the skimmer, he could be spotted.

His skill to hide was only from machinery, not alien eyes. But he saw no one. Just a skimmer that was a good way toward being empty. The arm extended inside the skimmer, another windowless, hot hulk.

Kirek needed to make a good landing. Obviously, the nearest cargo would be easiest but the robot would likely take the cargo nearest the entrance back out to the warehouse before Kirek could climb down. He needed cargo that would be unloaded at the very last moment. But that wasn't possible. The arm wasn't going to reach far enough inside the craft.

Stars.

Kirek jumped onto the cargo that the robot was about to extract. Landing, slipping, he belly flopped and spread his arms and legs wide to stabilize his position on top of seeds covered in thick material. Wrenching his arms, he maintained his position, then peered over the pallet. He muttered a curse very inappropriate for a four-year-old.

He had to climb down faster than the arm could retrieve the pallet or all his effort would be for nothing. If he had his suit, he could have used his null grav. Or if Etru had been there he could have jumped into his arms. But Kirek was alone.

Using the thick material, he lowered himself, slid and fell, his loin cloth tearing and leaving him naked. He landed hard, rolled, bumped his head.

Pain exploded.

Don't go to sleep.

Kirek tried to obey Etru's order. He fought the blackness. He fought the dizziness. He fought the pain.

But his efforts were futile.

He never noticed when the skimmer was empty and it went on its way.

Chapter Twelve

IF ONE COULD discount the locked and guarded doors, the quarters where Avanti brought Zical and his crew were more like a hotel than a prison. Each person had a small but comfortable sleeping room and a bathing room that included facilities to remove wastes in an odorless, efficient manner. They shared a communal cooking area, generously supplied with food and drink. While not as bracing as the air on the *Verazen,* the temperature was cool compared to the heat outside.

Zical had gathered his people, given them strict orders that their every word might be monitored by unseen listening devices and to be very careful what they revealed. Dora thought his precautions sound, but probably useless. These Kwadii had impressed her as ruthlessly efficient, but lacking in curiosity about their real intentions. From Avanti's clipped sentences, Dora gathered that the Kwadii dealt with all hyperspace intruders in the same manner—by execution.

Every time she thought about dying, her limbs turned icy, despite the heat. For all the Federation's technology, no one really knew what awaited the soul after death. Religious beings believed in many versions of an afterlife—a comforting thought, especially with little time left of what she'd hoped would be a long and fulfilling life. However, when she died, there might not be anything else. She tried and failed to imagine the nothingness, like before she'd been born.

Dora didn't fear death as much as she resented the Kwadii taking away her life. She'd barely learned how to live. Even worse, if they died, the mission to send the Sentinel back to guard against the Zin would fail. Would their deaths bring about the death of Tessa and Kahn and their entire new world? What would happen to the Federation?

As if she didn't have enough on her mind, she also worried about Kirek. Was he hungry, thirsty, alone? Had he survived and found help and friends on Kwadii? She'd like to think if anyone survived the Kwadii law, Kirek would be the one with the opportunity to live a full life. Yet, the worst part was not knowing. The lack of information haunted her as her mind conjured possibilities, all of them sad enough to bring tears to her eyes.

No one in the Federation would ever know what had happened to them—especially since Ranth couldn't send back a log. Dora wondered if the Kwadii would attempt to access the *Verazen*'s computer and whether or not the Kwadii could find Ranth—or if he lived. Before Ranth's disappearance, he'd installed security firewalls and protocols that would make forced entry difficult. Dora was probably the only Federation person who could crack his safety systems, but she had no intention of revealing her ability. The last thing she wanted was to send these Kwadii into Federation space where they could use their superior technology to prevent all hyperspace travel and bring trade among the Federation's billions to a standstill.

On a personal level, she desperately wanted to deepen her

relationship with Zical—now especially in the face of their impending death. Yes, she still wanted to make love with him, but she wanted to increase the emotional attachment that Tessa had told her could make the loving even better. She enjoyed their shared glances that required no speech to convey a thought. The more humans she worked with, the more special she realized Zical was. He wielded authority with compassion, tempered his orders with kindness, and led by courageous example. She didn't regret her decision to accompany him, but only wished they'd had more personal time together.

Despite her gloomy thoughts, her body still had needs. Dora helped herself to a long, cool drink of water to quench her parched throat, then availed herself of the bathing facility. Perhaps contemplating their execution was too much for her mind to bear, so she tried to ease the pain by distracting herself. She lingered over her bathing, focused on the sensation of water cleansing her skin and noted the puckering of her fingertips and toes. For a few moments, she tried to forget their dire situation and simply yielded to the cascade's sweet caress over her skin.

She was almost finished when someone knocked on her door. "Come in."

Dressed in a loin cloth, his chest bare, Zical entered the room, took one look at her nudity and carefully glanced the other way, but not before she noted the gleam of appreciation in his gaze and how his tone turned husky. "Get dressed. Avanti wants my help to prepare for the trial."

"More likely she's trying to find out how many more of us are coming through hyperspace so she can kill us all." Dora turned off the water, grabbed a soft cotton cloth and dried herself. Slowly. "So why do I need to dress?"

Tessa had told her Terrans preferred to bathe with water even after they had suits to keep them clean. And now Dora understood why. The sensual experience couldn't be duplicated by the suit. The drying was rather interesting too. The soft material soaking up water created a pleasant zing to her skin and she couldn't help thinking how much more pleasant the bathing and drying would be if she and Zical shared the cleansing ritual. But what was even more interesting was that although Zical clearly tried to turn his gaze from her, he kept glancing her way.

She liked his lack of control. She liked that he couldn't stop looking. She'd created this body specifically to entice him, gone to a lot of trouble to take his preferences into account. But now that she was provoking his interest, she wanted more. She still wanted his passion of course, but she also wanted him to think of her as all woman.

"You have a good mind. I thought you might help me analyze their laws."

"Okay." While Zical seemed determined to maintain a professional physical distance from her, she was very glad he'd sought her out because he wanted her opinion. And she was determined to do her best. She supposed he would consider her teasing him with her body the act of a wayward woman—still, she took her time, enjoying his covert glances and keeping back a grin of satisfaction. Their captors had supplied clothing and she wrapped a sarong around her hips, then tied on a pair of sandals. "You can look now," she teased, pretending that she hadn't noticed his accelerated pulse, or the slight flaring of his nostrils.

He turned around and, at the sight of her bared breasts, his eyes widened then narrowed and a flush rose up his neck. Now that they were about to die Dora supposed she'd never understand the Terran and Rystani inclination to hide their flesh.

On the ship she'd worn clothes because it was expected, because she wanted to fit in, but her own preference was nudity. And in her view, the Kwadii had adjusted well to their warm world by wearing a minimum of clothing. She dried her hair with the cloth, combed her fingers through it, and water droplets trickled over her chest. Zical seemed extraordinarily interested in a globule that dripped over her breast and clung to her nipple.

Just to distract him from their imminent deaths, she let the water droplet hang from her nipple and then teased him. "You're staring. But I don't mind. I like it when you look at me like that."

"Like what?" He glared at her as if he had more responsibility on his shoulders than he could bear.

So she teased him, hoping to lighten his burden. "When you look as if you can't decide whether to kiss me or lick me."

"What I ought to do is—"

"Yes?"

"Leave you here."

"But then you'd miss me and my analytical mind."

"Behave," he warned, but she refused to take his implied threat to leave her behind the least bit seriously. His wonderful eyes heated with a violet-red flame and for a moment the darkness in them was dispelled by light. Zical leaned forward. For a moment she thought he would kiss her, but instead he whispered in her ear. "Can they get to Ranth?"

So he'd seen the soldiers entering the *Verazen* too. She kept her voice low. "I don't think so. However, I wish we could communicate with him. We need help. And I'm worried about Kirek," she admitted.

"He's better off alone than with us," he whispered back.

Maybe. But at least they would die together. Kirek was alone and she hated thinking how frightened and forlorn he must be on an alien world where if the Kwadii discovered him, he'd likely face execution too.

She and Zical exited her room, strode down the corridor, and a guard led them through double doors and gestured for them to enter a conference room with a round stone table and many chairs with artfully curved lines. Fruits, nuts and cheese, plus a variety of drinks were laid out for refreshments.

Dora had expected to meet Avanti alone to go over their

defense, but someone else, a man, sat at the table. She estimated from his long white hair that he'd lived many years. His skin was white, his features unlined, as if he'd never spent a day in the sun. And unlike the men who wore loincloths, he'd donned trousers and a short-sleeved dress shirt of fine cloth embroidered with a fanciful gold and silver braid. One might have thought he was a man who spent his life doing no more than fussing over frippery, until she spied the strong muscles in his arms and the cords of power in his neck that could come only from vigorous athletic activity.

With a warm smile, and clever brown eyes, he rose gracefully to his feet at their entrance. "I am Rogar Delari Hikai, the prosecutor of the Fifth House of Seemar."

"The prosecutor?" Startled, Dora turned to Avanti for explanation. "I thought we were here to prepare our defense."

"We are. And Rogar will listen. It saves time when you only tell your story once."

"Is there a hurry?" Zical asked, clearly not liking Rogar's presence any better than Dora did.

"Rogar and his Risorians wish the execution to take place before their religious holy day of prayer," Avanti explained, but Dora required more information about the Kwadii to make complete sense of that statement. Apparently, Kwadii was home to at least two religious factions, and from the contempt in Avanti's tone, she didn't honor the Risorian beliefs.

"We would be more than happy to put off the trial until after your holy day," Zical offered.

"That will not be acceptable," Rogar informed them, gesturing for everyone to take seats. "Kwadii law requires a speedy trial to take place within two days of the treasonous act."

Avanti's tone turned to a sneer. "He intends to make an example of you, for political purposes. Our elections take place in less than a moon rotation and he would have the masses frothing to spend more of our resources on weapons, instead of social entertainments."

"Bah. Social entertainment is sinful. Selgrens have no morals, no ethics, no sense of right or wrong."

"You would have us work in your fields and factories all day and give us no pleasure to enjoy our nights?" Avanti's voice was cool.

Dora glanced from Avanti to Rogar, wondering how they could play one side against the other to their benefit. Never had she wished so badly for computer access to Ranth. They didn't have enough data to ascertain their situation, but this exchange was fascinating. And alarming. One moon rotation meant they had very little time left to live, to plan a defense—or an escape.

"We digress." Rogar frowned at Avanti and turned to Zical. "I assume you're pleading guilty?"

"You assume wrong." Zical spoke quietly.

"It doesn't matter. Our sensors recorded your transgression. The evidence against you is verifiable and conclusive."

"It's your laws that we question—not your findings."

Rogar spoke as if to a child. "You aren't Kwadii. You may not question our law. It's not permitted."

Dora was proud that Zical kept his tone reasonable. His effort to stay calm must have cost him, especially with the lives of every scientist and the crew at stake. Worse, she knew how much responsibility he felt not only to save his people on this mission, but those back home who depended on them to find the Sentinel. But although under enormous pressure, he didn't shout or rant, instead wearing his dignity wrapped around him as tightly as his loin cloth.

"We don't recognize your laws. We have no pact with you. And unless we form a treaty of peace, many more of our people will follow."

"It does not matter. We will execute them too." Rogar frowned at Avanti. "Haven't you explained the basics to them?"

"There is no point of law that I have not considered in their defense." Avanti's eyes shot poison darts at the prosecutor. "I'm sure they'd prefer to spend their last days without dwelling on their fate when it cannot be changed."

"Then why go through the farce of a trial?" Zical demanded, his tone determined. Dora ached to give her support and, beneath the table, out of sight of the Kwadii, she placed her hand on his thigh.

"The Selgrens think a trial is civilized. A Risorian would not have put you through the agony of a trial." Rogar spoke simply.

"He means he would have murdered you in hyperspace," Avanti clarified.

"Better that a few strangers die than our homeworld be destroyed again."

"Why do you people live in such fear?" Dora asked. "Who is this enemy that you seek to hide from?"

"We don't speak of them." Rogar closed a notebook and shoved back his chair, indicating the meeting was over before it had begun.

Avanti spoke with harsh emotion. "He thinks if we don't speak of them, we can pretend we didn't almost suffer extermination from the—"

A squad of men burst into the room and aimed their guns at Dora and Zical. The leader of the group stepped forward and handed Rogar a disk. "These people are in league with our enemy. Here is proof."

Alarm spread through Dora. Although Avanti's words had made it clear the trial would likely do them no good, Dora had always held out hope that Zical could convince the Kwadii that they meant their world no harm. But the accusations had just become severe, the mood in the room hostile.

Rogar popped the disk into a slot and a hologram formed over the table. Dora recognized the symbol immediately. It was the one over the door to the cavern where Zical had entered Mount Shachauri. She had also seen the symbol carved into the mountain in several other places, but they'd never deciphered the mark. However, in her mind the emblem would forever symbolize the Perceptive Ones.

At the sight of the sign, Avanti spat. "You carry the symbol of the Zinatti on your ship?"

Rogar disgustedly slapped his hand on the holographic machine, turning it off. "You conspire with the Zinatti. You deserve to die."

"The Zin?" Zical asked. "The Kwadii are at war with the Zin?" His gaze found Dora's. "Could the Zin and the Zinatti be the same race?"

"Do these beings come from another galaxy?" Dora demanded.

"Silence," Rogar roared. "We will tell you nothing."

Zical ignored the order. "The Zin are our worst enemy. They almost destroyed this galaxy. Our mission is to stop another attack."

"Lies." Rogar shoved back his chair and stood. "I would expect no more from those who would invite a Zinatti attack by flying recklessly through hyperspace."

Avanti slapped her palm on the table, temper sparking in her eyes. "Rogar, you have no reason to insult these people. They may be our friends. Perhaps if instead of hiding from the Zin, we could join with their Federation and the next time this galaxy is attacked, we might beat the Zinatti."

Rogar didn't raise his tone, but horror edged his words. "For a millennium our isolationist policies have kept the Kwadii safe. Your liberal notions are madness. You and your soulless Selgrens will destroy us all if we don't stop you." He glared at Avanti, who didn't flinch. "And we will stop you."

"Stars." Dora's eyes widened. "Are you saying that the Zin—the Zinatti—track us through hyperspace? That we placed our own people in danger?"

Zical already suffered enough guilt for accidentally starting up the machines that had recalled the Sentinel. Now the Kwadii accused them of blazing a trail through hyperspace directly back to the Federation, as if their ship had drawn the Zin a map. Horror at the menace warred with concern for Zical. No man should have to bear so much.

"Idiots." Rogar signaled for the soldiers to keep their weapons aimed at them.

"We likely are on the same side." Dora spoke slowly to Avanti. She didn't want to tell the woman about the Perceptive Ones and how Zical had accidentally recalled the Sentinel. No doubt Rogar would see it as yet another reason for execution. "My people hate the Zin. Our mission is to stop them."

"You can't stop the Zinatti." Rogar stood, spoke over his shoulder as he exited the room. "You can only hide and hope they do not find you."

Avanti gestured for Zical and Dora to leave the room with her, but stopped in the doorway. "The trial will be in two days. While my defense will be vigorous, if I fail, your execution will follow immediately. Prepare yourselves."

Dora's bones seemed to turn to sand, her muscles to water. How did one prepare for death? Her mind twisted and turned like a cornered jellyfish, but she saw no honorable way out. Dying before they completed their mission was unacceptable.

"I would like to study your laws," Zical requested.

"It will do you no good, but I will have suitable materials made available to you. I suggest you use your last days preparing to meet your gods."

ZICAL'S GUILT FOR putting his crew in such a tight spot to fix his earlier mistake drove him hard. If the Kwadii court had its way, they would all die, their mission a failure. He could barely bring himself to think past losing the lives of his crew and the scientists, never mind considering that he may have opened a hyperspace trail for the Zin, and that without the Sentinel it could lead them to conquer the Federation worlds at home.

The losses would be so devastating, the guilt so high, he

had to tamp it down just to keep a clear thought in his head. Focusing on survival not failure kept him going.

So he'd gathered his top people in the showers, hoping the splash of running water would hide the sound of this meeting from any listening devices. Dora, Cyn, Vax, Shannon, and Dr. Laduna stood in a close circle and Zical kept his voice to a whisper.

"My friends, the Federation is counting on us to complete our mission."

Dr. Laduna's gills flapped, a measure of his distress. "Captain, is it true the Kwadii will execute us in less than two days?"

His face grim, Zical nodded. He would not lie to the scientist. "While we live, we have hope. We have two days to formulate an escape plan."

He clapped his first officer on the shoulder. "Vax, find a way to disarm and take out the guards."

Vax met his gaze and dipped his head in agreement.

"Cyn, adapt useful survival gear from the machinery in our quarters. Drinking vessels, weapons, communication devices that we can use after we escape."

"I'll do my best, Captain."

"Shannon, work with Dr. Laduna to find a way to send a message home. We need to inform the Federation about the Kwadii and warn them about the Zin."

The Jarn scientist's scales paled. "And what will you be doing?"

Zical didn't usually explain himself but these were extraordinary circumstances. "Dora and I will go over the Kwadii laws and search for loopholes."

Zical had no idea if his people could accomplish the tasks he'd assigned. But working toward freedom was better than doing nothing but waiting to die. These people had given him their loyalty, entrusted him with their lives. Until he drew his last breath, he would fight to stay alive, to return to his ship and complete his mission.

"We may not have another opportunity to gather." He paused. "And once we go to trial, the security may tighten. So our best opportunity to escape may be now." He leaned forward, his whisper intense. "But I expect each one of you to do your best to live. We shall not give up. We shall keep up the spirits of our friends and help one another through this difficult time. We've escaped tight spots before, and I have every confidence we can do so again."

Zical's words brought fire back into their eyes, color into faces gone pale and hopeless. His people were the best. They also deserved the truth. "We are not giving up. Our mission is too important to do less than our best. I expect maximum effort and then some. Understood?"

He'd never been so proud, as his friends squared their shoulders, lifted their chins, and straightened their spines. And Dora was no different from the others in that respect. Although she obviously missed and worried about Kirek, as did he, their first priority had to be escape, and Dora clearly understood.

She'd come a long way in such a short time, supporting him and helping him as one of the team. He vowed that together, somehow, they would all find a way back to their ship and continue their mission. And if they failed, they would have given their best.

KIREK OPENED HIS eyes and wished he could go back to sleep and wake up in his own room with the scent of his mother's cooking. His head hurt. His mouth was dry as a sand worm's burrow and he had no idea where he was. The last thing he remembered was leaving Dora, falling in the skimmer. But from the look of this room, someone had moved him from the skimmer to a comfortable chamber.

Furnished with a bed, chairs, and a wooden cabinet with drawers, the room reminded him of holopics he'd seen of homes before the Federation provided suits. On a table next to his bed stood a tempting glass of water. He tried to sit up but hadn't the strength and he groaned in despair.

A woman entered the room. She had kind eyes, a wide bosom and hips, and a cheery voice. "There now. Let me help." She lifted the glass to his mouth and placed a tubular object between his lips. He bit on the tube, but nothing came out. "Suck on the straw," she instructed.

Kirek sucked greedily and water burst into his mouth and he swallowed before he lost one precious drop. He'd never tasted anything so good, but the woman pulled away the glass too soon.

"Easy now. Not too much at once. Let that settle and then you may have more."

Kirek looked around the room, puzzled. "Where am I?"

"I am Serri Jerhar and this is my home. My husband found you half dead in the skimmer. He wanted to take you to the authorities but I thought it better if you returned to the crèche on your own accord."

Serri obviously thought he'd run away from a crèche. And thanks to his loin cloth that had torn free during his fall, his nudity hid his origins. Many beings believed that the raising of children should be left to experts. Apparently the Kwadii believed so. And Kirek saw no reason to inform the woman of his true identity, as he pondered what his next move should be.

"Thank you. Please." He pointed to the water. "More."

She obliged, then looked anxiously over her shoulder. "My husband is a good man and he won't return from his shift until late morning. Young man, by then you need to be on your way. There's clothing for you there. Take it and go on your way. But first eat."

"Yes," Kirek agreed, realizing he'd been fortunate not to have been recaptured. He couldn't help wondering about Dora and the crew. Had they escaped? If so, they would have no idea how to find him. Kirek did his best to put the worry aside. He had more immediate concerns.

Serri shoved a plate toward him. "Eat," she repeated.

The food appeared strange, but Kirek ate everything she offered, drank more water, and began to feel more like his old self. His head still throbbed but after a good night's sleep and a hearty breakfast, he was ready to slip out the door when the kindly Serri placed a credit chip in his hand. "It's all I could spare. Go with the gods, child."

Once outdoors, Kirek saw that her pink rock home squatted in a cluster among others that looked much the same. Large leafy trees shaded a brick path and Kirek arbitrarily picked a direction. With food in his stomach, a loincloth to wear, and his thirst quenched, his spirits were up. His immediate goal was to remain free and gather information on the Kwadii.

With no destination in mind, Kirek left Serri's home and tagged after a bunch of children. They played a complex game with a ball and bouncing squares, paying no attention to him until the ball rolled away from them and in his direction. He kicked it back.

The kids were old and bigger than him. Their ragged clothes hung on bodies so thin it appeared they didn't eat regularly and their sandal straps were torn and retied in many places. He spied holes in the soles too. Miri and Etru would never have let him dress with so little respect for his appearance. Did these children come from a crèche? They looked as if they lived on the streets. Knowing better than to ask questions, Kirek trailed after them. He had no idea of their destination but figured that if anyone was searching for him, he could hide among the children, appearing part of their ragtag group.

But he didn't count on the kids' curiosity. One of the older boys with long hair that was clumped together like rows of corncobs planted himself in Kirek's path. "What ya doin'?"

"Nothing." Kirek looked at the ground and shuffled his feet, doing his best to appear nonthreatening, but apparently he'd chosen the wrong behavior.

"You a snoop?"

"Me?" Kirek had always been different from other children. He'd never fit in, except with his parents and on the *Verazen*. Just thinking about Dora, the crew, and the scientists made him feel even lonelier.

"You aren't from the crèche. And your clothes are too good to be a *banzoo*."

Kirek had no idea how this kid knew he wasn't from the crèche. Nor did he comprehend what a *banzoo* was. Although the kid was bigger and stronger, Kirek knew some dirty street-fighting tricks. But the other kids had circled him and he could neither beat them all, nor outrun them on his short legs.

"Where you goin', *deezer*?"

Deezer must be an insult. The other kids laughed. Kirek kept his answers vague. "I'm looking for a good time." He held up his credit chip, knowing the kid might take it from him. "And I'm willing to share."

The kid eyed the chip. "You heading to the carnival?"

"Yeah. Want to go?" Kirek offered, hoping to avoid a beating and at the same time use these kids as cover to avoid the authorities. In the back of his mind, he hoped to reunite with Dora and Zical, but he couldn't ask questions. These kids might turn him in for a reward.

"Maybe I'll filch that credit chip and leave you behind."

"That would be a mistake." Although quaking inside, Kirek grinned, knowing bullies often backed down when challenged.

"And why is that?"

"'Cause I'm good with machines. You stick with me and you'll win big." Kirek assumed that a carnival had gaming machines. If he was wrong, he might just end up broke and alone.

"What are we waiting for? Let's go." The boy clapped him on the back, almost knocking him down. "By the way, my name's Lew."

* * *

As promised, Avanti delivered a holochip with lengthy files of Kwadii law to the conference room a few hours later. Zical's head ached from the combination of trying to push aside his guilt over the failing mission while he tried to focus on obscure statutes. He was no law specialist and the convoluted sentences left so little open to interpretation that he was finally ready to admit defeat.

Dora had remained with him, but she didn't appear to be working too hard on deciphering the Kwadii statutes. Instead, she had a dreamy expression in her eyes, one that he'd been trying to ignore all afternoon. But he had been as successful at repressing his guilt and disregarding her expression as he had in pretending not to look at her beautiful breasts. Irritated with himself for needing a distraction from the burden of his responsibility, he closed the holofile. Vax hadn't found a way to overcome the guards. They were too well armed and backed up by lethal mechanical lasers. Cyn had made a few water bottles, which would do them no good if they couldn't escape. And no one had found a way to send word of their plight back to the Federation.

With so many seemingly unsolvable problems that appeared to lead to all their deaths and the failure of his mission, he needed a break, a distraction. But no matter how many times he told himself that Dora wasn't a solution, his mind seemed to require such a bountiful diversion.

With death facing them, he couldn't find an escape and his guilt and frustration mounted. How in the seven rings of Darnica was he supposed to concentrate with her sitting across from him half naked?

Yet he could no longer bear to worry over Kirek, his crew, the scientists, Mystique, and the Federation. His body recognized that his mind was too burdened by stress to find a solution that would keep them alive long enough to continue their mission. He needed a break.

Without his suit to suppress his natural urges, his groin ached from an excess of stimulation. And when Dora caught his gaze, he would have bet a month's pay that she knew exactly what was bothering him. But he didn't want to say a word and give her the satisfaction of knowing how badly he wanted her when he should be thinking of a way to avoid death.

"Yes?" One of her delectable eyebrows arched in speculation.

"This is getting us nowhere."

"Then why don't we do something more productive." She licked her top lip with the tip of her tongue in a most provocative manner, and his mouth went dry.

"I'm open to suggestions."

She stared him straight in the eye. "I would like to make love before I die."

"We may yet find a way off Kwadii," he protested, yet in response to her suggestion all his blood seemed to flow below his loincloth.

"You need a rest. You aren't sleeping or eating. You owe it to yourself and everyone depending on you to relax, so you can attack the problem from a fresh angle." She paused, wet her bottom lip, and continued. "And if these are to be our last days, I would like to spend them pleasurably."

She had a point. He certainly wasn't getting anywhere examining legal files. And he suspected Avanti was one sharp lawyer who would have enjoyed beating Rogar in court, not so much to save him and his crew but to best her hated adversary. No doubt she'd spent years studying to attain her position, and if she hadn't found a good defense for them, he probably wouldn't either. Still, to make love when he should be planning an escape seemed . . . irresponsible. And wonderful. Just the thought of having her made his blood quicken.

His guilt-laden and frustrated mind hadn't come up with a new thought in hours. A distraction might be just what he needed so he could return to the problem with fresh ideas.

Shucking responsibility had never been easy for him, yet this time, he didn't know why he was resisting. He could not think of one escape scheme that might succeed.

And he wanted her. Despite all their efforts, they would likely be dead within a week. Dora had given up so much to become human and making love to her would at least let her die with the knowledge that she'd lived a little. If he couldn't save them, why not at least give Dora some pleasure and himself too?

He let his gaze drop to her breasts and her nipples tightened in response. Stars, she was eager, available, responsive. What more could he want?

But she was a virgin, and some of his ardor cooled.

"Are you sure?" He raised his gaze to hers.

"Yes." Standing, she began to unwrap her sarong.

"I'll do that." He strode around the table, placed his hand on hers. "You can change your mind at any time."

"I won't."

She sounded so sure, so sensual, that he yearned to encourage those banked embers in her eyes to blaze into a frenzied fire. But she'd also said that she'd wanted a body and then had hidden in her quarters for months. So he had doubts. As if sensing she could banish the last of his hesitation, Dora reached her arms around his neck, brought her mouth to his, searing him with her lips, her bare breasts pressing against his chest in a sexual assault that made his senses reel.

His savage reaction to her had him taking her mouth with a rough fury. She gasped. Dora tugged him closer, molding her mouth to his, pressing into him, giving as much as she took.

Damn, the woman could kiss. She poured her desire into their fused mouths, stoking a need in him to have her naked, right there on the conference table. "A bed . . . would . . . be better."

"I want you here. Now." Her hands dropped to his loin-cloth, fumbled with the knots.

As bold as she sounded, her hands trembled. He clasped his hands on her waist, lifted her to sit on the table. His hips spread her knees wide and all the while he kissed her.

Her fingers gave up on the knots, stroked up and down his back, rushing him, urging him to hurry, to make love to her, as if she feared he would change his mind. He might have come to his decision quickly, but now that he was holding her, kissing her, the only thing that could make him leave would be if she sent him away.

Remembering that this was her first time battled with his need to pour himself inside her. With her legs straddling him, her scent enticing him, he had difficulty holding back. She'd waited a long time and endured much to arrive at this point and he wanted their lovemaking to be memorable. No, he wanted their time together to be the most spectacular experience in all her three hundred years of life.

Perhaps a tall order. But Zical was up for it. Oh, yeah, he was up all right and burning hard.

He pulled his mouth from hers. "We need to slow down."

"Why?" Part breathless, part demanding, part sultry petulance, her demeanor told him that she might have read every sex manual ever written, but knowledge and experience could be two very different things.

"Dora, your body hasn't made love before. The fit might take some getting used to."

"I'll be fine."

"I'm not aiming for fine. I'm aiming for sensational."

Dora giggled. Brazenly, she reached beneath his loincloth to stroke him. "I'd say you've already reached the mark."

Placing his hand over hers, he pulled her back. "Not yet." He set her hands on the table, then threaded his fingers through her hair. "I want you to remember every kiss, every caress." Combing his fingers through her hair, he stroked her ear, palmed her jaw and watched her pulse throb in her graceful neck. His voice turned husky. "Since we skipped the entire seduction process, let me make it up to you. Yes?"

"Yes."

She tried to brush her breasts against him, but he leaned back just enough to keep them apart. Frustrated, fascinated, she leaned her head into his hand and released a sigh. "You smell good. I never knew the sense of smell could be so . . . enticing."

"For both of us," he agreed.

Trailing his fingers down her neck, tracing her collarbone, he held her gaze. Anticipation flared in her eyes as he ever so slowly dipped closer to her breasts.

He'd intended to caress and stroke and fondle with his hands to excite her, but once her fullness filled his hands, he lifted a breast to his mouth and took the tip between his lips. Sucking gently, he heard her gasp.

"Oh . . . oh.   Ah . . . I   didn't   know . . . I   never imagined . . . that I could feel . . . so good." She threw back her head, arched into his mouth. "More, please."

Amid all his failures, Zical was glad he could give her what she asked for. Without hesitation, he gave her more.

Chapter Thirteen

DORA THOUGHT IF lovemaking was a flavor, it would be peppered and ambrosial. If lovemaking was a color, it would be paprika red. If lovemaking was a scent, the fragrance would be pungent spice with a finely sharpened texture, both creamy and steamy. And if a sound, lovemaking was pure unadulterated sizzle.

Every sense contributed to her spiraling emotions as Zical's expertise seduced her with one level after another of skillful stimulation. She tried and failed to quantify and identify each element. But like a finely cooked meal, or a masterful opera, the end result was so much more than the sum of the components that analysis failed her.

She morphed into a creature of sultry senses. Her pulse accelerated, her loins throbbed. Primitive mating urges took over and she arched her spine, thrusting her breast deeper into Zical's mouth.

Exquisite impressions zinged from her nipple to her core

as heat from his mouth streamed into her. His tongue laved the tip, feathering her with wondrous care, even as his teeth nipped her sensitive flesh and kept her from squirming.

Every nerve ending in her body was focused on her nipple, his tongue. She demanded more, her other breast jealous for his attentions. Sometime during his erotic kiss, he untied her sarong, leaving her open and so ready for him to enter her. But he had yet to move on to her other breast, and she finally understood what it was like to want him to keep doing exactly what he was doing, yet contradictorily to advance to the next tier.

When her nipple grew so sensitive that a moan escaped her throat, Zical finally released her flesh, only to give the exact same treatment to her other breast. Knowing what he was about to do, anticipating the rippling pleasure, had her reaching for him once again.

And again he grasped her wrists and placed her palms on the table's edge. She recalled that Rystani custom dictated that only the males touched, not the females. And Zical was all proud Rystani male. He obviously adored taking charge, setting this unbearably slow pace, and she would let him.

She didn't want to remind him that she wasn't born a Rystani woman. She didn't want to remind him that she was anyone but the current woman of his desire. However, holding still while he laved her nipple when she longed to skim her palms along his back, brush her lips into the cords of his neck, twine her legs around his waist, and tug him into her took more self-control than she'd believed possible.

Since actions were denied her, she attempted to urge him to go on. "You feel so good."

"Mmm."

He kept right on caressing her nipple with the tip of his tongue, paying little attention to her words. Dampness pooled between her thighs and her *synthari* required touching. When she tried to slip her hand there, Zical released her breast.

"Don't move." He placed her palms flat on the table.

"Wh-what are you . . . thinking?"

"That you need to hold still."

She lifted her palms. "No one could hold still with—"

"Sure you can." Again, he gently pressed her palms flat. Then he waited to see if she would comply.

She clamped her fingers around the edge. "I'll try."

He carefully brushed her hair back from her eyes and eyed her with satisfaction. "Much better."

"Easy for you to say." He wasn't the one clinging to a table, sitting there naked, ready to scream if he didn't make love to her soon.

"Open your legs for me." With no hesitation, she did as he requested. Finally, he was going to get on with it.

He trailed his fingers over the delicate skin on the insides of her thighs. "You've been waiting a long time to make love."

"Too . . . long."

"And how do you feel?"

"Needy. Impatient. Stars! What are we waiting for?"

A grin tugged at one corner of his mouth. "Don't you want me to appreciate every bare inch of you?"

"Not particularly."

His hands made sitting still almost impossible. He was being too careful, going too slow.

"I haven't even given you any compliments on how beautiful you look."

He was teasing her with words, taunting her flesh with caresses, and her head swam. Sunlight from the window glinted on one side of his face, casting half in shadow and adding highlights to the muscular sheen on his chest. He'd never looked more desirable and she yearned to touch and taste and do so much more than wait.

She clung to the table, reminding herself not to touch him. She couldn't close her thighs. Not with his hips keeping her

open. Totally at his mercy, she didn't know if she approved.
And yet the ache in her kept swelling, spiraling, taking her
to a place she most definitely wanted to be.

"I don't need compliments. I need you to . . . to . . ."

He cut off her words with another kiss. Eagerly she
opened her mouth and then she felt him ever so delicately
brush the curls of her *synthari*. A zing of pleasure caused
moisture to pearl. She shimmied her hips in expectation of
another caress, a deeper stroke.

As he thrust his tongue into her mouth, he inserted one
finger inside her *synthari*, which hugged him with welcoming heat. She would have gasped at the sensational feel of
him, but she had no breath, no words to explain how badly
she ached to move her hips, to take in more of him.

Slowly, he removed his finger, then thrust it back into her,
causing a stir, an uproar of raspy delight. His thumb opened
up her nether lips and found where she was most sensitive.
His gentle touch was like an electric current that hummed,
that tightened and clenched her muscles and caused a swirl
of anticipation. She'd never felt anything so delicious, yet
she couldn't stand the light pressure and ached for more of
his touch.

He broke the kiss and eyed her, clearly quite pleased with
his efforts. "So what do you think?"

Think? His thumb caressed her center and she gasped.
"How can I think when you . . . ah . . . oh-oh-oh." She could
feel pressure building, her muscles tensing. She was surely
about to explode.

"Good?" His tone cracked with raw heat, as if he knew
exactly how she needed more.

"Very . . . ah . . . good."

And he stopped. Withdrew his hand. He stared at her face
as she opened her eyes in passion-dulled confusion. "Zical,
please."

"Please what?"

"Keep touching me."

"I will," he promised, leaning into her, nipping her neck with tiny love bites, then lapping away the sting. "Trust me?"

"Yes."

"Then don't rush me."

She realized in his Rystani warrior way he was giving her a choice. A choice to do this his way. "You have no idea how . . . difficult . . . it is to sit here and not scream with the need you're creating."

"Seems to me you've recovered."

She had. While they'd been conversing some of the tension had eased. No longer feeling as if she were on the edge of combustion, she nevertheless yearned to proceed, to lose herself in the delicious haze of pleasure that Zical could create. She adored how he made her feel cherished and womanly, and she was glad they'd taken this time for themselves, glad he enjoyed being with her. And most of all, she was thrilled that Zical was the first man she was intimate with, because she cared so much about him. To her he'd become more than a friend, he'd become . . . special. She couldn't think about him without warm happiness urging her on. Tessa had been right when she said that making love was special when the emotions were involved. Dora admired this brave man who bore the burden of command with such honor and stoicism. Now, he'd gone out of his way to please her and make the occasion special. He couldn't possibly stop before taking her completely, not after he'd agreed to make love. So when he leaned down and captured her breast in his mouth, she released a sigh of pleasure and relaxed.

Not that she could relax for long. His mouth summoned every bit of the tension she'd thought had dissipated, stretching her taut, stoking her with an expertise that caused the embers he'd kindled to leap into dancing sparks that singed and burned and placed her on the edge of a deep chasm all over again.

And this time when his clever fingers dipped into her *syn-*

thari, she barely noticed that instead of one finger, he'd inserted two. But the extra thickness pleased her. He pleased her. She shifted her hips forward, parted her legs wider, welcoming every intimacy and fully believing that even if she died tomorrow, she'd never regret this night with Zical.

While she didn't understand how her heart could beat so hard when she was holding perfectly still, or how moisture broke out in a sheen on her skin while she did nothing but accept his every caress, she understood that comprehension wasn't required for enjoyment.

She'd built her body for lovemaking, and like a finely tuned starship, Zical had taken over as the pilot in charge. Left to her own inclinations, Dora would have preferred being more than a passenger along for the ride, but she was not about to question his methods. Especially when he felt so damn good.

But this lovemaking wasn't just about erotic sensations. She knew deep in her heart that she would respond like this only with Zical. Her emotions were all there, joy, acceptance, and a deep fondness for this man that she wanted very much to explore.

While she yearned to kiss him and trace her hands over all that savage-looking male flesh, she also relished submitting to his basic demands. And the more he asked, the more she wanted to give.

So even as she suffered the sweet torments of his tongue on her breasts, she knew there was no place she'd rather be than right here, right now. She'd created this body for him to enjoy, for them to enjoy, and there was no part of her flesh he couldn't explore. Nothing she would deny him.

"Zical?"

"Mmm?"

She liked being at his mercy. She suspected she'd also enjoy his being at hers. But the plain, simple truth was that she liked Zical, always had, always would. She enjoyed his company, period. Sharing her body with him was an extra bonus, a delight that made her happy, that made the physical pleasure almost secondary.

"Tell me . . . what would please you. And I'll do it."

He released her breast and trailed kisses up her neck. "You are to enjoy yourself."

"I would enjoy touching you too."

"Next time."

"There'll be a next time?"

"We have tonight," he murmured. "All night. And for your first time, I want you to think only about the pleasure I can give you."

"Okay."

He lifted her breasts until she overflowed his hands then flicked the nipples with his thumbs, creating a sizzle that caused her hips to squirm. "You like this?"

"Yes."

He plucked her nipples between thumb and index finger. "And this?"

"Yes . . . but . . ." She could do nothing, only take whatever he decided to give.

He plucked them again, causing the throbbing between her thighs to increase tenfold. "But?"

She licked her lips, uneasy. "I can't decide if . . . ah . . . ah . . ."

"If what?" He laved away the smarting with his tongue.

"If this is pain or pleasure."

"You want me to stop?"

"No."

She'd raised her voice and he chuckled, wickedly tweaking her nipples again. "There's a fine line between pleasure and pain."

"I feel so wanton. All achy . . . empty."

"Good." The satisfaction in his tone made her hunger for more of his loving. And finally, he stepped back and removed his loincloth. His *tavis* jutted proudly, thick and hard and ready.

She was too educated to wonder if he would fit. Her *synthari* would stretch to accommodate him. And she was so damp with her own moisture, she was certain he was going to slide his *tavis* inside her with ease. Instead he held his *tavis* at the thick base and rubbed the tip over her parted lips. She hadn't known anything could be so hard and soft at the same time or feel so absolutely awesome. The shock of his flesh rubbing her so intimately almost rocked her off the table.

His hand on her thigh steadied her. Her muscles were gathering, tightening, like a crossbow drawn too tight and about to snap. Her breath came in great gulps and then . . . the most marvelous sensations burst through her, a series of orgasms so intense, so hard, that a scream ripped from her throat. And it kept on and on, like one of those fireworks that shot higher and higher as it exploded again and again. And all the while, he kept rubbing her, milking her body of gasp after gasp of pure pleasure.

She had no idea exactly when the orgasms ceased, but eventually she realized he'd exchanged his fingers for his *tavis* inside her and held perfectly still, allowing her body to become accustomed to him. Without hesitation, welcoming his fullness, she wrapped her legs around his hips. She grabbed his neck for extra support. His hands clenched her bottom and then he pulled back his hips, thrust back into her. Hard.

"Yes." She groaned into his ear, a new tension already building. And this time she didn't hold back. Trusting him not to drop her, trusting him to instinctively know what she wanted, she simply held on. She was slick, ready. And his angle of insertion and extraction caused a lovely friction exactly where she needed it most.

His hands clenched her bottom. His breath blew raggedly by her ear, fanning her neck, and her breasts rubbed against his chest, the sensitive tips so tender, so connected to her, that when she exploded once again, her muscles fired, then collapsed, utterly spent. If not for Zical's strong hands around her, she would have fallen.

And still her Rystani warrior was not done. His stamina amazed her, worried her that she might not be his match. But then he braced her spine against the cool wall. And suddenly, magically, she was tensing all over again. The cool hardness of the wall contrasting with the heat of him against her chest, hips, and thighs not only revived her spinning senses but oddly cooled her down enough to heat up again.

She lost count of the orgasms. One blended into another until she lost all sense of self. She no longer knew where her body began and his ended. To her they were one. And when he finally spasmed into her, the surge of him triggered a flood of feelings. Joy. Contentment. Satiation. And an overwhelming need to hold him close and never let go.

Dora never had much recollection of Zical's tying her sarong around her hips, his donning his loincloth before he carried her from the conference room to the bathing room to his quarters. He'd lowered her to her feet and Dora didn't come back to herself until cool water rained down on both of them. Stunned by the experience, she gave up trying to find the right words.

Instead, she placed her arms around him, tilted back her head and smiled. "Thank you."

He chuckled and soaped up a soft cloth, his grin teasing. "Dora, I'm not done with you yet."

KIREK'S NEW FRIENDS didn't try to sneak past carnival security, so neither did he, although he could have easily slipped past the machines guarding the front entrance. While he didn't want to waste his limited credits, he also didn't wish to attract the attention of Lew and his peers, preferring to appear as if he were one of them.

So far, Kirek mostly kept his mouth shut and listened. He'd picked up a surprising amount of information during

their morning walk through the town to the city center. The
city had very different sections, those of wealth, Risorians,
who according to his new friends sat around improving their
spiritual nature in order to attain high positions in the afterlife. And Selgrens, poor workers who didn't believe in any
god and spent their free time in pleasurable pursuits.

Apparently Selgrens and Risorians didn't mix socially.
City center was Selgren territory and the surrounding parks
and nature trails were for those of a more spiritual nature,
who sought to improve their bodies through ritual exercises
and cleanse their mind with music.

Kirek had expected the carnival to be a roving group of
entertainers like the acrobats, jugglers, and trained animals
his parents had taken him to see on Mystique. But this carnival occupied a permanent location in Baniken's city center.

The pink rock exterior of the main building matched the
other nearby buildings. Yet Kirek heard the boys talking
about how the Risorians, the orthodox faction of deeply religious Kwadii, wanted to close the carnival down, but so far
the Selgrens had mustered enough popular support to keep
the entertainment centers open.

"Son of a Kinatti sand worm," Lew cursed, grabbing
Kirek by the arm and tugging him through the large crowd
of adults at the entrance. "If you stand there dawdling, we'll
never reach the games."

"Games?" To Kirek the carnival seemed like a haven for
every kind of vice he'd ever heard about, and many he
hadn't. Specific areas catered to sexual needs, and although
his curiosity at the profundity of variations spiked, his parents would not have approved of his exploring those sections where one could purchase everything from
prostitution to erotic fantasies to sexual scenarios for those
with more unusual tastes. Although Kirek's IQ was off the
scale, his parents lovingly protected him as they would have
any Rystani child. And while he had the curiosity of an
adult, his sexual inclinations were dictated by the biology of

a four-year-old child. So he didn't mind exploring the game section.

"Last time I was here, I won twenty credits on Galactic War Five."

"Really?"

"Yeah, we splurged on holovids for a week," Lew bragged. "Sucked down breen burgers and all the vips we could drink."

"Awesome."

With enthusiasm Lew whirled Kirek around a corner and through a double set of doors into a vast, dark room with hundreds of holographic games, seemingly all making noise at once. Kirek's first instinct was to clap his hands over his ears to muffle the din. But that wouldn't have been acceptable, and he needed to fit in with these Kwadii to avoid suspicion.

"Over here," Lew shouted to be heard over the din of shooting weapons, gongs, whistles, and applause, all coming from the players, their audiences, and the machines. Lew stopped in front of a gaming device, reached into his pocket and pulled out a credit chip. He read the balance then slowly replaced the chip in his pocket with a soulful shake of his head. "I'll watch."

Kirek placed his chip in the slot, then gestured to Lew "Show me how it's done."

Lew whooped with joy and pumped his fist, then settled behind the controls. Kirek quickly saw that while the game sported sophisticated sound and sensors, the goal was quite simple. Kill as many of the bad guys as possible in the shortest amount of time. To avoid too many winners, the levels became increasingly difficult, upping the stakes and the risk of losing one's credits.

Lew concentrated, moving through the first few levels with ease. He'd almost won back his wager when enemy fire nailed him. He kicked the mechanism and the machine warned him that violence was prohibited. Reluctantly, he turned over the machine to Kirek.

His hands barely fit on the controls. And he had to stretch

his fingers to reach all the buttons. When the machine recycled and started the game, Kirek had several close calls on the first level, but that was due to his testing his psi against the machine's trigger points.

Once he understood the high-risk points, the places where the game kicked in to take advantage of the player, he exerted a little psi pressure. And *whap*. He was moving through levels like an expert, putting aside his conscience, telling himself that Etru would understand his need to "cheat" with his enhanced psi to earn credits.

"Hey, guys." Lew excitedly called the others over to watch Kirek's game. "He's an expert."

"Who would have thought the skinny little kid's fingers could go so fast," said one of the boys behind Kirek, his voice filled with awe.

Kirek hadn't realized how fast he would draw a crowd. He should stop, but he hadn't had this much fun in a long time. Other kids usually thought him odd. He wasn't so much as accepted, never mind admired. And it was only a game with a bunch of kids. He didn't see the harm in playing, in using his psi to help him get past the codes that prevented big winners. The game was rigged to cheat these boys of their credits. It wouldn't hurt the owners to suffer a little payback.

When bells started ringing above his head and hologram fireworks burst around him, he realized he'd beat the game. Lew grabbed his hands and danced, jumping up and down, his voice jubilant, his eyes merry. "You won. You won. You won. That was great. You are evil, man. Evil."

"Thanks." Apparently "evil" was a compliment, and Kirek spoke quietly as the other boys wandered back to their own games. Lew plucked his credit chip out of the machine and handed it to Kirek. He was about to put it into his pocket, when the numbers on the chip caught his eyes. He'd started with ten credits. He now had four more zeros beyond the ten.

He hadn't expected the payoff to be so large. He also

hadn't considered that such a rare win would draw attention—the wrong kind. He should have won in smaller amounts, slowly building his stake. Instead, he'd made himself a target for theft, a target for the authorities.

Kirek's former excitement turned to ashes and left a bitter taste of fear in his mouth. He really should have been more careful and he vowed to exercise better judgment in the future. Although no harm seemed to have been done, he had an uneasy feeling, a prickle at the back of his neck that suggested someone might be watching.

Grabbing Lew's hand, he tugged him from the games. "Let's eat. I'm starved."

Lew didn't protest and together they strode toward a huge room filled with vendors hawking a variety of foods. The delicious aromas of cooked meats and spicy sauces filled the air. They stopped and bought pastries filled with sweet meats and sharp cheese and guzzled a fizzy orange drink that quenched Kirek's thirst but left him wondering if it had any nutritional value. But the feeling in his gut that he was still being watched was his largest concern, until he spied a poster on a wall.

The poster was an advertisement that included a likeness of two people he recognized. Dora and Zical.

Stars.

Kirek left Lew and zigzagged through the crowds to the poster. Without wondering if he was committing an illegal act, he ripped it from the wall. A security guard shouted at him and Kirek wadded up the paper and rammed it into his pocket.

"Run." Lew saw the problem. He could have left Kirek but he didn't. Kirek would have liked to think Lew was helping him out of loyalty and friendship but suspected it was the credit chip in his pocket that had Lew risking his neck for his new acquaintance.

However, Kirek willingly accepted help where it was offered. Lew knew the territory. This was his home ground and he led Kirek on a run through a warren of hallways until they lost the guard and stopped to catch their breaths. Kirek pulled the paper from his pocket and smoothed out the wrinkles. He couldn't read Kwadii.

"What's it say?"

Lew summarized. "It's an advertisement to watch the trial and execution of traitors."

Execution? The sweet meats and orange fizz in Kirek's stomach churned. The Kwadii meant to execute his friends. As his throat tightened with fear and grief, he fought to keep down his lunch. "How long until—"

"It's tomorrow. Want to go watch?"

Chapter Fourteen

SILENCE FILLED THE hover as Zical, Dora, his entire crew, and the scientists boarded. Since their capture, and even now on their way to their trial and execution, Zical had continued his search for a means of escape. But the Kwadii soldiers escorting them held so many weapons aimed at them that any attempt to flee would be met with instant death. During the last two days, Zical had learned that the Kwadii obeyed orders with fanatical adherence and didn't miss security details, using technical superiority to back up alert and conscientious guards.

Locked inside the windowless hover, Zical sat beside Dora, his mood somber despite his pleasurable night. Dora might not have been experienced when he'd begun making love to her, but she certainly was now. She'd been exceptionally creative and enthusiastic and their lovemaking had taken his mind off his failed mission for the duration of the night. But the experience had been bittersweet. The relaxation hadn't created any brilliant new ideas, as he'd hoped, and now the woman he'd grown to care for wouldn't live through the day.

Neither would his crew. Vax would never return home to help his aging parents. Shannon's brood of children and grandchildren would never know how she'd tried to keep up everyone's spirits. And Cyn, a credit to her heritage, would never be heralded as a heroine, her name in the hall of Scartar's bravest. All of their hopes and dreams, plus those of the Federation, were about to die with them. And failure weighed heavily on Zical.

He'd failed to right the sequence of events he'd put in motion. He'd failed to keep his crew alive. And worse, if the Kwadii were correct, their effort may have caused more harm, their journey through hyperspace may have created a trail for the Zin to follow straight back to the Federation.

Yet Zical was not about to give up. As long as his heart beat, he would seek a way to escape, to save his people and the mission.

Dora broke the silence with a quiet murmur in his ear. "Ranth's alive."

"How do you know? Can he help us?" Tamping down his hope, Zical turned to her, and the others started talking quietly among themselves, leaving them a cocoon of privacy.

She shrugged and her face clouded with wonder and confusion. "I've been reaching into the vault with my psi."

"Vault?"

"When we were still in hyperspace, at the first sign of danger from the Kwadii, Ranth locked himself away in a safe house that I call 'the vault.' When I tapped in, I sensed he might be there, but I didn't have the strength to contact him."

"So how is it possible that you can reach Ranth now? You aren't plugged in." Zical's hopes flared. If she could contact Ranth, the powerful computer might help them escape.

Dora shrugged. "We've always known that psi power is connected to sexual activity."

Zical recalled that when Kahn had trained Tessa to use her psi, he'd used sexual frustration in an attempt to encourage her psi to appear. Sexual frustration was a tried-and-true method of achieving psi ability. While the accepted method hadn't worked on the Earthling and Kahn had found another way, there could be no doubt that sexual experience could support psi connections. Although Zical had most certainly delayed his and Dora's orgasms, his intent had been simply to escalate the pleasure. Dora already possessed psi power, yet perhaps their activity had triggered or strengthened another part of her psi.

"You think last night—"

"Increased my psi strength. My contact with Ranth is not strong, but we linked. He's very much alive."

Zical supposed he didn't have to understand how Dora had attained a link, he merely needed to make use of her unique abilities. "Can you and Ranth infiltrate the Kwadii systems?"

She shook her head. "Not while Ranth's in the vault. We are still too weak."

"And if he comes out?"

"The Kwadii dampeners will kill him."

Some of his hope was dashed, but he still wouldn't give up until he'd explored every option. "How can we strengthen your connection?"

"Well, a few more nights like the last one might accomplish the goal."

Dora chuckled, and he marveled that she could do so when they were at the brink of death, but then the woman constantly surprised him. He'd feared Dora's innuendos and teasing about sex had been to cover up insecurities. Stars, had he been wrong. Dora reveled in her sensuality and she'd thoroughly enjoyed herself—as much as he had. And before the night had been over she'd proved to him that what she said was what she meant.

Frustration and discouragement swelled in his chest. "We don't have a few nights. We have only hours."

Dora entwined her fingers with his. "I know. But you'll think of something. You always do."

Her confidence jolted him. Ever since the Kwadii had imprisoned them, he'd been trying to think up an escape plan but hadn't succeeded. With their execution imminent, he had a responsibility to his crew and the Federation to keep trying until he'd breathed his last breath.

He'd tried perusing Kwadii laws again during the early morning when Dora had fallen asleep. He'd come up with zilch. And Vax and Cyn hadn't found a way to overcome the technology or their guards. Zical had seen no weakness in the Kwadii defenses and their security teams seemed prepared to counter every scenario. Nevertheless, when the hovercraft stopped, Zical kept his eyes open, his mind alert.

Followed by armed guards, they exited directly into an oval stadium filled with Kwadii spectators. When the audience spied them, their dull murmur rose to cheers and shouts. Loud music played over an audio system as if they were the day's entertainment, and Zical bristled. How dare these people act as if taking the lives of his crew and his scientists meant no more than watching a holovid?

With the overwhelming security around them, fighting their way free was not an option. The only thing he could do for his people was to concentrate on acting courageously—and in the end, bravery meant little when his failure condemned them to death. Teeth clenched, jaw set, he kept his head high, seeking even the slimmest opportunity to escape.

Avanti met them wearing her sarong and sandals, and in addition she wore a ceremonial silver sash draped over her shoulder. Her gaze was carefully emotionless, but Zical still sensed the tension in her shoulders, and he suspected she cared more about their fate than she tried to let on, especially after she took one of his hands and one of Dora's, then squeezed lightly. She gestured to a central podium, surrounded by chairs filled with dignitaries on two sides. The Risorians garbed in silver and purple splendor took positions along one semicircular table, the Selgrens in bronzed and unadorned attire on the other. The two sides appeared to square off as opposing factions—but in truth both sides wanted the Federation people's execution.

Avanti spoke quietly, her tone threaded with sorrow she couldn't quite contain. Her hopelessness showed despite her attempt to appear optimistic and that fed Zical's own pessimism. "The trial will take place on center stage."

Zical had decided they should wear their golden togas and loincloths because he didn't want to die in a borrowed Kwadii garment. He stepped forward and nodded to Avanti, ignoring the towering execution machine with the cruelly sharp blade as best he could, certainly not an easy task. Apparently, the Kwadii beheaded those they believed had committed treason and the executions would take place one by one.

Determined not to show his concern, Zical stepped forward. Horns blared and the cheerful audience hushed. Soldiers' hands tightened on their weapons, as if expecting Zical's group to recklessly charge them. Avanti touched a button. Nothing happened that he could see.

Dora leaned forward and spoke in his ear. "Their force fields are like nothing in my experience."

With Dora more attuned to the alien machinery than he, Zical had to take her word, because the force field was invisible. Avanti didn't appear to have heard Dora, but touched a second button. The force field changed from transparent to foggy with sparks of white and green. "Any living creature who comes into contact with this force field dies." When she touched a third button, she lowered the shield, allowing them to go by.

After they passed, a soldier repressed the third button, raising the shield behind them, trapping them inside the field. When Avanti reached her people at the stage's center, she was admitted past yet another field, this one sparking gold and silver, that kept the Kwadii separate from those who stood accused. Within moments Zical's people were caged within the bubble, which turned transparent again. Without weapons, without the law on their side, they were like *masdons* being led to slaughter. But they weren't beasts, they were people. And they had done nothing to wrong the Kwadii. In fact, he believed they were fighting the same enemy. Their peoples should be allies, but he'd have only one opportunity to convince them.

Zical had read about the proceedings. Rogar, the chief prosecutor, would speak, and Avanti would defend them, then Zical would have an opportunity to talk. He'd prepared his words, but Avanti had warned him they would do no good.

However, if this were to be his last day, he intended to speak eloquently in defense of his crew and his people. How ironic that all his life he'd trained as a warrior, but now he was left with no weapons—except words. He vowed to make his statement powerful. Dregan hell. His best would have to be good enough or they would all die, and the Federation would have to send another mission to reprogram the Sentinel to stop the Zin—if they had time.

The second irony, that they were accused of the crime of helping the Zin when their mission was to stop a possible invasion, angered him. As Rogar called the trial to order, Zical's determination increased. He had to listen to every word. Catch every nuance. And search for a loophole in Kwadii law.

"Let the great Tirips protect us, guide our decisions, and see true into our hearts." Rogar spoke at the podium, using an incantation that must be a prayer. He and the Risorians stood and raised their eyes to the ceiling, crossed their wrists over their hearts in prayer. Oddly, the Selgrens stayed seated, remaining silent if not quite respectful as they stirred and muttered among themselves.

Two factions, obviously two different religious beliefs. But Zical expected help from neither side.

When Rogar finished the opening prayer, Avanti took a

turn at the podium, speaking with a brilliance that clearly
came straight from her heart. "This trial is for the people. Let
us make wise decisions based upon facts, not superstition."

The Risorians took her words as an insult. As one they
stood and gave her their backs. At least that's how Zical in-
terpreted their actions. The Risorians' demonstration revealed distaste, like what one would exhibit to an unruly
child who didn't know better.

So the rift between these Kwadii went deep into many
facets of their society, religious as well as economic. During
his readings into the law, Zical had seen many references to
Tirips. The Risorians believed they were the direct ancestors
of Tirips, the Goddess of the Galaxy, and they spent their
lives improving themselves spiritually and physically. To
mimic the perfection of Tirips was to win a place by her side
in the afterlife.

The Selgrens who didn't believe in Tirips seemed to do
most of the hard work on Kwadii. Yet for a reason Zical
didn't understand, the Risorians appeared to have the upper
hand, most of the wealth and more clout.

While Zical didn't mind the Selgrens and Risorians bait-
ing each other and mocking one anothers' beliefs, he didn't
want them so angry they couldn't focus on the trial. However, he could do no more than watch the proceedings in disgust when a man beside Rogar approached the podium.

"Who's that?"

Avanti couldn't help scowling at the man taking center
stage. "He's Rogar's son, Deckar Rogar Delari Hikai, heir to
the Fifth House of Seemar."

Deckar wore simple clothes for a Risorian, but then he
didn't need to draw attention to himself with elaborate clothing. The man was taller than the other Risorians. As powerful as a warrior, he strode forward with a light step that
belied his size. With his black curly hair and muscular body,
he could have been mistaken for a Rystani warrior, if not for
his fair skin.

Next to Zical, Avanti tensed like a tigress. Her fingers clenched the table's edge hard enough to cause her nails to turn white. Her expression savage, her mouth in a terse line, she glared at Deckar with an animosity that suggested these two had a history of clashing.

"What's wrong?" Zical asked Avanti.

"That slimy son of a sand worm has a voice that can make a curse sound like a prayer."

"And?"

"He's the Risorians' best hope of winning the next popular vote."

"What does he have to do with our trial?"

"Once he states his opinion, every Risorian will follow his recommendations."

Zical fought to understand the ramifications of her explanation. "So won't the Selgrens vote with us?"

"Maybe the men. Too many of our women fear war and the Zin, and that bastard will play on those fears." Avanti sighed. "I told you from the beginning that we could lose."

Zical had thought they'd lose on a point of law—not because a handsome Risorian used his presence to play upon the audiences' fears. But as the words rolled out of Deckar's mouth as dynamically as any holovid celebrity's, Zical watched faces turn starstruck. The man's charisma held the crowd. As Avanti had predicted, many of the ladies appeared enthralled, and his charm was almost hypnotic as he described the violation of hyperspace, the Zinatti symbols that suggested the intruders were in league with the enemy. He made a clear, concise case that almost made Zical believe they were a threat to Kwadii and deserved the death punishment for treason.

"Death," Deckar exhorted the audience.

"Death," they shouted back, the roar so loud it would be difficult to find anyone who disagreed.

One scientist gasped. Another one fainted again, and Shannon caught her, supporting the woman protectively against her chest until Vax came to her aid. A few prayed, their lips silently moving. But most waited with their spines ramrod straight, and he'd never been prouder.

Zical had to give Avanti credit too. She tried. When it was her turn to speak, she told them that the Zin were their mutual enemy. She spoke of the Federation peoples' ignorance of how the Zin could track through hyperspace, but the crowd who would vote on their fate had clearly already made up their minds and did not believe in their innocence. Head high, eyes sorrowful, Avanti sat frowning to more catcalls of "Death."

Finally it was Zical's turn. Before he left for the podium, Dora gave his hand a quick squeeze. While the rest of the crew sat quietly, their faces white and grim, Dora's eyes sparkled with encouragement. She still held out hope.

Zical tried to concentrate on his speech and ignore the legalese. He spoke with passion of their mission, their quest to find the Sentinel guarding the galaxy, admitting that the sign of the Zin was aboard their ship, but not because they were spies. Their intention was to stop the Zin from returning. He pointed out in clear concise language that the Zin and Zinatti might be the same enemy. And hoping to prey on their fears, he told the Kwadii that if they stopped his mission to protect not just the Federation but the whole of the galaxy from an ancient menace, their people would suffer along with the Federation's billions.

The Kwadii audience listened to his words. He might not have been as eloquent as Deckar or as passionate as Avanti, but he was no less determined. He didn't know the Kwadii as well as Avanti, but all sentient beings shared the common trait built into their DNA—a need to live long enough to procreate and ensure the survival of the species.

And finally he spoke more about the Federation, a union of worlds that had much in common with the Kwadii. A political system that allowed freedom and differences in values and political beliefs. He spoke of his sorrow at leaving Rys-

tan after the Endekian invasion, of his pride in settling on
the new world of Mystique, and how their people were
counting on them to complete their mission. Lastly he spoke
of the millions of worlds within the Federation, its power,
and how if the Kwadii executed their citizens, the Federation
would consider it an act of war. And finally he suggested a
treaty of peace between their peoples, one that would allow
them to focus their goals and unite their efforts on eliminat-
ing the threat from the Andromeda Galaxy.

Zical finished as he'd started. To the sound of silence. He
suspected with gut-wrenching tension that his words hadn't
reached them. He returned to his seat and Dora smiled at
him. "You were brilliant."

He clenched his hands into fists, then forced his fingers to
relax. Although he appreciated her compliment, he feared he
hadn't done enough. And when the vote came in, he steeled
himself.

Avanti and Deckar approached the podium, their faces
shifting with emotions he couldn't read. Together they read
the verdict. "Death."

"Death," the crowd chanted. "Death. Death. Death."

As if Zical's crew expected the death sentence, they con-
soled the scientists. Cyn wiped away one of the women's
tears. Vax clamped a steadying hand on Dr. Laduna's shoulder and Dora held on to the woman who'd fainted earlier.
Brave to the end, they didn't deserve their fate, Zical
thought, and a lump formed in his throat.

Deckar raised his arms and the audience calmed. Soldiers
with weapons double-timed through a lowered force field
that snapped up again immediately after their passing.
Deckar's voice remained smooth and charming, but threads
of his power charged the area. "The prisoners will climb the
dais."

The soldiers approached. Black helmets protected their
faces, and armor guarded their bodies. Behind them the second force field crackled back into place. The soldiers had at-

tached long sharp spears to their weapons, in case the prisoners needing prodding.

Zical considered going down fighting. His warrior nature
fought with his abhorrence of senseless death. Taking the
lives of innocent Kwadii soldiers, men who followed orders
and who neither set the laws nor made the decisions, seemed
a senseless gesture of violence. Instead, he preferred to set
an example for his people. He would face his death with
courage and dignity.

Determined to be the first to die, Zical stood, angry that he
had failed, disappointed he couldn't finish his mission, sorry
that so many good people would die for no reason. When
Dora placed a hand on his shoulder, he swallowed the lump
in his throat. He would die first, and perhaps he could give
everyone else a few more moments of life to prepare, to say
their good-byes and whatever prayers would help ease the
journey.

Full of anger and sorrow, Zical took the stairs, and when
he reached the execution platform, two soldiers grabbed his
arms while others kept weapons aimed at him. They led him
to a machine, forced him to kneel. As a man tied his hands
behind his back, another offered him a hood. He shook his
head, refusing the blindfold, and filled his gaze with the
sight of Dora.

Stars. Even with tears rolling down her cheeks, she was
one beautiful woman. He wanted the sight of her to be his
last view of this world.

Music played. Deckar offered yet another prayer but Zical
didn't listen. His mind was too full of what he'd failed to accomplish. Leaning forward, he placed his head into the con-
traption that would soon release a blade to fall and lop off
his head. He cared not what would be done to his body. Rystani warriors believed that when the body died, the spirit was
freed. Deckar's prayer ended. The music changed. And
Deckar began to count backward from eight.

Zical didn't look down but kept his gaze on Dora. She'd

paled and her eyes were raised to the blade, her expression filled with horror and shock. Shoving past the others, she raced to the dais, shouting, but he couldn't hear her words over the roar of the crowd, lost sight of her when she moved out of his line of vision.

"Seven," Deckar counted, his voice amplified by a microphone.

Zical glanced above him and saw that the blade didn't fall and slice cleanly as he'd suspected. It was coming slowly, sawing to and fro. He steeled himself for a painful death, knowing that physical pain couldn't match the agony of failure in his heart.

"Six."

A commotion in the crowd caught his gaze and he watched the bubbling group of humanity to distract himself from the descending blade. He wished Dora had remained where he could see her. But despite trying, he couldn't turn his head and she remained out of his sight.

"Five."

A child stepped through the crowd and walked toward the force field. Stars. It was Kirek! He was heading toward the killer shielding. Zical shouted for him to go back, but his voice couldn't be heard about the noisy crowd. What did Kirek think he was doing? He should have stayed hidden. Even if he somehow navigated the field, the soldiers would shoot him down. Or he would suffer the same fate as the rest of them.

"Four."

Kirek stepped through the force field. The shield sparked rays of green, shooting a bursting aura of color over the audience. The crowd went silent. The soldiers' aimed their weapons on the boy, about to fire.

"Three."

Zical looked up at the blade and regretted that Kirek would witness such a grisly sight and suffer the same fate. He had only a few more seconds of life. He braced for pain.

"He's Tirips's Oracle," someone in the crowd shouted.

In the center of the stage, the Risorians' expressions changed from astonishment to awe. Many faced Kirek and crossed their wrists over their hearts. Deckar ordered the soldiers to hold their fire. Someone dropped the shield separating the Risorians and the Selgrens from the Federation people. Risorians fought past the Selgrens to reach Zical on the dais, chairs crashed, people elbowed one another, and the entire arena erupted into shoving and pushing and fighting. Within seconds a riot ensued.

Deckar continued his morbid countdown. Avanti was shouting for the execution to stop, but the blade was still sawing closer to Zical's exposed neck.

Kirek strode through the second field and another sunburst of gold and silver shot out in rings. The crowd oohed and ahhed. Many gazes rose toward the heavens. More Kwadii crossed their wrists over their hearts while Selgrens booed and yelled catcalls. Kirek joined the scientists and Dr. Laduna scooped the boy into his arms. And Zical's crew moved toward him as if sensing this might be their chance to free him. But they'd never arrive in time.

"Tirips's Oracle," the crowd chanted. People ~~normunwil~~ ~~and Mimou.~~

Oracle? Cold metal lowered to his neck. Zical clenched his jaws, determined not to scream in pain.

The blade stopped sawing, barely bit into his skin. The pain was minimal. Blood dripped down his stinging neck, but he was very much alive.

Suddenly Zical felt a woman's hands helping to free him. Dora's hands. She untied him, and her tears of grief turned to joy. Then she was holding him, hugging him, kissing him.

Zical tucked her under his chin, confused about the sudden change of events. "What happened?"

"I smashed the critical circuits."

He grinned. "Good thinking. Thanks."

She'd stopped his execution. During the chaos and confu-

sion, she'd reached him before any of his more experienced
crew. Bravely, she'd fought through the crowd, and he owed
her his life. Dora had saved him.

But why hadn't the Kwadii soldiers stopped her? And
then as a hooded cleric grabbed the microphone and spoke a
prayer from the podium, he finally understood. The Risorians believed Kirek was holy. According to the cleric's,
words Kirek had exhibited godlike vigor. The Risorians apparently believed the Federation people were the Oracle's
disciples. They would be spared.

But the Selgrens disagreed that Kirek was Tirips's
Oracle—hence the rioting. And Avanti hurried to him and
Dora, her expressive eyes full of concern. "Nothing like this
has ever happened. You've been spared, but as glad as I am
to see that you will live, many Selgrens do not believe in
Tirips."

"What are you saying?" Zical asked.

Avanti bit her bottom lip. "On Kwadii it's often difficult to
tell who is a friend and who is an enemy. Be careful. Be
wary. Trust no one."

While Avanti's pleasure that their lives had been spared
appeared genuine, she obviously didn't believe Kirek was
Tirips's Oracle. As usual, people believed what they wanted
to believe. The Risorians had deemed Kirek Tirips's Oracle,
yet after witnessing the same event, Avanti's Selgrens
wanted to destroy the boy, just like they wanted to destroy
the Risorians' beliefs that kept them in poverty.

Zical didn't know what to think. Kirek had walked
through the force field that would have killed a normal person. Thanks to Kirek's ability to avoid registering on machines, they weren't going to die. They might have the
chance to finish their mission.

The scientists and his crew had protectively surrounded
Kirek, welcoming him back with great smiles of joy. Despite
the death sentence on their heads, they sensed they would
now live due to Kirek's actions. The force fields that had

previously trapped them now kept them safe from the rioting chaos around the arena. Dora and Zical pushed their way past confused soldiers back to their people. Dora kept her arm around Zical's waist as if she couldn't bear to release him, and Zical picked up Kirek.

"You were very brave, little man," Zical told the boy.

Kirek flung his arms around Zical, careful not to touch his wounded neck, and buried his face in his shoulder. "These Kwadii scare the pee out of me."

Dora laughed, her tone light.

Zical shook his head and grinned. "Me too. Thanks for showing up at exactly the right time."

Around the arena, the soldiers gained control over the violence. Many Risorians celebrated and prayed, yet clearly many Selgrens remained disbelievers. Deckar ordered a cordon of soldiers around Zical, Dora, Kirek, their crew, and the scientists, and the soldiers escorted them past the force fields from the arena.

Although Zical's relief that they'd lived to continue their mission was as great as that of his crew's, he'd already begun to plan for the future. Zical wished to go directly to their ship and leave Kwadii before anyone discovered that Kirek was a brilliant boy with the power to remain unaffected by scanners and sensors due to his birth in hyperspace.

But Zical didn't have an pportunity to speak with Deckar for several hours. Their happy group had been bundled into a military transport vessel and whisked across the city. Many of the scientists who had been seemingly stoic about their upcoming deaths now cried with happiness. Others said little, the emotional burden and shock stunning them to silence. However, almost everyone had thanked and praised Kirek for his bravery and the kid was all smiles, but appeared weary.

They arrived at a military compound about an hour later. Soldiers made them comfortable in new quarters very similar to the ones they'd previously occupied.

Supposedly the guards were now there to protect them against Selgrens who would wish them harm, Selgrens who didn't want the Risorians to gain more political power due to new converts who'd witnessed the miracle of the Oracle. But when Zical had asked for weapons to defend themselves, the captain of the guard had refused his request, saying his men would protect them.

Located outside the city, the compound was made up of several bunkers, apparently a refueling stop for automated convoys, and Zical suspected they were now even farther from his ship than they'd been since landing. Yet his hope to reboard his ship was high.

These quarters were perhaps more comfortable, but no less confining. The captain of the guard had requested they remain indoors for their safety. Zical wondered if they'd be shot if they tried to leave. At the moment, he wasn't willing to test how far their new status would take them, especially since hiding in the open pasture and fields that surrounded the compound would be difficult.

However, as they'd entered the fenced and shielded facility, he'd noted the coming and going of many vehicles. And he made note of the entrances and exits, wondering if he and his people could escape on one of the transports. If only Dora could contact Ranth, the computer might be able program a skimmer to take them back to the ship.

He put the idea on hold until he'd gathered more information. Meanwhile, grateful to be alive, with a new opportunity to finish his task, he tried not to believe that they'd become a different kind of prisoner. When Deckar invited his crew and scientists to dinner in a large conference room, Zical accepted, eager to find out if they were finally free to leave.

"Welcome, my friends and most holy Oracle." Deckar crossed his wrists over his heart as he acknowledged Kirek. "Please forgive our earlier misunderstanding. We did not hear your words until Tirips showed your power."

"Then you now agree to see us on our way?" Zical asked,

finding it difficult to put aside the bitter taste in his mouth. Deckar had almost had him executed. If not for Dora's quick thinking and Kirek's stunt, Zical would not be sipping a glass of wine or about to partake of the feast laid out on the table. That Deckar had switched sides was due to his religious beliefs and Zical couldn't trust the man's sudden about-face.

This hour, Deckar believed Kirek was the Oracle. Who knew what he'd believe tomorrow?

Deckar spoke. "According to the scrolls, Tirips's Oracle must stay to help the Risorians convert the nonbelievers. You cannot leave."

Chapter Fifteen

KIREK LEANED FORWARD. "Converting the nonbelievers is your task. Not *ours*."

Dora appreciated how Kirek emphasized that they were all in this together. He'd saved them all, a child, a brave and valiant soul. She couldn't seem to stop touching the boy. With her hand on his shoulder, she smiled down on him with proud affection, glad he'd done so well on his own. The nod of his head and the way he forced his eyes open indicated he was about to fall asleep on his feet, and she suspected he'd had little or no rest the previous nights. And when she tousled his hair and found a lump on his scalp, she wondered how much he'd suffered while alone.

"Oracle, I plead to differ," Deckar flipped a switch and several holoscreens revealed riots. "This is Baniken." Deckar's somber tone emphasized the images of the city.

Selgrens had taken over the streets, looting shops in the local markets. Any unlucky Risorian they caught suffered in the ensuing violence. In one clip, a group of Selgrens surrounded a skimmer, overturned it with their bare hands, and beat the unlucky occupants with bloody fists as they tried to escape. In another image authorities moved into the unruly crowd, spraying the rioters with chemical deterrents that froze the rioters in place until another squad collected the bodies. Yet another screen showed a group of kids dancing on the property of a wealthy Risorian homeowner who pulled out a weapon and fired, leaving three children dead and four others wounded.

Apparently Kirek had set off a storm of religious controversy that was tearing the different factions apart. The Selgrens, nonbelievers in Tirips, worked hard and played hard. They resented the Risorians who owned the land and who in their opinions did little but try to better themselves in Tirips's eyes and who lived off Selgren labor. Kirek's appearance on Kwadii was like setting fire to rocket fuel, igniting explosive undercurrents.

"We need your help, holy Oracle," Deckar pleaded, his voice commanding and grave.

Dora stepped forward and tucked Kirek under her arm. Her every protective instinct was out in abounding force. Kirek had saved the Federation people this day and the haughty Kwadii had no right to demand the boy's help. "The Oracle is exhausted. He needs rest."

Deckar frowned. "But—"

"He must rest," Dora repeated, and not waiting for permission to leave, escorted Kirek from the conference room before anyone tried to stop her.

"Thank you." Kirek held her hand tightly, and once they were out of view, Dora picked him up and carried him to his new quarters down a long hallway. Although guards were posted at the exits, she suspected there might be hidden mechanical listening devices but had seen no evidence of them. While she didn't want to pester Kirek with questions when he so clearly needed sleep, one question nagged. After she reached his room, she decided a full shower could wait until morning and settled for washing his face with a soft cloth. She tucked covers around him, and sat by his side. Keeping her voice easy and gentle and low, she pried, "What were you thinking to accomplish when you walked through that force field?"

"I'd heard about the Oracle earlier today. After I won credits at a local carnival, we had to run away from authorities."

"We?"

"I joined a group of kids to avoid detection."

"That was smart."

"We hid in a Risorian place of worship, a *lepach,* the First House. A high cleric made us welcome, offered us water to drink, and told us stories. One legend was how Tirips's Oracle would walk through the field of death to prove his singularity."

"And if you'd failed?" she asked, amazed that he'd planned the effect he'd had on the audience. Still, the risk had been great.

"I knew I could nullify the force field."

"I meant, what if you'd failed to convince the Kwadii that you were the Oracle?"

"Then we would have been together."

Troubled, she smoothed the covers. "You would have died with us."

"Better than living alone." His eyes fluttered closed but his tone remained sure.

"Kirek, you could have had a good life here. You would have made new friends."

"It would not have been the same."

She leaned forward and kissed his brow, shaken by his words. "No. It wouldn't have been the same. Thank you for saving us."

Dora doubted the child heard her. His breaths had turned deep and even, his pulse steady and slow. But he'd made her think about human bonds, which were not so simple to understand. The strongest bonds seemed to be those formed early in life and those of blood and shared exploits that involved life-and-death encounters, undoubtedly bonds made stronger due to the shared intensity of emotions. It wasn't necessarily logical, but it was there all the same.

If she'd been stranded on this world, she would have probably made a new life and new friends. But not a friend like Tessa. It didn't matter if she and Tessa couldn't speak or spend time together for months or years. When they did reunite, their friendship would pick back up exactly where they'd left off, with no awkward silences, no fears about being accepted for exactly who each of them was. Their friendship would withstand the test of separation over decades because the bonds they'd forged were stronger than *bendar*. A new friend would never have known the old Dora who'd been a computer, would never know her in the same way that Tessa did.

This child had taken up residence in a corner of Dora's heart due to his goodness, his willingness to risk his life, and she wanted to protect and coddle him in return. Were these maternal instincts evolving from her human DNA? She didn't know. But he was precious, precocious, and she knew the attachment forming between them would last a lifetime. If he ever needed her, she would be there, without hesitation.

And what of her connection with Zical? She had known him when she was still a computer and had formed an initial friendship that had not only deepened over time but that had broadened in scope to include a physical side. Making love had been one of the most treasured experiences of her life. And she wanted more. More physical bonding, more emotional bonding.

But what did he want?

Would he have made love if he hadn't believed they were about to die? She didn't know. The man was stubborn, but now that he'd had a taste of what they could be together, would he push her away again and attempt to revert to their former relationship? Or would he agree that they needed to spend more time together to determine if they were a good fit?

Thoughtful, Dora stayed with the sleeping child, reluctant to leave him alone. Not the least bit hungry, she had no desire to return to the conference room to eat. She'd suffered enough stress for one day and didn't need to listen to more endless debates.

Earlier, when Zical had been about to die, she'd been almost resigned to their fate. But the moment she sensed she could save him, she'd been frantic to stop the machine.

She'd thought her heart would burst through her chest as she shoved past people, furious at the confusion that made the soldiers so slow to obey orders. She'd knocked aside one man with an elbow jab to the ribs, kicked another who'd tried to hold her back, using techniques that Tessa had taught her. Of course, without her suit, the skills were not nearly as effective, but her adrenaline had kicked in, giving her superior strength.

At that moment, when she feared she wouldn't stop the blade in time, she would have gladly traded places with Zical. He meant so much to her that she would have given her life for his. She had no idea if the strong emotion was love. Love wasn't supposed to make one hurt, but at the time, she could feel Zical's pain as if it were hers.

She'd seen the blade slice Zical's neck a moment before she'd smashed the circuits. When she saw his blood, an overwhelming fear that she'd been too late crackled down her spine. Her legs turned all rubbery. Later, the knowledge he would live had brought her such joy that she'd shaken and cried with happiness.

The turn of events and the emotional highs and lows had left her as exhausted as little Kirek. In Kirek's bathing room, she removed her toga, showered, and crawled under the covers on her living quarters sofa, wishing Zical were here to enclose her in his strong embrace.

She wondered if he would come to her. Closing her eyes,

she was certain she would dream of him, dream of his handsome grin, his sparkling alexandrite eyes, and his mouth closing over hers.

"DORA. WAKE UP." Zical wasn't sure whether it was the urgency in his voice or perhaps his strong grip on her shoulders that awakened her. While he would never hurt her, he was too upset to be gentle. Luckily, she was one of those people who merely needed to open her eyes and her brain was already in gear.

"What's wrong?" She sat up, letting the sheet drop to her waist and grabbed her sarong. "Won't the Risorians let us go?"

"Kirek is missing."

She raced through the open door to where Kirek had been sleeping. The room was empty.

Her fingers fumbled with the knot at her waist as she dressed. Her big violet eyes flared with red alarm, leaving no doubt of her outrage. "What do you mean, he's missing?"

"After the Risorians insisted that the Oracle make an appearance on the holovid to ask for a cessation of violence, I went to wake Kirek. When he wasn't here with you in your quarters, I thought he might be with the crew, but he wasn't, so I returned to wake you."

"I left him sleeping." Ignoring her sandals, Dora skidded into her sleeping room. Perhaps Kirek had wanted to shower and didn't want to risk waking her. But he wasn't in her bath. Dora's hands clutched her hands into fists, her face pale with worry. "Maybe he's visiting with—"

Zical shook his head. "I checked with Dr. Laduna too. He's not with the scientists. He's not in this compound. And the guards claimed no one has gone in or out."

"Damn it," Dora swore, using curses she'd picked up over the centuries and whose origin he did not benow. "I was sleeping so deeply. I should have stayed awake—"

"That's ridiculous." Zical read the fear in her eyes, a fear that matched his own. He tried to comfort her. "You couldn't have known someone would take him."

Although the boy had an intelligence as high as any adult's, Dora had mothered him and he'd responded to her like a son. Zical supposed the relationship had been good for both of them. In many ways they had a lot in common. Both possessed a keen intelligence that set them apart from the average person. In addition, both appeared to be outwardly normal, which wasn't indicative of their unique natures. Dora had been born as a computer and now lived as a human. Kirek was born in human form, but hyperspace had enhanced his capabilities. Between his powerful psi and his extraordinary IQ, he'd never really been a child except physically. While Dora still bonded with her machines and Kirek avoided the machines' sensors, they'd become true friends. Both had unusual abilities that set them apart, so it was no wonder they'd taken to each other.

Although Kirek might have fooled the machines into letting him depart, the guards here were very much human, however. Zical headed back to the sentries to ask more questions. Perhaps one of them had left his post and the other had turned his back for a few seconds. Or perhaps the guards could be conspiring with those rioters in the city. Fighting to hold on to his temper and keep his voice even, Zical kept his tone low. "If Kirek's not here, maybe one of the guards is lying."

Dora placed a hand on Zical's shoulder and he slowed. "There're other possibilities. Perhaps someone took him out another way."

"Then you don't think he left voluntarily?" Zical had to ask the question, pleased that Dora was thinking through her fears, not panicking.

Dora frowned in anger. "Leave voluntarily? Stars. Yesterday, he risked his life to save us all and you think he'd leave without so much as saying good-bye?" Her expres-

sion of anger faded to fear and frustration. "He told me"—
her voice broke—"that he'd rather risk dying with us than
living here alone. Does that sound like he'd just wander
off?"

Dora banged her fist against the wall, took another step
and banged again. At first Zical thought she'd gone crazy in
her grief. But then he realized she was taking the initiative,
listening to the echoes, checking the main hallway for signs
of a fake door or a secret passageway.

The crew and scientists gathered as word of Kirek's disappearance spread. They fanned out, all of them searching
for a secret entrance. Meanwhile, the guards must have notified Deckar of the Oracle's disappearance. With no regard
for his personal safety, the man ran into their compound, his
movements graceful, his giant legs sliding to a stop before
their group. Deckar was one unarmed man among many
Federation people and they could easily have killed Deckar
before the Kwadii soldiers could save him, but the real concern on his face for the Oracle's whereabouts put them all on
the same side.

Deckar's suspicious gaze sought Zical and Dora. "You
saw to it that he escaped from us once before, shortly after
your arrival." Clearly the the guards had filled him in. "How
do I know you haven't done so again?"

"You don't." Zical and Deckar stood toe to toe, both men
bristling with anger. The Risorian might have an inch on him
in height, but Zical's chest and shoulders contained more
power. As a trained warrior, not a dilettante, Zical could take
the Kwadii down—but he didn't want a fight. He needed this
man's help and spread his arms wide to emphasize his
words. "However, we had no reason to send Kirek away." He
shot Deckar a searching look. "We believe we're among
friends and that you would do no harm to the Oracle."

"That is so." The tension in Deckar's shoulders eased and
he relaxed his clenched hands. "However, there are others on
Kwadii who do not believe in Tirips."

"You think the Selgrens took Kirek?" Dora didn't mince words.

"There are many possibilities. There are rumors about a Selgren fanatic, L'Matti, who wants to prove the Oracle is a fake. He's determined to bring down Risorian control of the council."

"Would L'Matti harm Kirek?" Dora asked.

"I don't know. The Oracle's presence has disturbed many nonbelievers and you've seen the violence on the streets of our cities. If the Selgren L'Matti has the Oracle, he might try to make him recant, then release the retraction to true believers. And the clerics might be just as vigorous in their testing to prove Kirek is truly Tirips's Oracle."

"He's just a little boy," Dora protested, her tone quivering with anxiety.

Deckar rubbed his forehead. "To all Risorians, the Oracle is Tirips's messenger. The Goddess speaks through the Holy Oracle. It's unlikely, but possible, he was taken by our most sacred order of clerics who would test him to verify—"

"What kind of tests?" Dora interrupted with alarm.

"I'm not sure."

"How would the clerics gain access to this compound and smuggle him out?" Zical asked.

"The holy orders are secretive but reputed to possess unusual powers. Normally, they don't interfere in our jurisdiction. But Tirips's Oracle would attract the interest of those who don't normally deign to speak with the rest of us who aren't so devout."

Dora's brows narrowed. "These tests—"

"The sacred clerics will not kill him," the Risorian said, but Deckar didn't sound certain.

"What if the Selgrens have taken Kirek?" Dora asked.

Deckar shrugged. "They would want to prove he isn't the Oracle."

"And how would they do that?" Zical asked, not really sure he wanted to hear the answer.

"Selgrens are unpredictable. I have a diplomatic call in to the council. They have yet to respond."

Zical was unsure that a call to the council and the Selgrens was a wise move. Without knowing who had taken Kirek, Zical couldn't tell who was friend or foe.

In addition to Zical's concern for the boy's safety, Kirek's disappearance added complications to their mission and delayed their journey, a holdup that might ultimately prove costly. With the mission already behind schedule, Zical hoped it was merely a matter of another few hours until they found Kirek and departed Kwadii.

With his own seething frustration at delay upon delay, Zical wondered what else could go wrong. He'd thought it only a matter of time until the Kwadii released them to continue on their quest. By now the Sentinel was likely long gone from its post, leaving the Zin free to enter the galaxy. Any more delay might prove disastrous.

"You have my full cooperation," Deckar told them. "I've ordered sensor scans for this past day rechecked. We will thoroughly interrogate all the guards and examine any discrepancies in their stories. And I've sent search parties in every direction."

Dora's eyes were blank. "Thank you. But we need to search for him with our ship. If you could remove the dampeners on our computer, we could make faster progress."

"I don't have that kind of authority." Deckar dashed Zical's hopes that the Risorian would go along with Dora's good suggestion. "And without the Oracle, your status here is once again suspect."

"FIRST, WE ESCAPE." Zical had called a conference, and it was a measure of his leadership skills that their people followed him without question. Each of them longed to leave the planet and continue their mission. All were frustrated and on edge. Dora watched the faces of the crew and scientists carefully as Zical spoke, yet despite their eagerness to leave Kwadii, discipline remained intact and all seemed determined to follow his orders. "Once we're free of this compound, then we go after three targets. Dr. Laduna, you and your people must seek out the holy clerics and learn if they have Kirek."

"And if he's there?" Dr. Laduna asked.

"Rescue him and bring him to the ship." Zical turned to his right-hand man. "Vax. See if you can find out more about the Risorians. Try to discover if Deckar's been lying to us and if Kirek is among them."

Vax frowned. "You think Deckar has Kirek?"

"It's the most likely scenario." Zical spoke thoughtfully. "We're on his home turf. Who better than the Risorians to take the Oracle? Deckar may have kept him for his own purposes, or turned him over to their clerics."

"It makes sense to cover both possibilities." Dora nodded, anxious to put Zical's escape plan into action. They'd already waited hours for darkness to arrive, but with every passing minute, Kirek could be taken farther away and hidden better. To think an abductor had slipped right past her to kidnap him was intolerable. Logic told her Zical was right and it was not her fault for failing to protect the boy. She'd had no reason to believe Kirek was in danger. However, the thought still didn't prevent the guilt from slashing her, and if they didn't find him safe, she might never heal.

"Dora and I will seek out Avanti and the Selgren L'Matti. Even if the Selgrens don't have Kirek, she may know which of her people would most likely abduct him."

"But will Avanti help us?" Dora asked.

"We'll deal with her when the time comes," Zical said, suspecting Avanti had been sympathetic to their cause, but had tried to distance herself to protect her feelings when she'd thought they'd be executed.

Cyn spoke over her shoulder, but the fingers of his chief engineer were busy with wires that Dora had found behind a wall panel during a search for Kirek. They still had no notion of how or why Kirek had been taken from them, but the investigation for a secret passageway had led to the discovery. Cyn believed she could use the nexus of wires to create a feedback loop into the Risorians' security hologrids to make the Risorians who monitored their "prison" from headquarters believe that they still remained inside.

Overcoming four guards shouldn't be a problem. Success would depend upon coordinating the attack on both exits without allowing the guards to signal for additional help. From there, they would split up, making their recapture more difficult.

In human form, Dora had never been part of such an endeavor and she was shocked by her physical response to the anticipation of danger. Despite her weariness, she was extra alert. Her muscles were tight, her stomach hard and churning. At the same time, she was filled with hope. For the first time they'd found a weakness in the Risorian prison. Soon, they would be free of their captors . . . or dead. Dora tried hard not to think about the second possibility. She was determined not to show her fear or allow it to stop her from doing whatever was necessary.

Zical spoke to his team leaders. "After you complete your investigation, rescue Kirek and return to our ship. The first team that arrives must find a way to nullify the dampeners, but don't activate the plan until we all arrive. Since we don't have communications, we must move quickly. All of us must meet at the ship within two days. Hopefully, one of our teams will have rescued Kirek."

And if not? Did Zical intend to leave the boy behind? Dora's heart thumped painfully as she realized that they might not have a choice. They couldn't stay free on Kwadii for long and the mission must continue.

So many things could go wrong that Dora's head whirled with them. The Risorians might shoot them the moment they stepped outside. Even if they got away, they might never find

Kirek. The Risorians or the Selgrens could recapture them. And even if they succeeded, the likelihood of returning to their ship and getting away from Kwadii seemed farfetched. Then, if they made it back into space, she saw nothing to prevent the Kwadii from following and using the tractor beam to recapture them once again.

Yet she hadn't thought of a better plan than Zical's. She needed Ranth, wished she could use his massive brain power to help them solve some of the technical problems and to co-ordinate communications. But Ranth remained locked in his vault, hiding from the dampeners. The tenuous connection she'd shared with him was fading. Although she'd attempted to reestablish communications, she'd been so upset about the missing Kirek that her mind hadn't been totally focused.

Zical seemed to know how off balance she was. He hadn't asked much from her during the planning stages of their escape, but Dora was determined to contribute. However, compartmentalizing her emotions from her intellect as a human was a very complex process. Before she'd become human, she'd worried about her friends, but she could isolate those concerns so they didn't interfere with her thoughts. The human brain was more organic, one section spilling into the others. Although she attempted to focus on the escape, staying to Zical's left and slightly behind him during the walk toward the guards, worry over Kirek never left her thoughts for long.

She fretted about the tests his captors might put him through. Although he'd already survived being alone on an alien world, his childish body wouldn't stand up to adult stresses. The thought that anyone might hurt him sickened her. And she worried that Cyn's feedback loop wouldn't work to cover their escape from those monitoring from afar.

As if sensing her distress, Zical placed an arm over her shoulders. "Please, at least try not to frown."

Zical's arm comforted her and she drew courage from his sympathetic tone. Obviously, she could hold up better, and she tried a breathing exercise that Tessa claimed helped to neutralize muscle tension. Dora breathed in deeply through her nose and out through her mouth. If her muscles relaxed a bit, she didn't perceive a difference. However, since she'd tucked the top of her toga into her skirt's waistband, the exercise of expanding her lungs distracted the male guard by calling attention to her bare breasts.

Her inadvertent breathing exercise might be just the edge they needed. As a warrior Zical could take advantage of the guard's continued distraction. So she breathed deeper, then arched her spine, knowing the action would lift her breasts.

While the guard gawked at her chest in admiration, Zical flattened him with a one-handed strike to the throat. As the man fell, Zical released Dora's shoulder and front-kicked the second guard's chin. Both guards fell unconscious and Vax and a few scientists tied their hands behind their backs and gagged them, before lugging them into the conference room and locking them inside. Meanwhile Dora confiscated their weapons and changed into a modest Risorian garment to attract less attention. When the men returned, she handed one gun to Zical and the other to Vax.

Finally, Zical pried open the door. They'd waited until dark, but the temperature outside remained hot. The air smelled of sweet grass, herbal spices, and the overwhelming bold floral aromas of nearby flowering trees. Moments after she stepped outside, her toga stuck to her, but she nevertheless kept the top on while they raced across the Risorian turf.

Vax and his people were departing out the other exit and starting down a dirt path as the scientists headed away from Zical and Dora, using a building for cover before advancing toward the city. In preparation for the journey, they'd all drunk as much liquids as they could hold, but in this heat, finding water would always be a priority. Anyone who stayed outside all night would quickly dehydrate and weaken.

Vax led his team out the back entrance and planned to

head north. Dr. Laduna's group headed in the opposite direction. Zical was about to lead Dora west and into the woods when she spied a two-person skimmer. "Over there."

He shook his head. "We don't have the code."

"Maybe I can override it."

"It's too dangerous." He tugged her toward the trees.

She tugged back. "Walking through a forest in this heat is dangerous. Come on."

He allowed her to persuade him and stood guard, the weapon at his side. She popped the door and crawled into the driver's seat, wishing she could connect with Ranth and hoping no one saw the interior light that had switched on automatically when she'd put her weight in the seat. At the sight of a color-coded keypad, she grinned.

Within moments, she'd pried off the plastic pad and pulled two wires loose. It took only a few seconds to twist the wires together to complete the circuit.

"Hurry," Zical whispered. "Someone's coming."

She didn't look up but knew from his tone that she hadn't much time. "I'm almost done here." She snapped the keypad back into place and shoved open the passenger door. "Get in."

"You're driving?" He eyed her with dismay. No pilot ever liked anyone in charge of a vehicle except themselves, or perhaps another pilot.

"It would look strange if we suddenly switched places."

No alarms had gone off. At least none they could hear. And there were no signs of pursuit. The men in the distance kept walking and continued into a building. "The longer we go undiscovered, the more time we all have to get away."

Zical snapped a chest harness across himself. "Fine."

Dora gunned the motor, expecting to go forward. They boosted straight up.

"Damn."

Her stomach rose into her throat and she wished Zical were driving. To give him credit, he didn't try to tell her what to do, but clenched the weapon, his knuckles white. She had to figure out the stick fast before they crashed. In the Federation, most vehicles had simple controls. Move a stick right, the vehicle went that direction. Move it left and it went left.

However, the skimmer used a tricky combination of foot and hand controls that took a few tries to figure out. The vehicle was dropping fast, too fast. When they almost dived into a tree, Zical's breath hissed, but he didn't complain, even as branches scratched the skimmer's underside.

But once she finally gained control and put the skimmer into a sweeping curve over the compound before heading south toward the city lights, he made an odd choking sound, as if someone were strangling him.

"Are you all right?" she asked, looking back over her shoulder for signs of pursuit. But she saw none.

And she realized that he wasn't choking. He was chuckling.

"What?" She frowned. "What's so funny?"

"I was thinking about your breasts."

"Why?"

"They're a secret weapon."

"Huh?"

"That guard never stood a chance."

Zical kept chuckling, but Dora was damn irritated. She didn't see what was so amusing. For months she'd wanted Zical to admire her breasts. Now finally he was thinking about them—as a weapon. And he hadn't said one word of praise about her mastering the skimmer controls.

Men—they could be incredibly annoying.

She didn't know whether to be angry, frustrated, or upset. So she compressed her lips and concentrated on flying.

Chapter Sixteen

DORA FLEW OVER the city and looked for a place to set down the skimmer. In the dark, the pink buildings all looked as if they'd been cast from the same mold and their backlit windows reminded her that despite the riots in the streets, people ate and slept, made love, took care of their children, and argued with their mates. In the morning they would rise, bathe, and go to work in a comforting pattern of stability among family and friends and coworkers.

But Kirek would be alone. He'd left his parents and his world behind and now he was with strangers—strangers who, according to Deckar, might treat him badly. She'd hoped to find the boy quickly, but with no idea of who had taken him, a random search seemed unlikely to reunite them.

Her fear for Kirek's safety made her less cautious. Instead of setting down on the outskirts of the city where they would be apt to land unnoticed, she'd opted to save time by heading straight into the heart of Baniken. When she spied a wide-open park, she steered toward a clearing.

The skimmer suddenly jerked, the stick slammed into her hand. Her pulse sped and her mouth went dry. "Did I hit something?"

Zical peered out his window, his tone as casual as a tour guide's. "They're shooting at us."

Smoke spiraled behind them and the pedals beneath her feet turned to mush. "We're going down."

The skimmer spun, the engine sputtered, and she fought to turn into the spin. Gaining only a minimum of control, she veered toward the park, but they weren't going to make the clearing. She spied a pond and had to ditch that idea too. Spinning crazily, she fought the controls, tried to keep the skimmer from plunging into a straight dive.

"There." Zical pointed. "Land on the roof."

"If we miss, we're dead."

"If we land at ground level, we're dead," he argued. "They've mobilized an army down there. They've been tracking us."

Dora barely heard his words. One life-threatening problem at a time was all she could handle. More shots were fired and most of them missed, but several ricocheted against the skimmer's belly. Any moment she expected a projectile to slice through. The bottom must have been armored. No shots entered the cab.

But one cracked the windshield, shattering, the fragments torn aside to leave a gaping hole. Hot wind roared through the tiny craft, and as she tried to set down on the roof, it felt as though a giant fist lifted them up, then slammed them into a wall. She must have blacked out for a few seconds. When she opened her eyes, smoke poured through the skimmer. She hung by her shoulder harness, the craft tipped onto its side, all the blood in her head pounding.

Next to her, below her, Zical sat so still that she feared for his life. With a shaking hand, she felt for a pulse and relief washed through her at the strong steady thumps. Praying he didn't have an injury she couldn't see in the dark, she shook him.

"Zical. Come on. Wake up. We have to get out of here. Before the skimmer explodes. Or we burn alive." All the while she talked, she was unbuckling her belt, thrusting open the door over her head, wondering how in hell she could pull him up and out if he didn't recover consciousness.

Zical grunted, groaned. Even in the dim light, she could see his eyes open and then smoke swept through the skimmer and breathing filled her mouth, burned her eyes, and choked her lungs. She coughed. "You hurt?"

"Don't think so." His voice was groggy and he began coughing too.

Flames burst, a reddish-orange array of sparks and fire. In the light of the hellishly hot blaze, she grabbed the edge of the open doorway and pulled herself upward. From below, Zical boosted her feet with a strength that shot her out of the top, and tumbling free, she banged her shoulder and scraped her knee on the way down. Pain dazed her. Her knee hurt like stabbing knives, and she blinked back tears of frustration. She had intended to turn around on the top, reach in and help pull out Zical, but now she couldn't help him. However, a moment later he climbed out by himself and landed beside her, his face streaked with smoke.

"We have to go. Now," Zical ordered.

He helped her limp toward a rooftop door, lifted his weapon to pound on it, but when she tugged on the knob, it opened. They'd just stepped onto a stairwell when the skimmer exploded in a fiery roar that deafened them. Too late, she clamped her hands over her ears.

The ringing made her words seem as if they came from a distance. "Maybe they'll think we're dead," she suggested, taking his hand, determined not to complain about her knee that stung and burned like fire.

She turned to look over her shoulder and saw skimmers

about to land. Ignoring the pain in her knee, she descended
into the building with Zical, followed by yells of pursuit.

KIREK AWAKENED AND instantly knew he was no longer
with his friends. It was too quiet, too dark. Something was
very wrong. His mouth was dry, his tongue swollen, but not
from thirst. He suspected he'd been drugged, and by the
hunger in his stomach, he guessed he'd stayed unconscious
for at least a day, maybe more.

The last thing he remembered was talking to Dora and
falling asleep in the cool Risorian compound. He'd felt a
prick of pain in his neck. A shot? He touched the tender spot
and winced. Now certain he'd been drugged, he blinked
away the last of his grogginess, his alarm escalating.

Once again he was alone. And he hated that tears filled his
eyes. After reuniting with Dora and Zical, he'd felt as though
he'd come back to his temporary home. While Miri and Etru
were his family, Dora and Zical were like a dear aunt and un-
cle. Losing them a second time hit him hard. He wanted to
shout in frustration.

He'd thought that since the Risorians believed him the Oracle, they would release all of them, allow them to continue
the mission. Loneliness and frustration boiled up in Kirek
but he forced himself to use his best asset—his brain.

Think.

It was hot here and he strained to see in the darkness.
Slowly his eyes adjusted and he made out walls, a sofa where
he'd been sleeping, a desk. He appeared to be in an office or
study with an attached bathing facility.

He stood with care, letting his system fight off the remaining sleeping drugs, which had left his mouth dry and his
mind groggy. But his head was clearing fast. Fear and adrenaline and a need to survive had a way of readying the weak-
est muscles to fight or flee.

However, there was no one to fight, even if he'd been big

enough or strong enough to do so. He groped for the door handle and found it locked. Fleeing wasn't an immediate option.

Questions burned in his mind, the foremost being, Who had taken him and why? The Risorians had wanted him to call for peace. Had they separated him from the others in an attempt to force him to do as they wished? Or had another of the warring factions wanted the Oracle for a purpose of their own?

Clearly, whoever had taken him wanted something or he would be dead. That thought gave him the courage to explore the desk, where he found a computer system. "Computer on," he ordered, expecting the connection to remain dead.

When the vidscreen flickered on and the lights in the room brightened, he was pleasantly surprised. A man whose face he'd never seen before came up on the vidscreen. He possessed serious dark eyes with too many circles under them, lots of wrinkles, and a stern demeanor. With none of his body or clothing visible, Kirek couldn't guess which faction he represented.

"You are safe, Oracle."

Kirek folded his arms over his chest. "Why have I been taken from my people?"

"Oracle. We mean to commit no sacrilege, but our need to verify your singularity is great."

At the man's words, Kirek fought not to tremble. He recalled Deckar's words and the tests the clerics wanted him to pass. Tests that Deckar had implied would be unpleasant at best, and could possibly mean his death if he failed. However, Kirek knew better than to show fear. The Kwadii believed that Tirips's Oracle would not fear death ... or torture.

From his studies he knew that all religious doctrines were based on faith, and despite his distress at his circumstances, Kirek understood that a haughty attack might be his best defense among nonbelievers and believers alike. "You lack faith?"

"We seek truth."

"I don't listen to double-speak." Kirek deliberately insulted his captor and spoke in his most demanding tone, one he hoped didn't resemble a whine. "Bring me sustenance and drink. Then we will talk further." He turned his back on the vidscreen, hoping his tactic would work.

If he were full grown and a warrior like his father, when the door opened and someone brought food, he could attack, escape, flee. But limited by his child's body, Kirek had to depend upon his brains. While he could consistently fool scanners into false readings, he was certain his captors were aware of his abilities and would post living guards about these quarters.

He had three options. He could refuse to speak. He could lie and deceive. Or he could cooperate. As he waited for food, he mulled over his choices and decided he didn't have enough data to draw a valid conclusion. Refusing to speak wouldn't gain him much knowledge about his captors.

And if they caught him in just one lie, a deception could blow out what little faith these people seemed to have. Perhaps the truth would serve Kirek best. A slot in the wall of his room opened and he helped himself to the tray laden with food. Unfortunately, he saw no one and still had no clue as to who held him here.

Sensing the impatience of his captor to question him, Kirek ate slowly, hoping to provoke agitation in the captor that would lead to mistakes that might give him a clue how much to say. With his belly full, he set the tray back into the wall niche and returned to the vidscreen.

"What do you want of me?"

"You are Tirips's Oracle?"

"Yes."

"Why have you come to Kwadii?"

"I go where Tirips sends me."

"For what purpose?"

"To serve Tirips."

"And how do you serve?"

"In whatever capacity Tirips deems best."

"Oracle. Many nonbelievers doubt you are the Oracle."

"Did I not prove myself by walking through your death fields as your legends predicted?"

"Perhaps you employed superior technology."

Kirek turned around slowly, his arms raised in the air. "Do you see technology on my person? Do your sensors see more than flesh and bones standing before you?"

"The nonbelievers among us need more proof," his questioner stated, with a weariness that was difficult for Kirek to read.

Was the man tired of speaking in circles? Did he doubt every word Kirek spoke? Or was he irritated with his superiors for putting him in a position where he must question the Oracle? Kirek didn't know but kept his voice authoritative.

"Can you tell us why Tirips sent you now?"

"I am only the messenger. Tirips does not explain herself to me."

"And what message do you have for the Kwadii?"

"Tirips doesn't approve of her children committing violence against one another or against others. She would have the Kwadii at peace."

"So your task is to convert the Selgrens?"

"Putting words in the mouth of your Oracle is sacrilege," Kirek warned sternly.

"I apologize. I merely try to understand."

"Understanding isn't necessary. Obedience is." Kirek wearied of the conversation. He had no idea if he was truly Tirips's Oracle. Perhaps he was. He certainly had fulfilled the prophecy. After he and his friends visited the cleric, Kirek had known what must be done. Who was he to say Tirips had not put ideas in his mind?

"And what would Tirips have us do?"

"The Kwadii must find Nevanna or you will never have peace."

"Nevanna?"

"Yes."

"And where is Nevanna?"

"Tirips did not say."

"And what does Nevanna have to do with peace on Kwadii?"

"I do not know, but I have told you all. My mission is done and I must be free to go. Tirips has other plans for me."

"You cannot leave Kwadii." The man's expression turned to one of horror.

"Why not?"

"If you leave, legend says we will tear ourselves apart."

"Only if I leave in spirit will you fall. As long as the Kwadii believe, as long as you obey Tirips's laws, the Kwadii will survive."

"Oracle. We need you to help convert the Selgrens."

"Tirips has other plans for me." Kirek kept his tone even, his face grave. "To block my path is to block Tirips's path."

At his threat, the man paled, but then as if remembering his job, he squared his shoulders. "What proof do you offer of your singularity?"

Kirek had no answer and so restrained a heavy sigh and countered with a question of his own. "If Tirips herself stood here before you, what would convince you to believe?"

"Please answer my question."

Kirek closed his eyes. "Your questions tire me. Either believe or don't. The consequences are yours to face and do not matter to me."

What mattered was whether he would be kept here until his body grew weak, whether Kirek could hold firm until he was released. Kirek had no doubts that the interrogation would continue, that his every word was being recorded. Eventually the pressure and stress might cause him to make a mistake or error in judgment. One slipup and everything would be undone.

Kirek's best hope was that Dora and Zical would come to his rescue. But even if they could free themselves, how would they find him?

DORA AND ZICAL ran through a set of double doors and into a long hallway lined with soft flooring, recessed lighting, and a colorful mosaic between many closed doors. The building could be residences or offices or a school. She couldn't read the curlicue symbols on the doors that they raced past.

The corridor seemed endless. They turned right, left, and left again before the hallway widened. People, Risorians, she guessed by their elegant mode of dress, waited patiently in front of four sets of double doors. Hearts pounding, fearing someone would discover their real identities and shout for soldiers to arrest them, Dora and Zical slowed their pace and joined the back of the line.

Dora was certain that any moment, someone was going to recognize them, but in their Risorian clothing they didn't stick out. No one appeared to notice them except one small pink-haired child who hid behind her mother's legs. Couples spoke in low tones. Two teenagers couldn't keep their hands off each other, and a younger man helped an older woman stand, protectively keeping his hand on her elbow.

When the double doors ahead opened with an almost silent swish, the line moved forward. People entered a large hexagonal compartment and then turned around to face the opening. As the last ones to board, Dora and Zical were nearest the doors when they closed.

Dora expected the transport device to move sideways, but it dropped straight downward. She prayed that when the doors opened, the soldiers they'd seen outside wouldn't be aiming guns at them. When the compartment stopped moving, the doors opened on another level that looked like the one they'd just departed. But instead of soft lighting and mosaic walls, here the lighting was brighter and the walls were of pink stone.

Two people exited, leaving more room within. They dropped again, and this time when the doors opened, Dora stared wide-eyed and Zical had to tug her into the crowded transit station. She suspected from the large cavernous feeling they were underground. Crowds hurried to an assortment of platforms where long tubular pill-shaped compartments with seats whisked passengers out of the terminal while others entered to unload.

Despite the subterranean locale and huge overhead fans, the blowing air was quite warm. Dora spied a fountain where people stopped to drink and led Zical there. She drank deeply, the cool water on her parched throat quenching her thirst and rehydrating her body.

"Now what?" she asked, wishing they knew where Kirek was, but feeling less vulnerable among the crowds where no one paid them the slightest attention.

"Pick a transport," Zical told her. "We need to disappear before those soldiers think to look for us here."

As if saying the words had summoned them, soldiers marched down a set of moving stairs. Dora's pulse raced. Every nerve, every instinct told her to run. And yet her brain understood that running would call attention to them. She couldn't recall ever being so at war with her mind.

It was logical to stay hidden among the crowds. To move at the same speed as the others. But when she caught sight of those soldiers, her legs quivered with the need to flee. However, even when she lost control, Zical kept an arm around her waist, guiding her toward a transport and keeping their faces turned away from the soldiers.

She was grateful for their Risorian clothing. This planet didn't have offworlders. They executed them all.

Luckily, the crowds were thick enough for them to hide.

The terminal was shoulder-to-shoulder crowded, and people were too intent on arriving at their own destinations to notice strangers among them.

Zical plunged into the thick of the crowd toward a transport so overfilled that people had to stand. Dora noted the last cubicle didn't have windows and pointed her chin toward it. "Let's take that one."

"Fine."

They ducked inside, using the crowd for cover. Dora wondered what kind of payment was required for the fare, but there was no machine or slot for a credit chip barring their way. Perhaps transportation was free on Kwadii.

The moment they entered, the door closed behind them, and as Dora climbed the three steps inside, she expected to see rows of seats and other people. But the capsule remained empty, reminding her of a private luxury spacecraft.

There was a bed decorated with a sumptuous silver blanket with maroon threads and matching pillows at the far end and cooking facilities with a table at this end. She peered into a tiny cubicle and marveled at the compact shower and voiding lounge. And between was a comfortable seating area that contained a vidscreen, printed materials, sculptures, and two padded lounge chairs on swivels.

"This must be a private transport." Zical came to the conclusion the same moment she did.

"Without security?"

"The only locks I've seen on this world were the ones that kept us in."

Dora thought back to the doors in the building they'd just escaped. Zical was right. There were no locks. But could the soldiers track them in here as they had when they'd taken the skimmer? Or perhaps this compartment wasn't owned privately, but available for hire.

"We should leave." Zical began to turn back.

"Wait." Dora approached the vidscreen. "Computer on."

A woman's face peered back at her. "How may I serve?"

"We don't wish to be found."

"You require privacy mode?"

"Yes."

"Privacy mode activated."

Immediately all outside sound ceased to penetrate the transport's thick walls. Zical waited, hesitant to interrupt her conversation with the computer.

"What does 'privacy mode activated' mean?"

"You will not be disturbed. Doors are locked. I require a payment of—"

"Charge it to Rogar Delari Hikai, heir to the Fifth House of Seemar."

The machine would now ask for identification verification, a thumbprint, a retinal scan, a voice code. Dora thrust her psi into the wiring, adjusted a few circuits and withdrew. Normally she considered this kind of alteration an illegal entry, but these were desperate circumstances. Rescuing Kirek and completing their mission to reprogram the Sentinel to guard against the Zin was worth a little computer subterfuge.

"Account charged."

Zical grinned and took a seat in a lounger. "We are searching for Tiripo's Oracle."

"The Oracle . . . is being tested by the Selgren L'Matti."

Dora had never expected an answer. If the computer knew where to find Kirek, then Deckar must have known it too. So why had he pretended ignorance? Could Deckar be in league with Kirek's abductors? It made no sense for the Risorian to be in league with a Selgren. Perhaps Deckar hadn't truly known where Kirek had been taken when they'd last spoken and had no way to contact them since their escape. Or there might be another angle she had yet to consider.

"Can you take us to the Selgren L'Matti and the Oracle?" Dora asked.

"Yes."

"We need to leave immediately," Zical ordered, and the

compartment hummed, then settled into a soothing vibration as they began to move. "How long until we arrive?"

"Two days."

Dora frowned, worried that Kirek would be separated from them for so much time. And Zical had ordered the teams to meet back at the *Verazen* within two days. If they pursued Kirek, they would miss his own deadline. "That's too long. How fast if we take a skimmer?"

"Traveling by skimmer is forbidden."

"Why?"

"Skimmers pollute the air. Travel by sub is the quickest route to your destination."

"Fine. Take us to a sub," Zical demanded.

"What about your orders to rendezvous in two days?" Dora asked, glad he hadn't hesitated to go after Kirek.

"Vax won't leave without us." Zical sounded certain, so she put that worry from her mind.

"You are in a sub," the computer told them. "Would you care to implement see-view mode?"

"Can we see out without others looking in?" Dora asked.

"Of course."

"Then implement see-view."

Dora expected a vidscreen to appear in a wall, or maybe for the roof to show the sky. Instead, all the walls, ceiling, and floor turned transparent, revealing a sea of molten scarlet lava and burning gases of phosphorescent orange and golds.

"Oh, my. It's beautiful." She stared outside, marveling at a craft that could transport people through boiling lava. No wonder the Kwadii world was so hot. Beneath the crust flowed seas of smoldering lava that the Kwadii had harnessed and employed to transport themselves around their world. "I've never heard of this mode of transportation."

"Look." Zical pointed outside to a wide-winged creature with multicolored eyes that swam through the lava as easily as a bird flew through air.

Dora stepped closer to Zical. "Just think. We're all alone."

"And?" Zical's dark eyebrows arched upward with humor that touched his eyes and she caught a glimpse of longing behind his I'm-always-in-control, the-mission-comes-first demeanor. Was his desire real or an illusion she'd wanted to see? Yet, illusion or not, his glance captured her, drawing her in like a meteorite caught in the gravitational pull of a planet.

"We have nothing to do for two entire days."

"What about Kirek?" he asked.

"I'm worried about him too. But there's nothing we can do for him until we arrive."

"And?" Leaning closer, she brushed her fingers gently over his brow, his cheek, his jaw. At her tender caress, his eyes darkened, the deep violet turning molten, and his heat stirred her excitement.

Her words sounded carefree, light and breathy with desire. "Remember how I told you that sexual experience helps me to contact Ranth?"

"And?" He teased her with a low, husky voice that haunted her dreams. Only once before had he used that kind of heated tone, when they'd made love. And it seemed like a lifetime ago.

Her body quickening in anticipation, she grinned. "Well, don't you think we should try to strengthen the connection?"

Chapter Seventeen

A MAN COULD take only so much. Most Rystani warriors would have snapped long before now. Zical considered his caution a measure of inner strength. Most men would want Dora for her physical attributes alone. With her knockout curves, her gorgeous skin, and her flawless lines, she could have been a holovid star. To her credit she employed more than her looks to go after what she wanted. Her intelligence was off the chart. With all else perfection, her emotional vulnerability, her newness at being human, had held him back.

But Dora had changed and grown during this journey. Even as the blood roared in Zical's ears, he understood she no longer needed coddling. He recalled the very first time he'd heard Dora's sexy voice when she'd still been a machine and how it had summoned him on a primitive level. He recalled numerous conversations where she'd teased and taunted and insinuated how much she wanted to make love. He recalled how she'd been more than ready for her first sexual experience, proving that all her flirting had reflected her true nature, especially when she'd given as good as she took.

But she still didn't understand the primal savagery of his response to her. She had yet to experience making love to his true primitive self. During her first time, he'd held back.

As she teased him with soft words, taunted him with tender caresses, a bubble of need burst. She wanted to push him? Fine. He could even justify letting loose for the good of the mission because she believed orgasms strengthened her psi. Holding back no longer made sense, so she'd damn well better be ready for what she'd unleashed.

Hands that should have gently pushed her away yanked her closer, seeking out the silky curve of the nape of her neck. At his rough grasp, her eyes flared with surprise then burned with excitement while her contradictory textures of silky flesh over toned muscle intrigued, inflamed, and fascinated. Every cell in his body demanded he take all she offered. And more.

His voice came out roughened and harsh and he did nothing to ameliorate his savagery. "You want to make love to strengthen your psi in hopes of contacting Ranth?"

"Yes." She shimmied her hips against him, flung her arms around his neck, and attempted to tug his head down for a kiss. "But that's not my only reason," she assured him.

"And the other reason is?"

"I want you."

She didn't pretend and he adored that about her. "I'm glad you know what you want."

At the pure satisfaction in his tone, she boldly allowed a soft chuckle to escape. And then she tried to turn the tables on him by questioning his motives. "And will you deny that you want me for reasons all your own?"

"It is not your place to question my reasons."

"If you say so." She nibbled a path along his collarbone, shooting heat straight to his groin. Her inclination to touch when she wished, initiate whatever she desired, was not on his current agenda. And oh, yeah, he most definitely had an agenda. Capturing her wrists in one hand, he held them apart. "You've never understood Rystani ways. But you're going to learn them now."

"It's about damn time." Ever playful, she batted her eyelashes at him and made no attempt to free her hands.

"This is your last chance to change your mind."

"Like that's going to happen when all along I've been trying to—"

"Since we are not wed and you do not wear my bands, we'll have to improvise." He released one hand, tugged her behind him, and searched the sub for suitable material. During a Rystani marriage ceremony, a woman accepted bands that allowed her husband to control her body with his psi in the areas between those bands. Most men banded their woman's foreheads, wrists, and ankles. In return the brides were allowed to place one band on the husband. The man's band was symbolic—since with only one, there was no space between.

On their one night together, Zical had kept his passions reined. It had been her first experience and there was no point in following custom if one was to be executed as he'd expected. And while Dora was inexperienced, she'd been exposed to the customs and sexual practices of many worlds. However, he was Rystani through and through. He believed in the old ways.

Now she would experience what it was to accommodate his every desire. And she and Zical would discover her true nature.

She pointed to ties that held the pillows in place on the bed. "Will those do?"

Another woman might have fought the idea of bondage, but Dora not only seemed turned on by the notion, she was urging him on and making suggestions. Her willingness to comply stunned him, until he remembered that she had no idea how far he was about to go. Or how little say she would have during their encounter.

The notion of having her completely at his mercy shattered the very last of his reserve. She would be his. However he wished, in whatever manner he decided. The delicious power fueled his desire, pumping him with a savage need to plunder. Only a tiny speck of sanity kept him from ripping off her clothing.

Releasing her wrist, he folded his hands across his chest. "Take off your garment."

"Yes."

Dora could be more quickly naked than any woman he'd ever known. She had no modesty regarding her body, and he expected the clothing to drop to the floor within seconds.

However, a saucy smile twitched across her lips and she allowed her fingers to play with the knots at her shoulders that kept the garment on her body. As if sensing his impatience, she deliberately upped the tension by complying—even as she made him wait.

Ever so slowly, she untied the knots while she boldly held his gaze. And finally, when the knots were loose, she peeled down the top showing one inch of cleavage at a time. Clever minx. Once again she was attempting to take control. But she would learn

Before she slid the top down to show her nipples, he stopped her with a gentle tap on her wrist. "Hand me the ties."

He thought it fitting and symbolic that she should hand him the ties that he would use to bind her. At his command, she didn't so much as raise an eyebrow.

And when he tied her wrists behind her back, leaving her clothing covering the essentials but ready for him to uncover whenever he so wished, she did not struggle but leaned forward to ease his task. Oh, she seemed compliant, but her body was already stirring with needs.

And he had no doubt that before long she be wishing she'd obeyed him and taken off her garb at his first command.

* * *

Joy flooded Dora. Although she'd had a wonderful time during their previous lovemaking, she'd been aware that Zical had restrained the full strength of his sexual desires. He'd clearly been worried he'd overwhelm her with his need to dominate, and while she'd appreciated his concern, the savage man standing over her was ever so much more exciting.

She'd always suspected that although Zical appeared most civilized, at his core, he was pure Rystani. And Rystani men did not ask. They took. Demanded. Commanded.

They dominated.

And Dora was about to experience the full force of his sexuality. The quickening she'd felt earlier accelerated until pure anticipation filled her. She'd yearned to share his elemental nature. She wanted to take all he could give. Nothing was sexier than having his full focus, his every brain cell centered on her.

Dora thought that once he'd tied her hands, he would remove her garb and they would make love on the bed. But Zical had other ideas. Placing a hand on the small of her back, he led her to the sub's window.

"You will hold still or suffer consequences."

At his mild threat, her pulse escalated. She had no idea what those consequences would be, but from his sexy tone, she suspected he was looking forward to them and her excitement notched up another level.

Outside, the boiling lava flowed with spectacular gushes. And the pockets of gases revealed an ever-changing panorama. She spied several different creatures living in the hellish heat, but her mind did not stay on the view. Not with Zical standing so close, looming over her, his reflection, superimposed on the boiling lava scene outside, intense.

Zical stood behind her, his hands on her shoulders, his fingertips playing lightly over her exposed collarbone. She wanted to turn around and press her body against him, tilt back her head and invite a kiss. She wanted to place her arms around his neck and taste his mouth. But with her hands tied, she had to wait for him.

Dora didn't mind waiting because she knew *she* was worth waiting for. And she had no doubt that eventually this man would give her exactly what she needed. Out of billions of souls, he was the one who fired her imagination, and she trusted her belief in him. Giving him power over her cemented her faith in his true nature.

And so she forced herself to remain silent as he skimmed his suggestive fingers over her shoulders. And when his breath fanned her earlobe and his teeth gently nipped the sensitive curve of her neck, she restrained a sigh of satisfaction. She'd given her body over to his keeping to do as he wished.

And when his hands closed over her breasts and her clothing kept his flesh apart from hers, she did not fidget. Although she ached for his hands on her bare skin, she'd chosen to defy his order and understood she would now pay a price. Still, it was a more difficult lesson than she'd imagined.

His palms closed over her breasts in sensual circles, teasing her nipples through the cloth. She understood she was supposed to hold still. And she tried. Oh, she tried. But no one could possibly withstand the scintillating heat he'd kindled without squirming.

Despite her determination to obey his demand to remain still, she couldn't. Her hips rubbed his groin. And he immediately stopped stroking her breasts.

His tone remained mild as he roughly jerked the cloth up over her hips, leaving the material bunched at her waist. "I told you there would be consequences."

"I couldn't help it."

"I know." He chuckled, his tone warm and sexy, and therefore his next move took her by total surprise.

He slapped her bare bottom.

"Oh." It stung. And she tried to turn around but he held her firmly.

He slapped her right cheek. And she imagined two round pink flushes on her derriere.

"What are you doing?" she squealed, not so much in protest but total amazement.

The sound of the next slap startled her. The steamy tingle left her breathless. And unexpected excitement floored her as dampness seeped between her thighs.

As if he understood her confusion at her favorable reaction, he paused, giving her time to adjust. To tense. Slowly he massaged away the sting—but not all. And just as she relaxed, he spanked her again.

Her left side. Her right. Up high. Down low. Everywhere. This time he didn't pause, and as the sting spread over her entire bottom, she cried out. "Oh . . . oh . . . ah . . ."

Dora didn't like pain, but the slaps were easy to bear. Symbolic. She could let him do this, especially since the sting faded almost immediately, leaving the most indescribably delicious heat.

Finally, he stopped. "Ah, the sight of your pink bottom pleases me."

At his words, something inside her flared. Her skin was pleasantly warm, and between his earlier caresses and the heat he'd just applied, she realized that the tiny stings had caused the dampness of her *synthari* to slicken with sweet need. And she no longer cared if he never removed her clothing. She simply wanted him to take her amid all the luscious sensations he'd created, right now, right there from behind.

"Tell me how you feel," he demanded.

"The sting has faded, leaving . . . a tingling . . . ache," she admitted, more reluctantly than she would have liked.

"And you want me more than you did before?"

"It's strange, but it is so," she admitted, hoping he was done with this particular form of foreplay. Especially since it excited her and made waiting to see what he would do next a sweet torture.

"You have much to learn about desire."

She thought then that he might enter her body, but he stood behind her and again stroked her breasts through the material until she thought she would go mad with the wanting. The next time he told her to take off her clothes, she wouldn't be teasing him. Already she deeply regretted that his hands fondled her through the cloth when she so badly wanted them directly on her flesh.

Her breath came in ragged gasps, but she tried to hold still, especially since she now knew the consequences of disobedience. But he'd stacked the probabilities against her, and when she once again lost her battle to hold still, her bared bottom felt oh so vulnerable. And this time she knew what was coming, making the waiting for the sting so much more intense.

His first swat was sharp, the heat causing her breath to come in rasps. He spanked her twice. Paused. But she sensed he was not done. And the heat between her thighs, the ache for his touch deep in her *synthari*, left her wild to gyrate her hips.

"Spread your feet."

She did. And when he tenderly stroked her nether lips, she released a soft moan.

"You like this? You're slick and ready for me."

"Yes."

"But the sting is adding to your desire, yes?"

"I desire you enough."

She received two more sharp slaps for her response. "Oh . . . oh . . . oh." And soft whimpers of need told him more than she wanted to reveal, that she was enjoying his attentions, all of them. And the sharp bite from his palm and the heat of his caresses intertwined, creating increasingly higher waves of wild lust, each rolling sequence sweeping her further into a tide of desire.

He delved between her legs, delicious friction combining with the burn, escalating her need. Her legs trembled. Her hands itched to run them along his flesh to encourage him. But she was supposed to hold still.

"You didn't answer my question," he told her.

"Huh?" She couldn't think, could barely concentrate on his words. All the blood had gone to her *synthari*. Her mind was spinning at the fiery sensations.

"The slaps make you hot, yes?"

"Yes, but—"

Slap. Slap. Slap. She gasped at the heat, almost cried out for him to cease. Certain her bottom must be cherry red, certain she was about to orgasm from the rising temperature alone, she fought to free her hands. But she was bound tight.

And she realized that something in him had snapped. Always before he'd been in total control of his passions. Before he'd been careful. But now, he was no longer holding back. Because he couldn't. He wanted her too much to be careful. Wanted her too much to give her less than his full lust. And knowing he couldn't hold back heated her so that she was as tingly and warm inside as she was outside.

And then his hand returned to fondling her, found the center of her *synthari*. The slaps, the heat, the friction all combined to make her frantic for release.

She could not hold still. She was about to burst with the pleasure.

And he stopped.

"What are you doing?" Her voice rose with a plea and she cared not that she was begging.

He placed his hands on her waist, turned her around to face him, tilted up her chin. "I'm doing exactly what I wish."

Her stomach dropped to her toes. She'd never seen this side of him before. She'd always wanted to . . . but now she didn't know if she was . . . if she could . . . Stars. She couldn't think when she was burning up with the wanting of him.

"Ah, now you begin to understand what it is to take a Rystani warrior to your bed."

"Bed. I'd be happy to take you to bed. This is—"

"What I want. What I want from you." He jerked her

clothing down, let it pool at her feet. With the air caressing her breasts, her already pebbled nipples tightened. He eyed her with predatory satisfaction. "Do you want my touch on your breasts?"

"Yes." Her answer was automatic. But when it finally dawned on her through her spinning thoughts that he meant to tease her breasts until she could no longer bear it, she realized that it would be rational for her yes to turn to no. But her body craved the full measure of his passion. Since resistance wasn't even a remote possibility, she murmured, "Yes. Yes. Yes."

Her breasts seemed to swell under his touch, and the heat he'd kindled between her thighs, plus the fire on her red-hot bottom, had her twisting and squirming. "Please, Zical, I must . . . you must . . . please."

She no longer knew what she said. She couldn't think. Only feel. Desire ripped through her, holding her hostage.

And he had yet to remove his sarong.

She could only stand there and wait for him to do as he pleased. Even knowing he would not heed her pleas to plunge into her, she hadn't been able to refrain from asking. Words would not hurry him. And every time she'd tried to wriggle against him, he'd turned up the heat. He'd left her no options.

And although she desperately craved release, she reveled in his taking whatever he desired. Submitting empowered her in a manner she didn't understand and freed her to accept the pleasure in a way that made her feel more alive, more on edge than she'd thought possible. And there was no place in the galaxy she'd rather be at the moment then standing naked before him, waiting for his next caress.

He led her to the bed. Dazed with desire, she watched him pile one pillow atop another in the middle of the bed, confused what he would ask next. She didn't have long to wait.

He patted a spot next to the pillows, his demand almost as sexy as his kisses. "You will kneel."

She scooted onto the bed and kneeled. When he placed a hand on the flat of her back and guided her hips over the pillows, she finally understood. With her bottom tipped upward, her hands tied behind her back, he had total access to her *synthari*. But apparently, he wanted even more.

"Part your legs."

She struggled to do as he asked.

"Wider."

She could not see him but he could see all of her. And then he tied her ankles to keep her spread open for him. She would have been happy to accommodate his wishes, but he didn't want her to have a choice.

"Comfortable?" he asked.

Anticipation stretched her taut. She couldn't see him. Had no idea where he would touch her. Or if his touch would bring more wonderful caresses or the slap of his palm and fiery heat. Yet she liked not knowing. Her *synthari* had never ached so much. And at the tightness gathering in her belly, she suspected that her body could not accept much more stimulation before she spasmed with pleasure. "What do you want from me?"

She heard him moving to the bath, leaving her, and she fought to hold back a sob. Surely he wasn't abandoning her? Surely he meant to continue?

An eternity passed while she was strung taut, and she clung to the notion that he would soon return to do exactly what she'd wanted. He'd given her body a few minutes to cool down, adjust. And she gritted her teeth, realizing he was an absolute master at keeping her on a thin edge.

With his return, his weight depressed the mattress and the bindings on her ankles tugged her open wider. And then with absolutely no warning, his mouth closed over her *synthari*.

Stars. If not for her bonds, she would have jerked at the sudden heat of his wet tongue rasping over her most tender flesh. But she could not move. Could only remain pliant and appreciative.

He must be on his back. And that was her last coherent thought as his hands clasped her buttocks and held her tightly against his mouth—as if she could have gone anywhere.

Between her tied hands and ankles, she couldn't so much as wriggle. Not that she wanted to. His bewitching mouth, his playful lips, and his roving tongue would have had her hips bucking. Yet his hands on her tender bottom held her absolutely at his mercy—and he had none.

Panting, frantic for release, she could do nothing but accept the pitter-patter of her heart, the crackle of sizzling electricity that caused sweet purrs of encouragement from her throat. Expertly, he employed his clever tongue, and when she was once again about to explode, when one more caress would have given her release, he stopped.

And she wanted to curse him in every language she knew as frustration overwhelmed her, but her breath was too ragged for words. Her throat too raw for coherence. "I . . . can't . . . take . . . much more."

"You will take as much as I choose to give."

His words arrowed straight to her heart and she denied what her body wanted so badly, instead submitting, accepting his demands—even as she found it incredibly hard, undeniably sexy. "Yes."

Suddenly, his hands were massaging her bottom with some kind of oil that felt cool at first but quickly warmed her skin. "Ummm. That feels . . . ah." The oil trickled between her cheeks and his fingers followed, gently exploring and opening her. She ordered her quivering muscles to relax, but that was impossible. The oil was so slippery and his fingers were everywhere, under her, over her, inside her. Moving in and out in a steady rhythm.

Just one touch of his hand on her pleasure center would have given her release. But that was the one place he didn't stroke, and tease. Waiting for him to decide what to touch, where to touch, how much to touch, caused her stomach to tense. Her nipples were so tight.

"Tell me you want more," he demanded.

"More," she agreed.

And then he spanked her bottom with one hand while he continued to play with every exposed part of her with purring softness, coaxing hardness. The stinging slaps made her flesh smolder, his caresses on her delicate *synthari* altered from tender to decadent and throbbingly naughty.

"Again?" he asked.

"Yes." Knowing that if she'd had freedom to move, her bottom would have risen up halfway to meet the spankings, even as her hips wanted to buck to keep his fingers inside.

His alluring fingers methodically entered and withdrew, and with perfect timing, he spanked the curves of her up-turned cheeks until her entire body throbbed with expectation. "Oh, yes. Yes. Yes."

The heat. His fingers. Pain and pleasure rolled into one until she couldn't tell where one started and the other left off. Her head spun. Her fingers clenched. Her toes curled into the mattress.

And then he entered her with his *tavis*. She had no idea when he'd removed his sarong. Didn't care. Finally. Finally, he was inside her, filling her with torrid pressure. His hands came around and slid oil over her breasts and she cried out from the raw pleasure. And then she was spasming, the explosion starting deep in her center and radiating outward with electric force. But as he kept moving, thrusting, she didn't so much shatter as rocket. And the burn kept escalating, taking her higher, farther, in a series of eruptions that went on . . . and on . . . and on.

And still he didn't stop. His fingers found where she was most sensitive and he applied steadily increasing pressure. Each gushing spasm triggered another, each more violent, each topping the last. She totally lost herself. Her body short-circuited.

And she blacked out.

Chapter Eighteen

DORA EXPLODED INTO a world of brilliant colors. Cyan, turquoise, celadon, and golden ocher. Streams of color suffused her as if she floated among clouds. At first she thought she was dreaming. But this was like no dream she'd ever experienced. Color encompassed her, flooding through her and feeding her psi. As she reached out, the coalescent ribbons of color thinned until she sensed another presence in the swirling rainbow of shades.

Ranth?

Dora?

She wasn't speaking with her mouth but she heard him all the same. The connection was psi-linked with empathic overtones, allowing her to guess at his vigilance, yet he was most definitely happy to communicate. And beneath the wariness, she sensed Ranth's loneliness and fear, deep azure and indigo coloring his thoughts.

Where is this place? she asked, but as the henna and

cinnabar and honey faded along with his azure and indigo, she recognized Ranth's vault. But she was not on the outside looking in, she was inside with him. Somehow, she'd catapulted her psi exactly where she'd wanted to go. And she prayed she wasn't trapped. Because she couldn't remain separate from her body for too long or it might die, leaving her spirit with no place to return.

I created a doorway that would recognize only you, Ranth informed her.

Thanks. We're working on a way to free you from the dampeners. And Selgren L'Matti has abducted Kirek. We need any help you can give us to get him back.

I can link with you and leave through the doorway, but my powers will be limited.

Dora understood. The doorway Ranth had opened was a tiny bandwidth. He could operate only a puny part of his intellect through such a small crack.

Any and all help will **be** *appreciated. Stay linked with me as I withdraw.*

Compliance.

Keeping Ranth with her was like carrying Kirek. In the beginning, he was light and easy to take along the journey back to her body, but eventually she tired from the load. Determined to hold him close, she concentrated, but like muscles that had been pushed too hard, the psi link weakened.

Ranth shot her a virtual sigh. *You're losing me.*

Sorry. I'll come back.

Soon?

Soon, she promised but doubted he had heard her reply. The link sliced sharp and clean.

With a shocking thud, her consciousness ricocheted into her body.

It took a few moments to make the adjustment. She was lying on her back and Zical was bending over her, smoothing back her hair, concern in his eyes. "Welcome back."

She blinked several times and breathed deeply to regain

her bearings. Her body was deliciously satiated and Zical must have untied her limbs because they were now free. "What happened?"

He lifted her head and raised a glass of water to her lips. "You fainted."

She sipped greedily. "How long was I out?"

"Less than a minute." He set down the glass. "Did I push you too hard?"

"Not hard enough." She shook her head, unable to restrain her smile of contentment.

"You are not Rystani. I should not have—" He peered at her, his regret quickly passing as the words she'd just spoken finally registered. "What do you mean, not enough?"

"You pushed my psi over the edge. I contacted Ranth."

"You fainted and dreamed—"

"It was no dream. He left open a door in his vault. We left together, but I did not have the psi strength to keep him with me."

"So what happened?" Zical frowned, but she had to give the man credit, he was trying to understand what had happened. Another man might have thought her insane. And she appreciated that he didn't consider her words ridiculous, or worse, forbid her to use her new ability before listening to what she had to say.

"The psi link is like a rubber band. We stretched it until it broke. And when it snapped, I returned to my body. Ranth went back to the vault."

"You're certain?"

"I need you to push me further." She sat up, winced a little at her tender bottom, then eyed him with a speculative grin. "Think you're up to it?"

"I am." He peered at her, his expression full of suspicion because she had simplified her story. "But first we will bathe, have a meal and a rest. And then you will tell me exactly how dangerous your psi-traveling is."

"And if I don't? Will you spank it out of me?"

His fierce expression suddenly erupted into happy approval. "Did anyone ever tell you that you're incorrigible?"

AVANTI DIDN'T KNOW where to turn for help except to her enemy. She didn't even know if Deckar would accept her communication, but she didn't approve of her own people's methods, especially L'Matti's. So she beeped Deckar and waited impatiently for a reply. As one of the Selgren leaders, Avanti was not accustomed to waiting, but the violence on Kwadii was escalating, slowing everything from communications to transportation. Hospitals already overflowed with injured people. Schools had closed. Soon there would be shortages of food and medicine since the supply skimmers could not get through the riots.

And she worried about the Federation people. Would the Risorians free them and allow them to leave Kwadii?

Her holoscreen beeped and Deckar's too smug, too perfect face eyed her with one speculative eyebrow raised in ultimate confidence. Knowing she could never match the self-assurance in that metal-hard gaze, she strove to keep her fears hidden. Avanti, whose life was cobbled together out of uncertain alliances, and who schemed to maintain her position, tried to remain as composed as the Risorian—an impossible task. While Deckar had had the luxury of the best schooling, completing years of study of the arts, history, and political negotiation techniques, Avanti had only street smarts and a self-taught education that had more gaps and rough edges than she'd ever admit.

Although Deckar had to be astonished by her private communication, one would never know it from his cool expression.

"Avanti." Deckar greeted her with only a slight head nod to avoid complete rudeness. "Are you pleased that soon the Risorians will have no safe places to work and live?"

"I need your help." The words tasted bitter. Never had she

expected to ask the arrogant Deckar Delari Hikai, of the Fifth House of Seemar, for aid. Even speaking to him behind the backs of the Selgren Council was enough for her people to consider her a traitor.

She expected Deckar to sneer. Or summarily end the communication. He did neither. He stared at her, assessing her with intelligent eyes that burned and accused with barely concealed hatred. In total command, he let the silence stretch, his perfectly chiseled features giving away none of his thoughts.

Behind her back, she clenched her fists, determined not to beg. She would explain. He would refuse. And then she would go on, knowing that she'd given every option a shot, no matter how impossible.

Finally, he spoke, his charismatic tone soothing her, although his words were jarring. "And why would I want to help you?"

Jrek! She didn't want to be soothed. She held her head high, her spine bayonet straight. "Do you know L'Matti?"

"Who on Kwadii does not know of L'Matti? He's murdered four Risorians and openly brags of the killings. He owns over a fourth of the gambling and copulation establishments on Kwadii and has the morals of a Darvangian slug."

The distaste on Deckar's face appeared real. And Avanti hoped that the enemy of her enemy might become an ally. Clearly Deckar already disapproved of L'Matti, as she'd been certain he would. But would Deckar join her and risk L'Matti's wrath? It was time to find out.

"L'Matti is doing a true disservice to all Selgrens. He's kidnapped the boy, and I want to free him," she admitted, knowing that if her encryption program failed, she would lose her head for her revelation. While L'Matti wasn't officially a member of the Selgren Council, he often worked for them in secret. His pleasure palaces could be invaluable places to dig out confidential information critical to Selgren interests, and he'd bartered those secrets into a thriving empire and a position so powerful that she dared not speak against him among her own people.

And so she'd sought help where she could . . .

Deckar had been born into the Fifth House and as such had been trained from birth to wield political power with a skill that no Selgren could hope to achieve. Selgrens were too busy earning a living to waste an entire life studying to make themselves better in order to join Tirips in the next life.

But even as Deckar attempted to hide his reaction, for just one moment his shock at her words flashed in his eyes, before a hardness returned. "Your information is already old."

So Deckar's shock had not been over learning that L'-Matti held the boy, which he'd already known, but that she'd admitted it. But Deckar couldn't know L'Matti's plans. Only she knew, thanks to a well-placed spy inside his closet circle of advisors. "L'Matti means to test the boy, then kill him to prove he is not the Oracle."

"Killing him will make him a martyr. We will honor and worship his memory," Deckar intoned with the solemn rhythm of a cleric. His rigid tone caused anger to rise so hot it flushed her face. In the short time she'd defended the Federation people, she'd come to like and respect them. And she didn't support L'Matti's goal to refute the Risorians' beliefs.

"Why not help me save him?" she suggested, annoyed that Deckar was attempting to employ his mesmerizing voice to melt through her anger.

"And why would *you* want to save the Oracle?"

"I don't give a sandworm's slime if Kirek's the Oracle. I want him off Kwadii." She wanted him to be safe. "I want the violence on Kwadii to end for Selgrens and Risorians alike."

"And?" he prodded her, with piercing eyes and a gentle tone.

"And he's just a little boy." Jrek. Jrek. Jrek, she swore softly under her breath, regretting how easily Deckar provoked her. She hadn't intended to admit to a soft spot for the child. Showing weakness to a Risorian was always a mistake.

"What are you asking of me?" Deckar asked.

"Zical, the leader of the offworlders, and Dora, one of his crew, are traveling to the boy in hopes of freeing him as we speak. Without our help, they will fail."

"They are traveling without the Council's permission."

"The Council is full of narrow-minded leaders. The Federation is attempting to stop the Zinatti from entering this galaxy. We should help them on their way."

"You ask me to commit treason twice. Once to free an enemy, second to send the Oracle from Kwadii."

"If we do nothing, your Oracle will surely die. Is that what your Risorian religion teaches you? To be a coward?"

At her insult, Deckar's eyes flashed with fury; then he blinked away the rage as if it had never been. Clearly she'd pricked his ego, yet he kept his perfectly modulated voice under full control. "Do not think to manipulate me. I have no need to prove myself to anyone, never mind . . . you."

Her hand hovered over the disconnect button. "If you will not help, then—"

"I did not refuse."

How like a Risorian to talk in circles. "You haven't committed, either, and we are wasting time. L'Matti's defenses are strong. Taking the boy will be a difficult task."

"You know where L'Matti's keeping the Oracle?" Deckar demanded.

"Yes."

At least he had the good sense not to ask her to reveal her source of data. She wondered if he was recording this conversation, but she'd accepted that possibility when she'd sent her communication.

"Why come to me?"

"Why not? You believe the boy is Tirips's Oracle. Do you not wish to save him?"

"And your own people?"

"If L'Matti can topple the Risorian faith, it matters not to him if he darkens the souls of all Selgrens by killing a small boy in the process. Too many others agree with him."

Avanti didn't believe that Kirek was the Oracle and neither did L'Matti. The difference between them was that she wasn't so insane that she'd let an innocent child die to prove the Risorians were wrong.

Deckar's eyes narrowed. "Not all Selgrens agree?"

"Of course not. But there are spies everywhere. I do not know who among my people might carry back tales to L'-Matti."

"And if I help, if we rescue the Oracle, you then expect me to just let him go?"

"I expect more than that from you, Risorian Deckar. I expect you to aid in the offworlders' escape. No one may ever know that we aided the boy, or our heads will not remain attached to our shoulders."

"I see no profit in your idea."

"Besides preventing the murder of your Oracle?" she taunted him, but her hopes plummeted. She'd known winning his help would be difficult. She must have been wrong to think he had a heart beneath that cold façade.

"Perhaps it is Tirips's wish that he die. Perhaps only his death will bring peace."

His suggestion was outrageous. Even she who did not believe in Tirips couldn't believe he'd said such terrible words. Since he wouldn't help her for his religion's sake, she tried to appeal to the Risorian's fiscal interests on Kwadii. With the riots, their mines had shut down. They had to be losing a huge income stream. "If the Oracle escapes, tensions will return to normal. The riots will stop. Commerce will begin anew."

"Maybe so. Maybe not."

Avanti only had one more secret, one more argument to employ to convince him. And she wielded the intelligence information from her spies like a weapon. Hoping it wasn't a futile effort, she played her last gambit. "The Oracle has given L'Matti a message for us and all of Kwadii."

"Which is?" No emotion flickered across Deckar's face. He didn't so much as blink or breathe, telling her that the message might be even more important than even she knew. Had she nudged Deckar in the right direction? Invoked his curiosity?

"The boy will share his message once he is freed and back in space." This time, it was Avanti's turn to hold her breath as she awaited his answer.

ZICAL COULD BE very imaginative, and after Dora had urged him to top his earlier performance, he came up with a variation of a game children played on Rystan to learn computer code. But while Rystani kids employed their fingers to draw code on one another's backs to communicate commands, he'd used his tongue on Dora's most sensitive places. Using a combination of slow licks and long lingering tugs to spell out command codes that he insisted she decipher, he'd forced her to concentrate on the pleasure while at the same time distracting her, until she spasmed again and again and again, taking her further than she'd ever been.

And finally, she'd succeeded in not only contacting Ranth, but maintaining a permanent connection. Zical didn't understand how such a link was possible, but he didn't ask questions. After Dora had grown a body and transferred her personality into it, he figured she was capable of almost anything. And he was proud of her ability to adapt, even as she pushed the limits of her humanity. Of course, once she'd established and maintained contact with Ranth, their sexual intimacy ended and new plans began.

Although the sub would dock in a terminal where they'd never been before, Ranth and Dora had used the sub's computer system to map out the most direct route through the city to L'Matti's fortress. Their research also informed them of predictable areas where authorities might stop them at checkpoints, but Dora and Ranth believed they could use their combined psi to alter the computer's sensors to "see" them as ordinary travelers.

Meanwhile, in case they were wrong, Zical had fashioned a sheath to strap to his thigh that would hold a knife beneath his loincloth. With no case or container to hide the bulky weapon he'd acquired when they'd escaped Deckar's compound, he had no choice but to leave it behind.

However, he'd made good use of the drapery hardware, fashioning heavy rings to fit over his knuckles that would give him an advantage if it became necessary to use his fists. A search of the tiny kitchen produced a cleaning spray in a small cylinder, which he also tucked into the waistband of his loincloth. Although he didn't test it in his own eyes, most cleaning agents stung the cornea upon contact, and a tiny taste on his tongue proved bitter enough to swiftly spit out and then thoroughly rinse his mouth with water.

Dora looked up from the holovid, her gaze concerned. During their time together Zical had already learned that Dora didn't allow her thoughts to bog down with small problems. But her usually upbeat mood was somber now and he suspected she'd come up against a major problem in reaching Kirek.

"Tell me," he demanded.

"L'Matti guards his properties with many trained *Pirinja*, those Selgrens who study the warrior arts."

"I expected no less."

Dora gestured for Zical to look at the holovid with her. "We can't fight our way in." She pointed to guard stations along a heavily fortified wall that surrounded the building's perimeter. Around the edge, fast-running water flowed. Tall towers with armed guards could shoot down anyone attempting to climb the high walls.

Zical considered several ways to breach the exterior, tunneling, cannon fire, flying over in a skimmer, or bribing a guard to look the other way. He traced his finger on the projection, searching for weakness.

Dora pointed out the problems as if she'd read the Rystani book of military sieges, which she'd undoubtably once had stored in her memory banks. "A tunnel will take too long to dig, and since we don't have control of our ship and the cannonfire aboard, that is also impractical. A skimmer would be shot down and we haven't the time or the resources to bribe a guard. That leaves us fewer options." She looked to him. "What do you recommend?"

"That we attempt to sneak in. A place so large must allow many deliveries a day to stock their supplies."

And so they came up with a plan, but the discussion was interrupted. Their holovid suddenly filled with Avanti's somber face, and at the sight of her, Zical's worries multiplied. How had she found them? How had she overridden their sub's computer? Was she about to order them to surrender peacefully when they reached the terminal? Or was there unseen pursuit right nearby, hidden in the boiling lava?

As he considered signaling Dora to alter their course just minutes before their arrival to avoid recapture, Zical had to decide whether Avanti was trustworthy.

Avanti spoke in her usual blunt style. "You cannot rescue the boy by yourselves."

"Turn off the transmission," Zical ordered Dora, fearing it was being used to trace them.

"She already knows our location and has guessed our intentions," Dora told him, understanding his concerns. "We might as well listen to what she has to say since she must have gone to considerable trouble to find us."

"Fine." Zical agreed as if he had another good choice, but their options were sadly limited. Although Avanti had never lied to him, Zical didn't trust her, especially since a Selgren held Kirek.

"Deckar Rogar Delari Hikai, heir to the Fifth House of

Seemar, and I have made a pact to help you recover Kirek and escape Kwadii."

It took a moment for him to absorb her words, then stunned, Zical figured it must be a trick. The obvious hatred between Avanti and Deckar, the loathing between Risorian and Selgren, went so deep that Zical could not imagine them talking amicably to each other, much less making a pact, but he attempted to mask his rearing suspicions.

"When the sub arrives, remain inside and we will bring you Selgren clothing, weapons, and false identification."

"Why would you help us?" Dora asked.

Avanti's eyes glimmered with a fierce gleam of determination. "We don't have much time, but the rioting is tearing our world apart. Even the Risorian Deckar agrees that it is better for Kwadii if the Oracle departs. I told you I would help you and I keep my word."

"You and Deckar are going to help us rescue Kirek and to leave Kwadii?" Dora asked, clearly as skeptical as Zical was.

"Didn't I just say so?"

The woman's arrogance annoyed Zical, but it also gave him hope that she just might be speaking the truth. "We accept your help and will do as you say."

Avanti immediately cut the connection. Dora instructed the sub to return the hull to its original condition and the lava flows outside disappeared. Then she stood and stretched and he appreciated that she didn't question his judgment. He only hoped, for all their sakes, that he'd made the right decision.

However, as good as Dora and Ranth might be at fiddling with the Kwadii computer system, Zical preferred to have local allies. The right clothing, critical weapons, and, even more importantly, information that might be crucial to their success. He couldn't afford to refuse help from any quarter, even if he suspected that the Kwadii might deceive and betray them.

* * *

KIREK HAD USED every trick he knew to delay the use of
violence against his person. He'd had no sleep, little food,
and barely enough water to quench his thirst, and the deprivation made clear thinking difficult. He'd employed cir-
cuitous arguments, told long stories that had a moral that
barely applied to the point he was trying to make, and did
everything he could think of to make his questioner, Selgren
L'Matti, believe he was cooperating.

But L'Matti was wearing him down both physically and
emotionally. After the drugs and the questioning, Kirek was
a full day past cranky, his yearning to sleep was so strong
that he was having difficulty holding up his head.

L'Matti had resorted to playing loud, horrible sounds to
keep him awake in the too bright room. And Kirek had
been warned that if he fell asleep, L'Matti would see to it
that he never awakened. And all the while, L'Matti drilled
him with questions, repeating them until Kirek thought he
would go mad.

Kirek wanted to leave this horrible room, this awful world
where different factions were attempting to use him to grab
power. To stop L'Matti's torture, he had to say he was a
fraud, which would give the Selgrens power over the Risorians, but then he would also likely condemn the Federation
people to another trial and execution. Kirek imagined he was
back on Mystique, safe in his father's arms. He wanted to eat
his mother's home-cooked food. He wanted his suit to cradle
him as he slept. He was so tired of being hungry and dirty
and among strangers.

His chin dropped to his chest and he jerked awake. Surely
he could hold out for another hour. But he'd told himself that
three hours ago. Then two.

Kirek heard footsteps outside his door. Shouts. He should
be curious. He should be wondering about a rescue or thinking about an opportunity to escape. But his muscles
wouldn't carry him to the door. And the idea of escape
seemed impossible. He was so weak. He should go to the

door and place his ear against it to listen better. But he couldn't summon the energy. His eyelids fluttered closed.

And then the klaxons blared.

He clamped his hands over his ears and screwed his eyes tightly shut, his little body quivering. And he prayed that he would not say the wrong thing. He prayed that if he died his death would be quick and painless. He prayed that Dora and Zical would find a way to complete the mission without his help. He prayed that his parents would forgive him for not being there to help them in their old age.

Kirek closed his eyes. And slept.

Chapter Nineteen

SWEAT POURED DOWN Dora's back and between her bare breasts. She hoped the guards posted at L'Matti's building's entrance would attribute her perspiration to the heat and not her nervou. Even as every muscle tightened and she feared that the guard at the gate would betray them even after he'd accepted a hefty bribe to allow her and Zical to enter as part of a cleaning team, she held her breath and fought to keep her head down and her expression bored.

Beside her, Zical's broad back glistened in the early-morning heat. She feared the musculature of his powerful frame might give him away as a warrior, but the guards at the entrance didn't appear too concerned or alert. For once the heat was working in their favor. Clearly the pair of guards were eager to return to their station, a shaded post near the high stone wall that had to be at least ten degrees cooler than in the direct heat of the Kwadii sun.

Dora and Zical's mission was simple reconnaissance. Before they could mount a full-scale mission to rescue Kirek, they needed to know exactly where L'Matti was holding him. Avanti's information had been sketchy, but she'd suggested they head for the basement.

Entering the compound was almost anticlimactic. The guards waved them through and they tagged along with the cleaning crew ambling along a walkway and past a second set of double doors. Here, Dora paused, bending to adjust her sandal while she used her psi to alter the computerized security mechanism. One by one, the other Selgrens strode past a machine that scanned their DNA, matched it against a computer index, and allowed them to pass. The brief delay allowed Dora to change the recognition code so that the computer identified their DNA as being on the list.

She stood slowly and moved forward, and Zical followed, guarding their backs—just in case the bribed guard changed his mind when he realized that the computer had failed to stop their entry. But apparently, either the guard feared that stopping them now would be the equivalent of admitting his earlier dishonesty or he simply held no loyalty to L'Matti.

Once through the double doors, their group, which consisted of men and women of assorted ages, moved into an airless, stifling passageway. According to Avanti's intelligence, not only didn't L'Matti bother to cool air for his employees' comfort, he also refused to allow his employees to use his sumptuous hallways unless they needed to be there for cleaning and maintenance. And his preference to keep staff out of sight worked to Dora and Zical's advantage. They'd be less likely to attract notice within the narrow employee corridors that threaded like a maze through the building.

Dora grabbed a broom and a duster, and with the heavy implement in her hand, which could easily double as a weapon, she began to breathe again. The cleaning crew quickly broke into two-person teams, each pair heading in different directions.

She and Zical followed the dimly lit corridor until he pointed to a stairway. She nodded and they headed down. The air immediately cooled and she suspected that they were now underground. She tried not to imagine the immense building falling on top of them or the walls closing in.

Dora hadn't experienced any claustrophobia since she'd adjusted to her human body, or any twitches since landing on Kwadii, but something about the sinister atmosphere, her worry over finding Kirek and being trapped underground worked on her fears. Sternly, she told herself claustrophobia wasn't a rational concern, but when that did not the slightest bit of good to calm her anxiety, she focused on her need to find Kirek.

If it would save him, she would crawl through rubble to get to the boy. She couldn't imagine what he must be feeling. Being kidnapped, possibly mistreated, was far worse than when he'd simply been alone. He had to be scared. Desperate.

And Zical's quiet strength also helped to steady her. Their feet on the steps tapped softly in a soothing rhythmic pattern. Zical touched her hand that held the feather duster, slowing her. "Do you sense machines?"

"Everywhere." She leaned on the broom, cocked her head to the side, and listened. Her psi hearing noted the buzz of humming circuits.

"Can you tap in without being spotted?"

Dora placed more weight on the broom handle. She always had difficulty remaining a vertical and connecting to computer systems at the same time. She sent out a more direct and experimental psi ribbon, a strand so thin that it wouldn't set off the most sensitive detector. Bypassing the sophisticated security system, she pushed the strand with her psi and sneaked into the system, her method working on the same principle as inserting a key into a lock. She lucked out. Someone had just logged off the system and the password streamed by. She made a virtual grab, then used the password to dig deeper.

The password wasn't one from an especially distinguished user and the clearance only got her so far. However, she learned that the high security area was down two more levels, guarded by both *Pirinja* and more computer systems. She wasn't concerned about the computer. The armed warriors were another matter entirely. Down here in the cool air, she expected them to be more alert and more likely to question strangers.

She withdrew quickly, the return into her body abrupt. Jolting. Even with a firm grasp on the broom, she might have fallen without Zical's support. She ended up in his arms, leaning against him, sagging. Her arms tingled as if he'd been massaging her flesh while she'd been gone.

"You okay?" he asked, his concern coming through in an urgent whisper.

"Yeah, why?"

"You were so out of it. I feared you might not come back."

"Returning is always difficult," she admitted. "It's a shock to my system. I'm not sure why."

"Because human beings aren't made to share their minds with circuitry," he muttered.

She ignored his complaint. "We have to descend two more levels to find Kirek. And there are armed guards."

"I'm ready for them," he muttered and stalked off, his face intense, his pace quick, as if he couldn't wait to plant his fist in a guard's face.

She hurried after him, bent on convincing him that violence should be their last choice. "We may be able to bluff our way in," she reminded him. While on the one hand she liked that he worried over her, on the other hand, at times like this, his emotional concern could be annoying.

At the sound of a blaring klaxon, Dora's breath hitched. Her stomach curled into a tight ball and her mouth went dry as a sandworm's burrow. They must have been spotted. She raised the broom, determined to use it as a weapon. Beside her, Zical pulled a knife from beneath his sarong.

But no soldiers streamed into the dim passageway. She heard no hastily shouted orders. No marching feet. No curses. No panic. Abruptly, the klaxon ended and it was followed by the sound of a young boy's soulful shriek.

Kirek!

Were they torturing him? His scream was part anger, part frustration, and it chilled her to the bone to hear how weak he sounded.

Zical kept his knife out and proceeded toward the sound of the boy's voice. "Easy. He's still alive."

If Zical had intended his comment to reassure her, it hadn't worked. What had the poor child been going through?

When Kirek's wail ended as suddenly as it had begun, leaving them in harsh silence, Dora tried to shove past Zical in her haste to reach the boy. Zical blocked her progress, his voice hard and fierce, his fingers tight on her shoulder. "If we get ourselves killed, we can't rescue Kirek."

"You're right," she told him, even as she steeled herself against the renewed whine of the klaxon. At Kirek's next scream. She shuddered. Were they torturing him with sound? Swallowing her horror, she sought to reassure Zical that she wasn't about to panic and deprive them of the element of surprise. "I'm fine. Let's go."

Again the awful wail ended and Dora knew one thing for certain. Reconnaissance mission, or not, Zical's orders or not, no way was she leaving Kirek behind. However, she kept the thought to herself.

Zical cracked open a door between the employee passageway and the main ones. His broad back blocked her view, but when she angled lower, she could see beyond him. Four guards sat in a hallway outside a room where she assumed they were holding Kirek. The *Pirinja* played a board game and were obviously gambling. One man had his back to them but the others would have a clear view of their entrance.

Zical, Dregan hell, didn't hesitate. Plucking the feather duster from her hand, he used it to hide his knife. Then he handed her the canister of cleaning spray, opened the door for her, and let her enter first.

At the sight of them, the *Pirinja* immediately stopped their game and rose to their feet in lazy wariness. Clearly, these men were so certain of their superiority, they didn't immediately reach for their weapons.

Dora breezed inside, hoping they could bluff their way closer before the guards challenged them. The *Pirinja* might not be reaching for weapons, but they were suspicious nonetheless. The tension in their eyes confirmed that cleaning crews didn't come this way often.

"Good afternoon." She muffled her greeting and began sweeping the floor, edging forward slowly, while beside her Zical dusted a light switch.

"What are you two idiots doing here?" the highest-ranked officer demanded, thumping his fist on the table as he stood and causing the golden braids that hung over his shoulders to sway.

"Cleaning." Dora spoke in a surly tone, as if she were disgusted with her current task. "Selgren L'Matti's ordered the building to be cleaned from top to bottom." As the guard's eyes dropped to her breasts, Dora giggled, and made her steps bouncy, hoping the men's eyes would stay where they usually did—on her chest. "And this is the bottom, Right?"

"You can stay, but no men are allowed down here except *Pirinja*." Clearly the captain didn't like the looks of Zical's powerful body.

"Oh, pay no attention to him. He's,"—she whirled her finger by her temple—"not quite right in the head. Does what he's told like a beast. And I need him to lift me to clear the cobwebs by the ceiling."

Behind her, Zical hummed and fluttered the feather duster uselessly here and there, looking silly. And utterly harmless with his downcast eyes and stoic expression.

As Dora swept the floor, she worked her way closer to the table, careful not to send up clouds of dust that would make the men protest. While the *Pirinja* hadn't settled back into their game, two of them had regained their seats.

However, the captain remained standing, his narrowed eyes fascinated with Dora's large breasts. He licked his lips. "Come here."

Dora couldn't have been more pleased. She needed to be close enough to take him out and nullify the advantage of his weapons. And that was impossible until she advanced within arm's reach. She strode forward, making sure to exaggerate the sway of her hips, knowing the movement was provocative.

When the klaxons began to howl, Dora jumped and the captain laughed, clearly pleased that her nipples had tightened. He reached to cup her breast and she slipped away sideways as if she hadn't noticed his movement. "What is that noise?"

"Come sit on my lap and I'll tell you." He pulled out his chair with his foot, sat, and patted his knee.

She pretended to think about it, waving the canister, letting him get accustomed to thinking it harmless. "Sir, I have work."

The captain lost his patience. He snagged his arm around her waist and tugged her to him. Dora went with the motion and sprayed the cleaning fluid into his eyes, then tried to wipe it away as if she'd unintentionally sprayed him.

The man slapped away her hands, roaring with pain and fury. "Stupid woman. I'll have you strung up naked and whipped for that."

"Sorry. So sorry." Dora backed away a step, pretending fear. At the same time, Kirek screamed again. Zical attacked, moving so fast his strikes were a blur. Without hesitation, she slammed the broom into the captain's temple. He let out a woof of air and collapsed at her feet.

While Dora had been doing her best to misdirect the guard's attention, Zical had gone to work with his knife, his fists, and his feet. One guard dropped to the floor, his neck twisted at an unnatural angle. Zical slit the second one's throat and simultaneously struck the third *Pirinja* with a kick to the temple.

Dora picked up a chair, slammed it down on the captain's head to make sure he wouldn't get up. She didn't take time to ascertain whether he was mortally wounded or dead, not with Kirek wailing.

Knowing Zical could take care of the one remaining guard, she used her psi to unlock the door. Praying she wasn't too late, she stumbled at the quick transformation from machine circuitry to human brain, jolting back into her body as she entered the room and rushed to where Kirek had once again gone silent.

Even as she heaved through the door, she recovered enough to use her vocal cords. "Kirek. It's Dora and Zical. We came to get you out of here."

The boy backed away from her, his arms raised to block his face. "I am Tirips's Oracle, Do not strike me."

Stars. He was out of his head, eyes unfocused. He didn't recognize her.

She made her tone gentle. "Kirek. It's Dora, sweetie. We've come to take you away."

"Dora?"

Kirek lowered his forearms. At the sight of the black circles below his eyes and his shaking frame, Dora barely held back a gasp. She didn't know what they'd done to him, but he was clearly weak and totally exhausted.

"They wouldn't let me sleep."

She scooped him into her arms. "I've got you now. Sleep all you want."

FROM THE MOMENT Zical had heard Kirek's pathetic scream, he'd known they weren't leaving the boy behind. Even if he'd wanted to try to talk Dora into leaving and returning again with Avanti and Deckar to back them up, the stubborn hardness in Dora's eyes told him she'd never abandon the child. He adored her loyalty to Kirek. So her attitude was more than fine with him. Besides, holding back his fury would have been next to impossible. Anyone who would hurt a child didn't deserve to breathe another minute.

While Zical didn't take life without reason, he had no compunction about killing the *Pirinja*. And as he led Dora, who lovingly held Kirek, from L'Matti's building, he wouldn't hesitate to kill anyone who tried to stop their escape.

Earlier, Dora's performance had been brilliant. She'd extemporaneously thought on her feet, using her charms and intelligence to get them close enough to take out the guards. And she hadn't hesitated to back him up in the fight, either, displaying a physical courage that revealed just how much she'd grown from the woman on Mystique who'd been afraid to leave her room.

So when Dora suddenly staggered on the stairs, almost dropping the boy, he took Kirek from her arms, fearing that killing a man had finally caught up with her emotionally. But he was dead wrong. She had that glazed look in her eyes, a soulless expression that told him she'd sent her mind elsewhere. Holding the boy over his shoulder with one arm, he wrapped his other around Dora to support her.

Meanwhile, his concern fed his fury. What in stars was she doing linking with the computer system now? She needed to focus on her arms and legs and getting out of here before anyone discovered the dead guards they'd left behind. They couldn't remain undiscovered for much longer and he couldn't carry her and Kirek, too, never mind fight if he must.

He set Kirek down in the stairwell. Then he shook her. "Dora. Come back."

She didn't respond, and the thought hit him that every time he figured that she'd made progress in becoming a human, she did something to make him question that assessment. But this was the first time she'd placed their lives at risk. Concern and anger battled within him. By now he knew her well enough to believe she had good reasons for her actions, and that left him with nothing but anxiety. Had something outside gone awry? Had Avanti and Deckar betrayed them?

He chafed his hands up and down her arms. "Dora. We need you with us. Kirek needs you."

Nothing.

Zical covered her mouth with his. At first, she didn't move. But ever so slowly, her lips began to respond. Her eyes fluttered open. She jerked, spasming, and he realized that during their journey she'd gradually ceased her uncontrollable tics and spasms. He wasn't sure when she'd gained full control of her body, but now was not the time to discuss it.

"Dora?"

"Mmm." She tried to draw him back into the kiss.

But once he was certain she was all the way back and wouldn't fall down, he bent and picked up the sleeping Kirek. "We've got to go."

He considered it a measure of restraint that he didn't stop and demand to know what she was doing. This was no time for discussion. They had to get out of here. The sooner the better. He was about to climb the next set of stairs and return the same way they'd come.

"No." She pointed to the door on this landing. "I altered the security system. The guards expect us to leave the way we came. This way."

Zical didn't know if she was strong enough to carry the boy. But if he had to fight, he'd prefer to have his hands free. "Are you up for carrying Kirek?" he asked, and when she nodded, he handed the boy back to her. Then started to open the door.

"Wait." She drew a deep breath. "Ranth and I contacted Vax. He and Dr. Laduna have gathered at the ship with all our crew and scientists. The moment we are ready to leave, Avanti and Deckar will shut off the dampeners. Vax will fly the ship to this city's spaceport to meet us."

"You arranged all this?" He eyed her.

"With Ranth's help."

Dora had special abilities and a great mind. He'd been wrong not to trust her judgment, especially since she'd just saved his ass. Again.

"Okay. Which way?"

"Left."

Dora's plan went down as smooth as Osarian whiskey. They bypassed the employee entrance and walked out of L'Matti's building as if they'd been invited guests. Only one guard questioned them and Zical took him out before he sounded the alarm, leaving him in a closet.

"The dampeners are gone," Dora reported as they walked away from L'Matti's building. "Ranth is back at full strength. And with the security codes Deckar just gave Vax, our ship will land without attracting attention. Their computers will scan our ship and the readings will show a Kwadii ship returning from space."

"Good. How far to the spaceport?"

"Too far to walk." Dora peered to her right. A skimmer pulled alongside them. "Ah, right on time."

Avanti opened the skimmer door. Deckar was driving. "Need a ride?"

Within moments they were settled inside the skimmer. The hard part, rescuing Kirek, was over. But Zical couldn't relax. Until they left Kwadii and he was once again at the helm of his ship and in hyperspace, he wouldn't relax. Although Avanti and Deckar had made some kind of alliance, he couldn't miss the tension between them.

"How long until we reach the spaceport?"

"Ten minutes," Avanti said.

"Except we've got a problem." Deckar turned sharply to the right.

"What's wrong?"

"There's a skimmer block ahead. I'll try to bypass by changing our route."

But the change in course did no good. A net dropped over their skimmer, stopping forward movement. A voice came over the skimmer's speaker. "Exit the vehicle and keep your hands behind your heads."

DORA COULDN'T CARRY Kirek and place her hands behind her head at the same time. And she was reluctant to leave him behind. "Let's stay right here. Make them come to us."

"Why?" Avanti asked.

"Maybe we can negotiate."

Deckar shook his head. "They're as likely to blow us up as negotiate. Selgrens are violent."

Zical pulled his knife, his expression fierce. "If they want violence—"

"Put that away," Dora snapped. She peered at Avanti and Deckar. "Can't you claim we're on secret and official business?"

"One check into the computer," Avanti said, "and that approaching guard will know the truth."

"Let me handle the computer." Dora and Ranth went to work. Since Ranth was now free, he needed little guidance from her, allowing her to follow the conversation around her in a way she'd never done before. It was like listening to a conversation while a holovid program played in the background and she caught pieces of each.

While she and Ranth plunged into the Kwadii system and eradicated all efforts to capture them, she held on to Kirek who stirred in her arms. As a *Pirinja* yanked open the door, she and Ranth quickly and efficiently erased the soldier's orders to capture them.

"Why have we been stopped?" Deckar asked with all the authority behind him of the class who'd ruled Kwadii for ten thousand years.

"Orders, sir."

"I suggest you recheck your orders," Deckar demanded in

a commanding tone that expected immediate obedience. "We are on a clandestine mission of vast importance. You've drawn attention to our presence and placed lives at risk."

Avanti added her weight to the order. "I'll hold you personally responsible if you delay our departure another minute."

The *Pirinja* swore under his breath, apologized, and waved back a squad of men. However, he kept his weapon aimed at the skimmer, checked his wristvid for orders and frowned. "Something must be wrong."

"Something's very wrong," Zical snarled. "You, soldier, are stopping the Oracle."

The *Pirinja*'s gaze went from his vidscreen to Zical. As if sensing his presence was required, Kirek opened his eyes. "Dregan hell. Why has my sleep been disturbed? Is there no rest for Tirips's messenger?"

The Selgren soldier's skepticism pulled his lips into an ugly sneer. "My missing order is highly unusual. I must check with my superior—"

"We have no time." Zical tried to reach out and close the door.

The soldier placed a boot in the way and consulted his holovid. "You will please wait one moment. I could lose my rank if—"

"Here." Kirek flipped the man a credit chip.

The *Pirinja* caught the credit chip in midair. He eyed it suspiciously, then as he saw the credit amount on the chip, his eyes widened. Dora wondered where Kirek had acquired a large amount of Kwadii credits. "Sorry to have delayed your trip."

As the *Pirinja* closed the door and stepped back smartly from the skimmer, motioning his men to raise the net, she surmised the bribe had worked. Relief flowed through Dora as Deckar punched the engine and they zipped toward the spaceport. She hugged Kirek against her, smoothed his hair, and hoped he'd return to sleep. When she gazed down at his sleepy face, a smile flitted across his lips. And when she looked up, she caught Zical's burning gaze on her.

He was looking at her with a hungry expression of approval and need. She'd waited so long for him to look at her with that kind of regard, that for a moment she'd thought she was imagining it. But no. The burning in his eyes remained steady, and she realized that despite all the problems on Kwadii she would remember the planet with fondness. This was the world where she'd first made love. And this was the world where she and Zical had connected.

He'd picked a fine time to allow his passion to show. While in a crowded skimmer. While she held a child in her arms. While they fled for their lives.

During the last few days, she'd had little time to dwell on their personal relationship. And this was not the time either.

Deckar expertly parked the skimmer at the spaceport. And as they all exited the vehicle, Dora linked with Ranth and monitored communications. They'd already sent the spaceport's security detail to the far end of the tarmac to check out a bogus smuggling operation.

So far, no one appeared to have noticed their alterations to the Kwadii computer systems. And they remained alone on the pavement. As their starship landed, she held her breath, half-expecting someone to stop them, or worse, shoot the ship out of the sky.

But when Vax opened the hatch and it was time to depart Kwadii, Kirek surprised her by waking completely and wriggling from her arms. He held out a hand to Deckar and Avanti in an odd gesture. Then he gazed into their faces, and spoke solemnly. "If you truly seek to find *Nevanna,* you must join our mission."

"Join you?" Avanti asked.

"On the starship," Kirek told her.

Kirek's words took Dora by surprise. Until now, she'd believed Kirek was playing a role to help them escape Kwadii.

But now she was no longer sure. Why would he invite Kwadii from two warring factions to join their mission?

Did Kirek believe that unless the two leaders were aboard the ship, the Kwadii would stop them? Or could Kirek's mind have snapped during his sleep deprivation? Had he insisted that he was Tirips's Oracle for so long that he now believed it?

Fear for him triggered her every protective instinct. But Kirek didn't need her protection. His words had stunned Deckar and Avanti, their faces paling.

Deckar recovered first. "If you will have me, I will be honored to accompany you on this mission."

"Our mission is to reprogram the Sentinel and stop the Zin, not find *Nevanna*," Zical told them as a boarding ramp uncurled. "However, if you wish to join us, please understand you will be under my command and must abide by Federation law."

Dora was surprised that Zical hadn't refused to take these strangers along, but then, he'd held the boy in high regard since long before he'd been born. She remained silent, wanting to talk to Kirek in private.

Deckar and Zical strode toward the ship. Dora waited for Kirek, who still clasped Avanti's hand. The child gazed at her with wisdom too mature for the eyes of a four-year-old. "You do not believe in Tirips, do you, Selgren Avanti?"

"No."

Kirek winked at her. "But apparently your belief is not necessary, only your presence."

At Kirek's mischievous wink, Dora didn't know what to think. The child was asking Avanti to leave her world, to go on a mission of faith when she had none. Dora expected her to say good-bye and depart.

Zical and Deckar were already motioning them to hurry. They had to leave Kwadii quickly before the authorities realized they'd escaped. And still Kirek waited.

"It is difficult to leave one's world behind," he told her.

"But sacrifices must be made. And you have been chosen for the task."

"Come." Dora tugged on Kirek's hand. "We can't linger. You are only the messenger. If she chooses not to listen, it's not your fault."

"You are correct." Kirek released Avanti's hand.

Dora and Kirek hurried to the ship, leaving the Selgren leader behind them on the tarmac. Dora glanced over her shoulder once and caught a pensive expression on Avanti's face. With Kirek and Dora about to climb through the hatch, Avanti had mere seconds to change her mind.

Chapter Twenty

"CLOSE THE HATCH," Zical ordered, not the least bit surprised when Avanti stepped through the portal and onto the
bridge at the last second. She'd never struck him as a coward. He nodded in her direction. "Welcome aboard."

The hatch clanged shut. After boarding, Zical had taken a
moment to change into his suit and to temper his elation at
bringing his people on board. Although he'd always wish he
could have saved everyone, he considered losing only the
one panicked scientist after they'd first arrived a major
victory—a victory that would allow him to continue his
mission.

His responsibility to the Federation and Mystique was
never far from his thoughts. With his mission back on track,
he renewed his determination to find the Sentinel, to reprogram the machine so all peoples in this galaxy would remain
safe from the Zin. With renewed purpose, he strode onto the
bridge, pleased that his crew's determination hadn't wa-

vered. No one had even suggested they turn around and go home.

With the Kwadii dampeners off, their engine worked and so did their psi-controlled suits. It felt great to be clean again and able to move at the speed of thought. Living on Kwadii without their suits had been like living without one of their senses, and it was a measure of crew discipline that they hadn't complained. In fact they'd adapted, and he was proud of them all. Especially Dora. He'd begun to realize just how difficult it must have been for her to adjust not just to the lack of a suit, but to human form.

There was much he wanted to say to Dora, but right now his priority was to lift his ship back into space. Put the mission in the groove of hyperspace.

Zical glanced to his chief engineer. "Cyn?"

"Engines ready to go, Captain."

"Vax?"

"Dr. Laduna and his staff are set for departure," his first officer summarized. "Cargo and supplies are exactly as we left them. Water tanks have been topped off."

The exhausted Kirek had departed for his quarters but Dora remained at a computer station. She no longer needed hardware to tap into Ranth with her psi. But the blank expression in her eyes and the lack of emotion on her face indicated that she was linked, monitoring the Kwadii communications to ensure their liftoff would not be challenged.

His communications officer, Shannon Walker, sat at her station, but she had no job to do, since they planned to keep the Kwadii in the dark about their departure. Instead of asking for permission to depart the planet, she instructed Avanti and Deckar how to web in for liftoff. Since the pair had yet to learn how to use their psi or their new suits to nullify the g-force, they would require additional protection.

"Dora?" Zical prodded her into giving a report.

Her tone was flat, indicating her attention was split between the ship and her exalted computer. "Captain, the

Kwadii dampeners were developed by a race as old as the Perceptive Ones and are technically superior to ours. They power their machinery by converting both solar power from their sun and geothermal power from their lava flow, transforming it to negative energy on their moons. The result is a hyperspace defense system that can also be employed to enhance our journey as effectively as our initial boost from the Osarian black holes."

His hope rose joyfully to think that they might complete their mission much sooner than he'd anticipated after losing their original momentum, but he kept his tone even. "Are you saying the Kwadii system will accelerate us back to our former speed in hyperspace?"

"Affirmative, Captain."

"Will the Kwadii be able to come after us again?"

"We intend to drain their power almost dry. By the time they can recharge, we'll be long gone."

"What's required?" Determination to place them back on track filled him.

"Ranth and I will perform the calculations." Dora spoke in a voice so flat he had to refrain from wincing. The contradiction between his excitement and her cold, mechanical voice vexed him. Now that he knew how warm and giving she could be, her return to efficient crew member irked him.

While Zical needed her help, he'd always disliked it when she popped back into computer mode. However, he couldn't complain when she was doing her job so well.

"Commencing countdown to liftoff," Vax said.

Cyn, as usual, remained rock steady. "Engineering is a go."

The liftoff procedures settled Zical's elation at escaping Kwadii. During the last few years he'd become more at home in space than in his quarters on Mystique and the engine vibrations beneath his feet soothed him. The delay on Kwadii had cost him the life of one scientist, but it could have wrecked the entire mission. And even as the many tasks he needed to complete popped onto his vidscreen, he was glad to be back on course.

Kahn and Tessa must be worried by now and he needed to check in once they were safely away. Miri and Etru would want to reassure themselves that Kirek was fine. And the Federation would need particulars about Kwadii, especially about their beliefs that hyperspace travel might lead the Zin to the Federation. After Ranth and the scientists had carefully checked Kwadii libraries and data banks, Zical had no proof that the Kwadii belief that the Zin could find them through a hyperspace trail was anything more than superstition, so the mission would continue as planned. Zical had endless details, logs, and reports to file, but the person he wanted to talk to most was Dora.

He could no longer deny his attraction to her intelligence her beauty and her courageous nature. But he didn't wish to return to their old relationship, the kind they'd had before they'd landed on Kwadii. He wanted to openly express his affections. He wanted to seek out her company whenever he wished. If he had been Terran, he might have asked Dora to share his quarters. No regulations prevented crew members from forming social units, as long as they competently performed their assigned tasks.

However, Zical came from Rystan. And on his world, men didn't make love to women outside the bonds of marriage. He'd gone against custom once, making love to Dora, believing they'd be executed the following day. He'd flaunted custom again, when Dora had a need to increase her psi power, by making love in the sub. His reasons had been good, and if he had the same choice to make, he'd do nothing differently.

Holding her, loving her, living so closely with her through such trying circumstances, had convinced him of what she'd seemed to know all along—that they were meant for each other. The idea pleased him. Although the timing could have been better, and he wished they weren't on such a dangerous mission, if all went well they would spend the next day or two in hyperspace, more than enough time to settle things between them.

The liftoff jarred him from his thoughts, and as the ship soared into space, his heart lightened. He could still complete his mission. His crew was safe. They'd found and rescued Kirek. And along the way, he'd found someone extraordinarily special to hold close to his heart.

Dora had a unique way of looking at the world that complemented his more serious nature. He recalled how often she smiled, how she gave of her body during lovemaking, how she'd saved him with cool thinking when the Kwadii had been about to lop off his head, how she'd risked her life to save Kirek—all while keeping an upbeat disposition. Sure, her linking with Ranth disturbed him, but once their mission was completed, she would have no more need to lose herself amid computer circuitry. They could return to Mystique, build a home together.

Vax's voice interrupted Zical's musing. "Prepare for hyperspace."

The familiar sensations of color and sound reassured Zical. They'd overcome enormous obstacles and he was certain they would face many more. Yet his confidence and hopes of success had never been higher and he attributed his feelings of well-being to Dora.

Although he wanted to speak with her, the ship and his responsibilities were his first concern. It was many weary hours later before his shift ended and he turned in. Although he didn't expect to share his quarters before marriage, he was hoping Dora might visit him there. He'd come to think of her as a partner in this mission and valued her ideas as well as her company. But she wasn't asleep. At least not in his empty cabin, and it disappointed him that she wasn't there to celebrate their successful escape.

Zical threaded his fingers through his hair, glad he no longer needed to waste precious time shaving and bathing

since his suit once again took care of his grooming needs.
And yet, right now, the idea of sharing a water shower with
Dora sounded enticing.

Stars. The woman had taken over his thoughts. He supposed once they'd spoken, he'd be able to better focus on his
responsibilities. He wanted to succeed and bring everyone
back safely. With that goal in mind, he convinced himself
that seeking her out now might be best for the mission.

DORA AWAKENED FROM a wonderful dream to Zical's kiss.
"Mmm. I was hoping you'd come find me."

With Kirek snugly tucked away in her sleeping quarters
and the portal between the two areas closed, they had all the
privacy they required. Although they'd made love recently
on Kwadii, it seemed way too long ago, and she wanted to
try making love in hyperspace where sensations were especially sensitive. This time, they could concentrate on pure
pleasure and she needn't try to put aside her worry for Kirek,
the Sentinel, and if they'd ever escape Kwadii.

They'd made it back into space. And now she was ready to
reward the man who'd done everything possible to keep
them alive. His arms around her allowed her to snuggle in
ways she couldn't have done while she'd worn clothing instead of her suit. A simple psi thought here and there allowed for perfect pleasure, perfect pressure. And as she
fitted her mouth to his, her senses quickened.

She'd always dreamed of having Zical for a lover and had
feared that once they'd returned to the ship, he'd go back to
treating her as one of the crew. But he seemed to want her as
much as she wanted him and happiness zinged through her.
She couldn't wait to make love with null grav. The variations
were as endless as the imagination. And she already knew
from past experience that Zical could be quite inventive.

Her flesh tingled in anticipation of his touch and she used
her psi to turn her suit transparent. And then she pulled him

closer, kissed him deeply, showing him her eagerness to be with him.

"Are you awake?" he murmured sexily in her ear.

"Awake enough."

"Good." He pulled back with a wicked gleam in his gaze. "I thought we should talk."

"Mmm." She angled her head to kiss him again, thinking there were tricks to kissing in null grave that she needed to learn. And she yearned to steal a few moments from the mission to relax. He'd earned it. After their madcap escape and reunion with the crew, he'd seen to everyone else's needs. Now it was time for her to see to his. She placed her palm on the back of his neck to steady her floating body, let her fingers caress his speeding pulse. "Talk later. Do you know how long I've been waiting to make love in null grav?"

He nipped her ear and with a psi thought let his suit go transparent, signaling his willingness to make love. "How long?"

"Too long." She adored the long, clean lines of his warrior body. Loved the muscles in his powerful chest and how his strong arms could wrap her so gently in an embrace. But most of all she liked the glowing sparks in his eyes and the laughter on his lips.

With a psi thought she turned her own suit transparent, appreciating how his gaze raked her, interest turning the sparking gleam in his eyes to a fiery glow. Null grave did wonderful things for her breasts, lifting them, rounding their shape, and just the heat from his look had her eager for his touch. Her breasts ached at the thought of his hands on her, his clever fingers touching, teasing, and taunting. Yet she'd already learned that delaying caused anticipation and that anticipation increased their mutual pleasure.

But she didn't want only to give him a lot of pleasure. She wanted to challenge him to let go, to taunt him until he demanded what he wanted, until he took what he needed. She loved the power she had when she caused him to lose con-

trol of his passion. She liked pushing him, daring him to go
after what he wanted. And she was thrilled he wanted her—
and not just her body, which she'd created to entice his
senses—but she knew him well enough to comprehend that
he would never have come to her quarters if he wasn't attracted to the person she'd become. And his approval meant
so much to her.

Nude, she floated before him, considering the possibilities. Without gravity, touching became . . . interesting. She
no longer had to concern herself with weight. Every sensitive sliver of flesh, each delicate nerve, became more easily
accessible.

The basic laws of physics still applied in null grav. For
every action, there was an equal and opposite reaction. At
her caress to his neck, Zical would have floated away, except
she hooked her hand in his and held him steady. One finger
crook was all it took to move his weightless mass.

Except he placed a palm on the ceiling and slid below her,
attempting to place his hands on her bottom to capture her.
But she drew her legs up, twisted, rotated, came up behind
him and lightly nipped his butt.

"Ow." He complained but broke into a chuckle, even as he
twisted to take her into his arms.

His hands barely glanced along her hips, her thighs, streaking heat along her legs, but again, she flung herself away, using the pad of her foot to stream toward the ceiling, like a
swimmer doing a flip turn against the pool's wall. Without
hesitation, Zical zoomed after her, his reflexes quick.

Together they weaved and bobbed, playing a game of tag
that lasted exactly as long as Zical was willing to let her
tease him. He pursued her, grazing a finger down the inside
of her thigh, skimming his palms over her breasts, another
time licking her ear. And she in turn caressed his spine, nibbled along his neck, slid her hands along the strong muscles
of his thighs and buttocks.

And when he caught her in the middle of the room, his

timing was sheer perfection. He'd stopped their movement
so that they floated equidistant between six walls. With her
head toward one bulkhead and her toes pointed at the deck,
he threaded his hands between the curls at her thighs, the
slight tug shooting heat straight to her core.

And then with no warning his mouth closed on her *synthari*. Pure sizzling heat made her hungry and ready to taste
his flesh as he was savoring her, nipping and nibbling until
moisture pooled between her slick folds. With his *tavis* floating right before her, she eagerly took him into her mouth,
enjoying the fresh tang of his skin, the smooth flesh that
writhed under her lips and tongue. Floating, spinning
slowly, his mouth intimately pressed on her, her lips closing
over his rigid flesh, she burned from wanting him, arched to
take more of him into her mouth.

And as he electrified her with his lips and tongue and fingers, she let her tongue dance across his sensitive ridge, determined to drive him into a wild frenzy, pushing him to
want her as badly as she wanted him. Yet, wanting to delay
the pleasure, to make their loving last as long as possible,
she sucked, and stroked and teased, even as the pressure inside her demanded release.

She focused on his tangy scent, his turgid heat, his tight
sacs that she lovingly caressed, eliciting a murmured groan.
But he never stopped kissing her, and when she couldn't
keep her hips still, he locked her in place with his psi, keeping her exactly where he wanted.

When she thought she could take no more, with his psi,
he'd started rotating them slowly. Together, he spun them.
Dizzy, she closed her eyes and focused on the blood rushing
to her breasts, hardening her nipples, then emptying,
swelling her *synthari*. The stunning rush of her senses
heightened the frantic thrust of her hips. As her blood raced,
her heart pounding to keep up with the frenzied fervor, if her
mouth hadn't been so busy, she might have screamed.

Without gravity to distract her, the tug and pull of her

spinning flesh encompassed her. There was no dizziness, just the swelling and ebbing of her blood spiraling into every erotic aching cell that demanded release. As she gasped for air, trying to hold on, her heart sang with delight at the pleasure they could take in each other. And she basked in the knowledge that her power to excite and arouse him was as total as his over her.

Elated by her conviction that they belonged together, her need to have his arms around her, his *tavis* inside her, had her flipping, twisting in midair, parting her thighs and wrapping her legs around his waist. Burying her lips in his neck, adoring the feel of her breasts brushing his chest and his strong hands taking control of her hips, she gave herself up to her senses.

With her scent on his lips, his ragged breath in her ear, his *tavis* creating the most delicious friction, she tried to recall every precious sensory detail. His gaze that was as soft as a caress. The urgency in his hands, the tingling in her stomach. The vibrant chord he strummed inside her. Her feelings for him that had everything and nothing to do with reason. His psi that wrapped around her like a warm blanket. Her erratic heartbeat. Her gulped breaths. His husky groan in her ear, his electric tension that inflamed the rising blaze of need that burned white hot in her core. His bursting, shredding, and shattering pleasure that she rode with a joy that seared her heart and made her soul sing.

When her breath finally slowed and her heartbeat once more approached normal, she snuggled against his warm chest, content and happy. As much as she adored making love, the sweet aftermath was just as nice. She liked pillowing her head on his shoulder, liked the way he ran his palms over her back and bottom, constantly caressing as if he'd never tire of touching her.

"There's something I want to say."

She opened her eyes and peered into his, which looked too damn serious. If he was going to tell her they had to return to being captain and crew, then he shouldn't have made love to her. Because she couldn't go back to pretending she didn't want him.

"Mmm?"

"Are you sure you're paying attention?"

She peered at him warily, heart tensing. "Say it already."

"We should marry."

Maybe she was still dreaming. Or dizzy after that crazy spinning. She'd thought he said they should wed. She rubbed her brow and the last of her fuzzy passion cleared away. "Did you just say what I think?"

"We should wed," he repeated, the expression on his face expectant.

Stars! Dora didn't know what to say. She was at a loss for words and simply gaped. She'd thought he'd been about to tell her he intended to sever their physical relationship. That they couldn't make love like they'd just done now that they were back in space. But he wanted to form a permanent union.

He wanted to wed.

And Rystani mated for life.

Stars. Why hadn't she seen this coming?

"Say something," Zical demanded.

"I don't know what to say." She was shocked, honored, confused. She needed to sort out her thoughts and feelings. She needed to talk to Tessa. But they were too far from Mystique for a real conversation, even through the hyperspace com link, the time lag between a question and a reply could be days.

"Say you want to be my wife." Expectancy kept his voice tight.

"I don't know if I want to be anyone's wife." She said the words slowly, slowly withdrawing from his arms. "I haven't thought about the future. I've been so busy living in the moment, trying to adapt and survive that I just . . . don't know . . ."

Zical's eyes flashed hurt, then he quickly disguised the hurt with a tough veneer of hardness and a psi thought that clothed him in his captain's uniform. "Being human is planning for the future."

"I haven't thought that far ahead."

She hadn't thought past making it from one day to the next. She hadn't thought past saving Kirek and leaving Kwadii. She hadn't thought beyond finishing their mission. She hadn't thought past how much she enjoyed looking at his face, running her fingers through his thick hair, skimming her palms over his muscular frame, and how much she liked making love. She enjoyed their conversations. She enjoyed being with him. Why did he have to go and change things between them? But change seemed also to be part of being human and now she had more to consider than her own wants and needs.

They'd been doing so well as lovers. She'd actually been happy. But she saw that her reaction to marriage hadn't been one he'd expected and that her uncertainty was causing him pain. And his pain hurt her. Odd how that could be so, but she cared too much for him not to try and explain. She just wasn't sure she could put her confusion into words.

She swallowed the knot in her throat and licked her bottom lip, hoping she could make him understand. "When I was a computer, the present was always filled with billions of bits of new data. With so much to file and learn and absorb, I rarely thought past the present. And since I've become human, I've had difficulty coping with the moment I'm in. I'm having trouble getting past this mission. To think about my personal future is a whole different process."

"So marriage to me doesn't interest you at the moment?" His eyes flashed with hurt.

By the five seas of Jarn, he wasn't listening. "I have a hard enough time dealing with the present. To take on the future too—the idea of marriage to you is . . . overwhelming."

A smile cracked through his pain. "I was hoping you'd say I was irresistible."

"I need more time. It wasn't so long ago that I doubted I could live in this body," she reminded him, trying to choose each word with utmost care. "I thought all the spasms and twitching might be the organs rejecting my soul."

"Those twitches were likely caused by fear. But as you adjusted, you overcame your fears and the spasms stopped. You've come so far. Can't you take one more step? I know you're brave. You've proved it repeatedly." He hesitated. "Or maybe you just don't feel enough passion for me to make our union permanent?" His tone was gentle, but conveyed a world of disappointment.

"That's not fair. You ask about my feelings without stating your own. You've never said more than I have." She stared at him accusingly. He'd said nothing of love or even liking or caring. He'd simply said they should marry—but there was nothing simple about his statement. And she resented that he'd told her they should wed without even asking her opinion. Almost as if he'd never considered that she would refuse him. She supposed that was typical Rystani male behavior. But a small part of her wondered if he figured that since she'd once been a computer, she would be so grateful for his offer, she'd immediately agree to the union. More likely he figured that since she wanted to make love to him, she also wanted to wed.

But even worse than his attitude was the fluttery panic in her gut that her decision now affected more than her own life. They had more to discuss, and knowing Rystani custom, she supposed he was going to be even more upset with her shortly.

So she didn't dwell on what she'd given up to become human. Unless she died prematurely by an accident, she'd given up immortality to live a thousand years. To a computer one thousand years sounded like a short time, especially since there was so much more she wanted to experience. She wanted to visit Earth. And Osari. And Scartar. She wanted to see the Federation homeworld Zenon. She wanted to lie on a sand beach under a hot sun, learn to swim in emerald seas, and cook as well as Miri. She felt as though she were just learning to be human. Just learning how to communicate, how to make love, how to reach out to people and enjoy what they had in common. She wanted a few years to be selfish. Was that so wrong?

In her heart, she knew Zical was a good man. She cared about him more than any other man she'd met. He was honorable, brave, loyal. Special. But she didn't know if she wanted to spend all of her life with him. Suppose they grew tired of each other? Suppose she met someone else she liked more? She hadn't lived long enough to know what she wanted.

"We would make a good fit." He stated his case as if they were pieces of a puzzle, inanimate objects.

"A good fit?" Now he'd insulted her and hurt caused her tongue to loosen. "Do you think I'm so new at being human that I don't know the difference between getting along well and a grand passion?"

"I didn't—"

"And please don't take this personally, but I don't know if I want to follow Rystani customs."

"How else can I take it except personally? I am Rystani," he said with heat and pride and bitterness, his chin held high, his eyes narrowed on her in fierce concentration—as if he feared she might flee at any moment.

"And I think of myself as a woman, but not one from any particular world. Your customs . . . are not necessarily those I would choose for my own."

He shoved away from her, his expression harsh at her rejection. "If you wish to spend the rest of your life alone, then . . . I will leave you to it."

"It's not that simple."

"Seems to me you've made it very simple."

"What we've made is complicated."

"You don't want me for a husband. Nothing complicated about that."

"I need time to adjust to . . ." She hesitated to tell him more, gathered her courage.

"You need time to adjust to me?"

"It's not always about you." She flashed her own anger at him, letting her tone bite. "I need time to adjust to . . . the new life we made on Kwadii. A life growing in my womb." She curled her hand protectively over her stomach, still stunned at what she'd learned just today through her suit. The baby growing inside her was a miracle that changed not just her plans but her every thought. She didn't understand how she'd become so human, but the baby inside her already dominated her thoughts, colored her emotions, and somehow, someway, she already loved it. Unconditionally.

"What!" Zical's eyes widened with shock, happiness, worry. His lips softened and then his entire face glowed with joy. "You're pregnant?"

She couldn't contain her happy grin. "I wasn't sure until we returned to the ship, but when we were on Kwadii, we didn't wear our suits while making love." She pointed out what should have been obvious. She supposed he'd had plenty on his mind while on the hostile planet and that it was natural for him to have forgotten that the suits prevented unwanted pregnancies.

"We're having a baby?" Amazement rocked him and softened his tone.

"Yes." Dora had only found out a few hours ago. And she'd wanted to tell Zical at a moment when their lives weren't threatened, when their minds weren't distracted by the mission. She still wasn't certain what she thought about becoming a mother. However, her feelings for her unborn child were as strong as the ones she already felt for Kirek, and joy suffused her. However, ready as she might be to raise this baby, raising a child took twenty years or so—but Zical was asking for centuries.

"Dora, I know you said you haven't thought about the future, but now you must do so for our child's sake."

She tilted her head, surprised at the sudden vehemence in his tone. "What do you mean?"

"A child requires a mother and a father."

"You're the child's father," she agreed. "You contributed the DNA."

"Contributing DNA is not enough. A child needs a father's love and guidance, and not only is it wrong to deny me that role, you must also think of what is good for our child."

"I would never deny you parental privileges."

Zical came to her and took her hand. "Dora, I thought we were a good fit before you told me the wonderful news. Now, we can be a family. A real family. We should raise this child together."

Panic caused her to pull away. He spoke of his child in a loving tone and already she sensed his possessiveness. But surely she could be a mother and still do what was best for herself too? If she felt tied down and limited by a marriage, what kind of mother would she be?

"I'm not sure. I only know that I'm not ready for marriage. I need time."

"Do you doubt I would care for you and our child?" he asked, his earlier happiness fading to a bleak resignation.

She shook her head, wanting to be truthful, wishing she didn't feel her throat closing with tightness, her eyes about to overflow with tears, even as she knew that her uncertainty would cause additional damage. "I am not sure if I want to link my life to yours forever. I don't need a man to take care of me." Her voice dropped to a painful whisper. "It is my ability to commit to you that I doubt."

"You don't know what you can do until you try." Zical's eyes pleaded but his stiff and stilted tone told her that he was deeply disappointed in her.

"You don't get it." She took a deep breath. "The idea of becoming a mother is all I can deal with right now."

"Dora." Zical took her hand between hers. "I'll help you

all that I can. But please tell me you feel up to the task of motherhood. Or do you fear that responsibility too?"

"I'm not afraid." At her words, the tension in his shoulders eased. And she already wanted this child with a fierceness that made her breath catch. "It's just that I didn't picture my life taking this path."

"Neither did I. When I was a boy, I thought I'd grow up on Rystan. I never dreamed I'd have enough to eat or that I'd pilot a starship or that I'd father a child with a woman who was born as a machine. I never dreamed that my foolish exploration on Mount Shachauri could threaten life in the galaxy or that it would be our destiny to try and stop the Zin. We can't always choose our fates."

"I know that." She squeezed his hand and then released it. "Give me time to adjust."

He released a sigh of exasperation. "I'd rather we raise our child together, but if you aren't up to the task,"—his tone softened to gentle, fuzzy, sensitive—"I will raise and love the baby alone."

At his tender words, she wanted to cuddle in his arms and let out a sob. Already, she was too attached to the life growing in her womb to ever hand the baby over to him to raise after it was born. But it wasn't fair to take comfort from him when she couldn't promise him a future together. So she held back. Held back the tears of frustration that with all her intellect and all her planning and all her great knowledge of science, she'd forgotten the basic biological fact that when women and men copulated, they made babies.

She'd thought of having a child in the abstract. Much like she'd thought of someday having a husband. It was for a time in the distant future. She certainly hadn't expected to tie herself down with such responsibilities during her first year of being human. And yet she couldn't help the eagerness and excitement and love from spiraling. What would their child look like? What kind of personality would it have? Boy or girl?

She didn't care. She simply prayed that it would be born healthy and strong. And she wondered if she could be a good mother when she'd had none of her own to learn from by example.

After they returned to Mystique, Miri and Shaloma and Tessa would help her. As would Etru and Kahn. But of their family, only Tessa would understand her reluctance to marry Zical. And if she never married, likely only Tessa would remain nonjudgmental. But Dora couldn't make her decision based on how others would judge her. Whatever she decided, her baby would be loved.

Chapter Twenty-one

ZICAL AVOIDED DORA for the next two days in hyperspace. Although she often dwelled on her impending motherhood, she also worried about her future as well as Zical's. Since what Kirek needed most to recover from his ordeal was rest, he spent most of his time sleeping, and it gave her too much time to think. Mostly, she fixated about the future success of their meeting with the Sentinel.

After their escape from Kwadii, Ranth had run a self-diagnostic program. He'd discovered that while he'd hidden in the vault, the hyperdrive had been tampered with, slowing their progress. Dora knew Zical had questioned the newcomers on board, Avanti and Deckar, but she could think of no motive for them to attempt to slow the mission. They were spending all their time developing their psi to operate their Federation suits. She figured it more likely that when the Kwadii had put the dampeners on their systems, and Ranth couldn't protect the system while hidden in the vault, the dampeners had somehow adversely affected the hyperdrive.

Although repairs had been undertaken, Ranth estimated it would now require an entire extra week to reach the galaxy's rim, where they hoped to find a way to contact the Sentinel, then reprogram the ancient machine to return to guard the galaxy. The scientists were already discussing theoretical issues on how to locate the Sentinel.

However, now that they were so much closer to the rim, Dora wanted to attempt to gather more information. During the journey her psi had strengthened, and Ranth and she worked more smoothly together than ever before. Their reach into space was far greater, their ability to infiltrate distant star systems more manageable, and they'd broadened their communications networks to gather information.

And she hoped that since the Sentinel was now closer to the Milky Way Galaxy, she might contact the machine directly. The knowledge she could gain would be invaluable, and the task would also give her relief from thinking about Zical, his marriage proposal, and the baby growing inside her. Much more comfortable in the world of logic and statistics and program analysis than in dealing with her personal problems, she tapped into Ranth, hoping that with the hyperdrive repairs completed, he could give her his full power.

Ranth?

Linking.

Dora's mind merged with the processors, the hardware, her sensory array expanding until she could "see" from thousands of ship's sensors, monitor hundreds of thousands of random communications, take in so many details that it flooded her brain. To avoid mental burnout, she focused on keeping only the data she required, filtering out extraneous material. And as she linked with Ranth, she lost her sense of smell, her sense of touch, becoming lost in a system of intricately woven code.

And then Ranth's and her psi, powered up, shooting them through hyperspace, linking with machines from thousands, maybe millions, of other worlds. They ignored all data except that which pertained to legends of the Perceptive Ones, the Sentinel, and contacting and reprogramming the machines.

They found so little. On a planet called Haptarin was an outpost where the Perceptive Ones might have once spoken to the people on Mount Faragon. On Danjabo, she caught a reference to the Perceptive Ones in an ancient museum, noted a sculpture labeled *The Sentinel,* and collected odd bits of data that alone made no sense but perhaps when studied over time might aid their quest.

Stretching their new powers, they flung their psi ever outward toward the rim, where the stars thinned and the galaxy succumbed to the vastness of empty space between galaxies. Utter blackness, utter quiet cocooned them.

Silence.

Darkness.

Emptiness.

Without Ranth's link, Dora would have been terrified of becoming lost in the immensity of nothingness. And still they stretched their psi out toward the Andromeda Galaxy. Pushing. Seeking. And Dora's isolation increased as she let go of all sense of self. Hurtled through the great blackness until . . .

Ranth. What is that? She noted a tendril of alien intelligence. An iota of a psi tickle.

I am Guranu.

The words came to her clearly, the entity responding in pure thought. *Guranu. A resting place for the Sentinels during their long journey.*

The information excited and stunned. They'd assumed from the start of their mission that there was only one Sentinel. But Guranu had indicated there might be more.

Sentinels? There is more than one?

Guranu maintains contacts with thousands of Sentinels. Do you require aid?

We require communication and information, Dora requested, electrified by this contact, but worried that they couldn't maintain the link for long. The distances were simply too far, their powers weakening by the second. All along they'd thought that a single Sentinel, one machine, protected them from the Zin. To learn there were so many astounded her.

And then hope rose in her. Was it possible only one Sentinel had been recalled? And that the rest remained between the Milky Way and Andromeda galaxies still standing watch as they had for eons?

Guranu can link you and the Sentinels. Stand by.

Standing by, Dora agreed, wondering if their entire journey might have been for nothing. If Zical's presence at Mount Shachauri had only recalled one machine of thousands, they all might still be safe. And the crew could go home to Mystique if they could find another powersource. Dora would have liked nothing more than to speed them through hyperspace to return to have her baby with her best friend at her side. To be cut off from Tessa had made Dora grow, but she missed Tessa and longed to talk to her. About Zical. About the baby. About what Dora should do next.

This is Sentinel 17592. Why do you seek communication?

Have all Sentinels been recalled? Dora asked.

Yes.

Oh, no. It was worse than she'd thought and her hopes that all was at it should be burned out as quickly as a falling meteor. If all the Sentinels had been recalled, their task was now much more difficult. How would they find and contact them all? Somehow they'd have to find a way to turn all of them around—a seemingly impossible goal.

The recall order was an error, Dora communicated to the Sentinel. *All of you must turn around.*

The Sentinels do not listen to the enemy.

Enemy? The Sentinel thought they were the enemy? Then why had it given them the information they'd been recalled? Nothing made sense. Panic filled her. She tried to explain. *We are not the enemy. We are on the same side. The Perceptive Ones created the Sentinel to protect us from the Zin.*

You harbor an ally of the Zin. You are the enemy.

Dora sensed the machine's implacable will. Had the Sentinel's programming broken down, just like the Perceptive Ones' programming on Mount Shachauri? She sent a tendril down the link, hoping to infiltrate the system and discern the problem.

And struck a wall. A wall harder than *bendar*. A wall that hurled her and Ranth backward. And then blinding light shot out, only it wasn't simply light, but energy, pure hellish energy that destroyed two worlds near their starship, one to port, one to starboard.

Their ship shuddered, and sped onward, safe in hyperspace. But her own continued well-being didn't prevent Dora's horror.

Billions of innocent people had just died.

Dora jolted back into her body and immediately thought she might be sick. Slowly she realized that Zical was running his hands up and down her arms, a fierce glower of anger and concern on his face. She had no idea how long he'd been there but he must have been monitoring the link with Guranu and the Sentinels through Ranth.

Too stunned to talk, she didn't even ask him what he was doing here. Dregan hell. Two worlds. Billions of people dead within the space of a heartbeat. All because she'd contacted the Sentinel.

"The Sentinel may attack again." Zical spoke in a rush, but never raised his voice although every muscle in his neck tensed. It was a measure of his concern for the ship that he didn't ask if she was all right. As captain, it was his job to ensure the safety of them all. Yet she couldn't stop shaking, wanting his arms around her. Slowly she recalled she had no right to take that kind of comfort from him but couldn't get past the knowledge she'd made a terrible mistake.

"Ranth's been filling me in." Zical led her to the vidscreen where he showed her how close the energy burst had come to destroying their ship. "The Sentinel tried to kill us and missed."

"It's my fault." Slowly she gathered her wits.

"You didn't do anything wrong. The Sentinel made a mistake, not you."

She shook her head. "It said we're the enemy, and those worlds would still exist if I hadn't contacted the Sentinel."

Ranth added more facts in an attempt to assuage her guilt. "It's amazing that these great machines have lasted for eons. Sooner or later, parts wear down, energy dissipates. The Sentinel didn't recognize us, that's why it attacked."

With his ship in danger, Zical's tone was impatient. "Dora, get over the guilt. The Perceptive Ones' machine killed those worlds—not you."

"Billions of intelligent beings died. Mothers and fathers. Children. Entire races." Chilled, sickened, she had to fight to prevent her teeth from chattering.

"Making choices without knowing all the facts is part of being human."

Dora was beginning to hate that phrase about being human. Her stomach twisted into knots that had her crossing her arms over her stomach and rocking. How could she go on with her life after knowing what she'd done?

As if reading her mind, Zical answered her unspoken question. "You'll have to learn to forgive yourself. Sometimes the loss we suffer makes us appreciate the gift of what we do have. But right now, I need you with me, or more people may die. What are the chances of the Sentinel attacking us again?"

"I don't know," she whispered, her head aching as she tried to get past the horrible loss. "The Sentinel may not even know the attack failed. Or it could be reloading that terrible weapon."

"Why didn't the Sentinel recognize us?" Zical paced to and fro in her quarters, his hands clasped behind his back, his chin jutting forward with the determination to find a solution to the mystery of why they'd been attacked.

Dora had trouble understanding and thinking clearly with the throbbing in her head. "Either the programming broke down or someone changed it."

"A race as intelligent as the Perceptive Ones would have taken precautions," Zical said.

"Maybe they did. The machines the Perceptive Ones built on Laptiva for the Challenge still recognize that we are the true descendants. Our suits still work. It doesn't make sense that all these machines would break down in the same way. That attack wasn't from just one Sentinel, it was a coordinated group effort." She shivered, her tone as bleak as the despair inside her. If she hadn't contacted the Sentinel, billions of beings on two worlds would be going about their normal lives, eating, shopping, studying, working. Now, they were gone, two entire planets, utterly, completely disintegrated. For once she wished she could stop thinking. Shut down her brain. But the human mind didn't always do what its owner wanted. Despite her despair, she kept coming up with ideas.

"Maybe the Zin altered it and turned the Sentinels against us," Zical suggested. "We need to know. You'll have to tap in again."

He sounded as reluctant as she felt. Yet he'd gone ahead and urged her. Torn, overwhelmed by grief, she realized that even if he ordered her to contact the Sentinel, she would have to refuse. But she hoped it wouldn't come to a contest of wills, especially if she had to break her word that she'd obey his direct command. Better if she could convince him that contacting the Sentinel would compound their problem.

"If I tap in again, the Sentinels will probably attack again."

"Not if you convince them that we mean no harm."

"We have no way to convince them." And she wouldn't risk the lives of more innocents. The Sentinel was a planet killer. She would not be responsible for sending more people to their deaths.

Zical's eyes narrowed on her, his tone insistent but firm. "Dora, if you don't try, that weapon might turn on every planet in the galaxy."

"And it also may go back to ignoring us," she countered, her voice weaker than she would have liked.

"Right now, ignoring us is almost as bad as attacking. The Sentinels are supposed to be out there to protect us from the Zin. Without them . . ."

Dora gathered her wits. "Perhaps the Zin no longer exist. Perhaps they've expanded to other galaxies and are no longer interested in ours."

"We can't ignore the responsibility placed on us. My people have lost their home and settled on a new world. They've been through enough—"

"So has this crew," Dora reminded him.

Zical frowned. "This crew made their choice before the mission. We all knew the risks. If there's a way we can protect those on Mystique, we must. You and Ranth will—"

"No."

Zical ran his fingers through his hair in aggravation. His irritation might just erupt into a full-fledged order, she knew it.

But he held his temper and spoke more softly than she expected. "Then give me another alternative."

At his plea, her mind began to race. "The entity called Guranu claimed it was a resting place for the Sentinels during their long journey."

"A resting place? A graveyard for broken machines? Or a place to repair them?"

"It may be all or none of those things." She shook her head. "But I sensed Guranu is probably a giant space station between the Milky Way and Andromeda galaxies. Guranu told us it maintains contact with the Sentinels. It would make sense for Guranu to be a control center. Perhaps if we stop there, we can either figure out another way to reprogram the Sentinels to recognize that we are allies, not enemies, without risking more lives."

Zical stared at Dora, and she could guess the reason for his rising concern. The trip to the galaxy's rim was farther than anyone from the Federation had ever traveled. Without the two black holes that had boosted their initial journey, without the Kwadii system to aid their own hyperdrives, they could pop out of hyperspace between two galaxies without too much difficulty, but the problem would be the return trip.

"Ranth," Dora said. "Approximate Guranu's position and estimate the turnaround time to Federation space under normal hyperdrive conditions."

"Five hundred, eighty-seven point four three years."

"So if we go out there, there's a good chance that none of us will ever return home alive?" Zical asked.

Dora's hand went to her womb. "With an estimated life span of one thousand years, our child would be middle-aged by the time this ship could return to Mystique."

"Unless you wish to attempt to contact the Sentinel again, we don't have a choice." Zical's face was hard, stoic, but his eyes revealed a flash of desperation, and Dora gulped back tears.

The choice facing them was terrible. They owed it to everyone on Mystique to complete their mission. From the start of the journey, they'd been aware the odds would be against them as they traveled into unknown space, but that she'd have to choose between her own life and her unborn child's and the lives of everyone back home was a terrible dilemma. She already felt worse for the tiny life growing inside her than she did over the fact that if they continued their mission, the likelihood of them ever seeing Mystique alive again was almost nil.

How could she allow her body and the child she carried in her womb to die? But how could she abandon their mission and risk the lives of everyone back home?

ZICAL EXPLAINED THE terrible options to his crew on the bridge and allowed those off duty and the scientists below to sit in through the holovid system. Under usual circumstances, he might not inform the crew of their situation. But these weren't normal times, and with the stakes so high, he wanted to hear the opinions of those he trusted most.

Zical kept his shoulders squared, his chin high, knowing the others would take their cue from his demeanor. "So, people, we have to decide whether to turn back, risk another contact with the Sentinel, or venture between the galaxies in the hopes that Guranu may help us reprogram the Sentinels. I'm open to opinions."

Vax didn't hesitate. "We go to Guranu."

Zical had never appreciated his second in command more. Although Vax didn't have a wife or children on Mystique, his elderly parents still lived. But he'd always put the mission first, and Zical relied on his steadfast belief that they could make a difference by committing to what would essentially be a one-way trip.

Shannon, his communications officer, shot him a thumbs-up. "I'd like to go where no Terran has gone before."

"Cyn?"

His chief engineer frowned. "You're asking a lot of my engines, Captain. But we're good to travel."

Zical was proud of their selflessness. He only wished he didn't have to ask them to make this kind of sacrifice. And although his heart might break over the child that would likely never know a home planet or have the support of a real family unit beyond this crew, he could ask for no better companions and could do no less than his duty. He owed it to his people to make the ultimate effort. Too much was at stake to do less.

Dr. Laduna spoke up. "No. No. No. We're throwing our lives away for nothing. I don't mind dying for a good reason, but we have no idea if this Guranu can help us. We are gambling our lives on the thinnest of theories. We should turn around, go home. Reassess."

"With utmost resect, I disagree with Dr. Laduna," said another scientist somewhat heatedly. "We all knew the risks. We came out here to do a job. We should finish it."

Many of the other scientists cheered. Dr. Laduna shook his head, the Jarn's fish eyes sad and soulful. However, while the Jarn's was the only dissenting vote, the ship wasn't a democracy. The decision was Zical's and he made it with a heavy heart. "Ranth, plot a course for Guranu."

"Compliance."

They spent three days in hyperspace accelerating into the void. Cyn kept careful watch on her precious engines, but without even the smallest particles of matter to slow them, their speed encompassed thousands of light-years per second. Zical didn't even try to keep track of the vast distance in light-years. Instead he consulted the stars and verified their progress in massive sectors as they approached Guranu.

He occupied his time by keeping up morale with steady encouragement and sending back a detailed log to Mystique, even as he questioned if he'd made the right decision. During the middle of the night when he couldn't sleep, doubts assailed him. Doubts that they could successfully complete the mission. Doubts that he should ask so much from his crew. Doubts that he and Dora would live long enough to solve their problems. And Zical worked harder than ever during the day. While it might take weeks or even months for messages to reach home, at least the Federation would know what had happened to them and what they planned to do. So that if they failed, another course of action could be tried.

If Zical and his crew didn't succeed, the Federation would send yet another ship, ask another crew to sacrifice their lives. His determination hardened with every passing light sector. They had to succeed. As the time approached to drop out of hyperspace, Zical's anticipation skyrocketed even as the crew became slightly oversensitive. No crew had ever spent this long in hyperspace and the continued assault on their senses made them irritable. And with the gamble they were about to take, where the stakes could not have been greater, he wished to steady his people and had ordered Ranth to exit hyperspace within a half-day's journey from Guranu. Traveling the remaining distance in regular space would give them time to settle down and to explore from afar—although he wondered how much that would protect him, since the Sentinel seemed to have fired on his ship from half a galaxy away. Still, he'd rather approach the unknown slowly, giving their sensors time to analyze, his crew time to assess. With the fate of everyone he knew at stake, he and his crew could not afford to make errors.

And Zical worried that perhaps, just perhaps, the Sentinel had been correct when it called them an enemy. Ever since they'd left Kwadii and discovered the problem with the hyperdrive that had delayed them, he'd wondered if they had a saboteur aboard.

While Zical would bet his life that his crew was loyal, he could never be as certain of the scientists—whom he didn't know as well. And yet, what would any of them have to gain by slowing the drive? Why not just dismantle it? But perhaps they hadn't had time. Perhaps they wanted them to turn around as Dr. Laduna had suggested.

Or he might be suspicious for no reason at all. Without more to go on, he tried to put treachery from inside the ship from his mind. Between the Sentinels and Guranu he had enough real problems.

"Ten seconds to n-space," Vax warned the crew.

As the countdown to leave hyperspace and enter normal space ensued, Zical kept his eyes on the vidscreen. "Ranth, place long-range detectors on priority."

"Compliance."

"Five seconds."

Zical braced for the change, anchoring his body firmly to the deck with his psi. The ship wouldn't so much as vibrate during the transition, but the effect on the senses could cause an unwary traveler to stumble.

"Entering n-space."

Zical braced for the black emptiness of space, trying to prepare himself for the void between the galaxies. Out here there were no planets, no stars, no universal dust.

So he was astonished when the klaxon sounded. "Purple alert. We are under attack."

Chapter Twenty-two

DORA HEARD THE klaxon in her quarters. Kirek was with Avanti and Deckar, helping them to learn to use their psi and operate their suits, so she had no obligations to the boy at the moment. Even as Zical ordered her to report to the bridge, she used her psi to go there, her muscles tense, her nerves back on edge.

Now what? Had Guranu turned against them and attacked? As if they hadn't already had enough problems on this journey, they now had another emergency to deal with, and it seemed as though fate were stacked against them. Ever since Zical had first stumbled upon the ancient machinery inside Mount Shachauri, and their close calls on Kwadii, and the Sentinel firing upon them, she'd figured they were due for some good luck for a change.

But once she saw the viewscreen with warships dotting the void between the galaxies, she realized the alarm hadn't been another computer glitch—like the problem with the hyperdrive—as she'd first thought. Nor had their bad luck changed.

The crew were at battle stations, alert and calm, but for some reason unknown to her, Dr. Laduna was also on the bridge. And one of the crew held a weapon on the cowering scientist, who stared at the giant vidscreen with terror.

Her gaze went to Zical for answers, but she didn't interrupt his battle preparations. The captain stood on the bridge, his back to her, issuing precise orders, yet with uncanny precision he seemed to know the moment she arrived.

"Ranth?" Dora asked. "Why is Dr. Laduna under guard?"

"Those are Jarn ships."

"Jarn?" Dora turned to Dr. Laduna, and suddenly she understood who had slowed their mission after they'd left Kwadii. Dr. Laduna had tampered with the engines to allow the Jarn fleet to arrive ahead of them. But why?

Dr. Laduna's expression was grim and his entire body trembled. "I am sorry."

Zical finished giving orders, then turned from Vax to Dr. Laduna, his anger ready to erupt at the man whose people were responsible for attempting to stop his mission. Zical placed his hands behind his back and closed his fingers into fists, but he fired words like ammunition, his tone harsh. "Why are your people trying to stop us?"

"We had no choice." Dr. Laduna's fish eyes blinked at him, his amphibious scales turning an odd shade of green.

Rystani warriors did not take betrayal well. Zical's eyes burned, as if he had to contain the savage urge to pound the Jarn's head against a bulkhead until his brains spattered. But the captain held himself in check. "Explain."

"Eons ago, the Zin and the Perceptive Ones warred for supremacy of our galaxy. The battles were fierce. Billions of us lost our lives." Dr. Laduna's voice lectured with methodical precision as if he stood in a lecture hall, but his trembling didn't stop and his color turned even paler.

In no mood for a history lecture, Zical demanded, "Get to the point."

"The Zin pierced the Perceptive One's defenses, stormed the Jarn homeworld, defeated our soldiers, quashed our independence, and subjugated our world." The Jarn spoke quickly. "The Zin technology was superior to ours and they enslaved my people by encoding a self-replicating data chip into our DNA. That chip carries orders that every Jarn knows and must obey from the moment of birth."

Dora had no idea if such a thing were possible, but she wouldn't discount the possibility that the Zin possessed advanced technology far beyond what the Federation had today. Dora burned with questions and asked the one pressing on her conscience. "Dr. Laduna, the Sentinel detected your DNA aboard our ship from halfway across the galaxy and fired on us."

"That is their maximum range of detection."

And that would explain why the Jarn had penetrated the Perceptive Ones' facility on Mystique without attracting the Sentinel's notice. "But how is it the Sentinel didn't also fire on your fleet once it arrived here?"

"Our ships have a cloaking device to deceive the Sentinels."

Zical glanced at the menacing fleet of Jarn ships on the vidscreen, then back to Dr. Laduna. "What are the instructions in your Jarn DNA?"

"Our orders were to infiltrate the worlds around us, pretend we were one with the descendants of the Perceptive Ones."

"Why?"

"To bring down the Sentinels for our masters, the Zin."

Zical's eyebrows rose in skepticism. "You're saying that eons ago, the Zin anticipated our mission and planted this DNA coding inside the Jarn to betray us?"

"No one could envision that the machinery on Mount Shachauri would break down or that your entrance would accidentally trigger the ancient mechanisms to recall the Sentinels. Our orders are simply to destroy the Sentinels from within. We waited for hundreds of thousands of years, living peacefully among you, hoping that the opportunity to obliterate the Sentinels would never come. However, each time we spawned our young, we passed on our DNA and the coded chip, along with the Zin's commands to the next generation. Until this mission, we could not act. We didn't have the means."

Fury at the Zin's scheme and the Jarn's willingness to ally themselves with an enemy that had enslaved their world left Dora little respect for these people. Never had she been so angry, and that anger had her shaking to do violence. If she'd had the opportunity and the strength, she might have squeezed his scaly neck until he was no more.

Zical, however, remained calm. "So you were the one responsible for slowing us down in hyperspace so that the Jarn fleet would arrive before us?"

"Yes, Captain." The Jarn spoke in a rush. "Captain. We had no choice. If we fail to carry out our orders, the chip changes our body chemistry and we die."

"The chip can't be removed?" Horror at the Jarn problem softened Zical's tone, and it served to divert some of Dora's anger from the Jarn to the Zin, for putting an entire race in such a difficult position.

"The chip's part of our DNA. We've spent a millennium studying the problem, trying to remove it from our biology. Obviously, we failed or we would not be having this discussion."

"How does the DNA know whether or not you work with the Zin?"

"We don't understand the process. We only know that once a Jarn thinks of a task that the Zin consider an order, we die if we ignore it. We don't consider the Zin our allies, but our masters, whom we must serve and obey."

The Jarn had been used by the Zin, but, surely after so

much time a way could have been found to alter their biology—if only they hadn't kept the fact a secret. Dora frowned at Laduna. "Why did you not ask the Federation for help with your problem?"

"Our analysis showed that Federation science could not help us, and your most likely reaction would be isolation, or extermination. Besides, we most sincerely hoped that the Sentinels would remain in place forever. You must believe that we did not anticipate what has happened."

Dora's head was spinning. With the multitude of ramifications of genetic and biological sciences way beyond the comprehension of her human brain, she simply didn't know if Dr. Laduna was feeding them a far-fetched tale, or the truth. "Ranth. Analysis, please?"

"The Jarn DNA has a strand unlike that of any other living creature. It's both biological and chemical, yet part nanotechnology. Our scientists never understood the purpose for that particular sequence. It is likely the Sentinel's scanners detected and identified the Jarn DNA as the handiwork of the Zin and therefore concluded that we are the enemy. And it's also likely the Jarn fleet has a DNA cloaking device, since the Sentinel failed to attack them."

So the Sentinel's programming hadn't broken down. It had recognized what the Federation people had not—that the Jarn were an ally of the Zin. And so the Sentinel had concluded that since the *Verazen* had a Jarn aboard, they must all be the enemy. No wonder the machine had fired on them.

"So you see, Captain. We had no choice but to try and stop your mission."

"You could have sacrificed your world."

The Jarn hung his head in shame, then jerked up his chin, his eyes flashing defiance. "Is that the choice you would have made? To slay every man, woman, and child on your planet?"

Zical's gaze burned into the scientist's. "I don't know. Why did you tell me now?"

"Guilt." The Jarn shrugged. "Maybe I want your forgiveness. And to warn you."

"Warn me?"

"The Jarn fleet has already begun shutting down the Sentinels. It's only a matter of time until the Zin invade. My telling you their plan . . . is my death sentence." The Jarn's scales turned white. His double-lidded eyes closed and he fell to the deck.

One of the armed crewmen stepped forward and felt for a heartbeat. "He's dead, Captain."

Dora's lower jaw dropped. The Jarn had given his life to tell them the Zin's plan. If she hadn't been so upset by the sudden turn of events, she would have seen the obvious much sooner. Dr. Laduna wanted the Federation to stop the Jarn fleet, reprogram the Sentinels, and stop the Zin.

Dora's anger turned to compassion for Dr. Laduna's untenable position. He had had to make a dreadful choice. And now they had to find a way to get past the fleet and undo the damage the Jarn had done to the Sentinels, in order to stop the Zin invasion.

Zical glanced at her. "Dora, I need you to link with Ranth."

"What do you want us to do?" she asked, even as she linked with the computer, taking a bit of comfort in the instant rapport she shared with the machine and welcoming the numbing of her fears. It was a relief to leave behind much of her sadness over so many deaths on the two lost planets, as well as Dr. Laduna's betrayal and sacrifice, as she merged with Ranth.

"Incoming blaster fire," Ranth reported.

"Raise shields to maximum. Evasive tactics," Vax ordered. "Return fire at will."

Zical gestured to Dr. Laduna's body. "Place his body in a shroud and launch him out an airlock. I don't want his DNA aboard for the Sentinel to shoot at."

"Yes, sir."

Zical turned from the dead scientist to her, piercing Dora with a direct, hard gaze that revealed his determination. She knew he would never give up, no matter the high probability of failure.

And yet he didn't deceive himself or his crew either. "We can't outfight an entire fleet of Jarn."

Her gaze flashed to the vidscreen even as she linked with Ranth's sensor array. The Jarn were trying to prevent them from docking with Guranu.

Zical fired rapid orders at her. "Infiltrate the Jarn computer systems. Help me get the *Verazen* to Guranu."

"Understood," Dora replied, aware that Zical would do what he could to keep the ship flying. But against an entire fleet, the likelihood of success was close to zero. It was only a matter of time until the formidable opposition struck their ship, slowed their momentum, or hit a vital part of the *Verazen*. But failure meant that the Jarn's mission to turn off all the Sentinels would succeed, leaving the galaxy open for a Zin invasion.

Leaning against a wall, Dora took one last deep breath and then left her body behind, applying her entire attention to her task. Forcing the psi link to pull all her mind into Ranth, she didn't hold back even a tiny fraction of her self. She'd merged many times, but never before had she linked with every last particle of her consciousness. No longer could she feel her chest moving up and down with each breath.

No longer could she feel the bulkhead behind her back, the deck beneath her feet, taste the bitter fear in her mouth, or hear Vax and Zical devising strategy to keep them alive long enough to survive until she and Ranth could help.

Energy from Dora's body fed her psi. Ranth called upon his vast store of power and together they pushed toward the attacking fleet. With the shields of Jarn ships locked down tight, she and Ranth didn't try to push against the force fields or tug at the energy patterns, but searched for a crack.

Here.

Ranth led the way and together they wormed inside, through the hull, into the computer's heart. With a psi thought, Dora incapacitated weapons. Ranth disabled communications. Together they plunged into the core and fried the drive, withdrawing a nanosecond before the ship imploded, the hull squashed in hellish heat and melting metal.

One by one, they found the key to infiltrate the Jarn ships, but since the *Verazen* was so outnumbered, they required swifter measures to accomplish their goal. They had to be more efficient, faster, deal with more of the enemy in one psi attack. Even as Dora and Ranth contemplated the problem, a laser burst targeted their ship. Only a brilliant and severe last-second course change saved them from instantaneous death.

Together Ranth and Dora repeated the procedure on ship after ship, searching for a more efficient means to cause massive destruction. They took out a squad in nanoseconds but their efforts weren't enough. They weren't fast enough.

Ranth. We need to split up.

Your human mind cannot withstand partitioning.

Dora understood. The link between her body and mind might detach under the stress. If she weakened, she might never be able to return to her body and she would die. Even as she worried for her unborn child, she made the necessary decision, the only decision, her soul wailing at the necessity.

If we don't save the ship, I won't have a brain to worry about.

Compliance.

Ranth split their consciousness, weakening them, but they'd doubled their productivity.

Spilt again.

At four times their original speed, they tapped into ship after ship, becoming more efficient, deadlier, faster. And still the fleet closed in on the *Verazen*, ignoring their terrible losses, their Jarn will unbreakable as they flew into the death and destruction of Dora's and Ranth's lethal attacks.

Analysis, Dora demanded, the connection to her body almost gone. She'd become lost in the cyberspace of infiltrate, attack, disable.

We fail within thirty seconds.

Split again.

You cannot. You will die.

We have no other option.

Wake Kirek. Ranth suggested. *He will lend his strength to ours.*

No. He must be at full strength to get past the Sentinel's guard. Split again. Do it.

Dora's mind fractured into multistreaming ribbons. And each ribbon wormed through cracks in the Jarn shields, sought out command and control and altered the drive.

Disable. Destroy.

In the far recesses of her mind, she weakened, drew on last reserves of energy. Single-mindedly she held one thought first and foremost. One goal.

Demolish the fleet.

Save Zical.

He must live. And as she used the final supply of her humanity, she finally understood what Zical had been trying to tell her. On the verge of losing her life, she'd never appreciated living more. On the edge of losing her future, she wanted to live to bear her child. She wanted to raise their child with the man she loved.

She loved Zical.

Even as she destroyed and killed and attacked, she pushed herself harder, longer, to save him, his ship, his mission. She loved him. She fed on that love, letting the strength of the emotion push her past her last reserves, until the Jarn fleet was no more. She loved him. That's why she'd picked him out among the billions of entities. She'd always loved him, she simply hadn't recognized the emotion.

Now she was certain of her love.

And then like a burst of energy that flashes too hot, she was done. Finished.

Good-bye, my love.

ZICAL HELD DORA in his arms, hugging her close. Tears streamed down his face. Stars. He hadn't known that losing her would feel as if a part of him had been lost. Shattered. He hadn't known that his insides would churn like raw acid. That the agony would rip his heart to shreds.

She'd paid the ultimate price to take out the Jarn fleet and to save them all. And while her heart still beat and her lungs drew air, Ranth had informed him that it was only a matter of time before her body gave out.

She'd stretched her mind past the snapping point. Not even a healing circle could bring her back. There was nothing of her spirit left to gather.

He would lose her and it tore at him worse than any pain he'd ever suffered, worse than losing his first wife and unborn child, worse than losing his parents. He couldn't believe that once again he'd failed to protect his unborn child. What had he done to deserve such sorrow? No man should have to grieve over so many losses.

Even as he swallowed the lump in his throat, he regretted that Dora would never know that she'd embraced the totality of becoming human. Because nothing could be more human than to give one's life for others.

Yes, she'd risked her life to save Kirek on Kwadii, but, no matter how slim, they'd always had hope of success. But against the Jarn, Dora had known there was no chance for her survival. None. Absolute zero. Yet she'd gone ahead, putting the mission first.

Arms shaking, feeling broken, Zical held her inert body, missing the beautiful spirit he loved, the life in her dancing eyes that flashed red when she laughed with happiness and glowed violet with deep emotions while they'd made love. Never again would she tease or argue or advise. Never again would she chuckle or smile or catch his gaze from across a crowded room to share a moment.

The grief of losing her was a burden he would carry for all his days. Like a fool, he had wasted so much of their time together with his uncertainties and his doubts. Now, when it was too late, he wished he could have back all those days, to appreciate her as she should have been appreciated. As his tears fell unchecked onto her cheek, and he gently rubbed them away with the pad of his thumb, grief and sorrow clawed at him.

He wanted to rail at fate. He wanted to pound his fists until his knuckles bloodied and the outward pain distracted him from his anguish and heartache.

He didn't want to go on without her. He couldn't imagine going through his days . . . or his nights . . . without knowing she was close by. And now he'd never have the opportunity to change her mind about becoming his wife. Oh, how he yearned to join her. Depart this life. But then her sacrifice would be for nothing. To honor her death, he must live. He must complete this mission. Somehow he had to find the courage to go on alone.

But not yet. As Vax lew the *Verazen* toward Guranu, Zical held Dora close, breathing in her womanly scent, running his fingers through her silky hair, wishing that there had been some other way to overcome the Jarn. But there had been none. Dora had known she was the only person standing between the destruction of their ship and the total failure of their mission. She'd done what had to be done.

As he must.

He couldn't console himself with the complete victory over the Jarn. Not with what the victory had cost, taking from him the one woman so precious and dear to his heart.

Zical kept waiting for a measure of grief to subside and for anger to sear through the agonizing pain of losing Dora, but as he cradled her in his arms, he marveled at how she'd come to mean so much to him, capturing not just his heart, but his admiration and respect, in so short a time.

"Captain?" Shannon entered Dora's quarters, her voice hesitant and gentle. "Sir, Vax says we'll dock at Guranu within the hour."

Clearly, Vax had ordered Shannon to find the captain, but she was reluctant to interrupt his mourning. He nodded, hoping she'd go away.

Hesitantly, she placed a hand on his shoulder. "We'll all miss her, but we need you in charge, Captain."

"Thank you." He didn't need a reminder of his duty, yet her sympathy and kindness urged him to release Dora and shove to his feet. "Ranth, let me know when it's time to say a final good-bye."

"Compliance."

The captain led by example. His crew might sympathize and mourn Dora's loss, but they expected him to go on as he always had—at least outwardly. But inside, he'd never be the same.

No one had told Kirek what had happened to Dora. He'd been with Avanti and Decker through the battle, and had come back to their quarters to find Zical grieving over her body. At the sight of Zical's tears, Kirek had squeezed his own eyes tight, pretending he didn't see the captain's agony. Meanwhile, he'd contacted Ranth through privacy mode.

Ranth filled him in and Kirek cried his own tears. Dora could never replace his biological mother, Miri, but nevertheless he and Dora had shared a special bond that was more than friendship. She'd held him when he'd needed comfort, understood that his four-year-old body housed an adult intellect in a way most of the crew couldn't comprehend, and she'd risked her life to save him. Twice.

"Why didn't you inform me?" Kirek demanded of Ranth. "I could have added my psi to hers."

"Dora refused. She said you needed your full strength to deal with the Sentinel."

Had she believed her own words? Or had she wanted to protect Kirek from the battle? From causing death?

He shuddered and tried to contain the sobs welling inside him. Ever since he'd sneaked aboard, he'd known he would face danger, but he hadn't expected anyone to die in an attempt to protect him, especially not Dora.

He should have been there, fighting with her. Yet he suspected she'd known how much Kirek detested the idea of killing. Of fighting. Of violence. While he understood the necessity, he preferred to aid in other ways. Not because he feared injury to himself, but because taking a life seemed an abomination, a permanent blackness on the soul.

Kirek stared out the vidscreen for a long time, gathering his thoughts. And as the giant space station slowly filled the view, he felt fate pressing on his slender shoulders with a heavy weight. Guranu spun between the galaxies, shaped like a barbell with two rounded poles connected by a central axle where giant conical machines docked—the Sentinels. And there must be thousands of Sentinels attached to Guranu, all of them staring outward, their triangular bottoms like violet yolks in gray eggs.

Kirek's stomach tightened. Especially once he noted the dimensions of scale. In the vastness of black space with no planet or stars to use as comparison, he had no idea of the immensity of Guranu. But according to Ranth's precision sensors, each Sentinel was ten times as large as their ship. And Guranu was planet-sized.

The sheer immensity of the project was amazing. Guranu might be the largest man-made structure in the universe. And it boggled the mind to think that the Perceptive Ones had built Guranu eons ago and that the space station still functioned.

Despite his sadness over Dora, Kirek's pulse quickened. He'd always sensed that the Sentinels and he were linked by fate. But as the *Verazen* drew closer, that connection strengthened. It was as if the Sentinels were living entities. Collectively wise. All-knowing.

Yet the Sentinels were not perfect. A Sentinel had wrongly judged them as the enemy because of the Jarn aboard. And he reminded himself that the Sentinels might conclude Kirek was an enemy too.

Not only must Zical and his crew work past the Sentinels' sophisticated defenses, they had to reprogram the machines. And to reach the delicate computer systems that ran these machines, the task had to be done from inside. Yet if the Sentinels could destroy two planets from halfway across the galaxy, he couldn't even imagine what kind of powers would focus on anyone who tried to board.

Clearly, the Perceptive Ones would have taken all kinds of precautions, using technologies far beyond their understanding. But, Kirek's special gift was that he simply didn't register on machinery. He would have to go in alone.

And the idea chilled him to his bones.

Everyone was counting on Kirek. That's why Dorn had protected him. For this moment.

But suppose he failed?

Chapter Twenty-three

AFTER KIREK DEPARTED the *Verazen* through the docking port to Guranu, he couldn't maintain a link with Ranth, which meant he remained out of contact with Zical and the ship. Zical fretted over the boy going alone into Guranu and hoped for the best. He didn't doubt Kirek's courage, intelligence, or ingenuity, but the boy lacked strength, and Zical feared that he couldn't overcome any physical boundaries placed in his way.

Waiting for Kirek's news on the bridge, Zical didn't allow himself to pace, although he couldn't hide the tension in his eyes. And his crew knew him too well to bother him with inconsequential details. Time passed slowly. There was no talk. No action. The tension thickened as minutes ticked by, and it seemed like days, but it was only a few hours before Kirek finally contacted them through Ranth.

"I'm in," Kirek reported. "Ranth?"

"Linking." Ranth tapped into the psi communication and

gave Zical an update. "Kirek climbed aboard a repair bot and crawled from Guranu into a Sentinel without registering on the machine's sensors. He's turned off all offensive weapons. You're free to join him, Captain."

Zical broke into a smile of relief. "Kirek, great job. We're on the way."

"Captain, the Sentinel is monitoring our verbal communications," Kirek informed him.

"I understand." However, Zical didn't like it. Alien machines that had already proved hostile kept him wary and alert.

"The Sentinel has requested that you come alone," Kirek told him through the com link.

"Why?"

"I'm . . . not certain."

Zical could be walking into a trap. Perhaps the Sentinel was only pretending that its armaments were disabled. Once he entered, the machine could trap him, zap him, kill him. Now that they'd arrived, their next task was to reprogram the giant machine, starting with making it comprehend that they were not the enemy.

"Ranth, cut the com link to Kirek for a moment."

"Compliance."

"Is this a trap?" he asked the computer, hoping the Sentinel's sensors couldn't reach into their ship and monitor their conversation.

"I don't have enough data to give an informed opinion."

"Ranth, open communications. Kirek, I'm on the way." Zical figured that he'd led his people here. If the Sentinel took his life, then the engineers and scientists would know to be wary. It was no longer imperative he stay alive for the sake of this mission. If necessary, the others could carry on without him.

So he climbed through the hatch into Guranu, amazed at the orderly chaos in the smooth-floored corridor that appeared to continue in both directions for as far as he could see. Weightless bots of all sizes and shapes zipped by carrying equipment, but Zical had to scrunch down to fit his tall frame into the almost too-bright passageway. Squinting against the brilliant white lights, he adjusted his suit to allow less illumination to filter through, changed his nulligrav to a comfortable strolling level.

Which way and how far? he asked Ranth.

But the alien that was the Sentinel responded, obviously linking communications through Guranu. *Follow the blinking green light.*

The psi link revealed an ancient essence—wise, implacable, judgmental. But Zical also sensed an infinite patience and an indomitable will. He supposed an entity whose life spanned the eons would have many self-protective mechanisms. Had Kirek really fooled the ancient machine's sensors, or was that what the Sentinel wanted them to believe?

Zical wished Dora were with him, and not just for her instinctive comprehension of machinery and computers; he would have taken comfort in holding her hand. He shut the thought down. He must keep his wits about him, and dwelling on the woman he'd lost and how much he missed her company would only put his mission in jeopardy.

Zical followed the blinking green light to an intersection of two corridors. Apparently, he was to turn right and was pleased when the corridor both widened and increased in height, allowing him to stand upright.

More suited to your size? the Sentinel asked.

Yes.

This route is longer.

How much longer? Zical had the notion the Sentinel might send him in circles for centuries if he didn't question the directions. Perhaps he was paranoid. However, he didn't like being inside a machine. He didn't like machines that were left in charge of a galaxy. Odd, he'd depended on Dora when she was a computer—yet her taking human form and linking with Ranth had bothered him. When she'd stared glassy-eyed into space, ignoring everyone around her, she'd seemed to lose her personality and humanity—but that hadn't been the case. Dora had been just as human and his perception had been wrong. Yet his relationship with Ranth was comfortable. But even a surface psi conversation with the Sentinel made Zical feel as if he needed to look over his shoulder. As if an attack could come at any moment, from any direction.

Up ahead, Kirek waved, his small frame wriggling atop a bot. The space station and the Sentinel seemed to merge into each other with seamless precision, each section of the long corridor looking much like all the others.

Increasing his pace, Zical hurried forward. Kirek's expression looked relieved, the earlier tension when he'd set out for the Sentinel was now replaced by exuberance. Instead of using psi to communicate, Zical spoke to the boy, turning off the translator in hopes the Sentinel couldn't comprehend. "Are you certain all weapons are nonfunctional?"

"I am certain of nothing." Kirek hopped off the bot and pointed to a place where huge cables entered a compartment. "However, this is the mainframe and I've just isolated this Sentinel from all the others. It can no longer communicate with Ouranio cities."

"Good work."

The Sentinel interrupted their conversation, revealing it could comprehend spoken language. *You have disabled my weapons and communications, leaving me no choice but to self-destruct with you inside.*

No. Zical realized the Sentinel had tricked them. All along he'd suspected a trap, but he'd seen no option but to do as the Sentinel had asked. And since the machine still believed they were the enemy, he had to find a way around its logic circuits. If he could persuade the Sentinel to give them time, perhaps Ranth could find a way inside. *We must talk first.*

You are the enemy. I destroy the enemy.

We are allies, Zical countered. Meanwhile, he urged Ranth to seek a way into the machine. *It is true that the Jarn aboard my ship was programmed by the Zin. But the Jarn obey the Zin masters against their will.*

The machine paused as if to digest his words or perhaps to contend with another distraction. Finally it sent an implacable thought. *The Jarn seek to destroy all Sentinels.*

"Captain," Ranth said through the com. "Before we annihilated the fleet, the Jarn found a way into the Sentinels' programming. Dr. Laduna spoke the truth. The machines are slowly turning themselves off."

"Reverse the process," Zical ordered.

Ranth's tone was solemn. "I'm sorry, sir. I cannot do so without the Sentinels' help, but they are freezing me out. Very shortly, the only Sentinel that will remain awake is the one you are inside."

Zical shot his psi into the Sentinel. *We came to help.*

You are the enemy.

You are in error. Zical feared that with all the other Sentinels turned off and this one about to self-destruct, they had failed. The machine wouldn't believe his words. If only it could see inside him. An idea flashed into his mind. Twice before the Perceptive Ones' machines had scanned him as he stood in a golden cone of light. Hoping the Sentinel had the same capability, he straightened and demanded, *Test me.*

A deep scan will kill you.

If you self-destruct, you will kill me and the boy and everything your creators worked to protect.

Scan me, Zical ordered.

A golden cone of light shot down from overhead, trapping Zical like hard, sucking tentacles. Much like the light in Mount Shachauri, the light probed his mind, the alien presence shifting through the layers of his brain, burrowing deep to test his true essence, motives, and spirit.

Despite his horror at the invasion, Zical didn't fight the intrusion. He allowed the Sentinel to sift his memories and intentions, all of them, the good and the bad, permitting the machine to see they really were on the same side.

As his vision narrowed and he blacked out, even as he prepared to die, Zical hoped the Sentinel had dug deep enough into his core to find and recognize the truth.

ZICAL AWAKENED WITH every nerve in his body tingling, his hormones raging for sexual release. His first instinct was to search for Dora, but with the memory of her sacrifice, and Kirek's worriedly bending over him, he tamped down the cone's side effect, which this time wasn't so much a sudden charge of sexual need as much as a yearning to hold and love Dora.

Kirek's hand rested on Zical's shoulder. "Are you all right?"

"Zical spoke the truth, so I allowed him to live," the Sentinel intoned. "You are genuine descendants of the Perceptive Ones."

Zical shoved up on an elbow. "Will you allow our computer to reprogram—"

"Reprogramming is no longer necessary."

"I don't understand." Still groggy, Zical stood, hoping his head would clear, trying with all his might not to recall the last time he'd been probed by the light, when Dora had been in his arms.

"My system has already reprogrammed itself to fit the new data we retrieved from your scan. However, this one Sentinel cannot protect the galaxy from the Zin, so I am awakening the others. Soon we will all be back at our posts."

Kirek whooped and pumped his small fists into the air. "Captain, with your permission, I'm sending a message home to my parents."

Zical nodded and Kirek raced through the docking portal back to the ship, likely forgetting his parents would be very old, if indeed they even still lived, by the time his message arrived. Sounds of celebration from the bridge echoed back to Zical as Ranth relayed the news that the Sentinels would return to guard them all. Zical's heart ached with emptiness at the thought that Dora would not be there to celebrate their success. She, more than anyone, deserved to know they'd succeeded—but she never would. Although the rest of the galaxy, perhaps even the Jarn, would eventually be joyously celebrating, Dora would never know that giving her life had saved them all.

Vax spoke over the com link. "Captain, the Sentinels are waking and leaving Guranu. They appear on course for the Andromeda Galaxy."

"Understood."

"Captain," Cyn broke in, her voice excited, "the Sentinels' speeds are incredible. If we could find a way to tap into their power source—"

"I'll ask," Zical promised.

Relief that the galaxy would be set right staggered Zical, and if not for a psi thought to stiffen his suit, he might have fallen. He'd never expected the journey to end so successfully. And yet, how could he celebrate without the woman he loved at his side? He should be filled with elation, jumping up and down with jubilation, but success without Dora was bittersweet.

Can you help outfit our ship with your hyperdrive? Zical asked, more because his crew deserved to continue their lives than for any desire to return to Mystique, where every breath would remind him of Dora. He could not think only of his own selfish need to grieve and mourn, his crew deserved to live. With the Sentinel's knowledge and advanced technology, perhaps he could reward his crew for a job well done by returning to Mystique as quickly as they'd come and afford them the chance to continue with their lives.

Guranu exists for reprogramming. Since our parts do not wear out, Sentinels do not carry spares.

Zical would not give up easily. *Perhaps our computer and chief engineer could copy your schematics—*

You do not have the resources the Sentinel intoned. *However, my force field can wrap around the Verazen, and my drives could take you home. But my programming makes it impossible for me to aid the enemy. You must leave the Jarn survivors behind.*

Why not turn the Jarn into an ally instead? Zical suggested, hating to leave the battles survivors, who'd escaped in pods, to a lonely death.

I do not follow your meaning.

The Sentinel possessed superior technology. Perhaps the Perceptive Ones could counter the damage the Zin had done so long ago and Dr. Laduna's sacrifice could lead to the Jarn's salvation. *The Jarn are slaves to the Zin due to their genetic coding. Change the coding and the Zin will lose their ally inside the Federation.*

A suggestion with merit. Would you rather I send a pulse to free the Jarn of the Zin curse, or would you prefer that I repair the woman you mourn?

Zical's head snapped up. *You can heal Dora?*

I can restore her or the Jarn. Which do you prefer?

The Sentinel had just given him an impossible choice. Saving the woman he loved or an entire world. Even as Zical marveled at the wondrous technology, hope lightened his heart. Dora could live. Their child could be born on Mystique. All he had to do was choose to save her. Dora meant more to him than a billion strangers.

Yet, out of decency, Zical had to ask the question, *Why can you not do both?*

The Perceptive Ones' programming has limits. Saving both the Jarn and Dora exceed my parameters.

And the programming cannot be altered? Zical asked, his question rhetorical as sweat poured out of him, his suit barely able to keep up. The dream to have Dora back at his side was powerful, tempting . . . what he wanted more than anything. His ragged breath came in great gulps. If he could give his life to save Dora and their child, he would gladly do so. But that was not one of his options.

His gut churned with the agony of indecision. He'd rather fight a hundred battles than make such a horrendous choice. How could he measure the life of the woman he loved and their unborn child against billions of nameless, faceless Jarn? His heart constricted as a band of anguish tightened like a noose, flaying him until he might have had a gaping wound where his heart had once been.

He wanted Dora back so badly he could almost smell her sweet scent, taste her lush lips. To share their lives would be his fondest wish, his greatest joy—yet how could they experience happiness when choosing her over the Jarn would cost so many their freedom?

Make your decision.

He knew Dora would tell him to free the Jarn. She would tell him he couldn't save two lives at the expense of so many. Such a choice wouldn't be rational. But Zical would not miss the Jarn. He knew only one, Dr. Laduna, and his memories of him were mixed. Zical wouldn't wake up at night missing the Jarn. *You've given me an impossible choice.*

Choose.

Zical's throat closed on tears of despair. He shouldn't even be considering saving Dora. He shouldn't love her so much that he could deliberately cause billions to live as slaves for untold eons. But in the end, even as his gut wrenched and he raged in helpless fury, he couldn't leave such a world of Jarn slaves who were ready to bring down the Sentinels, an enemy living among the Federation.

Free the Jarn, he ordered, his words no more than an anguished whisper. Turning his back on the Sentinel, knowing that the decision had wounded his soul, a wound that would fester and never heal, he blundered back to the *Verazen,* his motor functions on automatic, his footsteps heavy, his hopes wrecked beyond repair, his dreams demolished.

"The Sentinel beamed a pulse through hyperspace," Vax informed him as he stepped aboard the bridge. "Ranth's analysis has concluded that the Jarn should now be free of the Zin."

Zical swallowed the lump in his throat, nodded, and headed straight to Dora's cabin. He wanted to hold her again, apologize for his decision that would lead to her death. As if sensing his sorrow, none of the crew stopped him along the way.

Ranth, Vax, and Cyn kept up a running patter, keeping him informed about the Sentinel's force field that would encompass the *Verazen* as well as the Jarn survivors and take them home. Kirek must have been on the bridge because Dora was alone.

She appeared to be sleeping peacefully. With her eyes closed, her breathing steady, he could almost fool himself into believing that nothing had happened to her. Her clear complexion, the delicate line of her jaw, the graceful lines of her neck and her beautiful body, seemed to mock the vacancy of her damaged brain.

Gently, he gathered her into his arms, holding her close. When her eyes fluttered open, intelligence sparked from her brilliant violet irises. Stunned, he watched her soft lips part, and she cleared her throat. "Hi."

Was he hallucinating? Had he finally lost his mind? Was the universe playing tricks on him?

Staring, hopeful, astounded, he could barely talk. "Dregan hell. Dora?"

"In the flesh." She wriggled against him, brushing her ample chest against his.

Pure joy blazed through him and he yanked her tightly against him, fearing he might lose her again at any second. "I thought . . . you were . . . gone. I thought I'd lost you . . . forever."

She grinned and wound her arms around his neck. "I'm not that easy for you to get rid of."

"Rid of?" He gaped at her, wondering how she'd healed. Ranth had told him her mind was gone. Had he wanted her to be back so badly that he was imagining she was whole? Seemingly her normal self? If he was talking to an apparition, he didn't care. He smoothed back her hair, cupped her chin and locked gazes, all his emotions and everything he wanted to tell her jumbling inside him. His voice choked. "I missed you so much."

He didn't want to question how she'd survived. He didn't want to think how lucky he was to have this second chance to show her how much he loved her. He simply held her tightly, rocking her, holding her, breathing in her scent.

The Sentinel spoke. "When you made the unselfish decision to free the Jarn, you proved your people worthy. Genuine descendants of the Perceptive Ones deserve to propagate."

Zical blinked back tears of happiness. The Sentinel had healed Dora. The terrible decision he'd made had been some kind of alien test. But he'd thought the scan had told the Sentinel everything about his character. "Didn't the scan tell you how I would decide?"

"Scans cannot read the heart."

"Thank you." Stunned for a moment into silence, he absorbed the enormity of the consequences of the choice he'd made. He'd never realized how much power he'd wielded in that decisive moment, how easily he could have chosen wrong.

Energy and glowing happiness zinged through him, and Zical wanted to laugh and talk and make love to this precious woman. He wanted to cherish her for the rest of his days. Most of all he wanted her to be happy.

"The Perceptive Ones would approve of you and your female. And you'll be pleased to know the Zin have not penetrated this galaxy. The Jarn are free. Your people are once again safe from attack. Now, I will take you home."

Every atom in Zical's body wanted to insist that Dora

marry him, but first he had something important to say. "Dora, I love you. When I thought I'd lost you, it was if I'd lost the best part of myself. I love you more than life itself. I don't care if you spend all your days linked with Ranth. Just give me your nights. I want to spend the rest of our lives together. If you aren't certain, I'll wait—as long as necessary. Just give me the opportunity to prove how much I love you."

Her eyes gleamed with happiness. "I'd like that."

"Which part?"

"The part where you prove how much you love me." She giggled, used a psi thought to turn her suit transparent. "In fact, I wouldn't mind at all if you started loving me right now."

She was so beautiful, this spirited, loving woman, that she stole his breath away. When she cocked her head at a mischievous angle and licked her lips with a provocative grin, his heart sped and his blood quickened, as he waited for her next saucy comment.

She grinned. "There's something you should know."

"Please don't tell me you miss life as a computer," he teased.

"Of course not. Computers can't make love." Her grin widened. "But I finally figured out that I love you too. I always have and I suspect I always will. Loving you is hardwired into my brain. I can't seem to help it. So it's a damn good thing that you love me back." She playfully teased his lip with the pad of her forefinger. "However, I have a few . . . concerns."

"Concerns?" he growled into her ear. "Like what?"

"Rystani men like to take control."

"So?" He clasped her waist to keep his hands from roving, but touching her seemed to cause his sizzling nerve endings to recall the stimulation from the Sentinel's mind scan. The alien machine always left him aroused, and Dora's wriggling, her words of love, all combined to make him burn for her.

"Sometimes a woman likes to be in charge," she warned him, her eyes sparkling.

"She does?"

"Oh, yes."

Following Rystani custom was no longer as important to him as keeping his woman happy. Oh, she hadn't agreed to marry him yet, but she'd already given him her love. For now, her love was plenty and would keep him a very happy man.

After trying and failing to give her his sternest expression, he chuckled. "Let me make sure I have this right. You want to take charge of our lovemaking?"

"Yes."

"Really?"

"Yes."

He laced his hands and placed them behind his head, a smile teasing his lips. "So, go ahead. I dare you."

Epilogue

Eight and one half months later

"PUSH." MIRI INSTRUCTED Dora.

For months Dora had been impatiently waiting for this moment, for the birth of her and Zical's twin daughters. With Miri standing between her draped thighs, and the healing circle that was Tessa, Kahn, Shaloma, Etru, and Kirek surrounding her head and shoulders, Dora was cocooned in love.

She'd finally admitted to herself that she wanted to spend the rest of her life with Zical and had consented to marry him. He'd accepted that she would always feel a special kinship with computers and claimed he loved that part of her too. He'd shown his acceptance of her differences when she'd refused to follow the Rystani custom of wearing the bands, and he'd married her anyway. Dora understood that his kind of acceptance was rare and precious, and loved him all the more.

Her husband now stood proudly among their family unit, with his hands on her shoulders, rubbing her with loving encouragement. Since Dora had borne the discomfort of carrying the babies for nine months, Rystani custom required the male to take his mate's pain during the birth.

However, the fathers found the agony easier to bear when it was shared among the family unit of the healing circle. So although Dora had no discomfort whatsoever, the three men, Zical, Kahn, and Etru, were bearing the childbirth pain through the psi link. Although Kirek had begged to be included, his father had protectively insisted that the boy's body was not yet strong enough to share the agony of labor.

Her abdominal muscles contracted again and Zical grunted. Kahn's lips pressed tightly together and Etru winced. Wishing to end the men's pain, yet unwilling to risk harming her babies by pushing too hard with her psi and her suit, Dora gave a little experimental squeeze.

"Dora, use more force," Miri gently instructed.

"But not too much," Zical cautioned, obviously willing to bear the pain to ease his daughters' way into the world, and Dora's heart swelled with pride.

He was a good man, a wonderful husband, and he'd be a terrific father. As a computer she'd picked him out, knowing he was special. But as a woman, she loved him with all her heart. As his suit barely kept up with the sweat on his forehead, as he bore the pain of childbirth for her and their children, she'd never loved him more.

Linking her psi with Shaloma, Tessa, and Miri, Dora reached out a mental link to her daughters. *Come, little ones,* she crooned. *It's time to begin your lives.*

The contractions increased in frequency, coming upon one another so fast that Dora could no longer have spoken if she'd tried. She was simply working too hard to spare any extra energy beyond the process of gently urging the girls from her body.

For some reason, despite the love surrounding their babies, the wonderful scent of fresh flowers, the dim lights, the encouraging Rystani melody, the girls wanted to remain in the womb. Not yet born, they already exhibited distinct personalities through their psi, one sensitive and shy, the other defiant in spirit. And despite Dora's, Tessa's, Miri's, and Shaloma's encouragement, the babies refused to cooperate.

Kirek's hand tightened on Miri as he linked and added his special encouragement. *Come on. You have a wonderful mother waiting for you.*

And a brave father, Dora added.

Tessa's mind linked and fed in more encouragement. *Friends are waiting to greet you and bestow their blessings.*

Dora might not feel any pain, but her body stretched to accommodate her children. She cajoled, coaxed, pushed.

And a new life entered the world.

Miri gently removed the firstborn, placed her in a suit that automatically shrank to her tiny size, then cleaned her. Dora reached eagerly for the baby, even as she gently urged her second daughter into the world. Miri took care of the details while Dora marveled at her daughters, two perfectly formed girls with alexandrite eyes.

Even as Zical protected her from the last of the birth pain, he grinned at her in proud, happy, and excited exhaustion. "You are amazing. These children are—"

"Going to be my best friends," Kirek proclaimed with a solemn face and a mischievous wink that took Zical aback and made Etru chuckle.

Then Zical tousled Kirek's head. "They will be lucky, indeed, to have you for a friend." He raised his eyes to the two men who'd helped him through the labor pain. "And I am lucky to share this moment with both of you."

Etru nodded with relief. Kahn clapped him on the shoulder and their women smiled as Zical's gaze quickly returned to the twins. One cuddled sleepily, sucking her thumb. The other stared at him curiously. Dora handed him the baby who was awake.

He took her gingerly and Etru showed him how to adjust the baby to a comfortable spot in the crook of his arm. "Are they supposed to be so tiny?"

As if his daughter understood, she stretched her little fists, slapping his chest as if to say, "Of course I'm perfect, can't you tell?"

Fascinated by the babies, Kirek obviously didn't want to depart with the others. But Miri took his hand, insisting the new family needed some time alone. And Dora assured Kirek he could return and visit soon.

After the others had departed, Zical wiped a stray tear from his eye and cleared his throat. Dora lifted her gaze to his, her eyebrow arched. "Yes?"

He leaned down to her, protectively cuddling their daughters. "Happy?"

She gazed back at the man she loved with all her heart, the man who had given her two amazing babies and a life where she felt . . . complete, wanted, needed, adored, cherished, and loved. "When I was a computer, I had emotions, but . . . they were never so intense. I feel as though I'm about to burst with happiness."

"Oh, you're bursting all right . . . with milk." Zical chuckled, kissed her brow, his gaze dropping to her breast where their youngest daughter had wriggled and latched on to her nipple.

As her milk let down and she nursed first one hungry daughter, then the other, Dora enjoyed the loving warmth in Zical's gaze. She'd created her body because she'd wanted to have sex with him. And even though sex with Zical was terrific, the best part of being human was to love and be loved.

She'd gotten so much more than she'd ever wanted and had no regrets about becoming human. Out of billions of people, Zical was her soul mate, the man she'd always loved. To feel such joy, to experience such love, was worth giving up her immortality. She had no doubt she'd made the right choice to become human. Rather than spending an eternity alone, she looked forward to a lifetime with Zical and her daughters.

Turn the page

for a sneak peek at the next Susan Kearney paranormal,
coming from Tor Romance in February 2006

The
Ultimatum

SOME SPECIES LIVED to make love. Why did hers require mandatory sexual encounters—not just to procreate—but to survive?

Once again Dr. Alara Bazelle Calladar's goal of creating the DNA she required eluded her, and she rubbed the bridge of her nose in disappointment. Her search to free Endekian women from the curse of their genetics was turning out to be extraordinarily complex and laborious. But all her effort would be worthwhile if she ever succeeded in putting women's hearts and minds, instead of their biology, in charge of when they had sex.

Under normal circumstances, finding a solution to achieve her goal was difficult, but during the beginnings of *Boktai*, Alara's female hormone levels made unclouded reasoning as elusive as a Denvovian sandworm who'd grown wings. As if in anticipation of a kiss, her lips already tingled and the increased blood flow from arousal had caused her breasts to become tender.

"Alara," her assistant and good friend, Maki, interrupted, her words echoing through the com system and over the lab's DNA maturation receptacles that housed Alara's hopes for the future of every Endekian woman. "You have a visitor."

"I'm busy." *Busy* was their private code word for put whoever was interrupting her work off until another day, a day when she wasn't so frazzled.

"He's . . . insistent."

"He?" Alara snapped her head up from the array of test samples, every one of them a failure. Science required patience and normally she had plenty. But with her blood simmering from the onset of *Boktai*, just the mention of a man caused her heart beat to escalate, her patience to dwindle.

"Oh, he's one hundred and ten percent male," Maki practically purred, and Alara imagined how the Endekian male would preen at Maki's compliment. He'd no doubt entered the reception area, puffed up with confidence that he was wanted and that he was worthy of female attention. Very likely, he wasn't. Endekian men didn't need to treat their women well, not when women had to offer up their bodies to them on a regular basis to stay alive. While it took a lot to impress Maki, she still wouldn't have interrupted unless she believed the man important.

"*Krek*," Alara swore under her breath, annoyed that in her current biological state she would react to a male just like every other Endekian woman with her hormones demanding sex. After inhaling male scent and male pheromones, she'd find him irresistible—even if he turned out to be an absolute idiot, or an uncivilized brute, or simply an unskilled derelict. In the early phase of *Boktai*, her enhanced senses would enflame her, deepening her desires, quickening her yearning until she transformed into a female she loathed—an undiscriminating female who required sex with every needy cell in her body.

Alara didn't want the temptation of a male in her lab, or in her life. Not unless she chose to invite him, but that wasn't damn likely. She had no use for men—not until she was caught deep in the clutches of *Boktai*. In fact, the few rare males who deigned to enter her laboratory were often those who sought to discourage her from continuing her work. Oh, yes. Endekian men were quite content with the status quo, and if Alara hadn't been a war heroine, the male-run government might have shut down her facility from the start.

Some heroine she was. While everyone else had died during the Terran terrorist's bombing of her city, her presence within an underground laboratory had saved her life along with her mother's. But due to an preposterous calamity of nature, Endekian biology tied a wife's death to her husband's. After the Terran bomb had killed father, her mother had suffered a slow, painful death.

Alara had gone on . . . alone.

She had raged, mourned and buried both mother and father. And then she'd repressed her grief in work. As the sole survivor of the vicious attack that had killed her parents, she'd studied harder and become more determined than ever to unravel the secrets of Endekian biology. She wanted women to be free of the curse of *Boktai* and an odd fame had given her the means to follow her dream.

She could never have foreseen the results of her survival, that the government would chose her as the symbol to rally the masses to their cause against the Terrans. Alara had used her new-found celebrity and government; connections to help fund her research. However, as the anger against the Terran attack abated, she'd become less useful to the government and had fallen out of favor. With the current unpopularity of her work, she wouldn't be surprised if her visitor was here to close her lab.

"Alara." Maki's voice dropped to a whisper. "He's bristling with attitude."

"Tell him I'm *busy*."

"I already tried." Maki's tone conveyed vexation. "He refuses to make an appointment."

"Well, use your imagination. Get rid of him for me."

"I'd be perfectly willing to take him home for the night." Maki breathed out a delicate sigh. "I tried. But he wants you. He said he's willing to wait as long as it takes."

"Oh, for the holy structure of atoms," Alara cursed and shoved back from the table. "He can wait all through the dark hours if he wants. I'm leaving through my personal entrance."

Alara picked up the disk to start her flitter and headed out the back of the building. She intended to go home, soak in a hot bath and take care of her growing arousal. Using self gratification to ease her cravings was only a temporary solution, one that would work for a short time and only if no males were present. Out of distaste, she would delay approaching a man for as long as possible to ease her need. Alara's personal physician had warned her that repetitive delays were detrimental to her wellbeing, that her cells required regular sexual activity with a male for healthy regeneration, and Alara fully understood that relief from her inborn biological drive to mate would be fleeting. Experience told her she couldn't hold out much longer and that within a day, two at most, she would lose control of her psi and herself and be forced to seek out a male partner.

With a quick retina scan, Alara unlocked her back door and stepped outside into the balmy dusk. Automatically she used her psi on her suit, the type worn by every Federation citizen, to shield her from the cloying humidity. Anxious to be on her way, she didn't pause to take in the city lights beyond her building and headed straight for her flitter, climbed in, inserted the disk and revved the engine.

"You were leaving without speaking to me." A deep male voice that was filled with vitality arrowed from the back seat and struck her full blown, causing her to jerk in surprise.

She held her breath, refusing to allow his scent into her lungs, but just the sound of his husky male tone kindled inevitable biological reactions. Her nostrils flared, automatically seeking his provocative scent. Blood rushed to her sensitive breasts and her suit cupping her skin seemed inadequate. Her pulse between her thighs quickened. Her flesh yearned for male hands to caress her, seduce her, satisfy her.

However, she was not yet so far into *Boktai* that her brain had abdicated completely to the demands of her body. She still maintained enough control to keep herself clothed, but thinking was becoming more difficult. The man had asked anticipated her escape. He had some nerve following her. Even if he recognized her needy condition, custom dictated that the female choose her mating partner, not the other way around, so she answered without bothering to conceal her annoyance. "This is *my* flitter. Get out."

"Not until we have a conversation," he countered.

Conversation? Ah, the combination of her needy cells plus the rumble of his voice must be clouding her thoughts. He was not here to mate. He was probably here to speak to her about the laboratory and her work. She refused to turn around. She knew the moment the receptors in her eyes detected his male shape, her hormones would elevate to the next level. In her worsening condition, he could be the ugliest male on the planet and if she stayed in his presence long enough, her will to resist wouldn't matter—she'd still find him handsome and her interest would flare into a kaleidoscope of basic need.

She spoke through gritted teeth. "Make an appointment with my secretary."

"I don't have time to delay. Neither do you."

"Exactly. We agree. I don't have time." Totally irritated by her reaction to him and how badly she wanted to climb into the flitter's cozy back seat and rip off his clothes, she practically growled, "Go away."

"Are you always so friendly?"

"Are you always so annoying?" she countered and took in a breath. Clean, musky male scent wafted to her nostrils, downshifted into her lungs and revved her olfactory nerves into third gear. *By the mother lode.* Why did his aroma have to remind her of sweet grasses and summer rain? Surely no other Endekian male had ever smelled so incredibly delicious.

She tried not to savor his wondrous scent and to distract herself with analysis. There was something odd about him. Something strange. Her mind tumbled and then settled. He didn't smell like an Endekian because . . . he *wasn't* an Endekian.

"Who are you?" Forgetting caution, she turned around. He was one giant of a man, one fantastic male specimen.

At the sight of bronze *male* skin molded over a powerful physique, her mouth watered. With his black hair clipped short to reveal a very *male* neck that was supported by cords of muscle, her gaze skimmed from his bold nose to his lush mouth to his dazzling cheekbones. But it was his compelling violet eyes, the color of precious nebula flame gemstones, that sought her out with male curiosity and which almost did in her rioting nerves.

Except his harsh expression stopped any inclination to move closer. He wasn't gloating with the usual I-know-you-can't-resist-me arrogance that she hated from the men of her world. Actually as he returned her stare, he appeared to be attempting to conceal distaste, but he couldn't hide his reaction in those grim eyes.

He held still, not crowding her. "Let me introduce myself. I am Xander from Mystique."

"You're a Rystani warrior," she accused him, still managing to keep her tone antagonistic, but barely.

Oh-*Krek*. He was one gorgeous hunk of a man. Even if she hadn't been entering the early stage of *Boktai*, he would still have been dazzling. Dealing with him now when she was in such a vulnerable condition was frustrating.

He spoke as if he had no inkling of what his presence was doing to her. "After Endekians invaded our homeworld, those of us who survived emigrated to Mystique." His tone was cold, his eyes direct. Despite the clamoring-for-attention need that she couldn't subdue, she shivered under his austere expression. But perhaps she was reading more into his demeanor than was there, coloring it with her own past.

She couldn't imagine any Rystani warrior had any love for Endekians. Her people had invaded his world fourteen Federation years ago and the rightness of their actions, the political reasons for war, had no bearing on the suffering they'd caused. Many Rystani had died in the invasion as had countless Endekian males. Her own brother had not come back from the war. When one lost loved ones—no reason was good enough to fill the emptiness, stop the pain, ease the sleepless nights. She ignored the sympathy and compassion that urged her to touch him and give comfort. Doing so would set her on an irrevocable path. It was bad enough to mate with an Endekian when neither participant had feelings for one another, but to mate with a man who had every reason to hate her people would be abhorrent.

She turned off the flitter, opened the door and exited her vehicle, hoping the fresh air would blow his scent away. But of course the weather didn't cooperate. When Xander unfolded his big frame from the vehicle, he revealed he was larger than she'd realized. Inside the flitter, she'd only viewed his upper half, but his flat stomach, narrow hips and long legs with muscular thighs made him seem more intimidating, more domineering, more male. If the battle for his world had come down to hand-to-hand fighting, if all the Rystani men were this large, his people would never have lost. Luckily for Endeki, they'd had superior technology and fire power.

Too bad there was nothing superior about her situation right now. As his scent swirled and eddied around her, her irritation with his determination to force her into a conversation warred with bubbling desire.

Even through her growing need she understood that he wouldn't leave until he'd said what he'd come to say. Rystani warriors had a fierce reputation. Known for their stubborn traits, she should have felt fear. She didn't. She should have felt relief that he wasn't here to shut down her facility. She didn't. She couldn't relax the tension that gathered inside her like thunderclouds before a storm, especially as she realized that the sooner they had their conversation, the sooner she could depart. He wouldn't allow anything less.

"So why are you here?" she asked, deepening her voice to compensate for the breathy teasing tone that her biology so urged her to emit instead.

"I need your help."

The only way she wanted to help was to find a private place. She imagined shadowy lighting, mellow music, hot sex and his mouth and hands roaming over her flesh. With determination she shut down the fantasy thoughts. "What kind of help?"

"Could we go somewhere more—"

"I'm not going anywhere with you." No matter how

strong her hormones, no matter how badly her cells wept for satiation, she could not have sex with an offworlder. She was already at odds with her government. Taking a Rystani into her bed would be seen as a betrayal by her people.

He chuckled, his tone so warm and inviting that she barely restrained a gasp of delight. At the change in his demeanor, she forced herself to listen while she tried not to stare at his full mouth, tried not to wonder what it would feel like to have his lips skim past her ear, down her neck.

As if he could read her thoughts, he frowned. "Is it true that you need merely look at a person to read his DNA?"

She shrugged and folded her arms beneath her aching breasts, hoping the light was too dim for him to see her hardening nipples. Why was he interested in her peculiar ability, albeit one she found useful, though her skill mattered little to the non-scientific community? "So what if I don't need a microscope to read DNA?"

He ignored her sarcasm. "It is said you can spot a flaw in the double helix chain at thirty paces."

She'd be willing to bet her last batch of test samples that Xander had never seen the inside of a lab, never mind looked through a microscope. He appeared to have spent his entire life outdoors, exercising and eating and growing muscles over his well-shaped bones. Ah, what she wouldn't give to spend more time with him. His intensity intrigued her and although she put her impression down to *Boktai*, she suspected under other circumstances he might still fascinate her. She'd noted a keen intelligence in his eyes, a glimmer of humor in their depths even as his voice carried overtones of compassion. Yet despite the intensity of her attraction to him, the offworlder's interest in her skill made her wary.

The war between his Rystani people and hers hadn't been over for very long. Although the Rystani had left their homeworld and emigrated to Mystique, Endeki still ruled Rystan. The peace between their people remained uneasy, and she suspected only the most dire of circumstances could have caused him to come here.

She eyed him, wishing the light was better so she could read his DNA. While chromosome combinations wouldn't reveal his motivation or his purpose for seeking her out, she had never before had the opportunity to examine Rystani DNA in a living male. Science would do her no good. She'd have to rely on her instincts and her chaotic senses.

"Why are you curious about my work?"

"I have no interest in your work. My interest is . . . in you."

Bloody Stars. Endekian men didn't speak with such directness. Then again, they didn't have to. They simply waited for a woman to choose and took their pleasure. Conversation was rarely part of the arrangement, so Alara found his bold declaration of interest in her odd, yet exciting.

Reminding herself that her brain couldn't possibly be functioning on all neurons, she eyed the big warrior with renewed caution. "What do you want?"

"I'd like for you to join me on a mission."

Before she told him that she was not about to give up her work to join him, or leave her friends and her home, she freed her curiosity and asked, "What mission?"

He shot her a charming, come-to-me smile that almost stole her breath. "I'm seeking the Perceptive Ones."

Despite his charisma, she snorted. "The Perceptive Ones haven't inhabited this galaxy in eons. They are legends. We aren't certain they ever existed, never mind that they still live."

"Have you no faith, Doctor? You wear a suit that was manufactured by machines the Perceptive Ones left behind." His voice turned earnest, youthful, and she suspected he was younger than she'd first thought. "They existed, all right. And according to ancient records, out near the rim is a system named Lapau, colonized by a humanoid race called the Lapautee. Not much is known about them. However, legend suggests their planet may be an outpost for a protector, a

Perceptive One. I'm hoping that since their machines lasted through the millennia, perhaps they did as well."

She didn't know if he was insane or on a grand quest. Either way, she couldn't help him. "I'm sorry. I must decline. I have my own work."

"This is important."

"And my work is not?" She arched a brow, daring him to put her down because she was female and her purpose inconsequential.

But he didn't. Instead he tried another tactic. "My mission to find the Perceptive Ones is necessary to saving the lives of billions."

She narrowed her brows, unswayed by his earnestness. "Then I wish good fortune to be on your side." She turned away to dismiss him.

He clamped a hand on her shoulder and electricity shot straight to her core. She barely restrained a gasp. The Rystani warrior's hand was gentle, strong and warm—warm enough to fire her flesh. Ruthlessly, she clenched her jaw and tamped down on her need.

His voice hardened in demand. "You will at least do me the courtesy of hearing me out."

Like she had a choice with his big hand on her? She forced herself to shrug it off, and no doubt sensing she would listen, he allowed her to free herself. He couldn't know that his touch had set off a storm of need so great that her ears roared. He was speaking, but at first she couldn't think beyond the rushing sensation that threatened her composure. But finally she regrouped.

"The Perceptive Ones are believed to have been responsible for seeding life in our galaxy with DNA."

"That's legend. It may not be true." She took deep breaths and as her chest raised and fell, she gave him credit, his gaze didn't once drop below her neck.

"My goal is go to Lapau in search of the Perceptive Ones and a pure strain of DNA."

"A pure strain?"

"For Terrans. They—"

"Terrans?" She felt the blood leave her face. She'd thought he was trying to help his *own* people, not the despicable race that had killed everyone she held close to her heart.

He continued as if he did not know of her hatred. "Terrans have polluted their planet and their DNA is damaged. Soon they will be dying by the millions. To save them, I'm looking for a pure strain of Terran DNA, without it . . . they will all die."

Groaning, she leaned against the flitter, raised her hands to her pounding temples. She had to think past the river of passion bubbling through her veins. Just mentioning Terrans to her had likely set off her fervor. Anger could trigger lust, the strong emotion set off signals, one emotion feeding the other.

She'd had no intention of helping this Rystani before. She certainly wasn't going to help him save cursed Terrans. She hoped they all died, and she would dance a celebration to the Goddess if she could rid the Universe of every last one of them.

Terrans had launched the bomb that killed her family, several friends and a coworker. Terrans had destroyed her life. She wouldn't lift one finger to save such a savage race. But she kept her reasons locked down tight.

"You don't need me," she argued. "Any scientist with a microscope can do what I do."

He shook his head. "We may not have the opportunity to examine each species in a laboratory. You can walk on their worlds and merely look—"

"That is where you are wrong. Even if I wanted to help, and I don't, Endekian females are not permitted to leave our homeworld."

Clearly stunned, he dropped his lower jaw and a muscle tightened in his neck. "Why not?"

She would not reveal her shame. She refused to tell him that their men didn't want their women to approach offworlders for life-giving sex. Selfish to the core, their men kept that pleasure for themselves. Still, she didn't lie, either. "It's the law."

Anger flickered in his eyes, whether it was for her inability to leave her homeworld or frustration that she couldn't accompany him, she couldn't discern. But all that male heat spiked her hormones another notch, flaying her with endorphins. *Krek.* Forget the scientific explanations. She was ready to pounce. On him.

She had to get away before she did something really stupid, like leaning into his chest, wrapping her hands around his neck and pulling his lips down to meet hers in a kiss. Like rubbing her skin against his. Like grinding her pelvis against his sexy hips.

Reminding herself he was a stranger, a Rystani warrior and forbidden to her, reminding herself that contact with him would ruin everything she'd dedicated her life to, would only keep her at bay for so long. Her starving cells demanded regeneration. She needed sex so badly she shook.

And damn him, she needed him to be out of sight so her gaze couldn't dwell on what he concealed beneath his plain black suit that molded to his frame with a precision that seared the image into her brain, branding her with a flaming heat. Moisture beaded on her upper lip and seeped between her thighs.

But she would not yield to her need.

She could not have an offworlder—especially one who was a friend to her worst enemy.

She would not succumb.

She'd remain strong.

Opening the flitter door, she eased inside, sensing he would not pursue her. Even as she escaped his presence, his words rang in her ears like a whispered promise. "Laws can be changed. We are not done, you and I."

Moon's Web

by

Cathy L. Clamp & C. T. Adams

SUE CAME OUT of the kitchen, favoring the leg that the little were-brat had bitten. I wanted to reach for her and bury my face in her shoulder-length auburn hair. She used to have honey-blonde curls, but we'd both made a change to match our new identities. It's odd. I can't seem to remember my life before I met her, but we've only known each other four months.

Sue isn't gorgeous, but she's pretty. Her heart-shaped face compliments a well curved body. She'd dropped some weight after a recent coma, when we could only feed her through tubes. She was looking damn good anyway, and I let my eyes reflect the thought. She caught me watching and blushed. I still think it's cute when she does that.

I breathed in her scent as she walked toward me. Rain-kissed plants and warm rich earth from a forest in summer mingled with the baked cinnamon smell of love. I would never get enough of her scent. It coursed through me like a drug, nearly shutting out coherent thought.

"Sue, let me see your leg." The words cut through the cloud of her scent. Bobby's voice was the sharp command of a cop. Of course, Bobby *is* a cop. He's part of Wolven, the law enforcement branch of the Sazi—call him double-o python. They're the nastiest of the nasty of each of the Sazi species. It's their duty to *permanently* remove from the gene pool any were-animal who breaks felony human laws or any of the big Sazi laws. Can't have a shape shifter locked up in jail during a full moon. The humans would find out we exist.

That is the ultimate rule of the Sazi: Keep our existence secret from the humans.

. . . coming in August 2005 from Tor Romance

Revenge Gifts

by

Cindy Cruciger

"You ready?" He looked directly into my eyes, and I definitely got the feeling that Howard was all business now.

Hell no, I'm not ready, but I'm not about to tell *him* that. Even though the big secret is out that I haven't had sex in ten years—maybe more now that I think about it—I've never fessed up to anyone about how bad the sex was when I was actually getting it. Yeah. Yeah. Yeah. I was a college kid. Sex was everywhere, so there's no excuse for not finding the big "O" with someone, or even by myself—but trust me, had I known the dry spell after college was going to be this long, I would have strapped a mattress to my back and gone to class naked until the goal was reached. Maybe.

I swallowed hard, "Ready."

He smiled that wicked little smile guys do when they know they are about to get lucky. I love that smile. It does things to my inner thighs. You have no idea. He stood up and poured two glasses half full of Merlot and walked over to hand me one. Tapping his glass against mine he leaned in to my ear and whispered, "So am I."

. . . coming in September 2005 from Tor Romance